The
King's
Disease

To Kissie.

Enjoy & thanks

For Meading!

# Other Books by Jeffrey S. Crawford

Fiction
*Finding Eden*

Non-Fiction
*Image of God*
*On a Ship to Tarshish*

# The King's Disease

Jeffrey S. Crawford

HILLSIDE HOUSE
PUBLISHING

*The King's Disease*
Jeffrey S. Crawford
Hillside House Publishing

Published by Hillside House Publishing, Springdale, AR
Copyright © 2020 Jeffrey S. Crawford
All rights reserved.

Cover Design by Mille Cooper

Unless otherwise indicated, Bible quotations are taken from the English Standard Version of the Bible. Copyright © 2002 by Crossway Bibles, a division of Good News Publishers.

---

**Library of Congress Cataloging-in-Publication Data**

Library of Congress Control Number: 2020942774
Jeffrey S. Crawford

The King's Disease
ISBN: 978-1-7327596-3-3

---

*Printed in the United States of America.*

*For my daughter,*
*Madison*
*As long as one and one are two...*

# PART 1

# THE LONG NIGHT

$T$*he king is sick.*

*Today marks the fifth month according to the calendar of my forefathers. When the illness began, it was thought to be a common drought of mind and body, typically lasting no more than seven to ten days. After the first month, the court began to express concern. The king's temperament seemed most affected. Fits of rage and ravings that make no sense to one of sound thought. He resisted any attempt by the royal physicians to provide care and he turned violent, ordering them out of his presence, throwing his golden chamber pot and its contents at them as they fled.*

*Those he trusts most, his inner circle of advisors, can no longer approach him. He only grunts and raves continually, always growing agitated the longer social contact persists. Even Heabani, the one closest to the king and the most trusted of all, has been cast out. In seeking to faithfully and accurately record the account of the king's illness I have pressed Heabani for details on its origins. He is quite certain it began in the month of Tašrītu when the moon shone at its fullest. It was on that night that the king returned from his walk along the flat roof of the royal palace, a most favorite location of the king to gaze upon the vastness of his kingdom, especially on this one night with the lights of the heavens showing at their brightest. "A curse! A CURSE...!" the king yelled as he stormed into his* bedchamber. *"The gods have unmade me...I am finished!"* He's not come out since.

Haebani insists it's a sickness of the moon. I personally believe in no such thing but his moods and temperament do seem to swing like the hammer of a great pendulum as the moon itself wanes and waxes. The height of his ravings always peaking as the moon itself peaks each month. But he always spirals down, never ultimately getting better.

So now, after five long months, it is clear — the king is sick. He is sick in mind, for sure. But he is also sick in body. Five months in his bedchamber, not once coming out to bathe or to freshen his clothing. His hair and beard grow long and matted. He is soiled as is his bedding. The whole room reeks of human waste and rotten food. Some days he eats but many he does not. The chambermaids refuse to attend to him out of fear. Royal guards do what they can to swipe old food and to clean up after the king, but such attempts are always cut short by the king's violence toward all who come near. He is still the king after all.

Everyone in this country worships their own gods and I have mine. Tonight, the priests are coming to burn incense and to offer sacrifices for the king and his healing. They will be praying to their gods for the king's relief and I will be praying to mine.

From the Journal of Meshach,
Royal court recorder for the king

Fifth day of the month of Addāru,
The nineteenth year of the king's reign (586 BC)

# CHAPTER 1

*The North Coast of Ireland, October*

The lone figure stumbled out of the woods onto the crumbled asphalt road. A wind whipped up and he felt cold, wet with sweat... and blood. *His* blood, or maybe it was Jorge's, or maybe it belonged to that...*thing*.

*Oh, Jorge...poor, poor, Jorge.*

He shuddered as he limped down the primitive road toward the glow of lights. Something was wrong with his right leg. Bad wrong. His jeans were torn and soaked with the sticky goo of his own blood. His left thigh didn't feel quite right when he probed it with his hands. Like a piece was missing. And the pain...the searing pain.

He had to make it to the small town. They could help him. Somebody would know what to do. It was late but someone would still be awake, right? He would pound on the door of each house until someone opened and helped him, and then...Jorge, they'd go find Jorge.

*We have to find Jorge. We can't just leave him out there. And the thing, whatever it is...there will be safety in numbers. And we will take guns.*

The moon had been high and full, but now clouds rolled in and the low hum of thunder could be heard in the distance. Rain was coming. He had to get to the village. They could help him. He stopped for just a moment and looked back to the woods. His bad leg gave out and he collapsed onto the road, hard, the pebbles of asphalt cutting into his elbows.

More blood.

And tired.

So tired.

He looked up into the sky, a prayer escaping from his dry lips - "Oh God, help me...."

A shake of his head. Once. Then a second time. Trying to clear the fog. He'd passed out when his head hit the tree. He'd been flung at least six feet into it, right? The last thing he heard was Jorge's scream and then everything faded away.

He'd been out, who knows how long. But when he came to, he was alone. All alone. Jorge was gone and he was a mess. He reached up to feel the back of his head where it had slammed into the trunk of the big oak. It was a matted mess, his hand coming away with a chunk of loose hair as he clenched his fist and then released it. His fingers were tacky from dried blood, so the hair just sort of stuck to his palm. That *was* his hair, right? Some of it looked darker and coarser than his own. He found himself staring out of curiosity. And then he shook his head yet again, trying to come back to the moment.

He had to keep moving.

He had to get up and he had to get moving again. He had to make it to the light.

To the town.

To help.

It suddenly struck him. *That* thing could still be out here. In fact, it likely *was* still out here...with him. Stalking him. Like before. That's what had happened to him and Jorge. They'd been stalked and caught, totally unawares.

What if it was playing with him? Like a cat with a mouse. Toying and playing. Pouncing and then letting go. But not really letting go. Just a game. To see the mouse limp and make its way toward its little hole in the ground. Its nest of safety. Watching from a distance with glee as the poor mouse made its way forward with the false hope of survival. What if he was the mouse and what if that thing out there was the cat? Playing with him.

His heart was suddenly racing, his breaths coming in quick, short gasps.

*I've got to get up, I've got to move! Maybe there is no hope, but moving is my only chance at hope.*

Balancing on the palms of both hands, he made to push himself up. Pain shot through his leg once again like a hot fire. And then forward.

*Step. Drag. Step. Drag.*

A roll of thunder, closer this time, the first rain drops beginning to fall.

*This is good,* he thought. *Harder to track me in the rain. Water washes the scent away, right? I've seen something about that on*

*Discovery Channel. And the clouds block the light of the moon. Make it darker. Harder to see me.*

A glimmer of hope was rising inside of him and he quickened his pace.

*But animals can see in the dark.*

He stopped and frantically looked back again. Was that a shape moving across the road? So hard to see now because it was getting darker. The clouds thickened and the rain was falling harder.

*That's right, animals have night vision.*

He had to move.

A first flash of lightning illuminated the outline of a small house just ahead. Hope swelled. If he could just make it to the house.

*I must look a mess*, he thought in panic. *Who would let someone covered in blood into their home in the middle of the night?*

He used his hand to wipe his face and smooth his hair. *Ouch!* New pain shot through the back of his head as he brushed over it. But the pain brought clarity. What exactly had happened? It was coming back to him now.

He and Jorge had spent the last couple of days in this same town. It *was* this town, right? Hard to tell right now - it was so dark and he was confused - but he thought so, nonetheless. The people had been friendly enough and there was much to see from this village along the Irish coast.

The first day of hiking was stunning, the weather perfect. He'd grown up seeing pictures of the majestic bluffs of Ireland as they dropped off into the Atlantic Ocean, but standing on the edge of one, over three hundred feet in the air, truly did take your breath away.

Heading back to their bed and breakfast, they had taken a shortcut across a field and stumbled upon four mutilated cows. The scene was grotesque. The bloated animals had been exposed for some time, covered in flies and maggots. They reported the find to the owners of the B&B, a nice couple – Vaughn and Patricia O'Leary – but they didn't seem too alarmed.

"Aye," Vaughn had said, "wild animals or wolves or some such. It happens from time to time."

"But the cows had not been eaten," Jorge mentioned to him later. "Don't wolves kill to eat? Those cows had just been...torn apart."

The pair pressed the owner to report it to the local authorities and Vaughn said he'd take care of it, but they questioned whether or not he really would.

And then tonight.

He and Jorge had headed out on a late afternoon hike to watch the sunset from the top of Masterson Peak. With the moon full, they'd planned to stay and take in a late-night view from the high point of the region, hiking back to town before midnight. And oh, how stunning it all was. The sunset was the best the two friends had seen on their backpacking trip across England, Scotland, and now Ireland.

They'd built a small fire and roasted hot dogs for dinner. Jorge pulled out his mini-Martin and began to strum tunes from his native Venezuela. The moon crested bright and full, revealing a unique beauty of the countryside all around. It had been a perfect day and with plenty of light in the night sky, the two had decided to head back to town shortly after 10:00 pm.

As they picked their way through the dense woods,

they'd gotten lost a couple of times but managed to find the trail after some backtracking.

"Rain's coming later tonight, Jorge, we can't afford to get lost too many more times," he'd chided his friend, all in good fun.

"Don't worry about me, amigo! Worry about yourself. Venezuelans always find their way home."

The smell was the first thing they noticed. Like a thick wave of musk.

The pair looked at each other, Jorge commenting that his skin felt prickly. And just like that, like some primal instinct, they knew they were being hunted.

Now, hours later - there really was no way to know what time it was. His watch had been torn from his wrist and in his confusion after coming to, he'd simply left his backpack behind. But he was almost to the dark house on the road. *Gotta get help,* was all he could think.

Then he realized it wasn't a house at all, but an old dilapidated shed for holding sheep or some other kind of animal.

Dread. And then fear.

And then he was walking faster down the road, past the shed. Other houses, real houses, came into view.

*Step. Drag. Step. Drag.*

The rain falling harder now.

The town center was still two or three blocks away and that's where the B&B was, but he needed help *now.* No time to wait. He chanced a look back over his shoulder once again and froze.

Was that? Yes!

In the distance, too hard to judge how far, but it was

there. Something in the road. The shape undefined, but...two eyes. Two *yellow* eyes... piercing the darkness and the rain. Fear shot through his body, draining him of what strength he had left. He whipped around and ran, dragging his way past one house.

Then two houses.

The third house shone a light in the front window. That was his target. His best chance of help. His best chance of survival. Bounding up the two wooden steps onto the porch, he reached the front door and banged hard with his bloody fist. Red smeared the white paint. He could hear footsteps moving beyond the threshold.

"Please God, let them hurry," he shouted through clenched teeth.

He was out of breath, his heart pounding.

In the light of the porch he looked down and saw more blood from his leg pooling on the wood planks. That's when he realized he'd been losing blood along the way.

Like a trail for the hungry wild to follow.

Like a cat being led to the mouse.

He felt light-headed.

The latch to the door disengaged and the handle turned.

As the door opened slowly, the warm glow of light and heat from the hearth poured out. A middle-aged man stood in the opening and stared at the late-night visitor standing on his porch.

Behind him a woman screamed and the visitor collapsed.

# CHAPTER 2

Phineas T. Crook sat on the balcony of his hotel room in his boxers and t-shirt. He was drenched in sweat.

Looking out across the Thames River, his gaze was fixed on the lights of the London Eye in the distance. He was shivering. His shoulders carried an uncontrollable quiver as his knees jiggled up and down.

"What is wrong with me?" he whispered, working the palms of his moist hands together. It was well after midnight; he hadn't bothered to check the time when he woke up. It was another panic attack, like so many he had suffered from the last three months. He inhaled deeply. Hold and count – one, two, three. Then exhale. Repeat.

A warm presence eased up behind him and he regretted disturbing her sleep.

"It's a beautiful night." A melodic voice instantly soothed him as a comforting hand rested on his shoulder.

"I'm sorry," was all Phin could manage to say. "I didn't mean to wake you."

"Nonsense," the voice replied quickly. "I've slept enough for a lifetime. Life is short. If you're awake, I want to be awake." She pulled a matching wrought iron chair over next to Phin's and settled in, her head leaning over onto his shoulder.

The two sat in silence as the moments ticked by, the beat of Phin's heart calming, his t-shirt drying in the slight evening breeze. She always had this effect on him. When Autumn was awake and with him, he was all good. His dearly beloved wife. His most precious earthly treasure. Who once was lost but now was found. A miracle of God that he did not deserve. And yet, they were together again.

"You had another episode, didn't you?" Autumn didn't really know what to call it. But her husband was suffering, and she struggled to understand the what and the why of it all. "We can talk about it if you want. Or not. Or we can just go back to bed, Phineas. I'm here, though. You don't have to worry anymore." She squeezed his arm tight.

And that was the heart of the problem for Phineas Crook - he worried constantly that he would lose his wife again. It had become a daily torment over the course of the last three months since she had been back with him.

"I know, I know," he replied, pulling away so that he could look at her. He never got tired of looking at her. Her silky brown hair, her milky smooth skin, but mostly her eyes - especially her eyes - their hazel tint. Now open to a world they had been closed to for the last three-and-a-half years. "In my mind, I know that all is well. That you are back and healthy and healed, but in my heart..." he stammered to continue. "In my heart, I'm scared, Autumn. I am scared to death that something is going to happen. That I'm going to lose you all over again."

A tear formed in the corner of Autumn's eye as she turned her head slightly toward the river. She could only imagine what the last three years had been like for her husband. For her it was but a moment.

The last thing she remembered was being shot in the stomach in downtown Oklahoma City. It was their sixth wedding anniversary and they had celebrated with a lovely dinner and a show. After that came the most amazing dream that seemed, to her, but a moment in time. But to Phin, it had been three years. A long, lonely, and tortuous three years. Three years of monthly visits to Second Life, Inc. in Plano, Texas, to visit Autumn. His precious E, as he loved to call her - the E standing for her middle name of Eden. Like the Garden of Eden, he'd always thought. Well, that now took on a whole new meaning after the events of the last year which had led to...now. She was back. It really was a miracle. Even the media called it that.

No patient of Second Life, Inc. had ever awakened. Oh, that was the whole point of the service, to provide a "suspended animation" type of care that could theoretically last until some point in the future when medicine could advance to the point that whatever led to a patient's near demise could be cured. But the technology and service provided by Second Life, Inc. was still very new and no patient had ever been revived.

Until Autumn.

And now she was back, her wounds healing on their own with remarkable speed. She was up and about within forty-eight hours and discharged from medical care within a week. Everyone wanted to know what had happened. The Crooks were inundated with media requests from the local news affiliates. CNN and Fox News picked up the story, as did the AP, which pushed it to all the national papers. 48 Hours wanted to do a special on the couple and their story. It was overwhelming to say the least. All Phineas and Autumn wanted to do was get away. And that's exactly what they did.

Phin's employer, Oklahoma Baptist University, had extended his sabbatical through the fall semester so the couple could reconnect. It may have only been a moment in time in Autumn's internal clock, but three years *had* passed. A lot had changed in the world. A lot had changed in *her* world. When she went to sleep, she had been a pastor's wife living in Oklahoma City. When she woke up, she was a college professor's wife living in a quaint little home on Broadway Avenue in Shawnee, Oklahoma.

The first time Phin drove her "home" it had felt so unreal. Walking up to a house that wasn't hers, yet it was. All the furniture, the pictures, and knick-knacks...their bed. It was all the same, but in a new place. Those first days were dizzying as she took it all in. Phin had taken Autumn on a tour of the OBU campus, introducing her to all of his colleagues and friends. It was as if his life had gone on while hers had frozen in time.

For Phin's part, it hardly seemed like life had gone on. Oh, time had continued to tick by, the days of the calendar flipping from one day to the next. But the life that Phin had grown to love and cherish, the life with his darling E, had come to a crashing halt - the only remaining remnant being his trips to see his sleeping beauty at Second Life, Inc. Her comatose, near lifeless body behind a shield of Plexiglass. But now she was back, just like before.

But not.

Life was now so very different and crazy. Everybody, it seemed, wanted a piece of them. To know the story. A story that in a very real and serious sense Phin was prohibited from telling.

The events surrounding the search for the Garden of Eden and real story behind Autumn's recovery were off limits, both legally and practically. What Phin and Autumn needed more than anything else was to be left alone. They needed time and they needed time away. So they'd simply left.

He didn't need to be back until the start of J-Term in January, and so the Crooks did what the Crooks loved doing most. They traveled. Boarding a plane with one-way tickets to Europe, they simply fell off the radar and had remained off the radar for the last couple of months. Their most recent journey had led them to a favorite city of theirs, London.

"You're not going to lose me again, Phin." Autumn had turned back to face Phin. Her tears gone, nothing but determination in her face. She was a fighter. Another characteristic Phin loved about his wife.

"You can't know that, sweetheart."

"Of course I can't *know* that, Phin. Nobody knows the future. But listen, I'm not going anywhere. What happened to me – to us – was a fluke thing. We could live to be one hundred and not be assaulted and me shot again. And the doctors all say that I am one hundred percent healed. They even said my body looks better than new in some respects. So, listen to me, Phin." She grabbed both of his hands and looked hard into his brown eyes, his floppy brown wave of hair mussed to one side. "We are going to grow old...together. Do you hear me? This. Will. Happen."

Phin felt embarrassed and his face flushed a bit. Why was it so easy for her to be the brave one?

"Oh, E, you are the best of me." The tension eased a bit in his shoulders. "I will say this." A bit of mischief appeared in his eyes and a sly smile returned to his face. "The doctors are right. Your body definitely looks better than new." He winked.

"Stop it!" She slapped his chest playfully. Phin drew her into a long embrace and kissed her gently.

They made their way back to bed and then eventually back to sleep. At least Autumn fell back asleep. Sleep was something that eluded Phin these days. Oh, he'd nod off well enough, but he always woke up prematurely, fear taking its cold hold. The first thing he would do is check to make sure Autumn was breathing, that she was still there with him. And then the second wave of fear would hit him. *Will she wake up? When the sun rises, will she?* He fought the urge to nudge her, just to make sure she was really with him. The last three years had taken their toll on Phin, and it seemed he was still paying the price.

As Phin lay in bed, his wife asleep by his side, he wondered when it would all end and life would return to normal. Was normal even still possible for the Crooks?

# CHAPTER 3

"Quit lagging behind!"

Malcolm Connor yelled over his shoulder. "The sooner we get there the sooner we can get out of this mess." The rain was coming down in sheets as the two young men slogged their way down the muddy trail that led to the beach. They each carried a battery-powered torch to illuminate the path that had degenerated into a slippery mess. More than once they each had taken a spill.

Behind him, Jamison Murphy slipped yet again, a round of curses pouring from his mouth. "I'm not even supposed to be out here tonight. It wasn't my turn."

"Stop yer yappin' already. Greg has the fever and so you're next on the list. That's how it works and you know it. It's not like no one's covered for you before," Malcolm reminded his partner. That quieted Jamison for the moment as he troweled a layer of mud off his trousers with his hand. The two trudged on, careful with each step.

Malcolm was the older of the two but not by much, only a year. They'd gone to school together and had known each other their whole lives. He'd always known Jamison to complain about the smallest inconveniences. Tonight, the inconveniences had come in triplet form.

First, he'd called Jamison to fill in for Greg Collins last minute, only an hour-and-a-half ago now. In Malcom's defense, he himself had only found out about Greg's illness about fifteen minutes before that. When he saw Jamison's name on the list as the "next" he had rolled his eyes.

Second, a storm had blown in, and harder than had been expected. It was never an easy hike to the cave, but in the dead of night and in the rain, well....

Finally, their shift had fallen on the evening of a full moon. Everything was inflamed when the moon was full. The tide was stronger. Storms were fiercer. And then "they" were always more agitated. On edge. Which is why the two of them had to do a shift change in the middle of the night.

Normally, on all other nights, the shift change occurred at dawn. But when the moon was full it had been decided that relief should be extended every four hours instead of every eight. And if your name fell on the night of a full moon – well, that's what had happened to Malcom and Jamison and, yes, it was inconvenient.

But such was the duty of the citizens of the small Irish township of Tiamat. Theirs was a close-knit community with outsiders visiting only for tourism purposes, and not many at that. As in most small towns, everyone knew everyone else's business. Few ever left for the world at large, and those who did always returned, usually choosing to work the family business, whatever that be, to get married, and then to die. And so it had been for many generations in Tiamat. The decision to have children, well that was a bit more complicated. While propagation was strongly encouraged, some couples didn't want to subject another generation to the peculiarities of life in their village. Others - most, actually - embraced the duty to procreate. The joy of children outweighing the trials, as they saw it.

All Malcolm and Jamison cared about at this moment, though, was getting their shift over with. But first they had to get to the cave.

"When are you and Marilyn getting married?" Jamison asked, trying to change his sour attitude by focusing on something different, happy.

"Next summer, but I'd be all for tying the knot sooner. I keep telling her that we just need to run away to Dublin and get hitched with the judge. But she'll have none of it." Malcolm laughed, recalling the numerous times he'd playfully gigged his fiancé with the notion.

"My mum says you two are a perfect match, Malcolm. I'm happy for you, truly I am."

This lifted Malcolm's spirits to hear such words coming from Jamison Murphy. It was no secret that he'd been sweet on Marilyn all the way back to grade school. Oh, they'd dated for a while, but she was forever turned away by his propensity for negativity. Malcolm was surprised that he was being so openly positive about his pending marriage to her. Maybe Jamison was finally growing up.

"Thanks much, Jami. I appreciate it, I do. I know you had hopes for you and Marilyn at one time."

"True enough. Marilyn's a real looker she is, but I've got an eye for Molly Walsh now. If you haven't heard, we've been seeing each other the last month or so."

"She's gotta be five years younger than you, Jami! And still in school, she is. Are you sure her father's gonna take a liken' to you dating his daughter?" Malcolm was surprised that any girl would be interested in Jamison. He didn't have the best reputation in town with young and old alike. For his part, he didn't like the way he talked about Marilyn being a "looker" and all, so he supported anything or anyone else that might divert his attention away from her.

"Oh, don't worry about ol' Bob Walsh. I've got him in my hip pocket, I do." Jamison chuckled. "Molly says that her and her da don't get on very well and that he can't wait for her to graduate, find a man, and move on. Well, I aim to be that man. Malcolm, she really does like me, I tell you. At least it seems like she does. And she's as ready to get out of her father's house as he is to get her out. Why, the first time I went over to meet her folks, it was Bob himself who opened the door and invited me right on in. Shook my hand real hard and was all smiles. Told me I was welcome anytime and that he was real excited Molly and me was a datin'."

"Well, alright, I suppose." Malcolm couldn't help but join in Jamison's newfound joy. He turned and shook his wet hand. "Best of luck to you both, Jami. Who knows, it might be a race to see which one of us gets married first." The two laughed in spite of the rain and wind, both of which seemed to be dying down somewhat.

It was another ten minutes until the two men broke free from the forest trail that descended the bluff to near beach level. The path was already becoming sandy although still mixed with dirt and mud. The storm was nearly gone and the clouds were thinning, the night sky beginning to lighten.

Malcolm's thoughts had turned inward again. The talk of girls and Marilyn and dating had him thinking again about his impending summer wedding. Marilyn wanted to leave Tiamat behind and move somewhere, preferably out of the country. She had a fascination with Scotland and was putting the pressure on him to at least consider it. But he just wasn't sure. His parents and the city elders really put the pressure on the next generation to stay and help the township stay alive and hopefully even grow. The reality of the situation was that it was just too hard and risky to leave. Oh, some did, but eventually all came back. Especially once they had children. And then there was the cave. The little secret of Tiamat. Actually, it would be a big secret if anyone on the outside were to ever find out. Which no one had...yet.

The two men followed their torch beams along the beach, staying close to the overhang of the bluff. The cave was just ahead, maybe another hundred meters, and they could make out a small fire just at the entrance. It was normal practice to keep one going for warmth on these cold fall nights.

"Who's on duty tonight?" Jamison asked, breaking the silence.

"Blake and Sheamus. The brothers."

"Well, they'll be glad to see us, I'm sure. One thing's for certain, their hike back will be a heckuva lot easier than our hike down."

"I don't know, it's still pretty muddy up there - "

Malcolm's words cut off as he walked up the small rise to the campfire burning just inside the cave's entrance. Something wasn't right. He'd felt it a few meters back but had tried to dismiss it.

"Hey, where are they – "

"Ssshhhh!" Malcolm cut his partner off. Setting down his pack, he eased his way toward the fire. No one was around and he strained to hear any sounds coming from deeper within the cave itself. He could make out scratches and what sounded like muffled grunts.

"Those guys better not be jackin' with us."

"I said be quiet, Jami!" Malcolm interjected again, this time holding up his hand toward Jamison while straining his eyes to see into the darkness. Seeing what he was trying to do, Jamison sidled up next to him, flipping on his torch.

The horror that lay before the young men paralyzed them both.

Jamison couldn't move.

It was as if his feet had been cemented to the ground. He was shivering, beads of sweat popping out on his forehead. He couldn't take his eyes off of the scene in front of him. Next came the sensation of warmth as his bladder lost control. The torch fell from Jamison's hand, landing with a loud crash on the rock floor. The light went out, plunging the pair back into an eerie darkness save the dying fire just meters behind them.

"Rrr...rrrr....RUN!"

# CHAPTER 4

"Get some bandages while I hold this towel in place. We have to stop the bleeding."

Ross McCloud pressed down hard on the thigh of the unconscious man. He'd been reading a book, trying to ward off his insomnia, when the bang on the front door had come. Startled, he had cautiously made his way to open the door, not certain at all what to expect. Mattie, his wife, had been rustled from her sleep due to the commotion and had come out from the back room to see what the need could possibly be at this hour.

"I'll be right back. Just keep the pressure on that wound," Mattie called back as she rushed to the closet and yanked down an old bedsheet. They would need more than the few bandages they had on hand.

The man was a mess, wet with dirt and mud and blood all over, but the leg was the worst. It looked like he'd been attacked by some wild animal. He was probably lucky to be alive. His blood loss was severe. Mattie started ripping strips of cloth, dropping down next to Ross to begin first aid in earnest.

"Here," she commanded. "Let me see what we've got."

Ross let her move in and take control. Mattie was good in situations like this, having volunteered at the local physician's office for the last decade. She was only a receptionist, but Dr. Kelly enlisted her help from time to time with various patients and she had picked up a lot of pointers on wound care along the way.

Mattie slowly removed the towel. The bleeding had slowed greatly from the pressure Ross had applied. This was good news. Cautiously, they cut away the man's trousers, and then with great care Mattie cleaned the wound with clean towels and warm water. The thigh muscle was more intact than she'd first thought, but the wound was still severe.

"Looks like it was ripped open," Ross commented with fascination. "Like he was just flayed. And look at all the bruises on his arms and torso." Even with his shirt still on, the rips and tears in the fabric exposed his pale skin. "His head's a mess too. Man, this guy really went through the ringer with something."

"Or someone." Mattie eyed him knowingly.

"Don't talk like that, Mattie," Ross replied with a stern tone. "We haven't had problems like that in a long time now. We've taken precautions. You know the system works just fine."

"Yes, you are right. It's just..." Her voice trailed off. "I wonder who he is." Mattie gently brushed his long black hair off of his forehead, using a rag to clean the grime from his cheeks. Their unconscious visitor had a kind face, a naïve innocence in his appearance. "There," she declared. "That's better."

She finished cleaning the wound, applying generous amounts of antiseptic the best she could before binding the leg with the strips of cloth from the bedsheet.

"Let's get some fresh clothes on him and then put him in Tommy's bed," Ross suggested. At the mention of their only son's name, Mattie stopped working and looked into Ross's brown eyes. The same eyes as Tommy's. "I know what you're thinking, Mattie, but he can't stay here on the floor. It's either Tommy's bed or ours."

The mention of their son touched a tender spot with both of the McClouds, a deep heartache. They lived a simple life in the small hamlet of Tiamat with Ross functioning as the town's gunsmith. He had a small shop on the square that had been passed to him from his father, who had received it from his father, and so it had gone, back for several generations. Between what the shop made and Mattie's modest income from Dr. Kelly's office, they did well for themselves. But their home was small - just a two-bedroom single story dwelling that had been passed to the couple from Mattie's side of the family. Small, but enough room for the couple and their son, Tommy. But Tommy was gone now and had been for some time.

"I know, but...it's just, it's Tommy's room and he's coming home soon." Mattie's heart churned. She had kept his room exactly the same as the day he left, his return inevitable.

"Not till later next year, the spring at the earliest. This is just for tonight, until we figure out what to do."

"What to do? We have to get him to Dr. Kelly for starters. I've only stopped the bleeding and bound the wounds. This boy needs stitches and probably a blood transfusion. Maybe even surgery. And then we need to let the town council know."

"I think that's an overreaction, dear. I'm not sure this is a council matter."

"Not a council matter? Excuse me, but we have a stranger in our home. A stranger to this town who's been torn apart. This was no accident. Someone did this to him." Mattie barked back at her husband. She had a gift for cutting to the chase.

"Not someone! Some *thing*. Or it was an accident," Ross shot back.

"We don't know that either. Not for sure. In fact, what we don't know about this young man and what happened to him is more than what we do know. That's why we need to inform the council. You know I'm right."

Ross did know she was right. He just didn't like it. The implications for what this might mean was a road he didn't want to go down. That none of them wanted to go down. The chances were that Ross was correct, that this was an accident with some wild animal their late-night visitor had run into.

"Okay, yes, we will let the council know first thing in the morning. Let's get him settled first, and then I will go and call on Dr. Kelly. He won't like it but I don't want to be responsible for another person's life any longer than is necessary."

27

Mattie still didn't like the idea of putting the stranger in Tommy's room but her husband was correct, Tommy wouldn't be home for at least six more months. Once this terrible night was over she could wash the bedsheets and return the room to the way it was. She washed the sheets monthly anyway so this would not be out of the norm.

They carefully lifted the young man, easing him to the spare bedroom and onto the bed. It was not easy work and they took extreme caution so as not to reopen his wounds. Next, they cut away his tattered trousers and shirt and Mattie gave him a warm sponge bath, wiping away the blood, grime, and mud from his body. Ross went and found some of his old clothes to redress their guest. Mattie drew a hard line with using Tommy's clothes. While Mattie dressed the young man, Ross cleaned up the living room and porch. Their guest had made quite a mess with his entrance.

Ross finally slipped on his canvas overcoat and walking boots, intending to head for Dr. Kelly's home. He was not looking forward to having to wake up the good doctor.

That's when he heard the shouting. Outside and in the distance.

"What's that commotion outside?" Mattie rushed into the living room, a look of panic on her face.

"No idea, I was just about to check." Ross pulled back the front curtain, straining to look down the street toward the town center. "There's someone out there. He's running from house to house, banging and yelling. I think it's Harv Connor but I'm not sure." Ross looked back at his wife, a puzzled expression on his face.

"This is crazy," she whispered. "What's going on out there tonight?"

As if to answer her question, heavy footfalls bounded onto the McCloud front porch followed by pounding on the front door – for a second time that night.

"Ross! Ross! You awake? Open your door," came a wild call.

It *was* Harv Connor, his gravelly voice unmistakable. Ross ripped open the front door.

"Ross! I saw your light on. Come quick. We're all meeting over at O'Leary's. It's an emergency." Harv was winded, his face shining with sweat behind his grizzled beard, eyes wide.

"What's happening, Harv? What's going on?" Ross questioned.

"It's the cave, Ross. There's trouble at the cave. Something's happened, that's all I know. But you need to come quick. I've got to find the rest of the council. Just come now." And with that Harv Connor tore off into the night.

Trouble at the cave.

Trouble in his back bedroom.

Trouble.

Ross looked at his wife one more time. That same knowing look they'd shared earlier returning to each other's eyes.

"I'll be back. Lock. This. Door." He made a move onto the porch and grabbed the front door handle, about to pull it closed.

"Wait," Mattie called to him. She shoved the cold steel of a stock and long barrel into his hand. "Take your gun."

# CHAPTER 5

"Everyone quiet down!" Vaughn O'Leary shouted over the wild talk of the group gathered in the parlor of the Lear House.

All seven members of the town council were present, along with a few wives and a smattering of other folks from the town who'd been awakened to the late-night commotion as Harv Connor had pounded and shouted his way through the streets. The council would normally meet in the town hall to conduct official business but at this late hour, and with the state of events that had occurred, it was easier to meet at the Lear House since Vaughn also functioned as the council's head. The shingle hanging outside the B&B bore the technical name of the establishment: O'Leary's Bed & Breakfast. But to the people of the township it was just the Lear House.

"I need everyone to settle down so we can sort out

what's happened down at the cave." Slowly, the side conversations subsided. The parlor was a small room with old hardwood plank flooring that creaked and popped continuously as people shifted their weight and scuffled around. Not everyone was standing though - the six or so marble-top, two-person tables were all occupied as well. During the day the parlor functioned as the breakfast part of the bed and breakfast.

"What exactly *has* happened, Vaughn?" It was Bob Walsh who called out from the back of the room. His daughter, Molly, had taken a liking to Jamison Murphy, who sat shivering at one of the marble-top tables by a window, a blanket draped over his shoulders. He was staring into a neglected cup of coffee. "Jami, my boy, what happened down there?"

"Where's Malcolm, Jami? What happened to my son?" Harv Connor's rough voice boomed. Harv was a confident, strong man, but he was clearly concerned for his youngest son.

"And what about my two boys, Jami? You and Malcolm were supposed to relieve Blake and Sheamus. Tell us what happened." Calvin Lynch was even more undone. The two brothers, his sons, were all he had left in the world after his wife had passed from cancer five years before.

"Yes, Jami, speak up!" another voice called.

"Come on, man. Talk to us," yet another demanded. The room erupted again in chatter, some yelling.

"PLEASE. Everyone has got to settle down. We will get nowhere if there isn't order." If there was one thing Vaughn O'Leary was all about it was order. He ran a tight ship at the bed and breakfast and carried an ease in his demeanor when it came to tense situations. This is exactly why he led the town council. He was not an overly tall man, but at just under six feet, he was taller than most residents of Tiamat. Like nearly all in the town, he had black hair and dark brown eyes that complimented his black goatee sans the mustache.

"What we need are answers." It was Bob Walsh again.

"Yes, we do." Vaughn replied. Directing his attention to Jamison Murphy, he placed a gentle hand on the young man's shoulder. In a soft voice he said, "It's okay, son. Tell everyone what you told me earlier. Take your time. You're among family here."

And then there was silence in the room.

The silence ticked on for a moment and Vaughn began to wonder if Jamison even heard him. The boy was clearly in shock. But slowly Jamison lifted his coffee mug and took a sip. As if the trance had been broken, he looked up, his eyes meeting Vaughn's. The innkeeper just nodded his head and smiled ever so slightly as if to communicate that all was well. But clearly, all was not well.

Both of Jamison's eyes became moist and a tear rolled down one cheek. His head rotated and his eyes met Harv Connor's.

"I'm so sorry, Mr. Connor. I'm so sorry," Jamison croaked. Harv Connor took a step toward the young man. Not in a threatening way, though. Harv could certainly come across that way. He was stout and stocky and very strong. His black hair was always mussed and his beard unkempt. But his move toward Jamison said *tell me more*.

"It's fine, Jami. Just take your time. What happened down there? Where's my son?"

"We..." Jamison began again and then stopped. Something clamped onto his mind, holding him back. But then he continued. "We left earlier to go to the cave. You know, it was our turn. Well, not mine...you see, it was Malcolm and Greg's shift. But Greg got sick so he called Malcolm, and Malcolm called me because my name was next on the list." Harv nodded as if to say, *this is good, keep going.* "So, we left and it was bad. The storm, you know. So, it took a little longer to get there with the rain and mud and all. I didn't want to go but that's not why I left him, Mr. Connor. I promise." Tears began to flow. "Malcolm joked with me and it made things better. He's like that you know. And so, we were good and I was okay with doing my shift, I was. So, the rain let up and we made it to the cave."

There was a slam of the front door and a rustling in the back of the room. "Let me through. Where is he?" A frantic female voice was pleading. People made way as Molly Walsh burst through and fell at Jamison's feet. "Oh, Jami, you're alive. You're okay!" she cried. Jami set his cup down and fell to his knees, embracing Molly as she clutched him, both of them sobbing.

Patricia O'Leary stood next to her husband and could only place a hand over her mouth. Others in the room were similarly moved. Jamison Murphy had a reputation of being carefree and brazen. Sometimes foolhardy and not exactly trustworthy. But overly emotional was not something that anyone knew Jamison to be. To see this young man sobbing and holding fast to the young Molly said something in and of itself as to what the boy had experienced. But then, as if awakened from a trance - perhaps it was new strength found in the embrace of Molly - Jamison rose to his feet and faced the gathered group, resolve showing on his face.

"Malcolm and I arrived at the cave." He began, passing his hand over his face to clear his eyes, wiping his nose on the back of his sleeve. "There was a fire at the entrance like normal but Blake and Sheamus weren't there. We knew something was up but just didn't have any idea." His voice cracked but he pressed on. "Didn't have any idea what was going on. We knew they'd never just leave. Not until we showed up. Blake and Sheamus aren't like that." He gave Calvin Lynch a knowing look.

"So, what happened next, where are my boys?" Calvin prodded.

"We decided to go to the back. Of the cave, you know. To check and make sure everything was okay. And maybe Blake and Sheamus were back there too. But..." Jamison stammered. Tension hung in the air. He knew that what he was about to say would change everything.

"Go on," Vaughn O'Leary urged.

"They're dead. I'm sorry, Mr. Lynch. I'm so, so sorry." Tears began to flow again, but tears of sorrow this time.

"Nooo..." A deep sigh of pain escaped from Calvin Lynch's throat and he stammered. Ross McCloud was quick to grab hold and settle him into a chair. The room began to buzz with chatter once again.

"And Malcolm. What about Malcolm?" Furman Hayes' voice called out, this time with the question. It was his daughter, Marilyn, that was engaged to marry Malcolm come summertime. She had also been awakened when Harv Connor came banging on Furman's door. Furman Hayes was on the town council and his presence was essential. Marilyn overheard the hectic conversation about trouble at the cave and she knew that Malcolm was supposed to be down there for his shift. She was immediately beside herself and wanted to come to the Lear House, but Furman had insisted she stay at home and wait until he knew more.

"We ran, Mr. Hayes. We ran as fast as we could, but the trail up from the beach was muddy and we slipped. It was so hard to get any traction." Jamison paused and looked around the room once again. "And we were *chased*." Another pause. "We ran and we were chased. At one point Malcolm fell and slipped off the trail. 'Just go,' he said. 'Keep going and don't stop.' He was yelling the whole time. 'Go, go, go!' So I did. I ran and ran. I've never been so scared in my whole life. Then I heard a scream. It was Malcolm. I turned to go back, but then all I could hear in my head was Malcolm telling me to keep going." The sobbing had returned as Jamison buried his face in his hands. "I'm so sorry, Mr. Connor. Mr. Hayes, tell Marilyn I'm so sorry. Really, I am."

The room was dead silent as the revelation of what Jamison Murphy was telling them and what it meant began to sink in. Furman Hayes had turned around and was facing a painting on the wall but not seeing it. Harv Connor just stared at Jamison.

"They're all dead, I tell you. All dead," Jami cried one final time before collapsing to the floor yet again.

# CHAPTER 6

Vaughn O'Leary stared at the young Jamison Murphy as he sat sobbing on the floor, held tight by Molly Walsh. If what he was telling the gathered group was true, then this was a worst-case scenario situation for the town. Somehow, they'd lost control and it was imperative that control be regained. As bad as things were, they could certainly get worse and would get worse without quick action. As the Tiamat council leader, it was on him to take that action.

"Harv, help me get him back up in a chair." Vaughn reached down and grabbed Jamison under his left shoulder while Harv Connor took the right. They settled him back upright while Molly pulled a second chair over and kept her arm around her boyfriend. Vaughn was about to address the group when Dr. Boris Kelly stepped forward, eyeing Jamison.

"Jami, what exactly do you mean when you say they're

all dead? How do you know?" Dr. Kelly was an astute man, details never passing him by. Even though it was the middle of the night, he somehow had appeared in the parlor of the Lear House in his standard black suit pants, white dress shirt with a black vest, and a black tie. His stereotypical round spectacles highlighted his dark brown eyes, accentuating their piercing nature. When Boris Kelly was looking at you it appeared as if he was looking *through* you.

"Because they just are, Dr. Kelly." Jami wiped his eyes again, regaining his composure. "If you saw what I saw -"

"And what exactly did you see, Jami?" Dr. Kelly cut him off. "Did you see Malcolm Connor killed? You said you heard him scream but did you see his body?"

"Well, no... but if you saw -"

"So, you don't *know* that Malcolm's dead, do you?" Dr. Kelly glanced over his right shoulder at Harv Connor. "You didn't really see that, did you?"

"No sir. I didn't."

"And what *did* you see, Jami?" Vaughn O'Leary asked this time. He knew where the good doctor was going with his line of questioning and he was grateful. That's what was needed right now...information. They needed to know more. "Take your time and tell us exactly what you *did* see. Not what you *think* happened. Take us back to the cave. What did you see at the cave?"

"Oh man...the cave..." Jami trailed off.

"This is important, Jami. Take a drink and clear your thinking and then take your time and walk us all back through it all." Dr. Kelly was treating Jami like one of his patients now.

Jamison did as he was told. He took a careful sip from the steaming mug on the antique table in front of him, drawing in a long, deep breath after he swallowed. It all worked to calm him down.

"Okay, like I said...me and Malcom got to the cave and Blake and Sheamus were nowhere around."

"My boys would never run off and leave the cave unattended. That's not like them." Calvin Lynch spoke up as if defending his sons.

"That's what we thought too, Mr. Lynch. That's why we went on toward the back. Of the cave, I mean. To see if they were back there checking on *them*." The room was again fixated on Jamison Murphy, hanging on his every word. "And they were back there, alright. But they weren't...oh, it was so bad! So, so bad."

"What was bad, Jami?" Vaughn prodded him again. "Keep going. I know it's hard but it's important that we know what you saw."

"They're dead." Jamison muttered.

"Blake and Sheamus?" Dr. Kelly asked this time. "You saw Blake and Sheamus dead. You saw their bodies."

"Yes...No...I mean it's not that simple. You don't understand."

"Help us understand, Jami."

"There was so...much...blood. It was hard to tell. There was a red flannel shirt, and a boot, and jeans, and...oh, it was so messy. And...he was being eaten!" Jamison's eyes bugged out wide at the last statement. There were gasps in the little parlor and no less than a few people began to cry softly.

Vaughn O'Leary went pale, frozen in place, his mind

working as if processing this news. Dr. Kelly was unfazed as he continued the questioning. "Who was being eaten, Jami? Was it Blake or Sheamus?"

"I don't know," he cried out. "I don't know. Sheamus I think, but it could have been Blake. There was so much blood...I think it was both."

"But you don't really know for sure, do you? You don't know. You're doing good, son." Dr. Kelly placed his hand on Jamison's shoulder in a fatherly gesture. "I have one more question, and this is important. Did you see the gate? Was it open or closed? We need to know what or who did this, so this is very important. Was the gate open?"

Jamison Murphy looked spent and defeated. His shoulders slumped. "I'm sorry, I never looked. I can't say. We were so shocked. It was horrible. I've never seen anything..."

"So, you don't *know*," Dr. Kelly trailed off. The doctor turned his attention from Jamison to the group. "Gentlemen...ladies...what we don't know is still more than what we do know. Vaughn," he addressed the Lear House owner, "I think it's imperative that we get a team together ASAP and get down to the cave to see exactly what has happened. And obviously this group needs to be armed. Whatever is going on down there...well, it's a major problem."

"We've also got another problem." It was Ross McCloud who interjected for the first time. He was leaned against a back wall of the parlor, the barrel of his shotgun resting on the hardwood floor as he clutched the butt. Heads swiveled toward the town's gunsmith, a man normally of few words. He looked tired and haggard with day-old stubble on skin that looked like it had spent too many days in the sun.

"What kind of problem, Ross? We've got our hands full here with this news from Jamison, I believe," Vaughn O'Leary countered. He and Ross McCloud respected each other but weren't on the friendliest of terms. They'd grown up together and were the same age, having been athletic competitors during their school days. At one point they'd both dated Patricia Combs, and she'd ultimately chosen the more charismatic O'Leary. But just the fact that the teenage version of Ross McCloud had had his eye on "his girl" was something O'Leary seemed to continue to carry.

For his part, Ross McCloud had moved on, falling in love with his dear Mattie. By his way of thinking he'd come out on the better end of things. Mattie was a good wife and mother and adored her rough-around-the-edges husband. As adults the two men were civil to each other – that was the best way to describe it.

"Well, I've got a young man up at my house all bloody and torn apart. Stumbled onto my doorstep over an hour ago, banging and yelling. Passed out as soon as I opened the door."

"Good lord, who is he?" Bob Walsh spoke up this time, questioning. He had worked his way over, standing by his daughter Molly, who was still comforting Jamison, rubbing his back in a slow circle.

"Got no idea. It's no one who lives here in town, that's for sure. Figured he might be one of those two boys who stayed at your place the last couple of days," Ross replied, looking at Vaughn O'Leary.

Vaughn didn't like the sound of this news. He was

contemplative for a moment, rubbing the back of his neck. "Yes, I've had two guests for two days. Both Americans. One white and one Hispanic."

"Well, the boy at my place isn't Hispanic. And like I said, he's all tore up. Lost a lot of blood. I figured he'd been attacked by something and was about to come wake up Dr. Kelly here when Harv came running down the street hollerin'. And now...well, with this news, I just don't know. But our problem just got more...complicated."

"Yes, complicated. That's an understatement," O'Leary replied. "The two staying at the House took off late afternoon today for a sunset hike to Masterson Peak. Clearly, they should be back by now and aren't. Okay, everyone listen up." Vaughn O'Leary had decided what needed to be done and he was ready to build a coalition. Facing his wife, he said, "Patricia, you and Ross head over to his place. Take Dr. Kelly with you. I need you to verify that the young man at the McCloud's is indeed one of our guests. If he is, then we've got to figure out what happened to him and more importantly, where his friend is." O'Leary didn't need to say what the group was thinking.

Patricia nodded, as did the doctor and Ross McCloud. They began to make their way out of the parlor as Vaughn O'Leary continued. "What we are going to do is put together two groups. One group will head down to the cave. The other group will head to Masterson Peak. Even if the young man at the McCloud place isn't one of my guests we still need to know where those two are. Maybe they're just camping on the peak but for their own safety we should escort them back to town. Both groups need to be armed so take your guns and if you need help, see Ross here. He can outfit you from his shop."

Ross nodded in reply and then spoke up. "I want to be in the group that goes to the cave, Vaughn. Count me in."

A pause as the two eyed each other. "You know that's not possible, Ross." The stare continued.

"I wasn't asking, Vaughn."

"I know you weren't, but you know the rules. If it weren't for Tommy –"

"Tommy's why I have to go."

"Tommy's why you *can't* go." Vaughn's voice rose just slightly. "And I can't either...because of Lucious."

Ross continued a hard stare. The room grew quiet as the two men appeared to be in a standoff.

"Look, Ross, I understand. I do. This isn't about you and me. It's bigger than that. We both have sons that are returning. Tommy in the spring and my boy sometime this month. Any day now. The rules are clear. We...can't...go."

Vaughn O'Leary was right. Ross McCloud knew it. The events of this night, whatever was going on outside the walls of the parlor of the Lear House - outside the confines of the simple hamlet of Tiamat - was bigger than the petty feud of their youth.

Ross broke his stare and simply turned and walked out the front door into the night, Patricia O'Leary and Dr. Boris Kelly following.

# CHAPTER 7

*Masterson Peak Search Team*

The four men each carried a shotgun and a tranquilizer gun, planning to use either depending on what or who they met.

Dawn was still a good three hours away and so the group carried battery-powered torches to illuminate their steps. A dank cold had settled in with a clear sky after the rain. Furman Hayes worked to hike the collar of his heavy wool coat up around his neck to stave off the chill working to seep into his bones. There had been more discussion about who was going to be in each of the two search parties before matters had finally been settled by Vaughn O'Leary.

*Always Vaughn O'Leary*, thought Furman.

Yes, he was the leader of the town council, and so it was his right and responsibility to have the final word, but

Vaughn O'Leary could be heavy-handed and manipulative, Furman knew.

Everyone knew.

In this case it was decided that two groups of four men would be sent out. Four because they could move faster than a larger party, but also four because it was big enough for protection.

"Safety in numbers," Vaughn had said.

He was right, of course, and that was the rub for Furman and so many others. Vaughn would always be Vaughn, but he was also usually right.

Eight men were summarily selected and then it came down to who was going where.

Everyone wanted to go to the cave. That made sense.

The thoughts of everyone gathered at the Lear House were on Malcolm Connor and Blake and Sheamus Lynch, and also the *others*. The answers to all their questions lay at the cave. Concern for the fate of his son meant that Harv Connor insisted - no demanded - that he was on the team going to the cave and that "no one can stop me."

Harv was a big, burly man, and even the wiles of Vaughn O'Leary couldn't steer him otherwise this night. Plus, everyone agreed that he should be one of those going to the cave. It was also decided that Calvin Lynch would be going. He too was a father, desperate to find out what happened to his boys.

For his part, the cave was where Furman wanted to go as well. He could still see the plea in his daughter's eyes as he left the house earlier, headed to the Lear House. She'd spent the previous day ordering invitations and working on other details for the summer wedding. She was beside herself in love with Malcolm and he with her. Furman needed to find out what happened to Malcolm for Marilyn's sake. He was the boy's future father-in-law after all. She would be desperate to know more.

But he was also a council member, Vaughn had reminded him. There were only seven council members total.

Vaughn O'Leary couldn't go, and neither could Ross McCloud. It was against the rules. Dr. Boris Kelly couldn't go because he was needed at the McCloud place to check on the mystery stranger who'd collapsed on Ross and Mattie's front porch. With Harv Connor and Calvin Lynch already decided as leaders of the cave team, it left only himself and Bob Walsh as the final two council members. So, it quickly became clear that he had no choice in the matter.

Masterson Peak it was.

To find, hopefully, the two guests that had been staying at the Lear House, safe and sound, all tucked into their sleeping bags. Bob Walsh was fine with this, of course. He had no business at the cave. His daughter, Molly, was dating Jamison Murphy and the two of them were back at the Lear House consoling each other.

If he was honest with himself, though, Furman Hayes wasn't at all optimistic as his group of four trudged their way toward the Peak. The cold that he felt this night had more behind it than just the weather. Something evil was in the air.

Bob Walsh was a quiet man, and as he followed steps behind Furman, little was said between the two. Bob drank a bit too much at times and overall had a disengaged air about him. Furman had been surprised that he'd allowed the relationship between Jamison and Molly to happen at all given Jami's reputation. There's no way he'd have let that boy near his precious Marilyn. But because it was Bob Walsh, well, it sort of just fit how things might happen in the Walsh house. He had to admit, though, that Jami and Molly did seem to make a good couple.

Furman looked back to check on his crew. Bob Walsh had his head down. Behind him were Greg Collins and Happy Flynn, both young, in their early twenties.

Greg was the one who was supposed to go with Malcolm to the cave tonight but had fallen ill. As soon as he got word that there was trouble, he immediately volunteered to help and had recruited his best friend Happy Flynn. Happy wasn't his real name, of course. His real name was Oliver but for some reason Furman didn't know, he'd gotten tagged with the nickname of Happy. Probably because he wore a perpetual smile on his face, if Furman were to guess. Greg didn't look well, Furman could see that much. By the way his shoulders sagged, he looked to be carrying a measure of guilt, as if what happened to Malcolm was all his fault. He also wanted to go to the cave, but that was out of the question given his condition. So, Masterson Peak with Furman, Bob, and Happy it was.

There were several routes to Masterson Peak, and the group had chosen the most common path straight out of the center of town. This was a well-worn trail of dirt, now mud, that was mostly open and exposed as it hugged the edge of Ashur Mountain while winding its way to the Peak. The plan was to follow the path to the top, check out the Peak, and if they didn't find anyone, to work their way back down through the woods that dumped out onto the road outside of town. This would put them close to the McCloud home.

The mountain trail continued its steady rise as the group trudged on. The full moon was bright and clear now, and although moving toward the horizon, it provided a nice amount of natural night light. The foursome climbed the open-air path devoid of trees, and Furman couldn't help but feel exposed. A slight breeze kicked in, coming off of the Atlantic Ocean, which could now be seen from their elevation.

It took just forty-five minutes to reach Masterson Peak. A patch of trampled grass with the remains of a small fire was not hard to find. The four gathered around staring. Bob Walsh finally stooped and poked at the burnt wood and coals with a stick.

"It's recent, that's for sure," Bob observed. "No doubt this is where the two spent the evening."

"I don't see anything else up here, Mr. Walsh." Happy Flynn scanned the area with his eyes and his torch.

"Nobody would stay around out in the open like this in that storm we just had. They'd head back to town or holed up in the woods." Greg Collins pointed toward the tree line. Bob Walsh stood and stared at the trees, only grunting as if in agreement.

"Well, no one made it to town, which is why we're out here," Furman asserted. "Not surprised, really. You're right, Greg, no one would stay exposed up on the Peak when they could find shelter in the forest. Alright men, let's work our way down and back to the road through the forest. We need to go slow and keep our eyes open. We're either looking for two hikers who are camping or for one who may be injured."

"Or dead," Bob Walsh finished. Happy and Greg stared at each other, eyes wide. Happy wasn't smiling anymore.

"Let's go." Furman Hayes headed toward the edge of the forest, the three others following. "Don't be afraid to make noise, boys. Something out here attacked whoever is at McCloud's place and I don't want to be sneakin' up on it. The more noise we can make the better."

That's when the howl tore through the silence of the night.

A vicious, primal howl that sounded too much like a warning to stay away.

Furman Hayes was not a man easily rattled, but even he found his scalp tingling, a rush of adrenaline shooting through his system. Bob Walsh's eyes went wide.

"What the..." Happy Flynn uttered.

"A wolf," Bob responded. "That's what it is, Furman. We've got a wild wolf out there and it's tasted blood." He checked his shotgun over, removing the safety. Happy and Greg did the same with their weapons.

"Look, just keep your tranquilizer guns ready everyone." Furman understood the apprehension...no, fear, that's what it was. But he also understood that there was the possibility this wasn't a wild animal at all.

"It's a wolf, Furman. Taint nothing else it could be," came Bob's matter-of-fact response.

"Yes, you're probably right, Bob. But just in case –"

"A wolf, Furman." Bob stared hard at Furman Hayes, letting his eyes speak for him.

Furman removed the safety on his tranquilizer gun and held it up. "Just in case," he responded in turn.

The four men stepped into the forest.

# CHAPTER 8

*The Cave Search Team*

Calvin Lynch paced anxiously. He was ready to move.
His two boys, Blake and Sheamus, dominated his thoughts.
He had to get to the cave, to see for himself what Jamison
Murphy had reported. And what *had* he reported, anyway?
Dr. Kelly was correct - what they didn't know was more
than what they did know. It's not that he didn't trust what
Jami had told the group back at the Lear House, it's just that
he needed to see, needed to know, for himself. The thought
of losing both his boys, or either one of them, was too
much for him to comprehend. Something bad had
happened at the cave, that was for sure. Something very
bad. Exactly what? That was the task his group of four was
charged with finding out.

Harv Connor stood silently with arms crossed, staring

into the night toward the direction they were headed. It was cold but Harv looked impervious to the weather. No doubt his mind was on his own son, Malcolm. Jami had been equally certain as to his demise as he was the Lynch brothers. But once again, it came down to what Jami had actually seen, which in Malcolm's case was even less. He'd heard screams, but that was all. The rest came from his imagination.

*That's right*, thought Calvin Lynch, *just an overactive imagination of a young man without much real-life experience.* He had to stay positive.

Harv's older son, Drake, was standing close to his father, checking his pouch of shotgun shells and the batteries in his torch for the third or fourth time. He was nervous.

Harv had gone to Drake's home, about a block from his own, to wake up his son once it had been decided that a group of four was needed to go to the cave, and that Harv would indeed be in that group.

Informed of the goings on and of Jamison Murphy's story, Drake wasted no time bidding his wife farewell and rushing to join the others.

Drake was a good-looking young man. Calvin couldn't remember his exact age but he had to be in his early thirties, probably about ten years older or so than his younger brother, Malcom. Married with a child on the way, Drake was more talkative and refined than his rough-around-the-edges father. He was also well liked by everyone in the community. Harv was a gruff man and sometimes hard to get along with, but he and Sarah had done a good job of raising their two sons. The three of them - Harv, Drake, and Calvin - were gathered on the northwest edge of town...waiting.

"What in the world is taking him so long?" Drake finally blurted out. The group was waiting on the fourth member, Jasper Collins, to arrive. When his own son, Greg, had insisted on going with the Masterson Peak group, Jasper didn't want to stay behind and had volunteered to go to the cave. His wife had come undone by it all. Whatever was happening this night, it was not good and she was afraid. They were all afraid on some level, but the thought of both her husband and son being out in the night with so much uncertainty abounding was too much for the faint-of-heart Dot Collins. Jasper told the other three he needed just a bit to settle her down and then he'd be right with them. That had been at least thirty minutes ago, Calvin figured. He checked his watch again.

"We need to get going, Calvin," Harv's rough voice chimed in. "I say we leave him behind. He can catch up if he really wants to come along."

"Five more minutes, okay?" Calvin was ready as well. He knew they needed the added safety of a fourth, but time was of the essence. Whatever trouble Malcolm and his boys were in, they needed help as soon as possible. "If he's not here in five we move."

Five minutes passed and Harv was done waiting. He spat a wad of tobacco juice onto the dirt by way of announcing that he was headed out. Drake and Calvin fell in behind. And that's when Jasper Collins came jogging up, his own shotgun at the ready.

"Sorry, fellas." He was out of breath. "Took longer than I thought. Dot is just not in a good way. A lot going on with her. Too much to explain, but all is well. Thanks for not giving up on me."

"We actually did, Jasper, but whatever." Harv gave him a look. Jasper, wide-eyed, wiped the sheen of sweat from his brow with a cloth he pulled out of his worn cargo trousers. "I'm walking fast. You all do your best to keep up." And with that, Harv Conner marched out of town, the other three right in line.

What would normally take half an hour was only a twenty-minute hike for the group to reach the muddy descent where Jamison had left Malcom behind. They had hoofed it hard. The trail was still wet and loose in places but not exactly pure mud. The breeze coming off of the ocean had made its way up the side of the cliff face and was working to dry the ground. This made for sure footing and quick speed.

Harv Connor slowed his pace considerably as they approached the final descent from the woods leading to the sandy beach path. He readied his shotgun and turned back to the group.

"Drake, get your shotgun ready, son. Jasper...Calvin...you two arm your tranquilizer guns. If we run into a wolf or wild animal Drake and I will take care of it. If it's...well, you'll know what to do," Harv trailed off. He slipped into a low crouch, shotgun held tight with both hands, his left hand holding a torch clutched up next to the barrel of the gun. Whatever direction he swung his weapon cast a bright light as well. Drake eased up next to his father in the same position - light, gun, and all. Calvin moved off to the right, away from the trail and into the undergrowth of the forest, just about three meters or so from Harv and

Drake. Jasper did the same on the left flank. This gave the group a wide blade of coverage as they crept down the slope.

It was damp and moist...and colder in here, Calvin could feel. He was not a woodsman in the same way Harv was, so he had been glad to let the woodsman lead the way. Harv did a lot of hunting and camping with his sons, so he was no stranger to these woods.

*SNAP!*...

Calvin swung his torch to the right. A rustle and commotion heighted his senses. His eyes worked to see into the distance, the flashlight only able to throw light so far.

"What is it?" Drake whispered.

"Don't know...just heard something is all."

The group turned their full attention to the right side and joined their light beams to Calvin's, scanning the thick growth. No one spoke as a moment passed.

Nothing.

"Squirrels or rabbits. Who knows," Harv finally offered. He moved his attention back to a forward crawl down the trail.

*Snap...Crunch...SMASH!!!*

Calvin swung his light back to the right, just in time to see....*what?*

"Oh, man!" he cried. He fumbled to ready his tranquilizer pistol and then...he dropped it.

"What? What is it...?" Drake swung his shotgun and light around.

There was more smashing and crunching.

"Something's moving. I saw —" Calvin frantically scooped his tranquilizer pistol from the leaves.

"What did you see?!" yelled Harv.

"I don't know! It was on all fours...but it was..."

"Nobody shoot!" Harv commanded as he bounded into the forest toward the sounds. Calvin and Drake followed but Jasper Collins seemed to be frozen in place. He stayed on the trail.

The threesome scrambled over logs and mounds of dead leaves. Thickets tore at their clothes and bare knuckles. Calvin's heart pounded in his chest as time moved in slow motion.

"I see it!" called Harv. He was a good fifteen feet ahead of the other two. It amazed Calvin how quickly Harv could move. "It's fast...but..." He stopped and lifted his gun.

BOOM!

The sound tore through the night. And then came the primal scream.

"I got it. Winged it for sure." Harv moved quickly in the direction he'd fired.

"Careful, Dad," called Drake.

Calvin lunged for Harv and grabbed him by the shoulder, pulling him back. "You fired your gun, Harv. That means it's a wolf or animal, right? That's why you fired your shotgun."

Harv hesitated. "It was on all fours...it was covered in hair."

"But was it an *animal?*"

Another hesitation. "Yes," Harv whispered through clinched teeth.

"You're sure, Harv? You need to be sure."

"It was an animal," he said this time, with more resolve. Harv tugged his arm away from Calvin and turned back. "Let's find it and finish it."

*Booooommmm!*

Another shotgun in the distance.

"Jasper!" Calvin said as he whipped around back toward the trail.

"HEY!" It was Jasper's voice in the distance. The group could just hear him through the growth. "I found him....I found Malcolm....hurry!"

# CHAPTER 9

Ross McCloud unlocked the front door of his house and stepped into the living room. He'd directed his two companions around the blood on the front porch.

*I'll have to clean that up first thing in the morning,* he thought.

Dr. Boris Kelly and Patricia O'Leary eased passed Ross as he shut and relocked the door.

After leaving the Lear House meeting, Ross had gone to his gun shop to issue tranquilizer pistols to the search parties as well as lend a couple of 12-gauge shotguns to Drake Connor and Jasper Collins; everyone else had their own weapons.

Dr. Kelly wanted to retrieve a small medical kit from his office, and Patricia excused herself to the private residence portion of the bed and breakfast to change out of her night clothes and robe and into something more suitable for traipsing across town in the dead of night. She stood now, in Ross and Mattie McCloud's living room, in black leggings and a gray sports top which accentuated her figure. She was a beautiful woman, for sure. Thoughts stirred in Ross, taking him back to his teenage years when he and Patricia had dated. In retrospect, he wasn't so sure that she wasn't just using him to make Vaughn O'Leary jealous. She could be sly like that...when it came to relationships. Nevertheless, Vaughn was who she ended up with. It fit. She was pretty. He was "pretty." They were the pretty people in town.

Ross had lost to Vaughn and it wouldn't be the first time. He'd been passed over more than once for leader of the town council. As long as Vaughn was alive, he'd probably retain that title. Oh, it wasn't that people were all that in love with Vaughn. Sure, people trusted him on the most important matters of Tiamat, but on a personal level, most just kept their distance. Vaughn had a way of getting what he wanted out of you, no matter what it was. It was a strange sort of charismatic power. Everyone recognized it. Nobody liked it. But nobody could resist it either. And Patricia was always right by his side. She was always very nice and sweet, and that was the problem. There wasn't any real reason to not like Patricia, except that she was married to Vaughn.

Mattie McCloud appeared, coming from the back bedroom. "Oh, you're home –" She stopped short, seeing Patricia O'Leary and Dr. Boris Kelly. "Patricia," Mattie said. She stood straight and stiff, offering the one-word greeting.

"Mattie," Patricia offered in like kind. The cold chill

between the two women permeated the room like a walk-in freezer.

"We're here to see the young man that interrupted your evening, Mrs. McCloud." Dr. Boris Kelly broke the tension, his tone all business.

"Yes of course, right this way." She stepped aside from the doorway, motioning for him to come. Dr. Kelly and Patricia moved toward the room as Mattie turned her attention to her husband. "Ross, what did you find out? What's going on at the cave?" She was obviously nervous to find out more, and had been anxiously waiting while tending to their visitor. Her questions caused the doctor and Patricia to stop, eyes on Ross McCloud, waiting for his response.

Easing out of his overcoat, he laid it on the back of a chair in the living room and looked at his wife. There was no easy way to say it so he just started. "We're still trying to figure it out. Jami Murphy's over at the Lear House recovering."

"Recovering? From what?"

"Something happened, Mattie. At the cave. He and Malcolm Conner went down there tonight to relieve the Lynch brothers. And well...it's not good. It's...." Ross paused, not knowing how to continue.

"It's what, Ross? Just say it." Mattie was shaking one leg nervously and biting the nail on her right thumb.

"Mattie, what Ross is trying to say is that there has been some sort of accident at the cave." Dr. Kelly took over. "When Malcolm and Jamison arrived for the shift change, something terrible had happened to the Lynch boys. We're not sure what, but they both left immediately to come back and report the matter to us."

"Well, what does Malcolm have to say?" she asked. "I know how Jamison Murphy can be. That boy's not reliable in any sense of the word. Malcolm Connor is who you need to be talking to."

"Well, that's just it," Dr. Kelly continued. "Something else happened to Malcolm on the way back."

"Something *else* happened?" Mattie was incredulous. "What do you mean something else happened?"

"The only one to make it back was Jami." Patricia spoke this time by way of explanation. "He was beside himself with fright. He told us that everyone was dead."

Ross McCloud let out a long breath. Why did Patricia have to say it that way? To Mattie?

"Dead." Mattie moved toward her husband, a frantic energy taking control.

Ross grabbed his wife and held her tight as she began to sob. "We don't know that, Mattie. Listen to me, we don't know. You said it yourself, Jami is unreliable. Whatever happened, he probably just got scared and ran."

"That's right, Mattie." Dr. Kelly's tone became more "doctorly" as he continued. "Whatever is happening, we will soon find out. We are sending a group down to the cave now to find Malcolm and to see what is going on. We'll know everything by morning. We must be patient. You can do that can't you, Mattie?" He laid a tender hand on Mattie's shoulder as she eased away from Ross, wiping her eyes.

"You need to go, Ross. You need to go with them so you can see and so we can know that everything's okay."

Her voice was pleading.

"I can't go, honey. It's not permitted."

Mattie looked down, her shoulders sagging. This was true and she had no choice but to accept it.

"Don't worry, Mattie. Harv Connor and Calvin Lynch are leading a group there now. Those two can handle anything that's going on at the cave. Harv knows the woods like the back of his hand. He'll find Malcolm and then we'll know what all is going on." Dr. Kelly sounded confident.

"What *is* going on, Doctor?" she asked. "A problem at the cave. Malcolm is missing. And I've got a total stranger in my son's bedroom. What's happening out there?"

"Yes, that's why we're here." Dr. Kelly moved to pick up his medical kit that he'd laid down. "I want to see the young man that came to your door tonight, I need to assess his condition. And Patricia's come to see if he's one of the two guests that's been staying at the Lear House the last couple of days."

"Of course, right this way Doctor." Mattie had composed herself, smoothing out her robe with the palms of her hands. "He's back here in Tommy's room. He's returning in the spring, you know." Her comment was meant more to speak hope into herself than to inform the doctor and Patricia.

"Yes, the spring, of course. We are all looking forward to Tommy's return." Dr. Kelly made his way past Mattie into the bedroom. "Tell me," he called back, "has he awakened at all?"

"Not really," Mattie said. The group filed into the room with the doctor and stood around the bed looking down at the mystery visitor. "He's mumbled a few things

I've not been able to understand. I was able to give him some water and he swallowed it."

"Good, that's good."

"There is one thing he's said a few times that I was able to make out. A name, I believe...Jorge, it was. He's said the name Jorge. It sounds Hispanic."

Dr. Kelly looked at Ross McCloud and then at Patricia O'Leary. "What do you think, Patricia? Is he one of your guests? Does he look familiar?"

She stared hard at the unconscious figure on the bed. "It's not easy. His head is bound in gauze and his face is...but yes, I believe it's him. And the name Jorge. That's the name of the Hispanic male in our registry. Jorge Ramirez. So, I don't think there's any doubt that this is the other one."

"Well, we should get his friend Jorge. I know it's late but we should wake him up," Mattie insisted.

"That's just it, honey," Ross chimed in gently. She wasn't going to like what else was coming. "Those two went on a hike to Masterson Peak earlier today and didn't come back. And now we've got this one in our house all tore up. We don't know where this Jorge is." Mattie just gaped at this news.

"But it's all under control," Dr. Kelly spoke. "We've sent a group to Masterson Peak also. They'll find this Jorge and between the two groups that are out, we'll figure out what's going on." He was doing his best to instill confidence. "Now let's look at the wounds on our visitor here."

"I did the best I could, Doctor," Mattie replied hopefully.

"Yes, yes, you've done a fine job here, Mattie." He smiled at her reassuringly and then began to undress the large wound on the young man's leg. He took his time looking over the various wounds from head to toe, but paying particular attention to the leg wound. He stared intently at it as if trying to solve a puzzle. With latex-gloved hands and a small flashlight, he got close with his face and scanned the leg wound from the upper groin area all the way to the knee. Moving very slowly, prodding it with his fingers at times, his only reaction was an occasional "um-hum," or an "interesting."

In time, he rose up and pulled his gloves off, wadding them up and stuffing them into his portable kit. "Very interesting, indeed."

"What's interesting?" asked Ross.

Ignoring the question, he said, "So this young man needs blood and stitches. Mattie, if you are amiable to the request, might I suggest that he remain here for a day or so? I want to type his blood and then give him a transfusion. He won't need much, but it should help his recovery. I need to stitch this leg as well, tonight if possible." He continued to stare at the leg wound as if trying to sort out a complex math equation.

"You said it was interesting, Boris." It was Patricia inquiring this time. "What's interesting?"

At the mention of his first name, or maybe it was Patricia's voice, Dr. Kelly broke from the trance he'd been in. Looking directly at Patricia he said, "I need to see your husband...immediately."

# CHAPTER 10

*Masterson Peak Search Team*

The forest was silent.

Not necessarily unusual for late fall headed toward winter. It was cold after the storm and so there were no insects buzzing or scratching. But this kind of silence felt different.

That was the word. You could *feel* the silence.

The wild howl earlier had surely sent whatever small wildlife was foraging at night for cover as well. The only sounds at all were the footfalls and crunching as the party of four crept forward, tensions high.

Furman Hayes looked back at the other three. Greg Collins was sweating profusely. He'd skipped his shift at the cave because he'd been ill but had insisted on coming along after he was made aware of the trouble that was afoot. Maybe that had been a mistake.

"You okay, son?" Furman directed the question to Greg.

"Yes sir," he whispered in return. He wiped the moisture from his forehead with the back of his hand. "Just a little hot is all. But I'm okay."

Furman wasn't convinced. He was trying to keep from shivering. Every step into the black depths of the forest seemed to send the mercury down another degree. The trees were thick, blocking any chance that moonlight would help direct their path. The thick darkness seemed to actually be pushing back on their battery-powered torches, limiting their reach. It was nearly like walking blind.

*Clap, clap, clap...*

"Hey, hey, hey! C'mon now, you beast, show yer-self." Bob Walsh broke the silence with the pounding of his hands together and a round of whooping.

"Is that so smart, Mr. Walsh?" Happy Flynn looked the most nervous of all of them. "We don't want to scare it off or make it mad, do we?"

"Oh, we won't scare it off, son. It's on the hunt and wants to eat, I can guarantee you that. And I ain't worried about making it mad. I've got a gun and it doesn't. Plus, if those two young men really are in here somewhere, they need to be able to hear us."

More clapping and more yelling.

And then another howl of horror.

This time it filled the space around them, much closer than when they'd first heard the creature from the Peak.

"Holy Geez, that's close!" Happy swung his light all around in a circle. His gun followed.

"Careful where you point that thing," Greg scolded.

"That's what I'm talking about!" The normally quiet Bob Walsh yelled into the night. "C'mon now! Here we are. Let's get to it."

Another howl.

Was it getting closer?

There was rustling and a *whoof* of something directly in front of them, right on the path they'd been walking. Two yellow eyes, bright and bold, like the flashing warning lights of a road sign reflected off of Furman Haye's torch as he shined it down the path. It was a mere twenty meters in front of them.

"There it is, Bob," Furman directed. "Right in front of us."

Bob's head shot down from scanning the trees, his 12-gauge pointed in the direction of Furman's light. "Gotcha!" he yelled, firing a blast into the night. The creature was faster than Bob's shot and was gone in a flash. But which direction?

"What are you doing?" Furman scolded. "You can't shoot, we don't know yet."

"It's a wolf, Furman. A nasty, blood-sucking wolf."

"We just don't need to kill something and then regret it, you hear?" Furman was mad. Bob Walsh was acting like a loose cannon and he didn't like it. Too much was at stake for their whole town. Bob had never sent anyone to the cave though. Maybe that was his problem. Maybe he just didn't "get it" because it wasn't personal. But he sure was acting like it was personal. Too personal. The normally quiet, withdrawn Bob Walsh, who most termed as disconnected from the cares around him, seemed, all of a sudden, like a man on a mission. So not only was it Furman's job to lead this search, but now he felt responsible to keep Bob Walsh in check. And he still didn't like Greg being out here sick, either. At least Happy was under control. He just seemed scared. But likely for good reason. This was not a good night for Tiamat.

"Let's get on down this path and see if we can find those two boys that are supposed to be out here." Bob resumed the trudge on down the path. More clapping and yelling along the way. The other three followed in behind him. Furman took up the rear, careful to keep an eye on their backsides. He didn't want to be snuck up on in the rears.

It wasn't five minutes before he heard Bob call from the front. "Found something. Get up here, Furman, and check this out."

Furman pushed passed the other two even as they were making their way to Bob, trying to get a look at what he was shining his light on. It was a backpack. Ripped and torn.

"Over here," called Greg. Only ten feet away was an orange The North Face coat. It had been shredded and had reddish-brown smears along the chest and sleeves.

"Oh man, is that blood?" Happy asked. "I don't like this at all. That scares the crap out of me."

And there was more.

As the group scanned the area, they found a second backpack, its contents scattered all over. A small bag of trash, cooking utensils, a hammock, cell phone, and other odds and ends. Happy even found an Ironman watch, its black band torn in half. And then there was the boot. A single hiking boot, the Merrell logo on the side, all nice and neatly laced up, bow and all. It was not torn or ripped in any way. It looked like it had just been pulled completely off of whatever foot it had been on. But how? And more importantly, where were the owners of all this gear? All of these thoughts and more went through Furman's mind as he studied the scene.

"Let's collect all of this stuff. Package it together best we can. Greg...Happy...can you boys carry it out for us?" They nodded in agreement and began the gathering process, using what was left of the two backpacks to stuff everything into.

"Furman, can I speak with you for a moment? Over to the side?" Bob asked. It was more of a command than a question. The two men moved off but not too far so as to stay in safe proximity to the other two. Bob continued, "I think it's pretty clear. That gear over there belongs to the two guests at O'Leary's place. They ran into trouble out here. Big trouble."

Furman nodded his head in agreement. There was no doubt about what Bob was saying. "That young guy down at McCloud's house has to be one of the two hikers attacked up here. Has to be. That means we've got to find the other boy, the Hispanic one, I think," Furman said.

"And we've gotta do a second thing," Bob replied. "Track down the wolf that did this...and kill it."

"Maybe so, Bob, but the priority is finding the other hiker. That has to be our focus right now."

"No sir," Bob shot back, but then caught himself. "I mean, yes, find the hiker guy. But, Furman, he's not even one of ours. Killing the thing that did this is number one. We can't let it get anyone else. Next time, it might just be one of ours."

The horrible howl broke through the night yet again. This time the direction was clear. Back up the path. The way they'd come. Back toward the location where Bob had fired his weapon.

"There it is," yelled Bob. "Let's go get it!" He tore off, up the path. Furman called to Greg and Happy and they all scrambled to keep up with Bob Walsh.

*Boom!*

Bob fired off another shell.

*He's acting like a madman,* Furman thought, as they raced on.

They caught up to him a few seconds later as he was standing in the path, scanning the forest, the smell of gunpowder fresh in the air.

"I saw it," Bob whispered. "Right off there in that direction, big and hairy it was, with yellow eyes." His light was sweeping the trees off to the group's right.

Another howl. This time further up in the distance, from where they had entered the forest.

More chills.

More adrenaline racing.

"It's at the Peak!" Bob proclaimed excitedly. "We've got it out in the open. Let's go, we have to hurry." He tore out again, sprinting this time. Furman could never recall a time in his life that he'd seen *this* Bob Walsh. The three worked to keep up with him but he was outpacing them all.

*Boom!* Another shot.

Greg tripped and fell and Happy stopped to pick him up. Furman slowed to stay with the boys.

This didn't feel right.

The howl they heard earlier was too far away for whatever they'd seen on the path the first time. And then howling *behind* them, in the direction they'd come from.

That's when it all came together for Furman.

*There's more than one out here.*

They broke into the clearing, coming right up behind Bob Walsh who was standing still, his gun raised to his shoulder.

Fifty meters away, at the Peak, standing on a rocky outcrop was the creature. The beast was silhouetted by the setting full moon in the background. Big and bold, the outline of its hair was visible, running down the sinews of its muscular body from top to bottom. Standing on its hind legs, head lifted to the sky, it rolled off the most hideous screaming howl.

*BOOOOMMM!*

The creature stopped mid-howl with a screech and fell off the back side of the rock.

"Got you, you mother!!!" Bob yelled with delight. He lowered his weapon, a mask of calm passing over his face as if "mission accomplished."

Furman ran toward the rock to verify the kill. His heart racing, a not-quite-right feeling still in his gut. He came to the rock outcrop and jumped up on it. His torch showed the unmistakable spillage of bright red blood. Bob had hit it alright. As he scanned the area below the rock, his light found its target.

Bob Walsh arrived along with Greg and Happy. Coming up next to Furman, Bob puffed his chest out. "Let's take a look at her," he pronounced.

Furman just stared, his light shining down. A bad situation had gotten worse. "We've got a problem, Bob. First...she's a he. And second, he's not a wolf."

# CHAPTER 11

*The Cave Search Team*

Calvin Lynch hurried toward the sound of the shotgun and Jasper Collins's cry for help. The thick layer of wet leaves and sticks made footing unsteady but he'd not slipped and fallen yet. Together with Harv and Drake Connor, the trio made quick work covering the distance through the trees back to the trail where they'd left Jasper.

He was not there.

Making a quick scan with his eyes, Calvin saw the wave of torchlight just off the path, opposite from where they'd emerged.

"There he is," affirmed Harv Connor excitedly.

"Over here...hurry!" Jasper Collins called again. He'd obviously seen and heard the commotion of the group as they bounded toward him.

"We're coming, Jasp! How's my boy?" Harv cried as he and Drake raced passed Calvin, both jumping a large rotten log, quickly swallowed up by the thickness of the trees. Calvin made the jump right on their heels. For the sake of Harv he hoped Malcolm was alright - for the sake of them all really. And then there was the matter of his own two boys down at the cave. He wanted to find Malcolm, but he had to get to the cave too.

Calvin caught up to Harv and Drake twenty meters off the trail. They'd both cast their packs off and shed their guns as they'd skidded to a stop on their knees next to a form on the ground. Jasper Collins was standing with a sullen look on his face, shone only in the dim light of their torches.

"Malcolm, my boy, it's me, your da." Harv's gravelly voice had all of a sudden taken on a tender note.

"We got you, Malcolm. We're here now." It was Drake prodding his younger brother with his voice.

Harv was doing his best to assess the condition of his youngest son. "I need more light." Harv looked to Jasper and Calvin. "Shine your lights down here so I can see." Calvin and Jasper complied, both aiming their battery torches across Malcolm's body. Calvin almost wished he hadn't.

"Oh my...lord...." Jasper covered his mouth with his hand.

There was blood. A lot of blood. Soaking Malcolm's jacket and trousers. His clothes were still on and intact but the form of his body didn't look quite right. He was broken and his left arm from the elbow down was...exposed. The sleeve of his down jacket had been torn completely away, exposing the flesh, except there was no longer any flesh. The ugly white of bone shone in the yellow light of Drake's own torch as he pointed it directly over his brother's arm. The skin and muscle had been stripped nearly clean, just a few fragments of tendon and gristle left hanging. But then his hand looked completely...normal, as if it could reach up at any moment and shake your own in a warm greeting. Calvin looked on in stunned fascination.

"Oh, Malcolm...my boy, my son..." Harv began to cry. "Wake up, Malcolm, come on my boy, wake up for me." Harv was gently rubbing his son's face with a calloused hand. Drake wept as well, not knowing what else to do. A calm stillness settled over the group, the two Connor men's soft sobs the only sound.

"Is he alive, Harv?" Calvin felt he needed to ask. If Malcolm was still alive they needed to get him back to town as quickly as possible and to the help he needed. Though some things were clearly beyond saving, he thought, eyes still fixated on the skeleton of Malcolm's left forearm.

"I think he is," Harv sniffed. He was careful to unzip Malcolm's jacket. Laying a hand on his son's chest, he leaned over, resting the side of his head over the boy's heart. Calvin and Jasper both had medical training as volunteer firefighters for the town, but were holding off in deference to Harv and Drake. Harv raised his head. "Yes, he's breathing and his heart is beating. Sounds strong, but...." He choked up again. "He's in bad shape. My boy's in real bad shape." He looked at Jasper, who still had a gloved fist balled up over his mouth. "What did you see, Jasp? How did you find him?"

Despite the cold, Jasper Collins had a sheen of

perspiration on his forehead under his gray wool cap. His eyes grew wide for just a split second as if contemplating. He looked at Calvin Lynch, who stared back with a look that asked, "Well?"

"After you all ran off after the...whatever it was..." he started, "I seized up. I don't know, just got scared is all. I'm sorry. But I got it back together and figured you all had it under control without me. I decided to do a perimeter sweep - thirty meters or so - and just see if I could find any signs of anything...of Malcolm or whatever. Save us some time once you got back. I thought it was a long shot really. I was up trail a ways and off in the woods when I heard some noise back in this direction, toward this spot."

"Noise?" Harv asked. "What kind of noise?"

"Like a rustling and a..." Jasper hesitated. "Grunting."

"Grunting?" Harv inquired again. Clearly, Malcolm hadn't been making any noise. He was out cold and had lost a lot of blood.

"Like an animal," Jasper continued. "I switched from my tranquilizer pistol over to my shotgun and made my way down. The closer I got...well, there was this stench...wild and I don't know...it was awful. And then I saw it." Jasper's eyes grew wide again as he relived the moment. He continued, more animated this time. "It was an animal...I think...it was covered in hair and so big. I don't think it was one of...but I can't be sure. It was dark and I started fumbling with my light as soon as I saw it. It was standing over Malcolm and it was..." Jasper hesitated to go on.

"It was what, Jasp?" Calvin asked. "What was it doing?"

"It was...feeding," Jasper whispered, his breathing

heavy. "On Malcolm." The reality of what Jasper was saying hit the other three all at once. "I fired off a shot and the thing took off into the woods."

Drake leaned away from his brother and vomited into the leaves. Harv let out a long moan while Calvin looked at Malcolm's bony arm with new understanding.

As if broken from a trance, Calvin dropped his gear and joined the Connor men on the ground. "Let me look at your boy, Harv." Harv Connor nodded and eased away, letting Calvin Lynch take over with his triage training. Calvin was gentle but thorough. From head to foot he examined all of Malcolm's limbs, applying gentle pressure to his abdomen. He verified the boy's breathing and heart rate, which was surprisingly strong although his breathing was shallow.

"He's taken quite a beating, Harv." Calvin began his assessment. "Been tossed around pretty violently, I'd say. He fought back hard it looks like, from the scratches on his palms and knuckles. He may have a few broken bones and some internal bleeding, I can't be sure. And then...well, his arm." He'd been hesitant to mention that part but it was unavoidable. "He's a tough one, Harv, I think he'll be okay, but we need to get him back to town right now."

Harv nodded in agreement, pulling himself to his feet, a look of resolve on his face. "Drake and I will do it. We can get him back to town. You've got to get to the cave, Calvin. You and Jasper, we can't waste any time." There was a fierce look in Harv Connor's eyes. Calvin knew what he was thinking and as a father himself he was grateful. "Your two boys are down there Calvin, and you need to get to them now. Whatever is out here roaming around...hunting...it's not good. I've found my boy and it's bad, real bad, no doubt. But I'm grateful he's alive and I mean to keep him that way. But it's time now for you to find your boys and get some answers as to what's going on out here...and down there." He pointed in the direction of the cave. "As soon as I get Malcolm to Dr. Kelly's, Drake and I will hustle back to join you."

"He's right, Calvin, and I'm in." Jasper appeared to have found his own sense of resolve. "We need to get to the cave and to your sons." He picked up Calvin's pack and handed it to him.

"Thank you, Harv...Jasper." Calvin looked at his two friends as he took the pack and began readying his own shotgun. He doubted he would be using the tranquilizer gun at all at this point. "I appreciate it. Let me and Jasp at least get Malcolm up so you can carry him proper."

The group made quick, efficient work of getting Malcolm ready for transport. Calvin bound his skeletal arm securely to his midsection and they made sure he wasn't bleeding freely. It would be a lot of work for only Harv and Drake to hike out with him as dead weight, but they'd manage.

Once ready, a quick look passed between the men with no words. Then they disappeared up the trail into the dark.

Jasper and Calvin looked at each other and moved on down the trail in the opposite direction, toward the beach and the cave.

They'd gone no more than five minutes when a terrible howl echoed up from the direction they were headed.

# CHAPTER 12

The lone figure looked to be in prayer.

The small library room was more than a little warm, the fire blazing strong in the stone fireplace. Vaughn O'Leary sat just off to the side, absorbing the heat. Morning was approaching, but this long night was not yet over. Despite the early hour and lack of sleep, Vaughn looked fully refreshed, perfectly dressed in brown corduroys complemented by a green wool sweater. A collared shirt poked above the neckline that dressed the pairing up just a bit, if not to also ward off any itching from the wool fibers of the sweater.

Reaching over to the end table on his right, he lifted the china tea cup from its saucer and took a sip of the hot liquid. Earl Grey. His favorite. Setting the cup back in its place, he resumed reading the ancient leather-bound book that had been resting in his lap. For the last hour, this is what Vaughn O'Leary had been doing. Reading and praying. Praying and reading. Or maybe he was meditating. It would be impossible for an outside observer to know for sure. Oh, Vaughn was a religious man, to be sure. But it was difficult to know whether he loved his god or himself more.

The events of this evening weighed heavily on the leader of Tiamat's town council. Theirs was a small, tight-knit community, and what affected one affected all. The residents of Tiamat didn't exactly live an isolated existence. Yes, they had attempted to for generations and succeeded to an extent, but such a thing had been impossible for some time now. The world had grown smaller, much smaller with the advent of the Internet and global communication via email, texting, and all forms of social media. What once was a too far, out-of-the-way destination in the northwest corner of Ireland had now become the sought-after destination for would-be adventurers and tourists. Thus, the reason for the Lear House or, for those who were outsiders looking for a place to stay it was known by its official name: O'Leary's Bed and Breakfast.

The Lear House wasn't on any Internet registry as a hotel or lodge, Vaughn had made sure of that. One could never find it and book a room in advance. It existed simply for those who stumbled into town and needed a place to stay. No one actually came to Tiamat for Tiamat though; it really was the countryside that drew them. By capturing all tourists, Vaughn was able to carefully steer their exploring, pointing them to the spectacular, postcard views of the Atlantic from the bluffs, or the main attraction, Masterson Peak via the Ashur Mountain trail.

It was always, *always* important to keep them from exploring the beach below the bluffs. It was imperative that no one stumble upon the cave. That was easy enough, declaring to those that inquired that no trail existed to the beach and that the few who had tried had slipped and fallen to their deaths. The way so treacherous that even their bodies were not able to be recovered. Or so they were told. This worked like a charm to steer folks to the places the residents of Tiamat deemed *safe*. Most who came stayed only a day or two although occasionally some stayed longer.

The two most recent guests had stayed the requisite two days when they had gone on their evening hike earlier in the day. They'd been cryptic when quizzed about their overall plans and length of stay. "Playing it day-to-day," they'd said. And while it was true that travelers were uninterested in Tiamat as a rule, these two had taken an unusual interest in their quaint little village. An interest that had made Vaughn uneasy. They asked too many questions: How old is the village? When was it founded? How many residents are there? What is the main industry? Where did Vaughn and his wife, Patricia, go for their post-secondary education? Are there any books in the town library on the history of Tiamat?

Vaughn looked down, once again, at the book in his lap. He closed it, caressing its cover. The two travelers made it a point to note that they'd been unable to find any history - or information of any kind for that matter - about Tiamat on the Internet. "It's almost like this place doesn't even exist," one of them had noted.

And now...one of them was likely at Ross McCloud's house, attacked and mangled. He had no doubt this would be confirmed once his wife Patricia returned. That meant their other guest was missing and possibly dead. Vaughn was mulling over all of this and more when the knock came at the door.

"Yes, come in."

"Patricia said I would find you here." Dr. Boris Kelly entered straightaway, easing the door to the library shut with a click. "We need to talk."

"Of course. Sit down, Boris, next to the fire. Come warm yourself." Dr. Kelly moved to the plush chair opposite Vaughn O'Leary and had a seat on its edge. He rubbed his hands together, holding his palms up toward the fire. The warmth of the flames did feel good. "Would you like something hot to drink, Boris? I have a pot of tea ready."

"Certainly. Tea would be lovely." Vaughn prepared a cup and returned to his own chair after handing the cup and saucer off to the doctor.

Boris Kelly took a sip, eyes closed, letting the hot liquid roll to his stomach, working its charm from the inside out. Satisfied, he opened his eyes, looking at his host. "The young man at McCloud's is your guest."

"Yes, I thought as much. I'd have been surprised if you had told me otherwise. What kind of shape is he in?"

"Well, it's not good. He's been attacked by...something." Dr. Kelly hesitated a quick second before continuing. "The main wound is to his left leg. The muscle of the upper thigh was compromised. Almost torn clean away from the bone. He's lost a lot of blood as well."

"Will he survive?" Vaughn asked, emotionless.

"I believe so. I need to suture his wounds and give him some blood. But yes, he should recover."

"Well, that is a shame." Dr. Kelly sat expressionless at Vaughn's reaction to his guest's likely recovery.

"There's something else you need to know," the doctor stated flatly. Vaughn lifted his own cup of Earl Grey toward the doctor as if to say *continue* before taking a sip. "The wounds on the boy's body are caused by claws - long claws - like an animal's...and bite marks."

Vaughn raised a questioning eyebrow. "And?"

"The bite marks are human."

Vaughn O'Leary thought for a long moment at this - his eyes working back and forth but not looking at anything in particular. Finally, he said, "Don't feel you need to try too hard to save him, Boris. It might be better for all of us if you didn't."

Dr. Kelly sat back, taking in a long breath. "That's not wise, Vaughn. To let him die. We don't need that kind of attention around here."

"We don't need the kind of attention he would bring if he wakes up either, Boris. He was asking too many questions before the attack. They both were. Can you imagine the kinds of questions that would be asked if he wakes up? Plus, the other one is probably dead or soon will be. He was surely attacked in the same manner. We can only hope that Furman and Bob won't find him up on the Peak and if they do, hopefully he's deceased."

"You really think dealing with two deaths is better than dealing with two attacked hikers?"

"Two attacked hikers who were already nosing around asking the wrong kinds of questions? Yes. Absolutely.

Look, we can take the bodies down to County Tyrone or Fermanaugh. Leave them in the woods. They will likely never be found."

"That just means people, family, and others will come looking for them. We will have more people asking more questions than just those two. Two Americans overseas don't just disappear without it being an international story."

"Then take them a county over and leave the bodies roadside to be found there. Just not here. If their itinerary is traced to Tiamat, then we show the B&B registry. They were here two days and they left. Nothing here to see. Move along."

"You're forgetting the bite marks. The human bite marks. Any medical examiner will see what I saw. Questions, Vaughn. Questions."

"But not tied to us."

"I disagree completely. My own oath as a doctor prevents me...."

"Your oath?" Vaughn O'Leary's voice rose. "Your oath? What about your oath to Tiamat, Boris? Before you are a doctor you are one of us. You *are* Tiamat! Your oath is to this town and to the legacy...to the burden we carry. We must protect both at all costs."

Vaughn O'Leary's counter was interrupted by a loud bang. It was the front door to the Lear House being thrust open. "Vaughn!" It was Harv Connor yelling. "Vaughn!" he yelled again as he stomped across the wooden floor. Vaughn O'Leary and Dr. Boris Kelly both shot to their feet. The door to the library opened abruptly. Harv looked exhausted, his hands and clothes smeared in dried blood.

"Oh good, Doc, you're here too. We found him Vaughn! We found Malcolm and we need help."

# CHAPTER 13

*The Cave Search Team*

It would be daylight soon, but not soon enough for Calvin Lynch. If he could will this horrible night to be done away with, he would, but not until he knew what had become of his two sons. Blake and Sheamus dominated his thoughts as he and Jasper Collins trudged their way toward the cave.

Several more times the awful creature had pierced the darkness with its howls. Each time, it caused the men to pause. Normal instincts would have compelled one to run and lock himself away in the safety of his own dwelling. It was that terrible. A night cry that preyed on the deepest fears imaginable. Fight or flight is what psychologists called it. But there would be no flight in Calvin Lynch this dreaded night. He would fight for his boys, no matter the cost. And despite the look of fear in his own eyes, Jasper Collins was by his side to help.

The sand on the beach path hugging the steep bluff had dried for the most part. As dawn approached, the clear sky to their left shown majestic with dotted stars. The breeze coming off the ocean was cold, though. Visibility was good which helped them make good time. They had to navigate two more points on the beach and then they would arrive at their destination.

And then Calvin saw it, the silhouette of the creature, maybe one hundred meters ahead. It was the yellow eyes that caused him to stop in his tracks. He held up his left arm, fist clenched, as a signal for Jasper Collins to halt.

Jasper was raising his weapon when Calvin reached back, seizing the barrel of the gun and lowering it. "We have to get closer," he instructed in a whispered tone. "Too far for a shotgun." A howl tore open the night again, but not from the creature in front of them. This sound came from directly above on the edge of the bluff. Both men's heads shot upward by instinct. But just for a moment, as they realized they couldn't afford to lose sight of the one only a football field's distance away.

Too late.

Bringing their heads back down, they saw that the yellow eyes had disappeared.

"Where'd it go?" Jasper asked.

"Gone...for now."

"I feel like those things are running around everywhere out here."

"Let's just get to the cave, Jasp. And keep a sharp eye out and your weapon ready."

The final distance to the cave was covered in short order and without incident, other than a few more howls, this time in the distance. The two men approached the rise to the cave's entrance with extreme caution. A smattering of trees surrounded the opening and provided nice cover for the cave. In the unlikely event an outsider was hiking by, the entrance would not be easily seen. The trees served also to take away a portion of the night light they'd been relying on. Their battery-powered torches once again fired up. Calvin Lynch and Jasper Collins had finally arrived.

The fire that was kept burning each night just inside the cave's entrance was out. Jasper knelt, passing his hand over the dark coals. "There's a little warmth in it but it's been out a while." Standing to his feet, he looked at Calvin. "Maybe I should go first. You know, just in case." He was thinking about what Jamison Murphy had reported to the town council back at the Lear House, unsure if Calvin was ready for what the cave might reveal as to the fate of his sons.

"I'm fine, Jasp. Let's just take care of business." Calvin steeled himself. The whole evening had been about getting to the cave - for him anyway. It seemed it had taken a lifetime to make it down here.

Seeing Malcolm Connor's condition, mostly his arm, had been a shock - a dose of reality as to what they were facing and what they might find at the cave itself. Oh, how he prayed not. In fact, Calvin Lynch had prayed the whole way down to the cave as they hiked. Prayed that Jamison Murphy was mistaken. Prayed that, overcome by fear, he'd seen something different than what he thought he saw. Prayed that when they arrived Blake and Sheamus would be nestled around the little fire cutting up and teasing each other as they were prone to do, but ticked off that Malcolm and Jamison had not arrived to take their shift and relieve them. He prayed for all of that to come true. But deep in his heart he wrestled with his own fear. Something had happened here tonight. Something horrible and awful. The condition of Malcolm was a testimony to that. And the fire was out. His boys weren't gathered around. There was no joking or teasing. There was nothing but silence and darkness. It was time to find out what was going on.

Both men swung their lights deep into the cave and made their way forward. They didn't have to go very far.

"Oh no...please...no...no, no, no...." Calvin rushed forward and fell at the heap of a body splayed out on the rock floor, tears welling up in his eyes.

"Is it...?" Jasper began.

"It's Blake," came the grieving reply.

"How do you...?" Jasper had to ask because the gore that lay before them made it impossible for him to know for sure.

"His shirt. And his boots. And I just know. Oh, my precious boy."

Blake Lynch had been torn completely apart. No father should have to see their child this way, Jasper thought. Anger boiled up inside of him.

"What did this?" Calvin wondered out loud. "This...this is inhumane. Barbaric and animalistic. But even animals don't kill this way." He looked up at Jasper as if he could provide an answer.

Jasper pulled a handkerchief from the pocket of his canvas trousers. He unfolded it and carefully laid it over

Blake's head and face, what was left of it, in a show of respect. "We need to find Sheamus, Calvin. We need to find your other boy." Calvin nodded and with great effort pulled himself up. He could do nothing more for his firstborn. Whatever did this, he swore to himself in that moment that he would find it and kill it...no matter *what*...or *who* it was.

The two men readied their torches and their weapons and walked toward the back of the cave. It was a deep cavern that traveled a good forty meters before it ended. Yes, they needed to find Sheamus. That was the priority of the moment. But they also needed to check on and secure the *others*. What lay at the back of the cave was the secret of Tiamat. As one who'd been praying all evening for his sons, Calvin now prayed that what lay at the cave's end was not responsible for Blake's death. If it was, then such an occurrence threatened to plunge their little hamlet into the darkest season it had ever known.

They continued on.

It was quiet and they didn't speak a word, their ears attuned for the slightest of sounds. They didn't want to be caught off guard by one of the creatures hiding in some black crevice, waiting for an opportunity to make another kill. The deeper they traveled, the colder the cavern grew. That was the nature of caves, but cold like this felt unnatural. Their footfalls echoed now. And then there was a shuffling sound, up and to the right. Calvin and Jasper shot their light beams in the direction.

*Scratch. Click, click, click, click, click...*

A scampering sound of claws clicked on a hard surface,

more shuffling - further to the right and still ahead. The light caught it this time and it froze.

"It's one of them!" called Jasper. "That means they're out. We've got to get it."

"Easy...easy does it." Calvin crept forward, his eyes not moving from the form in front of them. He had one hand out in front of him, his movements slow and easy.

*Pop!*

Calvin Lynch flinched, his shoulders rising and falling at the sound. "You got him!" he confirmed. Jasper lowered his tranquilizer pistol and rushed forward, passing Calvin, running to the side of the target. It had already collapsed and was near unconsciousness.

Amazed and grateful for how quickly the serum worked, Calvin asked, "Which one is it?"

"I've got no idea. Can't tell at all. Too much hair. Man, he stinks." Jasper wrinkled his nose.

"This means the gate's open." Calvin stated the obvious. "Let's go. We need to get it secured."

"You know he's not the only one," Jasper said, rising from the body that was now fast asleep. "If one got out, that means more got out. And Calvin...." He didn't want to say it but he had to. "You know there's a possibility-"

"Yes, I know," Calvin cut him off. "I know. But you saw my boy. There's no way. I just can't believe that one of them did *that*," he finished, motioning on toward the back of the cave.

"One step at a time. Let's get it secured, and then we can process what all happened here and to your son."

"And we still have to find Sheamus."

Jasper nodded in agreement as they moved on toward

the back of the cave. They arrived at the gate and just as suspected, it was open. More rustling and movement caught their attention on the left side where the cage bars were cemented into the rock of the cave. Jasper swung his light and tranquilizer pistol over. The figure sprang away, moving off of a pile of something laying on the ground.

*Pop!*

Another shot and another hit.

Calvin rushed over to confirm the hit and that's when his eyes caught sight of what it was their target had been standing over...and eating.

A bloody pulp of raw meat and denim shone in Calvin's light. He let out a guttural wail. "Please...don't let it be so."

"What?" Jasper ran over. "What is it?" He looked down, trying to understand.

"It's Blake." Calvin collapsed to his knees, defeated. "It's part...of Blake." His voice died off.

Jasper Collins lay a hand on Calvin's shoulder in comfort. After a moment he moved away to let him be. Calvin needed to be alone for a few minutes and Jasper needed to close the gate to the cage. He walked back over, only glancing at the body laying asleep on the cave floor, it's mouth bloody from the feast it had been partaking in. Jasper's stomach nearly revolted. He seized the heavy gate in both hands and clanked it shut, securing the lock. It had not been open very far, maybe only two feet or so, but it would have been enough. He shined his light into the cage at the others who were inside. Most of them were docile, which was their nature. An occasional crazed one dictated caution, of course. Jasper began to count them one by one.

He added the two that lay outside the cage, fast asleep. He would relocate them to inside the cage shortly.

As he counted them off, he quickly knew that something wasn't right. He did a double check in his head just to be sure he was seeing things clearly. It had been a hectic night and he was beginning to crash from an earlier adrenaline dump.

The adrenaline began to flow again, though - the result of his head count. "Oh no." He muttered.

Calvin had come up beside him. "What's wrong now?" he asked.

"Everything."

# CHAPTER 14

"I've sedated him so he won't wake up." Dr. Boris Kelly stomped on the pedal of his tubular trash can, causing the lid to pop open. He removed his blue latex gloves and tossed them inside. The group was in the exam room of the doctor's office just one block over from the Lear House. Vaughn O'Leary had joined Harv and Drake Connor in relocating Malcolm from the front porch of the Lear House to the town's only medical facility. He was thankful that no one was out and about at this early hour to see the four carrying what looked to be a lifeless body through town. But Malcolm Connor was very much alive.

O'Leary, along with the other two Connor men, had stood off to the side while Dr. Kelly performed his examination, spending most of his time on the exposed bone of Malcolm's left arm. "You say he's been unconscious since you found him?" the doctor asked.

"That's right," Harv answered. "He hasn't stirred or said a word. You don't think he's brain dead or anything like that, do you Doc?"

"Well, he was clearly thrown around and tussled quite a bit, but I don't see any real trauma to his head. His eyes respond to dilation, so no, I don't think we have any neurological issues. He's lost some blood, but the real issue, obviously, is his arm. I suspect he passed out due to the shock of his experience. I don't want him waking up in this condition. Not until I'm finished."

"Finished?" Harv looked confused.

"The arm has to go, Harv. I'm sorry, but it cannot be saved."

Harv Connor buried his head in his hands. He knew it would have been a miracle to save the boy's arm, but one can always hope in miracles. Hearing the finality in Dr. Kelly's words had washed all hope away.

"He's still alive, Dad. That's the most important thing," Drake consoled his father.

"Yes, you're right son. We've still got him with us." Harv moved over and put his hand on Malcolm's brow. "We've got to tell Marilyn and your mother. They're together at the Furman house." He looked up at Vaughn O'Leary. "I sent Sarah over to sit with Marilyn and Marilyn's mother. They'll be worried sick until they know he's alright." "Alright" was a relative term, he now knew, as he looked back at his son's skeletal arm with sadness but also anger.

"Tell us what you found out, Harv. Did your team make it to the cave?" This was the real reason Vaughn O'Leary had come along. He'd held off asking as long as he could, seeing how distraught Harv and Drake had been over Malcolm's broken body. He was concerned too for the young man, but his concern for all of Tiamat was greater. "And where are Jasper and Calvin? Please tell me nothing's happened to them."

As if snapped out of a trance, Harv's report came in a quick staccato-type fashion. "Yeah, Jasper and Calvin. So, we never made it to the beach path before we found Malcolm. And listen...something is out there. I shot it, but only winged it. Chased the thing into the woods for a bit, but it's fast, Vaughn, real fast. And there's more than one of 'em. Jasper saw one too."

"So, there's more than one?" Vaughn O'Leary asked to no one in particular. His mind was racing with thoughts.

"That's right. There's more than one for sure."

"Was it one of -"

"It was an animal. A wolf most likely." Harv cut off Vaughn's question before he could finish asking it, as if he knew it was coming. "Big and covered in hair. And fast, like I said. And I'll tell you this much as well. I'm goin' back out there to find the one that did this to my boy and when I find it, I'm gonna kill it." Harv Connor's eyes were wild. Drake stood up straight, joining his father's declaration.

Choosing not to challenge the wisdom of Harv's personal vendetta hunt, he moved on. "And Jasper and Calvin? What about them?"

"We sent them on to the cave. Calvin needed to find his boys, even more so after seeing what had become of my Malcolm. And we need to get back down there. We promised 'em we'd get Malcolm to the doc and all settled and then hustle back to join them. I know it's not ideal, for only two to be out there on the trail, but Calvin's good with a gun and that was the call we made." Harv Connor's inner conflict showed on his face. The well-being of his son obviously came first, but his dedication to his friend and the town as a whole was admirable. Once he secured the medical care Malcolm needed and was confident that his boy was stable, he'd be back on the trail.

Vaughn O'Leary and Dr. Kelly exchanged looks. "That was the right call. Plus, we need to know about the cave. What's happening at the cave tonight? I suggest you and Drake get a move on," Dr. Kelly encouraged. "Don't worry about Malcolm. I'll make sure he's taken good care of and we'll get word to Sarah and Marilyn that he's here with us."

The four men left the exam room, weaved their way through the small waiting room of the clinic, and out onto the sidewalk in front of the building. More was afoot this night than any of them had imagined. And there were still many questions to be answered. In fact, the only answer they had so far was that Malcolm Connor was alive, in spite of Jamison Murphy's certain declaration of his demise. He was alive, but he was not whole. And that led to new questions. What had attacked him? Was it truly a wolf as Harv Connor was so certain? And what about there being more than one? It's true that wolves are at home in this part of Ireland, but they are sly animals, rarely seen, and attacks by wolves are rarer still. So, while Harv may be right, there was a nagging feeling that something else, something darker, was moving through their little village.

"Someone's coming," Drake Connor announced to the

group, breaking up a discussion his father was having with the doctor.

A lone figure was approaching fast, running. It didn't take long for them to recognize Happy Flynn as he pulled up, breathing hard. "They sent me...to get you...come fast...we're on the edge of town." His words came in spurts between breaths.

"Easy there, son. Just take your time and tell us what you're talking about." Dr. Kelly worked to calm him. Drake Connor pulled a water bottle out of his pack and handed it to Happy who cracked open the white screw top and took a long swig.

"Thanks," he said, still catching his breath, wiping his mouth with the back of his hand. "They didn't think it was safe to bring it into town. Greg's not feeling so well, you know he was sick tonight. And Mr. Walsh and Mr. Hayes are arguing. Have been non-stop since we shot it. So, they sent me to get you."

"Whoa, whoa, whoa, Happy. Slow down. What's this all about?" Vaughn O'Leary stepped in, trying to ask.

"No time. You have to come now. All of you." And like that he ran back in the direction he'd come. The group had no choice. They followed on his heels.

The streets being empty, the pounding of the group's boots on pavement sounded louder than they actually were, like a mini-stampede covering the ten or so blocks down the main street of town called Akkadia Avenue. They took a right, running another eight blocks down Masterson Road until the shops and homes ended. Happy Flynn kept running another two hundred meters until he finally disappeared off the road, ducking into the woods. He was faster than the rest except for the young Drake Connor who was close on his heels, coming to a stop on the side of the road where Happy had disappeared, waiting on the older three to catch up.

Harv Connor and Dr. Boris Kelly had slowed considerably once they saw that Drake had stopped and was waiting. Vaughn O'Leary was in the best shape of all the town council members, his six-foot frame lean and muscular, above average for a man in his early forties. He came alongside Drake and was about to ask about Happy Flynn when Furman Hayes stepped onto the road like an apparition appearing out of nowhere.

"I'm glad it's you, Vaughn," Furman said by way of greeting. "The sooner you're in the loop on this the better."

"In the loop, Furman? You and Bob led the team to Masterson Peak. We identified the man at McCloud's place as one of my guests at the Lear House. Did you find the other one? The Hispanic guy?" Even as he asked, Vaughn's eyes had adjusted to the darkness of the night, having left the lighting of the town's streets. He could make out the orange glow of ember from what was likely Bob Walsh's tobacco pipe. His form, along with those of Happy Flynn and Greg Collins, were a matter of paces off the road, standing in a circle.

"No, we did not. We found something else and Bob shot it. We couldn't risk bringing it into town. We sent Happy to find you or the doctor."

Vaughn stepped off the road and over to the other three, Furman following. Bob Walsh flicked on a torch, revealing the somber faces of the group. At their feet in a heap was a dirty canvas tarp. No, it wasn't in a heap,

Vaughn realized. The tarp was laid on top of a body, covering it. Hiding it.

"Well, let's have a look, gentlemen. What's so important that we've got to gather in clandestine fashion in the woods?"

As he asked, Furman Hayes slipped passed Vaughn O'Leary, reached down and pulled back the tarp. Vaughn only stared, comprehending what lay before him in dim torchlight.

Dr. Kelly and Harv Connor arrived next, Drake leading them to the grim gathering.

Dr. Boris Kelly was the first to speak in somber fashion, "In the name of all that is holy, what have you all done?"

# CHAPTER 15

The sky was turning light in the East. Night was almost over and dawn came early this time of the year. But it couldn't come quickly enough for the group headed back to the cave. They were a party of four again. Harv and his youngest son, Drake, along with Furman Hayes and Bob Walsh. They would reconnect with Calvin Lynch and Jasper Collins and assess the true nature of what Tiamat was facing. Dawn may be coming, but the darkness of what they were facing was long from over.

The realization that Bob Walsh had shot and killed one of those that lived in the cave changed everything. He'd launched into a frantic defense of why he'd done it: *It's not my fault. Look at it, all covered in hair and stinking; easy to mistake for a wolf in the dark. It's supposed to be in the cage down in the cave for its own protection, not running around in the woods.* And then a final, *It's not my fault.*

In the end, it didn't matter whose fault it was. What was done was done, but the implications were staggering. They identified which one it was with the metal tag attached to a worn leather collar around its neck. That was the only way. It was impossible to tell otherwise. "Sid" it had read. They would have to notify Sid's family. They would be broken and furious - all understandable, of course. But the greater reality, and of far more concern in the whole, was that the cage door was open at the cave and they were out. The only question was, how many? Tiamat had not faced anything like this in anyone's lifetime. The guarding of those in the cave had always taken priority, and the measures put in place for their protection – of those in the cave and those in the village – had been adhered to with ferocious religiosity. The stakes were too high if any of them ever escaped. Now they had. And so, all of them were in danger.

As leader of the town council, the weight and expectation of the community over this most important of matters fell on Vaughn O'Leary. The decisions he made in the coming hours could very well determine the future and vitality of their community. He'd sent Happy Flynn running back to town to get his father's truck. They loaded the body into the bed, careful to secure the tarp concealing it. It was likely no one would be up and about, but the group didn't need to take any chances. Vaughn drove the truck back while the rest of the crew piled into the bed along with the body. He parked behind Dr. Boris Kelly's medical office in the alley. An addition to the clinic built several years prior served as the town morgue for the dead. The doctor had a loading dock of sorts back there for the local funeral home to come pick up bodies. The convenience for the town undertaker was appreciated. They made haste unloading the body and securing it in the morgue portion of the building. Dr. Kelly would have to return to it for a thorough examination after he took care of Malcolm Conner, followed by the mauled guest still over at Ross McCloud's house. It would be a busy day for Dr. Boris Kelly.

The team of four was quickly decided upon. Greg Collins, who was still sick and not looking well at all, along with Happy Flynn were sent home with strict orders to keep their mouths shut about what they'd seen. Once all was known and the cave secured, Vaughn would call a town meeting later in the day to explain everything to the residents of Tiamat.

Furman Hayes paused as the group emerged onto the beach path from the forest trail. Looking out at the ocean, he took in a long breath and let it out slowly. The sun was coming up in the East behind them, up past the bluff – the effect of which was that the sky over the water in front of them was beginning to lighten as well. A few seagulls were ducking and diving, plucking breakfast from the Atlantic's endless buffet. It would be a beautiful day. But there would be no time to enjoy it. The moment was broken as Harv Conner brushed passed him, moving with determination on down the path toward the cave. Furman followed in behind and the group quickly formed a line. Little had been said along the way. Tension rose every time a howl broke the silence of the march.

*It sure sounded like a wolf,* Furman thought.

And maybe it was. But then again maybe it wasn't. He didn't know what to think anymore and he was oh, so tired.

The long night was beginning to take its toll.

Approaching the rise to the cave's entrance, Furman caught the distinct smell of burning wood. The final steps of the hike brought them to a roaring fire. Jasper Collins was sitting in a chair warming himself. Catching sight of the group, he rose.

"Hey Jasp, got back as quick as we could," Harv Connor began. "Brought reinforcements too. Sorry it took so long. We got Malcolm to the doc and he's working on him now. But we ran into a problem -"

"The gate was open," Jasper said flatly, cutting Harv off.

"We know. That's the problem we ran into." Harv pointed at Bob Walsh.

"Bob killed Sid."

"I didn't know it was him," Bob began his defense. "It was dark. I had no idea."

"He's not the only one," Jasper tried to continue.

Furman stepped up, "What? Oh no, that's what we were afraid of. How many?"

"Five. Well, it started off as seven, but we tranquilized two that were still in the cave, just not in the cage. So now it's just five."

"*Just* five? That are out?" Furman asked, incredulous.

"Four now," Bob said somberly, reminding the group of the one named Sid that he had killed.

"Four..." Furman muttered again. He had not imagined that as many as four or five would have escaped.

"It's worse than that," Jasper broke in again. He'd picked up a couple more logs and tossed them onto the already raging fire, adding more fuel to its blaze.

"It's worse?" Harv asked this time.

"Calvin's in the cave." Jasper pointed over his shoulder with a stick. "He's with his boy, Blake. He's dead – Blake, that is. And it ain't good. He'd been chewed on. I couldn't even tell if it was Blake or not, but Calvin said it is and he's his father so I suppose he knows. We found a piece of him back by the cage, too." He said all of this with no emotion. Clearly, the trauma of what lay in the cave had gotten to him.

"What about Sheamus? Where's Sheamus?" Furman was trying to pull more information out of Jasper.

"Don't know," he answered, sitting back down in his chair. "Nowhere to be found. I guess that's a good sign. You'll know what I mean when you see the condition Blake's in. We'll need to go look for him, but Calvin didn't want to leave Blake until you all got here. Didn't want to risk one of 'em returning and...finishing."

Harv Connor made his way into the cave to find Calvin Lynch. He didn't have to go far before he found the grown man sitting on the ground next to his son. He'd laid a couple of blankets over the boy's body. The wool fibers had turned a dark shade from the blood that had soaked them. That was enough for Harv to know that all Jasper had said was true. Sitting down next to his friend, no words were said. Harv simply put his arm around Calvin's shoulder. That was not enough, but that was all he could offer.

Furman marshalled Drake Connor and Bob Walsh into action. "We need to go double-check the security on the gate. And also, the head count. If five - I mean four - are out, that means that there should be six in the cage."

"We need to know which six," Bob said. He was correct. A head count by itself was not enough.

"We'll go in with tranquilizer pistols, all three of us," Furman began. "Once they're down, we'll check the tags and record the names. Then we'll know which ones specifically are out and need to be found."

The men went to work. The gate was indeed secured, as Jasper had said. And there were six accounted for behind the bars. The stench of them all gathered together was off-the-charts awful. A metal supply cabinet housed sanitary gear for handling the creatures in cases where they needed to be touched directly. Masks and gloves were eagerly chosen by the men. With great caution – more than normal because of the circumstances – they unlocked the gate and stepped inside. The movement agitated the lot of them. Two of them seemed to be more subdued than the others, probably the two Jasper put to sleep earlier. Darts were shot into all six of them nonetheless, and in short order they were out cold.

The names were recorded and Furman found himself staring at them on the sheet of notebook paper he had used to make the record. It was divided into two columns. The left column captioned the names of the six, the ones in the cage. The right column contained five names with one crossed out - Sid. It was the four remaining names that Furman was fixated on. Any of them out roaming around was not a good situation, but two of the four names in particular stuck out to him, each for a different reason. They needed to get back to town as quickly as possible. They needed to get to Vaughn O'Leary.

Furman and Harv spent a few moments in conversation with Calvin Lynch. Yes, they needed to find Sheamus. Locating the man's only remaining son was top priority, but they'd done all they could do for now. The sun was rising and the group was spent. It had been a long night for all. What they needed to do now was return with the news of what they'd discovered, regroup with fresh bodies, and organize a proper search for Sheamus Lynch. Calvin reluctantly agreed, deferring to the wisdom of his two friends.

Their work in the cave was done. The questions they had come here for were answered. They gathered up their packs and gear and guns. With care and reverence, they bundled Blake Lynch's body into rolled blankets, securing them with rope. They made sure they had recovered all of Blake that they could find around the cave. Calvin and Drake would carry him. As soon as they got back to town, they would send an armed two-man team down to once again begin the shift work of keeping watch over the cave.

The group moved out for the long hike back to town. They emerged from the cave's entrance, leaving the warmth of the fire behind.

That's when the attack happened.

# Chapter 16

The creature pounced on the back of Drake Connor. Its teeth sunk deep into the shoulder of the young man who let out a scream of pain. Chaos erupted. The two of them, beast and man, fell to the ground, propelled by the force of the wild thing on Drake's back. They rolled down the rocky incline and an intense struggle for life and death began.

"Dad, help!" the young Drake cried.

Harv Connor along with the group began their scramble down the hill when they were cut off by the appearance of two more creatures. It was as if they had come from nowhere, like some sort of dark magic. Furman Hayes realized in that moment how perfectly camouflaged they had been. Their hair and filthy skin blending perfectly into the muddy and wooded terrain. They stunk though, and their foul stench now assaulted his nostrils in full force. Why had he not noticed that before? It was as if they instinctually secreted a putrid rank when agitated...or when ready to attack.

The group halted immediately. They were truly hideous things, surprisingly large and covered in long, matted hair. They hunched over on all fours, their long claws protruding from each of their four limbs, sharp and dangerous looking. They swayed slowly and moved with an unusual grace as they repositioned themselves in relation to the five men stopped in their tracks. They were mere feet away and any sudden movement might cause one of them to spring. There would be no time to raise a weapon and fire before the things were upon them. The only sounds they made were huffing noises joined with low guttural rasps. They were identical in appearance save the color of their hair - the one on the group's right on the darker side of brown.

The battle continued between Drake and the first beast while the rest of the men stood nearly paralyzed. That's when it occurred to Furman Hayes that he'd not moved at all, not one inch since their surprise appearance. It was as if he was frozen in place. He realized then that the rest of the men were frozen as well. Were the creatures causing this? Did they exude some kind of control over the group? Furman's heart rate was elevated and he'd broken out in a profuse sweat. What was happening to him?

He was even shaking - just a slight tremor.

It was fear.

Pure unadulterated fear.

Primal in its form.

The kind of fear that prey feels when being hunted.

The kind of fear that stops you in your tracks. Glued in place. Hoping, praying that your stature and lack of movement will conceal your presence and save your life.

But their presence wasn't concealed, Furman knew. And despite outnumbering them five to two, he believed they could not overtake the beasts.

Drake continued to scream for help. Furman was able to take his eyes off of the two creatures in front of them. Just long enough to see that the younger Connor had flipped his position and was now clamped on to the filthy thing, face-to-face. He was strong, Drake was, kicking and punching with all his might. The two rolled and fought on. But by taking his eyes off of the two beasts in front of him - for only that moment - to look at the struggle that Drake was in, it was enough, just enough to break the spell of fear.

Slowly, ever so slowly, Furman brought his shotgun up from his side. It was shaking. He was doing all he could to control it, to make it stop. No one else in the group was moving at all, still under the spell of fear cast by the awful things in front of them. Why hadn't the beasts attacked them yet? What were they waiting for? It was as if they had some fiendish plan they were working out. But it didn't make sense. They could likely have their way with the group, as stunned and unmoving as they were.

The shotgun rose higher, still shaking somewhat.

Furman forced himself, with all the energy he could muster, to not look at the two beasts stalking in front of them. He knew that if he did, he would lose his courage and he'd be done for. They all would.

The gun was nearly waist level now.

The creatures began to paw and scratch at the ground. They could sense movement in the group as well. Furman's movement. They didn't like it. He was trying to control the shaking in his right hand, that in turn was causing the gun to quiver. The creatures huffed louder, one of them releasing a bark of sorts.

The sound stopped Furman from moving.

He was stuck, frozen in position, gun level at his waist, only his right hand wrapped around the firing mechanism. If he could just get his finger to squeeze the trigger. But what was he aiming at? Nothing. That was the problem. Drake screamed again and this time the scream was different. He was losing the fight.

With all the strength and courage and willpower he could muster, Furman Hayes squeezed. He squeezed and squeezed the trigger as hard as he could.

Nothing.

It wasn't enough.

So, he prayed.

Furman Hayes wasn't much of a religious man, but in that moment, he prayed to God. He wasn't sure for what, just for more.

*BOOM!*

The gun fired and everything changed. He didn't hit anything, the shot from the gun going wild as the weapon flew backward out of Furman's hand. But it was enough. Enough to cause the one attacking Drake to stop. Enough to snap the other four men out of their paralysis and into action. Harv Connor fired his own gun wildly as well. The two creatures blocking their way instinctively sprang away and ran. And they kept running, down the beach path and toward the woods. Seeing that his protection had fled, the one mauling Drake broke away and followed his companions. Harv gathered himself and was able to get off two more targeted shots, but it was too late. The distance too great to land a hit.

"Drake!" he screamed, scrambling down the hill to his son's side. Furman along with the rest of the group followed close behind, save Calvin Lynch who stayed with the body of his own son.

"I'm okay, I'm okay," Drake was insisting as they gathered around. He was on his hands and knees trying to push himself up, but Harv wouldn't let him. Getting down on his own knees, he cradled his son to the ground.

"Take it easy, boy. You're bleeding. We need to check you out."

Drake complied, rolling to a sitting position on his rear end, knees up with his arms draped over them.

"Somebody get him some water!" Harv Connor cried out.

Jasper threw his pack on the ground and pulled out a canteen, handing it to Harv who gave it to his son. Drake took a long drink and then Harv used the rest, pouring it liberally over the bite wound on Drake's shoulder.

It was a vicious, bleeding wound, already soaking his shirt and jacket. But it could have been worse. Drake flinched but he did not cry out. He was a tough young man. A quick assessment showed numerous other scratch and claw marks but nothing too serious and no broken bones. He was sore when he finally rose to his feet. "Let's get a wrapping on that bite mark," Harv indicated to no one in particular. It was Jasper who once again produced, pulling a small first aid kit from his pack with some gauze and tape that they used to quickly cover the wound.

"Let's get out of here," Furman urged. "We're in no

shape for another encounter. We need to report all of this to Vaughn and the council ASAP. Drake needs to see the doctor about that bite, and..." He hesitated before continuing, the true sadness of the moment hitting him again. "We need to help Calvin get Blake back home." He glanced back up the hill at Calvin Lynch, a somber look on his face, still standing guard over the body of his son.

"I'm sorry, son." Harv gave Drake an enveloping but gentle hug. "I'm sorry I didn't get down here quicker to get that thing off of you. It was like I was stuck and couldn't move."

"Yeah, that's right," Jasper chimed in. "That's exactly how it was for me. Those things were standing there in front of us and I wanted to run, but I couldn't get my legs to move. I couldn't get anything to move."

"Same with me," Bob Walsh added. "I wanted to fire my weapon but my arms were locked at my side. Never felt anything like that before."

"That's how it was for us all," Furman explained to the group. "It was something about those things. They exuded some kind of aura or, I don't know what you would call it. But it affected all of us. Once I was able to take my eyes off of them, I was able to raise my own gun and fire it...barely. Like Bob said, never felt anything like it before." The others nodded in agreement.

In a matter of moments, they had gathered themselves and their things and were headed across the beach path toward town. The sun was fully risen now and the sky was bright. Morning had arrived. Furman Hayes was feeling a bit at ease in the morning light, until a final howl tore across their heads from the bluff above them.

They stopped and looked up. A creature stared down at them from over three hundred feet up. It was the final of the four that were loose. The creature sprang away from the edge of the bluff, disappearing into the woods. But not before they got a good look at it. This one was different. He was less hairy than the others, enough so that he could be recognized. A sick feeling spread through Furman Hayes' gut. He could almost taste the bile in his throat.

It was Vaughn and Patricia O'Leary's son.

Lucious O'Leary.

# CHAPTER 17

The buzz of activity in the parlor of the Lear House was like a stirred-up hornet's nest. All seven members of the council were present: Vaughn O'Leary, Harv Connor, Dr. Boris Kelly, Ross McCloud, Bob Walsh, Calvin Lynch, and Furman Hayes. Several of their wives were present as well, but not all. Sarah Connor was with both her sons, Drake and Malcolm, who were at Dr. Kelly's clinic. Mattie McCloud was still at home tending to the young man who'd disrupted their night by collapsing bloody and unconscious in her living room. Jasper Collins was not on the town council but he was present because of his role in the happenings at the cave earlier. But his wife, Dot Collins, was taking care of their own son, Greg, who was growing more ill after returning from the search of Masterson Peak. In addition, numerous other people from the town had crammed their way into the Lear House. It was standing room only as the mass of bodies spilled into the two converging hallways, up the staircase, and even into the kitchen area.

Word had spread quickly, post breakfast. It was just now past nine o'clock in the morning. Vaughn O'Leary stood at the front of the parlor by a bank of windows. He was in an animated discussion with his wife, Patricia, pointing wildly at him while Dr. Boris Kelly stood close by watching. The three of them had been huddled up for some time. The clamor of voices, all in side conversations, was intense as folks worked to find out more information.

Wild animals had attacked Jamison Murphy.

A stranger was found dead in the streets.

Something was going on at the cave.

All sorts of rumors mixed with threads of both truth and misinformation.

"We should have gathered at the town hall." Dr. Boris Kelly stepped in to break up the argument between the O'Learys. He was not one to raise his voice, but was forced to now because of the volume in the room. "This is getting out of control, Vaughn. You've got to speak to the group now and calm everyone down."

The council members had all gathered and consumed a quick breakfast once the cave team had returned. There was much to report and a lot of information to sort through and assimilate. The plan had been to call a town meeting after lunch, but over the course of the last hour, people began to trickle into the Lear House looking for Vaughn O'Leary, wanting answers. He'd put them off long enough.

Vaughn put his hand on Patricia's shoulder as if to say, "We will finish this discussion later," but she just shrugged away, clearly unhappy. Nodding to Dr. Kelly, he took a stand on an antique chair made of oak. He cupped his hands around the sides of his mouth and called out above the noise, "Everyone quiet down! Please, everyone settle down." The room obeyed quickly, the side conversations dying away. Everyone's attention turned to the head of the town council. "I know you all have heard rumors – stories – of what went on last night. We're going to gather at the town hall after lunch. Be there at one o'clock for a full account of what we know."

"I'm not waiting that long," a voice called from the back. "You need to tell us now, O'Leary."

"I've heard the cage was left open at the cave," the voice of a woman cried. This started another round of murmuring.

"Is it true?"

"Tell us now. We demand to know now!"

This was clearly not working. There was no way the group was going to let him wait until afternoon to give a full report. Vaughn O'Leary had no choice but to speak now.

"Please, please!" His powerful voice boomed. "Of course, I will tell you all *now* what we know. But help us spread the word to everyone else. A full briefing at the hall after lunch. One o'clock sharp." This seemed to appease the cluster of packed bodies that still continued to grow as a few more trickled in.

"My friends," Vaughn began. "My brothers and sisters, please listen carefully and do not interrupt until I am done. I have some very grave and serious news to report to you this morning that impacts every citizen of Tiamat. We have done our best to gather as much information as possible about what happened in the late hours of last night all the way into the early morning hours of today. I will tell you all we know as of right now. There is still information to assess and decisions to be made and we will know more after lunch, so please come to the hall at that time. But here is where matters stand.

"Jamison Murphy and Malcolm Connor were scheduled to relieve the Lynch brothers, Blake and Sheamus, at the cave late last night. Before they arrived, however, something happened that frightened the young men and they made every effort to return to town. Jamison made it back but Malcolm did not." A stirring spread throughout the room. Harv Connor stared straight ahead, unmoving as Vaughn continued. "At the time that we were hearing from Jamison about all of this, we became aware that one of the two guests who had been staying here at the bed and breakfast had stumbled onto the porch of the McCloud home and collapsed. He'd been...attacked...by something." More stirring and murmuring, but Vaughn powered on. "The second guest was not accounted for and our last knowledge of the two men was that they had gone for a late evening hike to Masterson Peak. So we quickly formed two parties. One to go look for the missing guest and one to go to the cave. What I am about to share with you next will be hard to hear so I must have your attention. It is important that you hear clearly as to what has happened. The group that went to the Peak was unsuccessful in finding my missing guest. I can tell you that he is a Hispanic young man named Jorge. If anyone sees him or knows anything about his whereabouts, please let me know personally and immediately. But what I must share with you now is more important than the missing young man. This group, the group that went to the Peak, shot and killed what they thought was a wild animal. A wolf. But it was not...it was Sid Buckley."

The room erupted in commotion. "It's true then! The gate is open." More than one person yelled. Several ladies began to cry - friends of the Buckley family.

"Enough!" Vaughn O'Leary thundered, his face a mask of red as he powered over the top of the noise. "This is no time for hysterics or chaos. We must have clear thinking and action. I said that you must hear me out. All the way out, because I am not done. There is more to tell." This worked to calm the group yet again. "Obviously, the gate at the cave was open but we had a group headed there anyway. I am relieved to report that this party found Malcolm Connor on the trail. He was alive but he'd been attacked by something. He is recovering now at Dr. Kelly's clinic." Glancing at Dr. Kelly and Harv Connor, he carried on without saying any more regarding Malcolm Connor's condition. "The team arrived at the cave." Another pause, knowing what he was about to tell the crowd. "What they found is most disturbing. The gate was indeed open. And worse still, Blake Lynch had been killed. Mauled to death would be the best way to put it, I suppose."

"Where's Sheamus?" someone asked, choking up.

"We do not know. It's likely he ran and is hiding. We have to find him. But we secured the gate, and shift work at the cave has begun again with a fresh crew."

"What was the head count, Vaughn? How many are out?"

"Yes, tell us the head count. How bad is it?" Several

voices around the room were all asking the same question at different volumes.

"Please, please," Vaughn O'Leary pleaded. He held both arms above his head in an effort to quiet the crowd. "I know this is very hard. What happens at the cave impacts us all, I know. So hear me out, please. Yes...we are in crisis mode because some of them have escaped. Sid, of course, is dead. But we have four more that are out and running loose."

"Four!" People cried over and over.

"May God help us," more whispered. The room filled with similar sentiments and pleas to divinity.

"What are we going to do about this, Vaughn?" A loud voice carried over all the others.

The crowd stopped talking. A sea of faces all looked at Vaughn O'Leary, waiting for an answer. Waiting for him to lead. As he looked back, he gazed into each set of eyes. Some with tears. Some with anger. Some with doubt. And in some, many actually, he saw fear. Fear of what was happening. Fear of what was to come. Fear of the unknown. But also fear of the *known*.

The cave.

The gate.

The four that were out.

How would this end?

Vaughn O'Leary was acutely aware that not everyone in Tiamat liked him. There were actually very few who would go so far as to call him friend. But all respected him. Some even feared him. And that kind of respect has to be earned, he knew. That kind of respect has to be maintained. The words he uttered and the decisions he made going forward would determine not only the future of Tiamat, but also how he would be remembered by generations yet to be born. Vaughn O'Leary made up his mind in that moment that he would be remembered as a man who was respected and feared. Not by some, but by all.

"We are going to hunt them down and catch them. We are going to put them back where they belong. In that cave behind those bars. We are going to restore peace to Tiamat. And if they fight us...we will kill them."

Vaughn O'Leary stepped off of the chair and walked out of the parlor as the stunned crowd parted like the Red Sea.

*Respect and fear,* Vaughn thought as he walked out of the Lear House and onto the street, smiling to himself as he went.

# CHAPTER 18

It was late afternoon in the town of Tiamat. The sun would be setting soon. Five men were gathered around a large rectangle oak table in the kitchen of the Lear House, the shades drawn on the windows to the outside and the door leading to the parlor closed. Privacy is what the group needed now more than anything.

Patricia O'Leary set a stoneware plate of biscuits in the middle of the table along with a carafe of coffee to replenish the cups that the men clutched in their hands. She cast a knowing eye toward her husband as she moved to excuse herself from the room and the conversation, a raised eyebrow communicating some unknown message between the couple.

"You did a good job at the town meeting, Vaughn. I think most folks are calm and gonna be okay tonight." Ross McCloud wasn't thrilled about praising Vaughn O'Leary so openly, but it was true. Rumors had spread like a flash flood through town, threatening to wash away the peace and tranquility of the life they had preserved for hundreds of years in this little corner of Ireland.

By the time the appointed hour of one o'clock had arrived, the town hall had been packed. Standing room only. Tensions were high as was the temperature in the room with so many bodies packed so closely together. None of the group of five around the table could ever remember another meeting like it. Tempers driven by misinformation and fear were high. There was shouting, pointing fingers, blaming, and even some shoving. At one point the whole event threatened to dissolve into chaos.

And then Vaughn O'Leary took control. If one didn't know better it would have been easy to think that he actually allowed, maybe hoped for, the frenzy to break out so that he could be the grand savior. In any event, that's exactly how it went down.

Vaughn stood on a table at the front of the hall and called out to the town. They stopped and listened. He laid out in calm fashion the state of matters related to the cave and those that dwelled there. He played the crowd like a master musician.

At one point, when speaking about the mauling of Malcolm Connor and the death of Blake Lynch, he even produced a few tears. The town followed suit. They ate a full course meal right out of his hands. Vaughn O'Leary had always exuded a strange form of charisma over the people, which was why he was continually chosen to lead the town council. But the four joined with him around the table now had never seen anything like this version of Vaughn O'Leary before.

You could despise Vaughn O'Leary on the one hand, but you had to admire him on the other. He had saved the town today from internal combustion. Now it was up to this small group gathered in Vaughn's kitchen to save the town from the rest. Namely the four cave dwellers who were loose in the forest plus the coming outside attention to Tiamat because of two Americans – one missing and one clinging to life.

"Thank you Ross," Vaughn replied to the compliment. "I think it went well too, but our focus now, gentlemen, is not just on keeping the town safe tonight, but going forward. Tomorrow night, and the next, and so on. We must contain the problem and clean up the mess."

He spoke as if this were some construction project that had gone off the rails and needed to be put back to rights. Not something that involved real people and real families and the whole future of their village. That kind of cold disassociation bothered Ross McCloud and most likely the others, but he said nothing.

The other men around the table represented the bulk of the rest of the town council. Harv Connor sat at the opposite end of the table from Vaughn, taking big gulps of coffee from his cup. To his right, and just opposite of Ross, was Dr. Boris Kelly. He looked calm, only taking an occasional sip from his cup. He sat back with one leg crossed over the other. Sitting next to Ross was Furman Hayes. The cup in front of him remained full; he hadn't taken a single drink, although his large hands were wrapped around the mug as if to keep them warm. The other two remaining council members were absent. Calvin Lynch was home alone mourning the loss of his son, Blake. It was critical to Ross McCloud that finding Sheamus be of the highest priority. He couldn't imagine his friend's life if Sheamus, too, was dead. That would mean the loss of his wife and two boys all within the span of five years. Bob Walsh was absent as well. He'd been the focus of much anger during the town hall meeting when it was made known that he'd shot and killed Sid Buckley. Sid's mother had melted into a screaming rage. It had gotten very ugly, very quickly, and Bob simply stormed out and had not been seen since.

The rest of Ross's mental energy was focused on his own son, Tommy. He knew it was a possibility that he'd escaped the cave, but when it had been confirmed by Furman that Tommy McCloud was one of the four still loose, well, it had been almost too much for Ross to take. He and Mattie had waited and endured over six years of separation. Six long years. They were so close now. Tommy was set to return in the spring. The light at the end of the tunnel had begun to shine in the McCloud household again.

And now this.

It was still unclear *how* all of this had happened. How the gate had been left open allowing for the escape in the first place. If they could find Sheamus, maybe they would have some answers. But right now, it didn't really matter how or what went wrong. All that mattered was getting Tommy and the others back to the cave safely.

"Let's talk about our plan of attack, so to speak," Ross began. "Harv and I have been talking about the best way to catch the four that are loose." He nodded to Harv, who set his now empty mug down. Harv was an avid hunter so this was his wheelhouse. Hunting.

"We will send out two teams per night. Each team will consist of five men. That way if somebody in the group gets ambushed or attacked by one of...them...then someone can stay with him or try to get him back to town, and that will still leave a group of three to continue the hunt."

"Let's be clear what we mean by hunt," Vaughn interrupted. "We're using the tranquilizer guns exclusively. No live ammo. We don't need another incident like what happened with Bob and Sid. No more killing. Am I clear?" Everyone nodded. Despite what he'd said earlier, Vaughn had no intention to hunt to kill. It had all been for effect.

"Absolutely," Ross replied. "I spent the afternoon at my shop cleaning and prepping our entire stock of Pneu-Dart tranquilizer guns. We've got enough to outfit the two teams each night that Harv talked about, plus I'm issuing several around town, mostly to folks who live on the outskirts in case they hear or see anything suspicious at night." In the same way that Ross was concerned that no harm came to Tommy, he also knew that Vaughn was equally concerned about his own son. "Don't worry, Vaughn. We won't let anything happen to Lucious."

Vaughn stared hard at Ross for a moment, his fists clenched. One of the rules of the cave was to not talk openly about those who dwelt there. Calling out names personalized it too much. It was already hard. No need to make it harder.

Vaughn relaxed and carried on as if he'd not heard the

name of his son. "Harv, how are we going to go about actually finding them?"

"We won't find them as much as we will let them find us. They'll be out and about at night exclusively. They're nocturnal. During the day they'll be hunkered down, hiding and sleeping. But at night is when we have our shot. We'll be out hunting, but so will they. For food. So, the plan is to help them out. We'll scatter wild game – rabbits, squirrels, anything really – out around the perimeter of town. As long as it's bleeding, they will come. They're drawn to the smell and taste of blood." This whole way of talking sent a chill up Ross McCloud's spine. He didn't like to think of his son in these kinds of terms. This was another reason they never talked about those in the cave. The more they could separate themselves mentally from what or who was in the cave, the better.

"It won't take long," Harv went on. "Maybe a few days, but they'll get hungry quick. The lights of the town should draw them toward us, and then when they find what we've laid out...*POW*." Harv raised his hand - finger pointed at Vaughn, thumb in the air like a gun - as he made the sound.

"We've also put in place a curfew." Ross broke the tension. "Once the sun goes down, no one out in the streets. No one. I don't think it will be hard to enforce. People are scared."

"Which is why the sooner we can contain the problem the better," Vaughn inserted, using the language of a foreman on a construction site once again. "That leaves us with the search phase of the project. What's the plan to find Sheamus?"

"Daytime search teams. We can send out smaller teams during the day because it will be safe. I've got four teams of three men each set to go out first thing tomorrow morning and as long as we need until we find him." Harv Connor was indeed good at this.

"And don't forget about the missing American. Jorge is his name, I believe," Ross said. "We need to find him too."

This elicited a look between Dr. Kelly and Vaughn. There was something between those two that Ross couldn't read.

"Yes, well...thank you, Ross. I'm not sure that we'll find him. Based on the condition of the young man at your house, it's likely that the other one was attacked as well and is dead."

"But that doesn't mean we can't still find him. Are you suggesting that we don't even try?" Ross was incredulous. "And what about Sheamus? Using your logic, we might as well not look for him either because Blake was attacked and killed."

"No, no, no, Ross. I'm sorry. You read me wrong. All I'm saying is that Sheamus is one of ours. He's Tiamat. The Americans aren't. They're outsiders. It's not that they aren't important. It's just that the one missing is probably dead and the one at your house may not survive either." Vaughn looked at Dr. Kelly who just looked down and away at the mention of the mauled guest at the McCloud home. "Our priority is to take care of our own first. To find Sheamus...to find Tommy." It was Vaughn's turn to say a name. The name of Ross's son. It had the impact Vaughn had hoped for, defusing Ross McCloud immediately.

Vaughn O'Leary was back in control of the situation

once more. Controlling the conversation. Controlling the focus. Controlling the town. Tiamat was his. He would make sure it stayed that way.

That's when the door to the kitchen swung open, banging against the doorstop. Mattie McCloud was out of breath. "Oh, good, I found you!" she managed to get out.

"What's wrong, dear, what has happened?" Ross sprang to his feet. Everyone's attention swung toward Mattie.

"It's him. The man at our house. Your guest, Vaughn. He's awake...and he's talking!" Mattie McCloud exclaimed with a big smile.

No one looked in Vaughn O'Leary's direction. But if they had they would have seen.

Very clearly.

He wasn't smiling.

# PART 2

# SIX DAYS LATER

*The king has returned!*

*It was a glorious feast last evening in honor of the great king of Babylon. The festival hall was full of family, advisors, and court officiants. All the king's favorite dishes were served and he ate like an animal, although an animal he is no more. The curse of the last seven years suddenly lifted, and without warning. It has not yet been a full three days since he simply stood up in the outdoor pen that had become his new home, and walked back to the palace. On his own and in his right mind. He was a mess, of course. Filthy and weather-beaten. Nearly unrecognizable because of the length of his hair and beard, but the animal nature that had overtaken him was absent.*

*I was in the great Hanging Garden, reading and meditating on a portion of the Torah, the Holy Word of my God from my ancient homeland (it seems like another life, so many years since I called Israel home. Babylon is where I lay my head now and likely will for the rest of my days), when the king himself walked past me. Servants were scurrying at his sudden appearance. Someone had laid a robe over his shoulders to cover his naked form. The king stopped as he passed me, sensing my presence I can only assume. He looked at me with his piercing dark eyes and I knew then that he had returned. Then he said to me the most stunning thing in my native tongue of Hebrew: Yahweh Shalom. The Lord is peace. Never before had I heard the great king, a man of many gods, invoke the name of my God.*

*The miracle of his transformation continued at the banquet. For the great king stood at one moment in the middle of the feast and called the court to his attention. He gave a speech that left all those in attendance without speech.*

My kingdom has been restored to me. My majesty and splendor have returned to me. Now I, Nebuchadnezzar, praise and extol and honor the King of Heaven. For all his works are right and his ways are just. Believe me when I declare this truth. Those who walk in pride, he is able to humble.

*The great king of Babylon was speaking about my God! Is it possible that he has become a follower of the one true and living God? Praise be to Yahweh if this be so. Time will tell. In the midst of our joy upon the king's return, the court physicians report problems within the king's family. It appears a number of his relatives, cousins I believe, have developed the fever. Not unusual by itself but they've begun to act out since the king's return. I will have to investigate this and write more of it.*

From the Journal of Meshach,
Royal court recorder for the king

Tenth day of the month of Addāru,
The twenty-sixth year of the king's reign (579 BC)

# CHAPTER 19

Phineas Crook was a like kid in a candy store. He lifted the raw block of briar wood to his face, pulling in a long draw through his nose. It carried only the slightest of scents, barely discernable. Such was the case with briar, which actually was part of the root system of a shrub and not a tree at all. Most people wouldn't know that or even care. Autumn Crook certainly didn't.

"I know you love this stuff, Phin. But I just don't get it."

"That's because you don't appreciate the finer things in life," Phin replied with a teasing wink.

"Finer things? All I see are blocks of funny-shaped wood and loud machines, cutting and sanding them into all kinds of shapes to be sold at inordinately high prices to thick-headed men who will actually be fool enough to pay the prices. Who will then stuff a gross old weed into them, set it on fire, and then puff on the smoke for the next hour until they are a smelly mess. No thank you. Give me a sensible ladies' boutique selling reasonably priced accessories that will accentuate my beauty any day." Autumn lifted the palm of her hand to bounce the bottom of her dark brunette hair. She was playing with him in return.

"You really have a way of stealing my thunder, Mrs. Crook. What you fail to see, my dear, is that this..." Phin straightened up, arms spread, taking in the whole of the factory. "This is Mecca! I've waited my whole life to come here."

*Here* was the Dunhill Pipe Factory. Phin and Autumn had taken the short drive to the northeastern London district of Walthamstow. Having spent the last week enjoying London proper and the surrounding area, Phin had finally convinced Autumn to take this short side trip with him. They'd done all the touristy things – the London Eye, West End theatre district, a journey north to Stonehenge, time on the sandy beaches of Brighton. They'd shopped, eaten fine food, slept a lot. They'd even taken a day to journey back to Oxford for a picnic in Christchurch Meadow where they'd first met ten years ago. Ten years ago for Phin. Only seven years ago for Autumn. She'd lost three years of time as she slept in a stasis tube at the headquarters of Second Life, Inc. in Plano, Texas. But that was all behind them now. This second honeymoon of sorts, was serving its purpose. Phin and Autumn were reconnecting after the trauma of the last few years and the miracle which brought her back. It was time to live life, to experience new things, which had begun by reliving some old things. Phin and Autumn loved Europe and had done most everything on their itinerary before. But this time it was like a reset.

One thing they had never done, however, was tour a pipe factory together. Phin didn't have a lot of hobbies, but one thing he did enjoy was sitting on his porch in the evenings and firing up a bowl of his current favorite tobacco – which happened to be Sutliff's Vanilla Custard at the moment – in one of his small collection of eight pipes. He owned two Rattray's which were Scottish in origin, an Irish Peterson, a Churchill of unknown origin because it was a gift with no stamping, a couple of Missouri Meerschaum corn cobs, and two other basket pipes. What he didn't have was the highly coveted White Spot, referring to the logo stamped on all Dunhill Pipes. A Dunhill is universally considered the Mt. Everest of pipes. The best of the best. And the price point proves it, which is why Phin didn't own one. A White Spot started at $400 and could easily run to over $2,500. Way out of the salary range for a college professor.

The couple was scheduled to leave the next morning for Rome, and Phin insisted this was their last chance. They had to tour the factory that day. Autumn had given in after some playful resistance. In truth, she liked the smell of the burning tobacco when Phin smoked his pipes. Cigarette smoke and cigar smoke were intolerable to the elegant Autumn Crook, but there was something more refined about a pipe, she thought, and its aroma was wholly different, and pleasant. She normally found herself on the front porch next to her husband with a good book while he enjoyed a smoke. She wasn't necessarily crazy about spending the morning touring a pipe factory, though, but she would do it for Phin.

She enjoyed the look on his face and the enthusiasm in his step as they made their way from one section of the factory to another. His eyes sparkled like a six-year-old on Christmas morning coming down the steps to see what Santa had placed under the tree. They observed the selection process of the aged briar blocks according to the quality of the grain, followed by the cutting and drilling of the selected blocks. This was where the shape of the bowl began to reveal itself.

Various artisans were in the process of sanding and shaping dozens of pipe bowls and shanks. All of these steps were done by hand in the fashion of Alfred Dunhill himself going back to 1910 when the first factory was founded. Even Autumn found herself fascinated by the process. She had no idea the detail and standards that went into a simple tobacco pipe. The crafting of the stem, or the mouthpiece, was of particular interest. She was amazed how the vulcanite rubber was molded and shaped by hand before being polished to a high gloss finish. Again, all by hand. At one point she got lost in her own exploration and had to catch up to Phin who was talking to a craftsman named Lance, who was covered in tattoos on both arms, and was in charge of the final staining process of each briar.

"How exactly is the color chosen for a pipe?" Phin was asking. He was hovering over a tray of finished pipes of various colors. Some were shiny black with a hint of blue, others had tinges of red or plum mixed into the various shades of browns and tans. It truly was an exotic array.

"Some of the colors are classic Dunhill. Our stains are

handcrafted and patented and we produce them year in and year out. But others are more limited edition. The avid collector is always looking for something new and unique, something none of his other friends would have. So, we work to accommodate both markets."

"Fascinating," Phin replied. "I'm overwhelmed, really. I fear I'm going to get home and realize I missed something important."

Laughing, Lance replied, "You can always come back, my friend." He reached out his hand and Phin shook it with vigor, thanking him for the conversation.

The tour ended where it began, in the showroom. Surrounded by hundreds of pipes of all shapes, sizes, and colors, Phin nearly foamed at the mouth.

Autumn eased up beside him, taking his arm and laying her head on his shoulder. "Are you done yet?" she asked. "Get it...*done* yet...as in *Dun*-hill?" She poked him in his side, getting a reaction that caused him to pull away.

"You are so ridiculous sometimes, you know it?" He put his arm around her, pulling her close. "Thanks for doing this."

"What?"

"Coming here with me. I know it's probably silly to you, but this is just the coolest thing. I've read about this place for years. My old professor at Oxford, Dr. Brumfield, owned a White Spot. I'll bet he'd had it for over forty years and it was still a thing of beauty. These pipes are meant to last a lifetime and be passed on to the next generation."

The allusion to children churned Autumn's heart. Phin felt it too. They'd tried to have children for two years prior to the accident that stole her away for another three years.

Their inability to have children had been a source of stress and even some conflict. Nothing serious, it was just an emotional thing for them both. Autumn's healing had been a miracle for sure. She'd been restored to perfect health, just as she was before the accident – in every way. Including her infertility.

"Why don't you pick one out," Autumn whispered to Phin. "Which one speaks to you?"

Phin only chuckled. "No ma'am. I don't think so. Too expensive. It's nice to look, and even touch." He reached up and stroked the polished finished on a dark brown bulldog before pulling his hand back. "And sometimes that's enough." He finished with a smile. "Come on, I'm hungry. Let's get out of here - head back toward downtown and get a bite to eat at that little bistro in Hatton Garden that caught our attention."

"Okay, if you're sure."

Phin was already pulling her by the hand out the door. The little Saab they had rented to troll around in was parked across the street at a meter. They immediately noticed a Bobby writing a ticket for the windshield.

"Oh no," Autumn muttered. "Hey, hold on a second. We're here!" She released Phin's hand and dashed toward the police officer.

Everyone knows that in England people drive on the "wrong side" of the road. It takes a little getting used to for Americans traveling through the country. This also means that when crossing the road you have to look to your *right* and not your *left* for oncoming traffic. It's an easy thing to forget.

In the rush to stop the cop from writing a ticket, Autumn did forget. That's when she stepped in front of a speeding bus.

# CHAPTER 20

Phineas Crook's hands were still trembling. He couldn't raise the overfull glass of water sitting on the little brown slatted table in front of him without spilling it, so he didn't even try. Instead he focused on his breathing, attempting to slow his heartrate down. Autumn sat across from him with a furrowed brow, deep concern etched on her face. The waiter of the Bleeding Heart Bistro, a young man by the name of Frederick according to his name tag, made a pass by the couple for the third time in an attempt to take their order. Autumn gestured with her hand once again that they were not ready.

It was a stunningly beautiful day in the city. Phin and Autumn had chosen a small outdoor table for two nestled up next to the brick wainscot of the building, not so much to enjoy the weather as to give Phin the fresh air he so desperately needed.

"You're having a mini panic attack, Phin," Autumn

finally acknowledged. Her voice was soothing. "You just need to calm your nerves. Take deep breaths. It's okay. I'm here with you." She reached over and took his water glass, poured a third of it on the sidewalk, and returned it to him. She took Phin's hand and placed it around the glass. "Here, try and drink something."

Phin obeyed. The wave seemed to be passing, not so much from the water as much as Autumn's warm touch. The shock of Autumn nearly being crushed by one of the iconic red London Routemaster buses had worn off. This was something more. Yes, this was a panic attack. *Another* panic attack.

The bus driver had seen Autumn dart in front of her and had hit the brakes of the twelve ton missile, buying Phin just the split second he needed to lunge for his wife. Like a linebacker in the NFL sacking the quarterback, Phin performed a perfect form tackle on his wife, his momentum propelling the couple out of the way as the bus came to a rattling stop that would clearly have been too late were it not for Phin's aggressive move. The couple hit the pavement hard and rolled to a stop. The passengers on the bus were shaken but not more than the driver herself who sat, white knuckles glued to the steering wheel. Phin and Autumn were scuffed up but not too badly. Nothing that would require medical attention. The only good that came from the incident was that the Bobby writing the ticket for their rental car came running to check, and when he realized what Autumn was trying to do, tore up the ticket and sent them on their way in short order with a, "Have a nice day."

That's what Autumn was trying to do now - salvage their last day in London. The panic hit Phin about halfway to Hatton Garden, forcing him to pull over so Autumn could take over the driving duties.

The waves of panic or terror or whatever it was had become increasingly common for Phin. He would wake up in a night sweat, his heart pounding out of his chest. Or some crazy thought would strike him related to losing Autumn...again. The fear was always based around his wife, his precious E. He was smart enough to know that the thoughts were driven by irrationality, yet he couldn't stop them. Autumn was encouraging him to see a counselor and he'd about decided to do so. As soon as they returned home to the States, he would find someone. Someone to talk to. Someone to help him understand, and hopefully take it all away.

But what had happened outside the Dunhill Pipe Factory was different. That had been *real*. If Phin had not been paying attention, or if he'd been a second too late, or if the bus driver had not hit the brakes of the bus, or if a hundred other somethings Phin couldn't think of now, had not happened, at just the right time, and in just the right order, then...well, then he would not be sitting at a bistro about to "enjoy" lunch. He'd instead be in the morgue of some local hospital, reliving the events of nearly four years ago. But this time, there would've been no miracle. There'd be no finding his lost Autumn Eden. She'd be gone...lost to him forever.

"Come on, let's order something." Autumn picked up the menu in front of her and opened it, her words and movement snapping him out of the trance he was in. "It's such a nice day, don't you think? What a gift for our last day here." In the time they'd been sitting, several other couples had found seats at the smattering of tables with red cushioned white chairs. The arrangement spilled from the sidewalk onto the brick-paved, dead-end street along the side of the Bleeding Heart. It was so quaint and so London, not necessarily touristy but more local in its draw.

"Why don't you order something for us both? You know what I like." Phin took in a long, deep breath and tilted his head to look at the blue sky. A slight breeze was blowing. Emptying his lungs, he willed his cares into the breeze, hoping it would carry them away.

"Why don't I get the salmon and cod fishcake and I'll order braised rabbit for you and then we can share." Autumn motioned for Frederick who seemed more than ready to receive their order. After taking notes of all, he politely excused himself, indicating their food would be delivered shortly.

Phin's mood lightened considerably. Autumn scooted her chair closer to his so she could rest her hand on his knee. "Let's talk about something. Something not serious. What do you want to do when we get to Rome?"

"Well," Phin began. "We could always drive to Milan and visit the Savinelli Pipe Factory. It's only six hours away."

"Oh my gosh...you've got to be kidding me. I said something not serious and that is definitely *not* serious." Autumn laughed with genuine joy. She had her Phin back.

Over the course of the next half hour the talk was light and pleasant. Autumn got Phin laughing and he returned the favor. Theirs was a playful, intimate love and to anyone observing they would have looked like a newlywed couple.

The food arrived and they dove in, their appetites peaked after the tension of the morning. Phin loved that Autumn enjoyed to eat. She wasn't one of those women who ate only dainty salads and quiche in insanely small portions. Girl food, Phin called it. No, she could pack away a good ribeye with the best of men on any day. Yet, her figure remained perfect. If his wife was anything, it was disciplined. She was up every morning before sunrise - usually somewhere in the five o'clock hour - and out hitting the pavement for one of her four-mile runs. Even during this vacation of sorts, she kept the routine. When at home in Shawnee, she had found a Kenpo Karate gym where she enjoyed working out and volunteer teaching. Altogether, she was in the best shape of her life and more than capable of taking care of herself in most situations.

After lunch, Phin found himself rubbing the top of her hands as they rested on top of the table, staring into her majestic eyes. They were hazel in color but had a way of changing shades to suit whatever Autumn was wearing for the day. In this case, tapered jeans with white New Balance shoes along with a light blue quarter-zip athletic top which pulled out just a hint of blue in her eyes. She was perfect by Phin's way of thinking and so much more than he deserved. He felt underdressed and slovenly next to her in his own pair of Gap jeans, Birkenstock suede sandals, and an untucked crimson hoodie shirt. What she saw in him, he'd never know.

"Thanks for marrying me, E," he said, using his preferred term of endearment. "Thanks for loving me in spite of all my faults. You are amazing, you know it?"

"Oh, you're just being sweet." She turned her hands

over, taking both of his into a clasp. "You are my hero, Phin. My lover and my protector. My best friend. I wouldn't be here with you right now if it weren't for you. For your faith in me – in us. You brought me back."

"God brought you back, my dear. All I did was not give up."

"Well that was enough. And you're right. God did it. That means He's not done with me. With us. You have to believe that. God didn't just bring me back in order to tear me away again. You must trust this and allow yourself to rest easy. You must allow yourself to live, Phin."

She was right. Phin had allowed his fear of losing Autumn again to lock him down. But how to overcome that which scared him the most, he did not know.

"The thing is this, Autumn. Yes, God brought you back. It's a miracle. But you won't live forever. None of us will. Something I've always thought about when reading the Gospels is that every person that Jesus healed...eventually died. All the blind people. All the lame people and the people with leprosy. They would all go on to die. Right? Even Lazarus, who Jesus brought back to life...even he eventually died. A second time. The thought of dying once is enough for me. How bad would it be to have to die a second time?" Phin was trying to make a joke but his overall point was serious. "So yes, God brought you back to me. But you will eventually die, Autumn. For real and for good. And you won't come back this time. I will die, too. We all will. And I have no idea when or how or which one of us will go first. It could literally be anytime. None of us are guaranteed another day. I've already experienced life without you, Autumn, and it was awful.

Horrible. I don't ever want to do it again." This time there was no joking as the tears began to well up in Phin's eyes. "Just the thought of losing you locks me down. It paralyzes me. And every day, I see hazards that could take you away from me. Just one wrong step – like in front of a bus – and you are gone."

This was the clearest admission of Phin's fears that Autumn had heard from him yet. "This is good," she affirmed. "You need to articulate your fear, Phin. Call it out. Name it. And now that you have, we can crush it."

"But how? How do we crush it?"

"By living!" Autumn exclaimed. "We live life. Today. We live life today. Don't worry about life tomorrow. It's not here yet. Maybe it won't come. I don't know and I don't care. But what I have is today. I lost three years of my life. Asleep. Remember? I woke up and the world had moved on without me. My parents are three years older. *You* are three years older. I've got a niece who was ten when the accident happened, and now she's a teenager, Phin. A teenager! I've missed three Christmases. Three sets of birthdays for everyone I love. I'm tired of missing life, Phin. No sir! No more missing out on life for me. I have today. And I choose to live today." She squeezed Phin's hands hard, her hazel eyes on fire as they stared into his. "I *want* you...I *need* you to live life with me, Phin."

Phin was overwhelmed by her strength. He could feel the power of her will flowing from her into him. Emboldening him. Filling him up with life. How this was possible, he did not know. Autumn Eden Rose Crook was a remarkable woman. Yes, he could do it. He could live life...today. For her. With her. He stood up, leaned across the table, and gave her a long kiss.

The moment was broken as the other outdoor patrons began to clap, one young man in a French-styled beret even whistled and blew kisses back at them.

Phin sat back down. "I guess we made quite a scene," he said, blushing. Autumn picked up her napkin and used it as a fan, cooling herself from the steamy moment.

Phin's phone rang and he worked it out of his back pocket. "Hello?" he answered. There was a pause as he listened to the voice on the other end. "What? What are you talking about? Are you alright?" Phin stood and walked a few steps to the side, not wanting to be heard by the other people who obviously had no problem eavesdropping. There was a clear look of concern on his face. Autumn watched intently, trying to decipher the conversation. She heard him ask, "Where are you?" A few more words were exchanged that she couldn't understand and then, "Yes, of course. Whatever you need. I can be there tomorrow. Don't worry, I'm on my way." He disconnected and returned to his seat.

"Phin, what was that? Who were you talking to? I heard you that say you were on your way."

Phin eyes were focused on nothing in particular, his mind racing. "It was Jason Morris."

"Jason Morris?" Autumn was trying to place the name. "Oh...Jason Morris. Isn't he your former student? The one who went to the Garden of Eden with you? You two are close, I know. What's wrong, Phin?"

"I don't know for sure. He's in some small town up on the northern coast of Ireland. He's been attacked and is in bad shape." Phin's eyes finally found their focus on his wife's. "He needs my help, Autumn. I have to go."

# CHAPTER 21

Phin made his way through the Irish countryside in a brand-new Ford Ka. He'd never heard of a "Ka" before because it wasn't for sale in the United States. The brownish-gold colored compact was very European in style and very small. It was the best the Hertz agent at the Dublin airport could do for him on short notice.

Autumn sat next to him nestled up next to the door frame, wrapped in a thin gray travel blanket, reading a novel on her Kindle. He was making good time on the N2 highway, which was about to become the A5 highway once he crossed into Northern Ireland in just a few more miles. The four-and-a-half-hour drive would put them at their destination sometime after lunch into the early afternoon hours.

The weather was on the cool side but good, no rain in the forecast. Since leaving Dublin proper, the road had meandered through predominantly rural country, which characterized most of Ireland really. A patchwork of farms and plots, one after another. The towns they drove through were small, very small, each consisting of one main street, lined by old businesses and homes. A few side streets crossed the main street, and then they were out of town and back into the country.

As soon as Autumn saw the concern on Phin's face after the call from Jason Morris, she knew matters were serious. She didn't kick back on the interruption to their travel itinerary at all. To the contrary, she insisted they leave immediately while also insisting on going with him. They were partners in life, no matter where that might take them. Plus, she had always wanted to explore the island of Ireland. They'd both traveled Italy and been to Rome many times. This would be a new adventure.

Closing the cover on her Kindle she looked toward Phin. "Go over with me again what Jason said to you on the phone. What exactly did he mean when he said he was attacked?"

"Some sort of wild animal, I think. He and a friend of his, a guy named Jorge Ramirez, were on a hike about a week ago when they were both attacked in the woods. Jason said his leg is in bad shape and a local family has been taking care of him. He's getting to where he can move around some, but he's got no idea where Jorge is and he feels like the people taking care of him are keeping information from him. He sounded really scared."

"Well, I'm sure he is scared. The whole thing sounds horrible. He probably needs to get to a proper hospital for treatment. I can't imagine being that far from home at his age and something like this happening to him. What exactly were he and his friend doing up here?"

"Well, he and Jorge met at the archaeological dig he was doing in Israel last summer. I'd set Jason up with some of my contacts in-country to really give him an experience he'd never forget. He just fell in love with Israel from day one. I knew he would. The last I heard he had stumbled into some interesting research on the Jewish exile to ancient Babylon. Said he and Jorge were going to do a deep dive into a theory they were working on. Do some traveling, etc. That's really all I know."

"Well that tells me just about nothing as to why they were hiking the north woods of Ireland," Autumn replied sarcastically.

"Hey, you asked and I'm just telling you what I know. Which, granted, isn't much. Who knows, maybe they got bored reading about ancient Babylonian history and decided to take a break up here in Ireland. Remember, we're talking about two guys in their early twenties. It's no big deal to just pick up on a whim and take off to wherever the wind is blowing."

"Well, you're right. I get that. I just hope Jason's friend is okay. It doesn't sound right at all that it's been a week and he doesn't know what happened to him."

"No, it doesn't. First thing I'm going to do when we get there is talk to the authorities and find out what exactly happened and what's going on. But here's the part that really puzzles me: Jason said that he asked to use his cell phone but they told him it hadn't been found. Apparently, Jason lost it in the attack. But when he asked to use *their* cell phone, they claimed that they didn't own one and that a recent storm had knocked out landline service to their whole street. It's like they didn't want him calling anyone."

"Well, how did he call you then? Phin, this doesn't sound right to me. Who doesn't have a cell phone today?"

"He's apparently staying in the bedroom of this couple's son who's away on some sort of trip. When Jason got to where he could get out of bed, he started snooping around and found a cell phone in a drawer. It was dead, of course. He thought that was really strange after they told him they didn't have cell phones, so he kept it a secret - that he'd found it - and he charged it overnight. That's when he made the call to me yesterday. He made it very clear that I shouldn't call him back because he didn't want the phone going off. He doesn't want the people he's staying with to know he had it."

"The whole thing smells fishy to me."

"Yes it does. We just need to get there."

"And where is *there* again? What's the name of the town?"

"Tiamat. It's pronounced, *tia* and then *mot*. Tiamat."

"Tiamat. Got it. And it's up on the northern coast, right?"

"That's right. Probably another couple of hours away. But I'm about ready to stop for lunch if you are. There's a little town up ahead called Aughnacloy. Not a whole lot after that for a while."

Autumn and Phin rolled into the small town and quickly found a wonderful little restaurant called The Diamond. They ordered sandwiches and salads and enjoyed some small talk with the owner. It made for a perfect pit stop.

Between bites of sandwich Phin pulled out his phone to review the route to Tiamat on Google Maps. Before flying out of London he'd tried to do a little research on the village but found very little. He could see that Tiamat is located in the extreme northern part of the Republic of Ireland in the county of Donegal; the part of the country that wraps around over the top of the separate country of Northern Ireland.

Ireland being an island with two distinct countries has made for some interesting history, the most recent of which was the time of the late twentieth century called The Troubles, when Protestants and Catholics in the British state of Northern Ireland clashed bitterly, resulting in the deaths of thousands. A tenuous peace existed now, but when doing searches of Ireland this was what came up on Phin's phone first. There was just very little information at all about Tiamat itself.

No travel reviews.

No accommodations listed on any of the hotel websites.

Nothing - except that he knew it existed and where on a map it was located.

It was as if Tiamat was a black hole in terms of information. *Aw well,* Phin thought. *We will see for ourselves soon enough.*

Back on the road, Autumn decided to change the subject. "What are we going to do if we can't have children?" she asked sadly. She knew the subject was touchy but it was something she thought about.

A lot.

Phin's shoulders sagged even as he clutched the steering wheel of their tiny rental. "Hey, don't talk that way, okay? We agreed to see a doctor once we get back home. We can try in vitro fertilization and I'm sure they've got all kinds of new things they can do today to help couples like us."

"I know," she replied, turning her head to stare out the window. "It's just...I don't know. I have this feeling that no matter how hard we try it's just not going to happen for us. I mean we've been trying for two years...well, before the accident we tried for two years. And since I've been back...nothing. I'm starting to think that God just doesn't want us to have children."

"I don't believe that." Phin reached over and took Autumn's hand. "Listen, I've been doing a lot of thinking too. I think we should consider...adoption." Phin let that sink in before continuing. "There are lots of kids out there, Autumn. Thousands - at home and around the world - that don't have a family. We could do it, honey. We could take a child that has no home and be their home. We could be a family."

Autumn was solemn. "I've thought it about it too. I just...I want to have my own child. *Our* own child. At least one."

"You're always telling me to trust God. And I think you are right. We have to trust God. In all things. Maybe he will give us kids of our own. And maybe the child that he wants to give us is a child no one else wants. If God gives him or her to us, whether through birth or adoption, that is the child he wants us to have."

"We'll see," she said, squeezing his hand. "We'll see."

The Irish countryside continued past them both,

Autumn looking silently out her side window, Phin looking out through the windshield. They crossed the border out of Northern Ireland and back into the Republic of Ireland. Phin had always wanted to see the famous northern coast of Ireland, to stand upon its majestic bluffs and gaze out onto the Atlantic Ocean. That dream was about to become reality. What Phin didn't know was that the line between dreams and nightmares is sometimes closer than one could ever imagine.

# CHAPTER 22

It was 2:30 pm when Phin and Autumn rolled into Tiamat. They'd turned off of the loop called the Wild Atlantic Way and followed a more primitive paved road to reach the little village.

Phin had no idea what to expect, but Tiamat was certainly small even when compared to most of the other Irish villages they'd driven through earlier in the day. Yet, it was typically Irish in nature. The first structures they drove past were homes, old homes - constructed mostly of natural pale stone and mortar, topped with wood shingle roofs that looked ancient. Phin thought they must be three or four hundred years old at least. Once again, typical for this part of the world.

The asphalt was broken and chunky in places and their little Ford bounced around until they got closer to the center of town where the road improved considerably.

Homes turned into businesses and carried a more modern flair. The street sign said they were on Akkadia Avenue, which looked like the main street of town. It was an unstriped two-lane road but with parking available curbside all the way down. Most of the buildings were two stories, a few reaching three stories. It was likely the owners ran their businesses on the first floors and lived upstairs. A variety of colors adorned the smooth masonry and block-covered buildings. Driving slow, they eased past The Kranky Barber Shop, which was bright red and of the three-story variety. The next business butted right up next to the barber shop and was a launderette service painted in a drab tan. The Imperial was a boutique of sorts, its building painted lime green on the first floor but pink on the second. McCloud's Gun Shop was simply painted white. And so it went, on down the block, like a patchwork quilt with no rhyme or reason.

Phin wondered what it would be like to live in a town like this. To know every person, young and old, and to know their story. And for everyone to know you. Moore, Oklahoma, where he and his older brother, Remus, grew up, was not a big town either and it was probably like Tiamat in that way - easy to know and be known. But it was a metropolis compared to this little hamlet - and most of the towns in Ireland for that matter.

*A town like this could hold many secrets*, he thought. *And hold them tightly.*

He had this odd feeling that he and Autumn might be driving into the middle of one of those secrets in trying to locate his protégé, Jason, and find out what exactly had happened to him.

They reached what must have been the center of town where the prominent feature was a large roundabout. It was so big in its circumference that it created the look of a traditional town square of sorts. The grass was green in the middle with beautiful landscaping and a bronze statue of some figure in the middle. Only one other street came into the roundabout and out the opposite side. It was called First Street.

They made their way around and exited, staying on Akkadia. Traffic was almost nonexistent. They'd passed only one other truck since arriving, although numerous parked cars lined the street. People were out walking, making no effort to hide the craning of their necks as Phin and Autumn drove past. There was something about the people he saw that Phin felt was strange. But he couldn't quite put his finger on it.

"You get the feeling we stick out?" Autumn asked.

Phin chuckled uneasily. "I feel like we have a spotlight following us. This place is already giving me the creeps. It's not like it's that different from the other towns we drove through, it's just...I don't know. It feels different. Maybe it's because I know that Jason is here somewhere and needs us."

O'Leary's Bed & Breakfast caught the eye of Autumn as they came out of the traffic circle.

"Look," she pointed. "I'll bet that's where Jason and Jorge stayed. I haven't seen any other hotel or accommodation of any type except for that."

"Yeah, could be. We'll have to come back to that."

They'd decided that they would drive all the way through the town, just to get a sense of the layout. They had no idea where Jason was but wanted to locate the local police station or constable's office to ask for help. Just a few buildings down from the B&B was a local medical clinic. A two-story gray building with a fancy hand-painted sign that simply read: The Doctor Is In.

"We definitely need to stop there, Phin. They surely helped to treat Jason if it was as bad as he said."

"You're right. Let's get all the way to the end of this street and then we'll come back."

A few blocks later, the businesses ended. The road became primitive and narrow once again and more old homes were all that was left. Eventually those ended and only trees and woods were left to greet them.

Phin made a three-point turn in the tight road, grateful for the compact nature of the car for the first time.

They made their way back to the doctor's office. A pickup truck, a Volkswagen, and another very old car - the type of which Phin didn't recognize - sat in the parking slots in front of the town's clinic.

They drove up and found a spot two doors down in front of an ice cream parlor called The Creamery. There was no meter to feed so they just locked the car and walked back toward the doctor's office. An older man with a slight limp passed them. He was dressed in baggy carpenter pants and a beaten brown corduroy coat that came down mid-thigh. His hands were in his pockets and as he passed Phin and Autumn, he only grunted in reply to Autumn's happy greeting. He made a quick glance back at them and then picked up his gait until he rounded the corner.

"Not the friendly sort around here, I guess." Phin shrugged as he mounted the steps to the doctor's office. He pulled on the old wooden door, painted glossy in a fresh coat of dark green. It was very heavy but glided open with ease. A traditional lobby greeted them. There were dark brown wooden chairs to sit in - the kind that you didn't want to sit in for too long because they weren't very forgiving on one's backside. An antique loveseat looked more inviting. A few potted plants were placed around the space and a table with a collection of National Geographic magazines was positioned in the middle of the seating area.

A woman that looked to be in her early thirties lifted her head from behind the counter, her brown eyes betraying surprise on her face. "Oh...uh...yes, how can I help you?" She stood to her feet, looking very nervous. She was dressed in khaki slacks with brown flats and a floral blouse. Her Irish accent was quaint yet striking at the same time.

Phin stepped forward with a smile on his face, trying his best to channel all the charisma he could muster. "Good afternoon, my name is Phineas Crook. *Doctor* Phineas Crook."

She didn't need to know that he wasn't a medical doctor, Phin thought. "My wife and I are looking for a young man named Jason Morris who was likely treated here last week. He would have had injuries from an animal attack, we think. We're wondering if you know him or his case and could help us locate him."

"Okay," she said slowly, clearly thrown off by Phin and Autumn's appearance in the clinic. "Let me see...what did you say his name was?"

"Jason Morris," Phin repeated.

She began to shuffle papers aimlessly around on the desk, trying to avoid eye contact. Phin was convinced she knew exactly who Jason was and probably *where* he was. Her nervous posture and meaningless movement of paper on the desk was a ruse. She was stalling, trying to decide what to do. Clearly, she or they weren't expecting anyone to come looking for Jason this soon.

"I think you need to see the doctor. Yes, Dr. Kelly can help you. Please excuse me." And just like that she hastened from the desk and through a closed door behind her.

"Boy, that was weird," Autumn commented, walking over and picking up a copy of National Geographic.

They could hear a few muffled voices and in just another moment, a door to the side of the room opened. It surprised both Phin and Autumn, as they had expected the girl to come back through the door behind the desk. But it wasn't the girl that reappeared.

A smartly dressed gentleman led the way with two others following. He was dressed in black slacks, a starched white shirt and black tie with a black vest. He was clean shaven, displaying a thick head of jet-black hair, with deep olive skin and dark brown eyes accentuated by the round glasses he wore.

An older man followed, dressed simply in work clothes with his arm around a younger man, most likely his son. All three had features that could have made them family, though, which Phin found curious. His thoughts quickly shifted gears when the young man came into view, moving past the doctor with the help of his father. He heard Autumn take in a sharp breath.

"Harv, you just use that kit I gave you. It has everything you need. Change his bandaging once a day. It's important to keep the wound clean. Infection is what we're watching for now." The doctor turned his attention, placing his hand on the side of the young man's ashen face. His left arm was only a stump covered in a thick white wrapping, ending right at the elbow. "You're going to be fine, my boy. You hear me? Don't think about it too much right now. Just rest and concentrate on healing. Let that pretty little girl you're engaged to come over and take care of you." The young man only nodded and he and his father shuffled around Phin and Autumn. Phin rushed to open the door for the pair as they exited. The one named Harv nodded and said thanks. He too gave Phin a suspicious glare as he made his way down the steps.

"What's this I hear from my assistant about you looking for someone?" The doctor asked loudly.

Phin shut the door and hurried over to the doctor. "My name's Dr. Phineas Crook, and this is my wife, Autumn."

"Dr. Boris Kelly," the doctor replied, taking Phin's extended hand. "And what kind of doctor are you, *Dr. Crook?*"

"Uh...well, I'm a college professor, actually." Phin smiled like a kid caught with his hand in the cookie jar. His little plan to impress had been thwarted.

"Oh yes, of course. I understand," Dr. Kelly replied with a tinge of smugness. "And you're here for the young man that we treated last week, I assume? Jason is his name."

"Yes," Phin answered. "That's him. Jason Morris. We have a lot of questions about what happened to him and also the friend he was with, a guy named Jorge Ramirez."

"I'm sure you do have a lot of questions, Dr. Crook."

The doctor's demeanor took on a dark tone. "Perhaps it would be better if we spoke privately...in my office."

# CHAPTER 23

"Your friend is very lucky to be alive."

Dr. Kelly sat behind the large mahogany desk in his private office. He was leaned back in an aged leather highbacked chair, the fingers of his hands tented in front of him. He was the picture of astuteness and formality. Phin and Autumn sat in leather chairs on the other side of the desk, taking in the coziness of the office. Pictures of a young woman, perhaps his wife or daughter, sat on a credenza behind the doctor. An iPhone sat in a dock playing classical music softly to push back the quiet space. Mozart, if Phin wasn't mistaken. He often played similar music while studying in his own office on the second floor of Montgomery Hall on the campus of Oklahoma Baptist University.

"If you don't mind my asking, Dr. Crook, how did you

find out about Mr. Morris's condition and that he was with us here in Tiamat?"

It was a strange question, Phin thought. The doctor was fishing for something. What, Phin did not know. He decided to be forthright. He had nothing to lose by his estimation.

"My wife and I were vacationing in London the past week or so. I became aware that Jason was here in Ireland somewhere with his friend, Jorge. Jason's a former student of mine and we've remained close since his graduation. We have a certain...bond, if you will. He means a great deal to me. As does his welfare. He called me yesterday to tell me of his condition and asked for my help."

Phin waited to see the doctor's response.

"I see," Dr. Kelly began. "He called you, you say. On a phone." It was more a statement than a question.

"That's how most people do it these days...on a phone," Phin replied with a bit of sarcasm. "Jason mentioned that he'd been trying to make a call for several days but had trouble obtaining a working phone. I found that curious, doctor." Again, Phin was testing – watching the doctor closely for any sort of reaction.

"Yes, well, we've had issues with our local service. Storms have been fierce at times this fall season. I'm sure you understand. Don't you have storms with, let's see...tornadoes? Yes, tornadoes are common in Oklahoma, I've read."

"Oh, yes," Phin replied with a big smile, slapping his knee. "We've got tornadoes and bad storms back where I live. We also have cell phones." Phin pointed to the docked phone behind the doctor.

"Of course you do." Dr. Kelly smiled. "It seems one cannot go anywhere in the world these days and not be connected. That is if the towers are operational. Unfortunately, our towers were down this week as well. A very bad storm you understand."

The cat-and-mouse game was getting nowhere, Phin decided. The doctor was being coy on purpose. Phin chose to push the doctor using a more direct manner. "Where is Jason, Doctor? I'd like to see him please."

The smile on Dr. Boris Kelly's face vanished. "He's not here. He's staying with a local family."

"Yes, he mentioned that to me. Perhaps you'd be so kind as to point us in the right direction. We're not from around here, you know."

"I think it might be best if you spoke with the head of our town council. His name is Vaughn O'Leary. He owns the local bed and breakfast. I'm sure you passed it on your way in. It's only two doors down. An easy walk."

"The head of the town council," Phin repeated. He looked at Autumn. *Why was this so hard?* his face read. She raised an eyebrow in response. "And the head of the town council...this Vaughn...."

"O'Leary."

"Vaughn O'Leary. He's interested in Jason Morris and his friend. Why?"

"Let's just say it's complicated."

"Complicated," Phin repeated again. "Yes, it certainly does seem...complicated." Phin was growing frustrated. "What exactly happened to Jason, Dr. Kelly? What's wrong with him?"

"Well, as a patient of mine, I am prohibited from

speaking about his condition unless it is to family. Our health care system has its own privacy laws much like your HIPPA laws in America. I'm really not at liberty to share with you more than I already have. As I said, the best thing for you to do, I think, is speak to-"

"Vaughn O'Leary," Phin finished for him. He was getting nowhere with Dr. Boris Kelly.

Dr. Kelly leaned back in his chair with a smile as if to say, *we're done here.*

"Thank you for your time, Doctor." Phin and Autumn rose, as did Dr. Kelly. "I'm sure once I've located Jason and gained his *permission* to speak regarding his health and condition, I'll have more questions for you."

"Yes, of course. I'll be happy to help in any way I can."

Phin didn't believe him.

Exiting the building onto the sidewalk, Autumn couldn't wait to jump in. "What was *that* all about?"

"I've got no idea. He's hiding something, that's for certain. Maybe this Vaughn O'Leary will actually tell us what's going on."

It was a short walk, indeed, to O'Leary's Bed & Breakfast. Just two doors down, as the doctor had said. It took them less than sixty seconds to cover the distance. They passed their car, still secure in its slot, and took a moment to glance at a gathering of people in the grassy middle of the traffic circle. Phin guessed maybe fifteen or twenty people, mostly men but also a few women. It looked as if the men were splitting off into smaller groups of three, and a couple of older men were giving them instructions and handing out papers that looked like maps. It was hard to tell from a distance.

The whole scene was curious and all at once alarming when Phin caught glimpse of what looked like a handgun being checked by one of the younger men. Autumn saw it too and squeezed Phin's arm, pointing. One of the older men giving instructions must have seen Phin and Autumn because he moved quickly to the one with the gun, and in a very animated fashion stepped in front of the man, blocking their view. Phin caught what looked like the man motioning over his shoulder with his thumb toward them. A few in the group looked Phin and Autumn's way. When the older man stepped away the gun was no longer in view. Feeling as if they'd been "caught," Phin and Autumn turned and walked up the steps and into O'Leary's B&B.

It felt like stepping back in time as they entered the lobby of the bed and breakfast. Everything was adorned in antiques. The wood-planked floor creaked and popped as Phin and Autumn walked across it toward a chest-high check-in counter. The whole place smelled like Phin's grandmother's house back in Oklahoma. Not a bad smell at all, just old and quaint. Phin and Autumn smiled at each other and instantly felt at ease.

A little boy, no older than six or seven years old, came tearing around the corner. He was carrying two small spaceships in his little hands. A Star Wars X-wing fighter and a Millennium Falcon. They looked to be in some kind of dogfight. The boy came to a screeching halt in front of Autumn, stopping and staring back up at her.

"Well, hello there," Autumn said in a chipper voice. "What is your name?"

"Patrick O'Leary and I'm not supposed to talk to strange people," he croaked out in a shy voice. The black-haired, brown-eyed boy was so cute with a bowl cut to compliment the bangs that rested just above his dark eyebrows.

"Well, we aren't strange people, Patrick. At least I'm not. He can be a little strange sometimes." She leaned over, lowering her voice to a whisper and motioning toward Phin. "But he's mostly harmless, I promise." She straightened back up and resumed a normal volume. "I'll bet your parents were talking about *strangers*. And yes, that is very good advice. You shouldn't talk to strangers. And we definitely are strangers to you. So maybe we should talk to your parents. Are they around, Patrick?"

"Welcome to Tiamat!" A pleasant voice caused them all to jump. A woman, neatly dressed in fitted jeans, loafers, and a gray sweater appeared behind them, entering from a side room. "Patrick O'Leary! What are you doing out of bed, young man? I swear if you aren't the healthiest looking sick boy I've ever seen. Excuse me," she directed to Phin and Autumn. "He's out of school today with a slight fever. Which," she continued, directed to Patrick, "seems to have disappeared." She stepped up, putting her hand on the boy's forehead. Then leaning over, she kissed him on the cheek. "Why don't you run up to your room and play while I take care of these nice folks."

"They're strange people, Mommy."

"Patrick!"

"It's okay," Autumn said. He's a lovely boy. Cute as a button. You are very lucky."

"Thank you very much. And please excuse our little Patrick. He tends to say what comes into his little head. My name is Patricia O'Leary." She extended a hand in welcome to the Crooks. "Welcome to our quaint little town and to our bed and breakfast."

"Yes, welcome indeed!" A booming voice startled Phin and Autumn for a second time. A sharply dressed man, with slicked back black hair and sporting a crisp goatee had come up from behind them silently through the front door. "You must be the Crooks. My name is Vaughn O'Leary. I've been expecting you."

# CHAPTER 24

"Papa!"

"Hello Patty, my boy." Vaughn O'Leary scooped up his son, who'd sprinted into his arms. "Oh, let's take a look at you." He held the boy away from himself, appraising him like the proud father he clearly was. "My oh my, you look to me like you've made a full recovery. Mrs. McCraery sent me home with your homework and said she's looking forward to having you back in class tomorrow." Patrick O'Leary stuck out his bottom lip in disappointment. Vaughn sat the boy down, tussling his hair. "Run off to your room now and take these papers from your teacher with you. I need to take care of our guests."

Patrick turned to leave the room when Autumn said to him, "Nice to meet you, Patrick. The next time we see each other we won't be strangers any longer." She gave him a wink, which produced a smile.

The boy took his time walking up the stairs, looking back at Autumn the whole time. Just before he disappeared around the corner of the landing he called back, "You're pretty." And then with a giggle he was gone.

"I'm so sorry," Patricia O'Leary apologized.

"He's just precious," Autumn replied. "You are so blessed to have him."

"Yes, we are...blessed is the right word I suppose." There was something in Patricia O'Leary's response and behind her eyes that Autumn couldn't quite read. A sadness perhaps.

"As I said," Vaughn broke in, breaking the moment. "I was expecting you. Dr. Kelly called me while I was over at the school visiting with Patrick's teacher. He said you were headed this way and so I made haste to return. Why don't we step into the parlor. Patricia, dear, would you be so kind as to prepare some coffee for our guests?"

"Oh, none for me, thank you," Phin said. Apparently, phone service was magically working just fine now. "I'm not a big coffee drinker but water would be wonderful."

"Water is fine for me as well, thanks so much," Autumn responded in turn.

The group moved into the parlor, which looked as if it doubled as a dining area for the bed and breakfast. Beautiful bow windows looked out onto the roundabout. Phin noticed that the people who'd been gathered there were now gone. Two ancient curio cabinets sat on opposite walls and contained what looked to be very old trinkets. Antique marble-topped tables for two were scattered around the room along with some low-profile cushioned seats for two, also antique. Everything in O'Leary's Bed &

Breakfast was very old but in excellent condition. The owners obviously took pride in maintaining their establishment to the highest of standards. Sitting at one of the tables, Vaughn pulled over an extra chair to join the Crooks. Patricia arrived with two glasses of water and then excused herself from the room.

"You're interested in one of my guests, I understand - Jason Morris," Vaughn began.

"Yes, we are," Phin replied. "Jason is a former student of mine. A protégé of sorts. We are very close. When he phoned and told me he was in trouble, we came right away. The doctor - Kelly, I believe was his name - was nice enough, but he seemed to go out of his way to not really tell us how Jason is. He insisted that we talk to you."

"Of course. Doctor-patient confidentiality is the issue, I'm sure. I imagine you understand. But the good doctor knew I was not bound by such constraints, which is why he steered you to me."

"How exactly *is* Jason, Mr. O'Leary? And what can you tell me about what happened to him?"

"Oh, please, call me Vaughn. We aren't as formal around here as we might appear at first glance."

"Thank you, Vaughn. So, about Jason."

"Yes," Vaughn O'Leary began with hesitation. "Well, it's somewhat complicated."

"Those were the words that Dr. Kelly used," Autumn chimed in. "What exactly is so complicated?"

"We are a small town, Mr. and Mrs. Crook."

"Phin and Autumn," Phin cut him off. "We aren't as formal as we may seem either."

Vaughn smiled and continued. "As I said, we are a

small town. Not much happens of any excitement around here. We get very few visitors, and when people do come, they stay a day or two - see the sights, what few there are - and then they move on. Such was the case with Mr. Morris and his companion. But then there was an accident."

"An accident?" Phin questioned.

"Yes, accident. Or I should say, an attack of sorts. From a wild animal. Most likely a wolf. They are known to roam these parts but are rarely seen. We've not had any trouble in years and certainly have never had a visitor attacked by one. Jason is very lucky to be alive. The quick work of one of our residents, along with the expertise of Dr. Kelly, saved his life. To be frank about it, the whole incident has been very upsetting to us all in Tiamat. This is not what we want to be known for."

"What about Jason's friend - Jorge Ramirez?" Autumn asked.

"Yes, Mr. Ramirez. That is part of what makes this situation so complicated. The problem we are facing is that...well, we cannot find him."

"So, he *is* missing," Phin said, sitting back, running a hand through his thick mane of hair.

"Yes, unfortunately. The two men went for an early evening hike to the top of Masterson Peak. It's one of the draws for the few visitors that we do have. The view of the Atlantic is spectacular from there, I must admit. My understanding is that they were intending to stay and watch the sunset and then return back to town after dark. What I can tell you is that Mr. Morris made it back but in grave condition. His friend has not been seen since. It was obvious that Jason had been attacked and we can only assume that the same fate befell Mr. Ramirez."

"My goodness, man!" Phin exclaimed, a little more forceful than he intended. Nevertheless, he *was* shocked. "It's been a week since all this happened. What are you doing to find him? Have you contacted the authorities? What about his family? The U.S. Embassy? Who all knows about this?"

"Please, Mr. Crook...Phin...we are taking this very seriously. Our means of communication have been limited with the recent storms we've had."

"So I heard," Phin said, trying not to sound too put off.

"But we've been very diligent in our attempts to locate Mr. Ramirez, I assure you. We've got search teams combing the woods day and night. In fact, you may have seen a group about to head out. They were organizing in the traffic circle a few moments ago. It's very easy for one to get lost in the hills and woods around here. We are very optimistic that we will find him, though."

"But what if he's hurt? Or worse..." Autumn asked, her voice trailing off at the implications.

"As I said, we're optimistic. It has happened before that people get lost and we have to send some locals to find them."

"But a week, Vaughn. Seven days. I have to tell you, I'm very concerned," Phin admitted.

"As are we, I assure you."

"I think I'd like to speak to the authorities, if I may. The police or constable, whatever you do here in Tiamat for law enforcement."

"We don't have a police department or constabulary in

Tiamat. All matters related to the law and violations of the law are handled through our town council, of which I am the head."

Phin was incredulous. "Let me get this straight. This town has no formal law enforcement agency? I've never heard of such a thing. Who takes care of matters when someone breaks the law?"

"Oh, we do have a formal law enforcement agency, Mr. Crook. It's the town council. The town council handles all matters of the town. And by that, I mean *all* matters. Including matters of the law. I know it may sound strange to you, but we are a small town. There's fewer than four hundred residents in Tiamat. Everyone knows everyone here. And we all take care of one another. It's been this way for more generations than any of us can count. We've simply had no need for a police department or anything else for that matter, other than a town council. I suppose as the head of the council, I am the closest thing we have to a chief of police. And I *am* elected by the people of the town. This is why Dr. Kelly insisted that you come speak to me. As I said, I'm sure this all sounds strange to you, being from America and all, where violence is a daily occurrence, but such is not the case in Tiamat. This is how we do things and for us it simply works."

"It works," Phin mused out loud. "Until it doesn't."

"Excuse me?" Vaughn asked, not following.

"It works until it doesn't. Until a young man is attacked and nearly killed and another goes missing for a week and you can't find him. Pardon me if I'm overstepping my bounds in saying this, but it sounds like this is bigger than what you can handle."

Vaughn O'Leary stared at Phineas Crook. Like gunfighters facing off, one waiting for the other to make the first move. Neither flinched.

Finally, Autumn broke the stalemate. "Can we see Jason, Vaughn? Surely you know where he is."

Vaughn O'Leary tore his eyes from Phin's and turned his head toward Autumn. And just like that he released a charismatic smile. Like a politician, Autumn thought. A sleazy, slick politician. All smiles, but never to be trusted with anything of real value.

"Of course. I'm sure you would like to see your friend. And I'm sure he's anxious to see you as well. Come, let me take you to him."

# CHAPTER 25

The walk to Ross and Mattie McCloud's house took fifteen minutes. Vaughn O'Leary had suggested they drive the short distance to the edge of town where the McClouds lived until he saw the size of the Crook's rental car. It was a beautiful day, the weather in the low 70s, so a nice stroll through town was just right for Phin and Autumn. They'd spent the morning in a plane followed by a long car ride so no complaining from them.

Their presence seemed to draw more stares from the local folks who were out and about, even with Vaughn escorting them. There was still something strange about every person they had encountered so far - including the random people they saw on their walk through town. Phin couldn't quite put his finger on it. He had traveled all over the world and functioned in all kinds of cultural settings – exotic food, languages, dress, customs, etc. Wherever you travel in the world, you quickly discover that people live life differently than you do. But different is not a problem. Different is just different. But here in Tiamat it wasn't about being different. Something felt...off.

As they walked, they left the business section of town behind. Staying on Akkadia Avenue, the buildings turned into houses - the really old stone and block homes Phin and Autumn had driven past on their way into town. Most were very small and simple, with tiny stoops and porches, but well maintained. It struck Phin that despite the age of the town, nothing in Tiamat seemed to be dilapidated or falling into ruin. That certainly set this village apart from the others they'd driven through earlier that morning. The quaint little towns of Ireland were like most small towns in America, Phin thought. Some old, some new, some well taken care of, and some not. Here, though, everything had an appearance of perfection. Like a postcard, Phin realized. Maybe this is why Phin felt "off" about the town. But maybe not - what he sensed felt deeper.

The threesome made small talk with Vaughn O'Leary asking a majority of the questions – mostly about Phin and Autumn. Phin's job as the holder of the Sam and Martha Goodman Chair of Preaching and Pastoral Ministry at Oklahoma Baptist University seemed of particular interest to Vaughn. He drilled Phin with a quick round of questions about Baptist beliefs and protestant theology. He was a difficult man to read and Phin intended to probe with some of his own questions until Vaughn asked Autumn if she liked being the wife of a college professor. She stumbled over her answer. It was complicated to explain to someone they had just met that although Phin had been teaching for three years, she'd only known him as a professor for four months. When doctors had slipped her into a cryo-tube at Second Life, Inc. in order to save her life, she'd been the wife of a pastor. When she woke up three years later, she was the wife of a college professor. She truthfully didn't know what it felt like yet. After a stop and start answer that made not a lot of sense, Autumn moved to a change of subject.

"Tell us about your family, Vaughn. Patrick is such a precious little guy. Do you and Patricia have any other children?"

"Oh, yes we do," Vaughn replied without skipping a beat. "We've got one other son. Lucious is his name. He turned twenty-five last month. He's a remarkable young man. We are proud of both our boys."

"Twenty-five?" Autumn remarked with surprise. "That's quite an age difference between the two boys. How old is Patrick? Six, seven?"

Vaughn laughed, shaking his head. "He's seven years old. Yes, I know, it's a big gap. All I can say is that Patrick is the surprise of our old age."

"You hardly look old," Autumn teased. "You and your wife can't be over forty." It was true, both Vaughn and Patricia looked younger than what one would expect for parents of a twenty-five-year-old.

"Let's just say Patricia and I married young and began our family young. We wed right after secondary school and Lucious was born the next year. We got an early start for sure. Patrick, on the other hand, caught us off guard. Don't get me wrong. We wouldn't have it any other way."

"Well, he's a fine young man. Perhaps we can meet Lucious while we're here."

There was an awkward pause before Vaughn replied. "Lucious isn't here. In Tiamat. He's away. Traveling. It's common for our young people to take a number of years after school to do some traveling. You know, get out – see the world. Then they always come back. Always. They discover that there's...let's see, how did that girl from Kansas in that old American movie say it? Dorothy was her name, I believe. *There's no place like home.* Isn't that right?"

"The Wizard of Oz," Autumn confirmed. "That's the one. And yes, I can assure you, there's no place like home." She reached over and took Phin's arm as they continued to stroll. "So how long has it been since you've seen Lucious? You must miss him terribly."

"Oh, we do. But he's returning to us very soon. Anytime, actually. Patricia and I are very excited. We've a big party planned to welcome him back."

In short order they arrived at the final home on the street leading out of town. In fact, they'd already passed what they thought was the last home half a block or so back. Only a stable for animals and what looked like storage sheds lay between that home and the one they approached now. It was clear that this was the marker for where Tiamat began and ended. There was nothing but a few more sheds, and then road lined with trees, for as far as they could see.

"And here we are," Vaughn announced. He stepped up onto the small wooden porch and knocked. After a moment, footsteps could be heard and the door opened.

"Good afternoon, Vaughn," came a woman's voice that

cut short at the sight of Phin and Autumn standing behind the head of the town council. She was a plain looking woman with kind brown eyes, a large flock of jet-black hair pulled up high off her olive-toned neck. She was dressed casually in a simple skirt made of light blue cotton and an oversized black sweater. It didn't exactly match but she was probably not expecting visitors.

"Good day to you, Mattie. I suspect Ross is still at the gun shop?"

"Yes, he is. He usually gets home around six."

"Well, I apologize for stopping by unannounced but we have some guests I needed to bring over straightaway. They are friends of the young Mr. Morris."

"Oh, my!" she said, surprised. "Yes, of course. Come in, please. Come on in out of the street." She motioned them all in, a look of nervousness in her movements. She was smoothing out the lumps in her sweater as Phin, Autumn, and Vaughn stepped across the threshold into a plain but nice living room. Phin caught the smell of an old fire emanating from the fireplace from the night before. A burning candle was also adding to the scent of the room. Sandalwood, if he was correct. Mattie McCloud gathered up a few papers from the couch and chair, urging them to have a seat, offering the customary coffee or tea.

"We hear you've been taking care of Jason, Mrs. McCloud. We are grateful for your hospitality. But we'd like to see Jason if that's alright." Appreciative of her hospitality, Phin had remained standing along with Autumn. This was not a social visit for them. They'd come a long way on a moment's notice and now that they were so close, they wanted to see Jason Morris for themselves. To verify that he was alright and to find out what was really going on.

"Dr. Crook!" A voice called from the back room. There was banging and shuffling, a frantic nature to the commotion. "Dr. Crook, I'm here." And just like that, Jason Morris appeared in the doorway. He was hobbling on a homemade cane made of some sort of wood. A checkered red and black flannel shirt was untucked, and the jeans he was wearing were cut off on one leg revealing a thick layer of bandaging. Except for that, he looked like the Jason Morris that Phin had sent off to Israel right after graduation in the spring. He was a handsome young man with close cut sandy-blond hair and bright blue eyes.

"Jason," Phin exclaimed with joy. He rushed over, the two men enveloping each other in a warm embrace. "How are you, my friend?"

"I'm fine. I'm fine. The McClouds have taken good care of me, but I am sure glad to see you." Jason cut off at the sight of Autumn Crook who was standing back, watching the two of them with a glowing smile on her face. "Autumn...," his voice said and then faded. "You brought Autumn," he said to Phin.

Phin was all smiles. "Yes, I did. I thought it was time you two meet. My favorite girl and my favorite student."

Jason hobbled toward Autumn, a look of wonder on his face. "It is *so* nice to meet you, Mrs. Crook. I apologize...I just...I've seen your picture in Dr. Crook's home...I mean your home. I never knew. Never thought it was possible. But here you are. Praise God. What a miracle."

Vaughn O'Leary and Mattie McCloud looked on in curious fascination, not sure exactly what it was they were witnessing.

"It's nice to meet you too, Jason," Autumn said. She gave Jason a warm hug of her own. "I've heard so much about you as well. I hope you're okay. How is your leg?"

"My leg? Oh, it's fine," Jason said, shaking his cane as if it was an annoyance. "My leg's not the problem. Listen," he directed his attention back to Phin, "I'm so glad you're here. You're not going to believe what I've discovered. I've got a lot to talk to you about and I need your help. Both of you."

Mattie McCloud gave Vaughn O'Leary a worried look. But Vaughn didn't look worried, he looked angry.

# CHAPTER 26

"I don't have any idea how they found out that he's here," Mattie McCloud hissed through clenched teeth. She was loud in the kitchen as she opened and closed cupboards, pulling out cups for the hot tea she'd promised her unexpected guests. She'd taken offense at Vaughn O'Leary's accusations of sloppiness in keeping an eye on Jason Morris. No outside contact under any circumstances had been the admonishment. The last thing the residents of Tiamat needed right now was any other tourists, and certainly no one coming to look for or help Jason and his missing friend.

Ross McCloud had disconnected his home phone from the landline and they'd taken extra care to keep their cell phones on them at all times, claiming to Jason that the towers were down and that the town was cut off to outside communications. They'd known that the ruse wouldn't work forever but at this point they were just biding time – one day at a time. It appeared now that they'd run out of time.

"Well, he's only been in this house, Mattie. Nowhere else. It's not like he can just run down the street and borrow the neighbor's phone." Vaughn moved aside the lace curtain covering the front window and peered out at the three of them – Phineas and Autumn Crook, with Jason Morris – in the street just off the front porch. Phin glanced up, right at Vaughn, who jutted back from the window. He already didn't like Phineas Crook. The man would be trouble if he stayed too long. And one more hour was too long as far as he was concerned.

"He didn't make any call from this house, I tell ya." She was adamant. "Here, take a look at my phone if you don't believe me. The unlock code is: 4923. You won't find anything going out or coming in." She took her phone from a pocket concealed in the fold of her skirt and flipped it right at Vaughn's chest. He jerked back as he caught it.

"I believe you, just calm down." He set the phone on the counter without looking. All I'm saying is that he made a call somehow and he hasn't left this house since he stumbled onto your porch a week ago. I'm just not sure Ross wouldn't be so careless as to leave his phone laying around. He's not exactly a detail guy." Vaughn moved back over to the curtain to attempt another stealth look at the threesome. They'd moved a step further from the house since he last took a peek. It was clear they'd positioned themselves so as not to be overheard by the two of them inside the house. "How close are you to finishing with the tea, Mattie? I need an excuse to go out there and break up their little meeting."

"I'd like it very much if you didn't rush me, Vaughn. You've already come into my home and accused me of not being competent to take care of my own business." Mattie continued to stomp and make more noise than necessary, slamming the tea kettle onto the burning stove.

"We're all on the same side here, Mattie. We need to act like it."

"Let me hand you a mirror then, Vaughn O'Leary. And you can say those words again if you like. Because the only *side* I've ever known you to be on is your own side."

That was enough for Vaughn O'Leary. He wasn't about to stay confined to the McCloud house and take this kind of disrespect. Even if it was from Mattie McCloud herself. He turned and made his own noise, stomping across the living room and out the front door. He made sure he slammed it by way of adding an exclamation point.

*****

Phin, Autumn, and Jason began their conversation on the porch of the McCloud house. Jason was eager to talk to them, people that he trusted. He'd been sequestered for a week now and was about to go stir crazy, all cooped up inside. It was obvious to the young man that the McClouds were intentionally keeping him away from people. The only other person he'd seen besides Dr. Kelly - who came around once a day to check on him - was the owner of the bed and breakfast where he and Jorge had stayed, Vaughn O'Leary. Jason was convinced the man was hiding something. He suspected that whatever had happened to him and Jorge had something to do with Vaughn O'Leary and the whole town of Tiamat, he just could not imagine what. But now he was among friends.

Becoming quickly aware that they were likely being eavesdropped upon, the group had moved off the porch and out into the street. Phin tried to help Jason with his leg but he refused. It felt good to be outside, breathing fresh air. The leg was bad but it wasn't so bad that he couldn't move around. In fact, he felt that after a week of bedrest, moving around would be good for it.

"I can't tell you how glad I was that you picked up when I called yesterday, Dr. Crook." Jason sounded relieved, like the weight of a thousand pounds had been lifted from his shoulders.

"Jason, how many times do I have to tell you - it's Phin now, not Dr. Crook. I prefer my *former* students to just call me by my first name."

A big smile was on Jason's face. "I'll call you whatever you want...Phin. I'll kneel and kiss the ring on your finger. Whatever you want. I'm just so relieved you're here."

"It looks like they've taken good care of you, Jason," Autumn observed. "Have they done something we don't know about?"

"Oh, no. They've taken great care of me...physically. Mrs. McCloud is so caring and gentle. I think I remind her of her son. I've been staying in his room because he's away on some kind of extended trip. Been gone for several years it seems. But he's set to return in the spring they say."

"Vaughn's son is away as well. Says it's common for the young folks around here to leave for a period after school. Explore the world, he says. I imagine the two of them might be traveling together but who knows," Phin surmised. He was thinking on this bit of news about the McCloud's son, trying to connect the dots, if there were any to connect.

"Well, if I grew up here, I'd sure want to get out. And I'd probably never come back. I mean it's nice enough and all, and beautiful. But look around, there's nothing here. And where can you go in the world these days and be totally cut off from the outside world because of storms? I don't believe it, I tell you. As soon as I found their son's old cell phone buried in the nightstand, it had no problem getting a signal. Something's not right. Why in the world would they want to keep me from calling for help?"

"You're exactly right, Jason. None of it makes sense. We've felt like they've had eyes on us since the moment we drove into town." Phin looked over at the house and saw someone looking at them through a part in the curtain that covered the front window. The shape moved quickly away. "Here, let's step a little further from the house. I don't think they can hear us but -"

"Have they said anything about Jorge? They said they're sending search parties out each day, but I don't know. I can't tell what's going on from inside of there." Jason cocked his head toward the McCloud home. There was a tinge of panic in his voice when mentioning Jorge.

"I think that's right. We saw several groups forming up at the center of town earlier. Looked like they were getting ready to go out," Autumn added.

"What I can't figure is why they haven't called in help from surrounding towns or even the government. I'd think with a missing person at stake, a foreigner no less, they'd have a formal command center, search dogs, maybe even a helicopter," Jason went on. "And nobody has interviewed *me* or asked me what happened. I was the last person to be with Jorge. It just doesn't make sense."

"One thing's for sure," Phin said, still keeping one eye on the window of the house. "They're a tight-knit group in this town and like to handle things themselves."

A loud bang sounded and Vaughn O'Leary appeared on the front porch, having slammed the front door. He looked less than happy - a scowl appearing on his face - like he'd been sucking on a lemon. He marched down the few steps that emptied onto the street.

"My presence is needed in town," he announced. "If you folks need anything at all, I'll be at the bed and breakfast shortly." And with that he gave a nod and quickened his pace down the street, back toward the center of town.

"That guy's the lynchpin to the whole operation around here," Phin commented. His brow was furrowed like a chess master sorting out his next move. "He's the head of the town council which also functions as the town constable. He's essentially the law around here. And he just happens to own the bed and breakfast -"

"The only place a visitor can stay in town, I might add," Autumn said.

"That's right," Phin continued. "Nobody comes or goes around here without going through Vaughn O'Leary."

"So, what do we do?" Jason asked, agitation in his voice. He felt helpless.

"Well, to begin with, we don't leave until we figure out

what's going on. If I need to make a few calls to rattle a few cages - get us some help in here - I will. I've got a feeling our friendly de facto leader of the town won't like it, but I think whatever happened to you and Jorge is bigger than him."

"Why exactly did you and Jorge pick this of all places to vacation, Jason? If you don't mind my asking." Autumn had been curious about this. Of all the beautiful places to visit in Ireland, why such an out-of-the-way hamlet?

"Oh, we weren't on vacation, Mrs. Crook -"

"Uh-uh-uh..." she cut him off, chiding with her index finger. "I'm with Phin. First names only, Jason. We're all friends here. Just call me Autumn." She ended with a smile.

Jason smiled in return. He was indeed relieved to have friends with him after a torturous week of recovery and confusion. "I got it. I'll do my best."

"So, what do you mean you weren't on vacation? Why else would you come all the way up here?" It was Phin's turn to ask.

"Research," Jason answered with a sparkle in his eye.

"Research?" Phin and Autumn asked simultaneously.

"That's right," he exclaimed. "Oh, I wish had my notebook. It was in my backpack which was lost in the attack. Vaughn says they've not found it or any trace of our belongings while searching for Jorge. But I've got most of it up here." He tapped his head with the hand holding the handmade cane. "And boy, have I got a story to tell you!"

# CHAPTER 27

The trio of Phin, Autumn, and Jason had moved fully across the street from the McCloud house. They were off the road and sitting under a large and very old oak tree. It felt like breaking out of prison to finally be outside, but Jason was still in full recovery mode from his attack and needed to sit down. It was a stunningly beautiful day in north Ireland as the afternoon waned. The sky was blue with a gentle breeze coming from the south. A pair of birds flitted around on the ground close to the tree, playing with each other. Jason felt like he'd been reborn.

"So, Jorge and I met this past summer while I was working on the dig in Caesarea Philippi. He's from Mexico but he's been working on his Ph.D. in Old Testament studies from New Covenant Seminary in Denver. Anyway, one of Jorge's professors connected him with a man named Avi Cohen who works for the Israeli Ministry of Foreign

Affairs. Avi got us access to the dig tunnels under the Temple Mount in Jerusalem. A private off-the-books tour. We couldn't believe it. This would have been late August or so. Our tour was conducted by the head of the tunnel project, a Dr. Harris Kaplan. I don't know why but he took a real liking to me and Jorge and invited us to stay for a few weeks and work in the tunnels with them."

"That's incredible," Phin interjected. He sat cross-legged, leaned in toward Jason, like a child eager to hear more. "They don't let anyone except sanctioned Jews work down there. Just too much potential for political conflict."

"That's why we couldn't say no. It was the opportunity of a lifetime. They ferry out buckets of debris laced with artifacts every day. We were in a brand new section dating to the post-exilic period. The Jews of the Babylonian captivity started coming back to Jerusalem around 538 BC, after Cyrus the Great conquered all of Babylon in the name of Persia. Basic history, right? This return would go on for over a hundred years, with Jews trickling back to their homeland. Now remember, these Jews returning had never actually lived in Israel themselves. They'd been born and lived their whole lives in Babylon. Oh, they were one-hundred percent Jewish for sure, but they'd been *Babylonianized*, so to speak." Jason paused, proud of the new word he had just invented.

"So, these Jews that came back brought with them all sorts of materials from Babylon, you know - clothes, pottery, jewelry, cooking utensils, that sort of thing. All of it distinctly Babylonian. And they also brought back with them scrolls. Parchments of all kinds. Some of it was poetry, some of it story, some of it myth...and some of it *history*." Jason put a heavy emphasis on the last category.

Phin's eyes went wide. "What do you mean history? You found something, didn't you, Jason? What did you find?" He was almost beside himself to know more.

"Not just history, Phin. We found a library. A whole collection of scrolls containing a detailed history of the events near the end of the Babylonian Empire all the way through the early years of the Persian Empire after Cyrus took control of the known world. All written by a Jewish historian named Malphious." Jason paused again to let this news sink in. He was enjoying this moment. The pupil had become the instructor.

Phin stared at the ground, deep in thought, working it out like a mathematician trying to solve an impossible equation. "I've never heard of a historian named Malphious," Phin finally admitted, looking up at Jason.

Jason was looking back at Phin. A big grin on his face. He had more to share and was letting the moment play out. "No one has. No record of a Malphious anywhere in the historical record. But...you've definitely heard of his father." Jason stopped and let it hang there, enjoying the tension of it all.

"Well, spit it out man!" Phin couldn't stand it any longer. "Who's this famous father of the unknown Malphious?"

"His name is...Mishael." Jason leaned back against the oak tree and crossed his arms, waiting for Phin to work it all out.

Phin sat staring at Jason Morris, his face wrinkled up, puzzled. "Mishael," he whispered. "Mishael," he said again.

"I've never heard of Mishael," Autumn blurted out.

"Shhh..." Phin held up his index finger, quieting his wife. A gesture she didn't appreciate but she let go.

Phin's jaw fell open, his eyes growing wide. He'd worked it out. The math problem was solved. "No way. You've got to be kidding me."

All smiles from Jason. He slapped his knee. "Yes sir! Serious as a heart attack. Can you believe it?" he shouted, louder than he intended.

"Excuse me," Autumn butted into their private party. "Who exactly is Mishael? I've never heard of him."

"Oh yes, you have." Phin turned his attention to his bride. "He's in the Bible. One of the most famous stories in all of the Bible. Incredible." Phin ran his hand through his floppy brown mane of hair in wonder. He could see that Autumn was still struggling. "The book of Daniel, Autumn. You remember the story. Ever since you were a kid. Sunday School. VBS. Come on!" She looked at him, still not getting it. "The story of Daniel and the fiery furnace. Good grief, do I have to retell it all? You remember Daniel, right?"

"Yes, of course -"

He cut her off, unable to control himself. "So, Daniel was part of the Jewish royal family taken into captivity after the conquest of Jerusalem in 605 BC. He would have been a teenager at the time, deported to Babylon to work in the court of King Nebuchadnezzar. This is all in chapter one of the book of Daniel. But remember that Daniel had three teenage friends, also part of the Jewish noble class. These three, along with Daniel, formed a unique bond because of their captivity. The story of the fiery furnace occurs in chapter three. King Nebuchadnezzar became angry at Daniel's three friends because they refused to bow down to a gold statue that he had created of himself. So, he bound them and threw them into a furnace as a form of public execution. But the miracle of the story is that a fourth 'person' appeared within the furnace. I personally believe it was Jesus Christ. A Christophany – an Old Testament appearance of the Christ. Some say it was an angel. But regardless, the appearance of the fourth individual brought with it saving power. The three teens did not burn. In fact, they survived without even a hint of smoke on their bodies or clothes. It was a miracle."

"Yes, I know the story, Phin. Like you said, heard it my whole life. The three boys were Shadrach, Meshach, and Abednego. But what does that have to do with...wait..." Autumn paused, snared by something in the recesses of her memory.

"Uh huh..." Phin said with a smile. "You've almost got it. Shadrach, Meshach, and Abednego are their names, alright. Their *Babylonian* names. Not their Jewish names. The Babylonians made it a practice of changing the names of those they carried away into captivity. It was their way of stripping their identity, taking away their will to fight. It obviously didn't work with these three or with Daniel."

Jason jumped in to complete the circle of thought. "If you go back to chapter one of the book of Daniel you will find the Jewish names of the three teenagers. Shadrach's name was Hananiah. Abednego's name was Azariah. And Meshach's name was..."

"Mishael!" Autumn finished excitedly.

"Amazing." Phin voiced the sentiment of both he and

Autumn. "You're saying that you found the historical writings of Meshach's son. A man named Malphious."

"That's exactly what I'm saying. And, brother, you won't believe what's in them."

The enormity of this discovery hit Phin like a sucker punch. Not only would the history of Malphious provide yet another archaeological confirmation for the veracity of the biblical book of Daniel, but the contents of that history could potentially fill in the blanks of the historical record that scholars have been scratching their heads over for centuries.

"Phin, you're not going to believe this, but Malphious records an exodus of the Babylonian royal family. An escape...just as the Medes and Persians descended upon Babylon and conquered it."

"What do you mean an exodus?" Phin asked. He was puzzled as to where Jason was going with this surprise revelation. It was common practice in the ancient world for conquering nations to execute, imprison, and deport the members of the royal family of the country they had just subjected to their rule.

"What I'm saying is that the Babylonians knew how the game was played. They had subjected the Assyrian Empire to execution and deportation when they came to power. Then they conquered the Judean remnant of Israel which was how Malphious's father, Mishael, ended up in Babylon. Now it was the Persian's turn. They were set to conquer the Babylonians. That meant the necks of all Babylonian royalty were on the chopping block – so to speak. They didn't want to endure the same fate they had subjected others to, so...they planned an exodus."

Phin worked this all over in his mind, his hand rubbing the three-day-old stubble on his chin. "But Daniel chapter five records the Medo-Persian invasion. The Babylonian king, Belshazzar, was killed the night the city was breached by the Mede military."

"Belshazzar was a fool king," Jason shot back. "Malphious even calls him such. A fool king who was drunk on wine and power nearly all the time. The city of Babylon was under siege by the Medes and Persians and he refused to see reality, that his rule had come to an end. But not everyone in his court was so foolish. Malphious's own father, Meshach, led the effort to preserve the royal family. He was eighty years old at the time the Medes and Persians moved in. He'd never forgotten the torment of being ripped away from his own land and family so many years ago when he was a teenager. So, he made arrangements for Belshazzar's court and family to flee. And then he convinced them to move just as the Medes and Persians descended. They were ferried out of the city and into the night as the slaughter of Babylon took place behind them. It's an amazing story all recorded in the scrolls we found."

"He must have been a remarkable man to have such influence." Autumn had been listening in rapt attention. The wheels of her own mind spinning.

"You know where they went, don't you, Jason?" Phin had caught on to his young protégé's excitement. An ancient mystery waited to be solved and he'd found the master key to unlock the box.

"Not exactly, but..." Jason replied, the gleam in his eyes unfading. "Meshach, himself, left with the royal family. He left his own son and family behind, because he knew that

Malphious would be safe as a Jew. The Medes and Persians would have no interest in the Jewish people. He didn't want Malphious and his family to be uprooted. Babylon was their home now; the only home they had ever known. As for Meshach...well, he felt obligated. Compelled by God, Malphious writes. It was his mission to see the royalty of Babylon to safety - the royal family whom he so faithfully served his whole life. There's actually a census in Malphious's writings of those who left the city. Over two hundred and fifty men, women, and children. Meshach had worked it all out with the help of the court topographers. They would head west, cross the Mediterranean, and continue on. As far as they could go. To an unknown land. An *island* of which there was very little knowledge. And they would rebuild, living out their lives in obscurity...and safety."

Phin could not believe what Jason was suggesting. The thought was beyond ridiculous. He rose to his feet, brushing his backside off with his hands. "It's impossible, Jason. No way that what you are aiming at is what really happened. We've got to be at least three thousand miles from modern day Iraq...or ancient Babylon...you know what I mean."

"Have you noticed something different about the people around here?" Jason asked, still sitting, that silly smile pasted on his face.

"Besides the fact that they watch us like we've got the plague or something?" Autumn let out a huff.

"They're all the same." Jason began, answering his own question as Phin and Autumn looked on. "Not *exactly* the same, but where it matters most. I know you've noticed it.

Black hair. Brown eyes. Olive skin. Very Semitic in appearance. We're in *Ireland*, Phin. Ireland. I know it's a caricature but not a single person in this town has fair skin or red hair. Not a one. I'm telling you, the people around here...they all come from the same family of origin. And it's not Irish."

In the flash moment, it all came together for Phin. This was the missing piece he'd been trying to place. As crazy as it sounded, Jason was right. He had to be right. And he had the historical record to prove it.

The people of the town of Tiamat were the descendants of the ancient Babylonian Empire.

# CHAPTER 28

*Be careful with Vaughn O'Leary, I don't trust him.* That was the final warning Jason Morris had given Phin. They hugged the young man and helped him back to the McCloud house and to the care of its gracious host. They said their goodbyes, but only for now. Phin promised to be back in the morning to check on Jason and to get him out of the house again. Mattie McCloud inquired if they would be leaving soon with Jason, suggesting nervously that there was better care down the road in Donegal.

Phin didn't make any promises.

He had more to think about now.

A lot more.

If it was true that the residents of Tiamat had all descended from the ancient royal family of the Babylonian Empire, then that could explain the secrecy, the suspicion of outsiders, and the reason very little about this tiny corner of north Ireland was known, save its existence on a map.

But it didn't explain everything.

Two visitors had been attacked.

One was missing.

Surely, they weren't above getting help from the surrounding villages. They couldn't be so isolated that people living in the surrounding area weren't aware of their existence and didn't have dealings with them. It just didn't make sense. Something more was going on.

Phin knew that Vaughn O'Leary was the key. He was more than just the head of the town council. More than the face of local law enforcement. More than the owner of the only place a stranger could rent a room for the night. Oh, he was all of that for sure, but he was also more than that, Phin was convinced. Vaughn knew more about what happened to Jason and Jorge and for some reason he was holding back. It felt to Phin that what Vaughn O'Leary - and probably everyone else in town - wanted more than anything else was for Phin and Autumn to load Jason Morris into their cramped Ford Ka and drive away, never to return. But, of course, that was impossible.

Jorge was still missing. He'd been missing for a week. Phin was astounded every time he paused to think about Jorge - at just how unbelievable it was that there was not an all-out search for the missing American that involved the surrounding localities, the government, and even the media. It was almost as if Vaughn O'Leary didn't want anyone to know that they had a missing person's case on their hands.

So, why not?

What was the big secret in Tiamat that was bigger than the life and safety of an individual?

It had to be more than the secret of their heritage.

Whatever the reason, Phin knew that Vaughn was the one man he needed to get to know better. That led to Jason's warning: *Don't trust Vaughn O'Leary.*

Jason and Jorge had been in town only two days before their attack. But they'd come for a reason. To see for themselves if the people of Tiamat might be descended from Babylonian royalty.

The history of Malphious didn't exactly lead them to Tiamat like a road map. It didn't quite work that way. Malphious didn't travel with the group that fled. He'd stayed behind in Babylon. But he did record a proposed route. Across the Mediterranean and onward to a westernmost island located on "the edge of the world," the text had said. You couldn't get more "west" and more "edge of the world" to an ancient traveler than modern-day Ireland. At least that's how Jason and Jorge had reasoned it out. What the aging Meshach didn't know was that within a year after fleeing to the edge of the world with a ragtag group of wanted people, Cyrus of Persia would declare that all Jews were free to return to their homeland of Israel. The son, Malphious, had never been to his ancient home. He'd heard stories from his father about a land flowing with milk and honey. And then there was the spiritual pull - something all Jews felt when it came to the ancient soil of the Holy Land. It was this divine pulling that led him to make the return to Israel with his family.

In his writings, he longed that his father had stayed and returned home with them. He speculated further about the fleeing Babylonian's final destination. His father, Meshach, had said that they would travel all the way to the sea, until they could go no further. Perhaps then they would be beyond the reach of Darius the Mede and Cyrus the Persian. Their great hope? A place of safety and peace.

It was a gut feeling. A hunch. Jason and Jorge had decided to take a journey along the coast of north Ireland. A long shot, they knew, and much of the trip was just for the fun of it all.

But then, they'd found Tiamat. The impossible had been confirmed. Maybe. They still needed proof. The kind of proof that Vaughn O'Leary could give. If only he were willing. Phin guessed he wouldn't be.

"It's uncanny. The people here really do all look like they come from some place other than here." Autumn held Phin's hand as they made the stroll back toward the center of town. They were both looking at the residents of Tiamat through a new lens. The lens of the history of Malphious. A young man, whose biblical father had led the royal family of Babylon to the edge of the world. Could it really be this town and could it really be this people? Well, their descendants, anyway?

"I'm still trying to wrap my head around it all. I knew something about the folks here puzzled me but I just couldn't quite nail it. But it's undeniable. Every single person we've seen – they all have black hair and brown eyes and the darker skin tone that characterizes modern-day Iraqis." Phin had taken extra care to focus hard attention on each person they passed as he and Autumn walked. The residents of Tiamat certainly took no issue looking at them, so how could they be offended if he returned their stares?

"I'll bet they've never intermarried with any of the local peoples of this island. That's the only explanation for what we are seeing here."

"You're right, hon. But think about what this must mean. If we have a group of people, directly descended for over twenty-five hundred years, who've lived in this one spot all this time..." Phin was thinking hard, processing as he talked and walked.

"What are you getting at, Phin?"

"Somewhere around here would be tombs. Burial grounds. What I'm saying is that located very close to where we are standing would be the entombed remains of the family of King Belshazzar of Babylon. Of the Bible. Think about what this would mean to the world of archaeology."

"Something tells me they don't want the world of archaeology, or any other world for that matter, coming around here. But it sure does change the way you look at things."

Phin and Autumn made their way across the grassy traffic circle. It was already after four o'clock in the afternoon and the sun was moving quickly toward the horizon. It would be setting soon - before five o'clock - being this late into the fall season. They passed a group of school-aged children kicking a soccer ball in what looked like a pickup game - mostly boys but a few girls. They'd thrown down their school bags and jackets to mark off impromptu goals. The kids stopped and stared as Autumn and Phin skirted the boundaries they'd marked off. It was as if they'd never seen anyone from outside their village before. Phin was mesmerized by the symmetry of the group. Black hair of various lengths and all with brown eyes. Classic middle-eastern features. He chuckled to himself, realizing it was so obvious now that he knew what to look for.

No one was present at the front desk of O'Leary's Bed & Breakfast. The house was quiet save a padding of small footsteps running on the second floor. Patrick was probably playing with his spaceships, Mrs. McCraery's homework finished. Autumn took a seat in the parlor, pulling out her phone while Phin went exploring for the owner.

There was nothing about the bed and breakfast - or any of the architecture of Tiamat for that matter - that hinted at Babylonian influence. It all looked distinctly Irish, just like every other town they'd driven through early that morning. The only exception being that the town was in pristine condition. Nothing was run down. Every building well maintained, the grass cut and manicured, from one end of town to the other. It really was a living postcard.

Phin found himself sidling down a hallway that ran past the stairs and behind the front counter. A door was cracked at the very end and he detected a shuffling of paper. He wasn't sure why, maybe it was just the Crook instinct at play, but he felt himself move into stealth mode. It wasn't easy because of the tendency of the old planked floor to crack and pop. But Phin was good at covert movement when necessary.

He came right up to the door and ventured a look. A wall of shelving loaded with books was unmistakable to miss. *A library*, he thought.

And then a surprise.

On the floor at far end of the room, stuffed in a corner next to the shelving, was a small mound of personal articles – clothes, a boot, the corner of an iPhone, and a backpack. He took in a sharp breath. The door swung wide, catching Phin off guard. He awkwardly stumbled back. Vaughn O'Leary filled the door frame with a scowl on his face. Phin chided himself for being caught unawares. He was better than that.

"Oh...Vaughn...I thought you might be back here. No one was at the front. I hope you don't mind." Phin stammered over his words. He was acting like a child caught doing no good.

Vaughn stepped quickly into the hall, closing the door behind him. The unhappy look on his face remained. "The bed and breakfast is also our home, Mr. Crook. Our private home. Guests are welcome in the common areas, of which this is not one."

"Yes, well, my wife and I would like to check in, if you don't mind. We've decided to stay for a while. Take in the town and the area...and help with the search for Jorge." Phin studied their host's reaction, and then finished with, "I assume you have availability."

A switch flipped in Vaughn O'Leary. A transforming smile and affable nature were immediately present. "Yes, of course. Follow me. Let's get you and your lovely wife settled." He set off at a quick pace toward the front desk, calling over his shoulder, "How does the best room in the inn sound to you? It's called our Room With a View – looks out over the center of town."

Working to keep up, Phin replied, "Yes, that, uh...sounds wonderful."

Vaughn was behind the front desk filling out a form when Phin caught up to him.

"What should I put you down for? One night? Two, perhaps?"

"I think we'll stay as long as we need to." Phin was coy, trying to break the false charisma that oozed from the man.

Vaughn didn't reply for a long moment. "Mr. Crook, if you're worried about the missing young man, I can assure you that we are doing all we can. We really don't need your help. In fact, it might prove to slow matters down."

"It's been a week. Surely our presence would only help at this point." Phin smiled back. He was trying to goad the man without being obvious.

Another pause. He was thinking. "I must insist," Vaughn began with controlled firmness. "We do things our way in Tiamat. It will be best for all involved to let us take care of matters ourselves. I'm sorry, Mr. Crook, but you will simply have to trust us. Now, let's see. Here's your room key. The lock can be a little tricky but if you work with it, it should be fine. Breakfast begins at 8:00 am. I hope to see you then." It was clear the discussion was over.

"Oh, and one more thing, Mr. Crook. As I shared with you earlier, we've been having some trouble with the local wildlife around here lately. Wolves have been raiding our chicken houses, cattle, and other livestock. Happens from time to time. We've got it under control, but for everyone's safety, we've instituted a town curfew. No one is allowed out after sunset. Which...is less than an hour from now." Vaughn glanced at his watch and when he looked back up there was an intensity in his chocolate eyes that Phin had not seen before. "I ask you, Mr. Crook. Please heed my words very carefully. For your own sake and for the sake of your lovely wife...do not go out after dark."

# CHAPTER 29

The sunny day had turned into a cloudy night.

A wet chill filled the air around Tiamat.

In the distance, but still close, an otherworldly howl echoed. The search parties would be on the move toward the creature, but the beastly sound still gave Dr. Boris Kelly chills. He inserted the key into the front door lock of his office and after securing it stepped off the porch onto the sidewalk. He took his time looking up and down each end of the street while buttoning his black wool peacoat.

No one was out and about.

*Very good*, Dr. Kelly thought.

The curfew was working. People were staying indoors where it was safe.

In the week since the escape from the cave, there had been no other "incidents." No attacks on any citizens. Lack of opportunity would have been the biggest reason.

But the creatures were active, evidenced by three things. One, their incessant howling. At times the pack would cry out from one direction only. Then hours later it would sound like they had surrounded the town, their howls working in chorus from one end of the village to the next, like some sort of hellish communication.

Two, the carcasses that had been laid out as bait had been effective – sort of. The beasts had been drawn close, but they'd never once moved in for a meal, and thus within trapping distance of the search parties. It was as if they knew they were being hunted.

Three, various livestock penned on the outskirts of town had been attacked and eviscerated. Some eaten but much left behind, a rotting mess. As difficult as it was to imagine, it felt like the creatures were leaving the town a message: *we are smarter than you*. When you put it all together the beasts were indeed smart. They were calculating, elusive, and terrible. Their omnipresence had plunged the peaceful town into darkness. An unholy reign of terror is what it was.

Dr. Kelly hiked up the collar of his coat, nestling his neck against the softness and warmth of his lambswool scarf. Following another glance to his left, down to the far end of the street into the blackness beyond, the doctor turned and hastened the two doors down to O'Leary's Bed & Breakfast. Were it not so close, he wouldn't had ventured the distance without an armed escort.

He let himself into the inn and headed to the library where he knew he'd find Vaughn O'Leary.

He was expected, of course.

It was time for their nightly chat.

A debriefing, of sorts, of the day's activities and progress...or lack thereof. As he passed the front desk, light coming from the parlor caught his attention and he stole a glance, catching the eyes of the Crooks who were finishing dinner. He nodded by way of greeting and hurried down the hall. The bed and breakfast was apparently now a bed and breakfast and dinner.

He rapped gently on the solid wood door with the knuckles of his first two fingers.

"Come in, Boris," came a muffled voice beyond. Dr. Kelly turned the knob and eased himself into the library, securing the door behind him. "Ah, my good doctor! Right on time as usual."

Vaughn O'Leary was sitting in his plush arm chair, a small fire crackling away in the fireplace. He set aside the book he was reading and picked up his teacup and saucer. Dr. Kelly eased into the chair opposite of Vaughn's and began working the teabag in his own steaming cup, already set out by his host, waiting for him. And such had their routine become.

"Well, it certainly has been an interesting day," the doctor began. "I noticed our unexpected guests have checked in. Decided to stay for a spell, I assume."

"They have indeed. I suppose it was too much to hope that they would simply pack up the immobile Mr. Morris and leave for greener pastures." Vaughn seemed relaxed, as if he'd resigned himself to the inevitable.

"Not with the missing American still out there somewhere. It was just a matter of time before others came, you know. We're fortunate we made it a week before someone came looking for them."

"Not fortunate, Boris. Sloppy. I tell you, Ross McCloud is a fool. An idiot. Has been his whole life. The good Mr. Crook got a phone call. Now, how do you suppose that happened? Carelessness, I tell you. Had we handled matters another way, my way..." Vaughn trailed off, letting the implication hang in the air. He was pointing a finger at the doctor.

"That young man woke up on his own, Vaughn. Don't lay this on me. He's strong, very strong, with a will to live. And my Hippocratic oath prevents me from doing harm."

"I never suggested you do harm, Boris. You just didn't have to be so helpful."

"I didn't do anything, O'Leary." The doctor was getting frustrated, choosing to use the town leader's last name. "Mattie had already dressed his wounds, and then he simply woke up."

"That's what I'm talking about...The McClouds. That imbecile Ross and his simpleton wife."

"They're good people, Vaughn. And it does us no good to be fighting amongst ourselves. We need to keep focused on moving forward. Fixing the problem and getting everyone around here back to a normal flow of life."

"So, what do we know? I'm told that there's been no progress since we captured the one." Vaughn was referring to the creature whose tag read Marco. He'd been cornered by one of the search parties just at dawn three days prior. He'd gorged himself on a lamb he'd slaughtered belonging to the McBrides. The search party stumbled upon him by accident really. With the sun close to rising and with a full belly, he'd grown sleepy. He was not paying attention and stumbling around when a tranquilizer dart pierced his neck.

He was down and out within seconds. From there he was quickly bound and returned to the cave. Mission accomplished.

"I heard the same. No sign of the remaining three at all."

Silence dominated the next moment save the popping and hissing of the fire. Vaughn took a sip of his tea. They always spoke of the beasts in vague, nameless words. But the *three* had names. And they had families. Tommy McCloud. Vance Talley. Lucious O'Leary. The last being Vaughn's own son.

He wasn't surprised that the three left were making it difficult to track them. His son was smart, the most intelligent of the bunch, by his way of thinking. He, no doubt, was the leader of the pack. He didn't know whether to be proud or disgusted. Proud of what his boy was doing - out thinking and out maneuvering the best hunters in the village. Or disgusted at the thing he was. But it would soon be over. Very soon, as he thought of the calendar. Lucious was supposed to return any day now. They would be back together as a family once again, their seven-year nightmare over.

"They won't make it easy," Vaughn finally spoke. "We may need to consider doubling our teams at night. Really put the press on them. We should also ask those with livestock to donate live animals. We need to quit with the dead rabbits and other small game we've been using to lure them. It's not working. They know what we're trying to do. We have to outsmart them, Boris. Do something unexpected. Catch them off guard and then...take them."

He finished with a forceful slap of his hands. Dr. Kelly startled at the sound.

"You talk about them as if they're organized. As if they're coordinated and planned in their movement."

"They are, I tell you! You have to consider who's a part of the group." He was referring to his own son.

"They are not a *who*, Vaughn. At least not anymore. They are a *what*. Primitive. Devolved. Savage. You're suggesting there's a mind behind the pack. I just can't go there."

It would do no good for Vaughn O'Leary to push the issue. The doctor was a fool too. In his own way. No one saw things like Vaughn did. There's a reason he was head of the town council – the head of the whole town. He was better than all the rest. And deep inside, they all knew it. Ah well, he would just have to steer and manipulate his neighbors without them knowing it. He was good enough to do that as well. He glanced up over the top of his tea cup. Boris Kelly was looking at him.

"What about our guests? The Crooks. What is the plan for dealing with them?" Dr. Kelly asked, having decided to move on.

Vaughn smiled in return. As always, Dr. Boris Kelly was leaning on him for the plan. Everyone leaned on Vaughn O'Leary when a plan was needed. Yes, they really did know, deep down inside, that he was better than them. He was the best of them.

"The Crooks could be a problem. I don't like the husband, Phin. He has a look in his eye that I don't trust. There's more to him and why he is here than he's letting on. The young friend of his, Jason Morris, he's a nosy one too.

Was asking too many questions before all this happened. I've a feeling that the apple of the pupil hasn't fallen far from the tree of the teacher. Dr. Crook might force my hand, and if he does, he won't like the outcome. But his wife is the key to controlling him, I think. There's a protective nature about him toward her."

"All husbands are protective of their wives, Vaughn. Same as you toward Patricia," Dr. Kelly noted.

"He's different. Their relationship is different. There's a fear in him when it comes to his wife. I can smell it. No, if our friend Phineas Crook starts to get out of hand, I think a focus on his dear Autumn will be all it takes to reign him in."

# CHAPTER 30

His eyes burned a bright orange. Vaughn O'Leary sat facing the fire, its flames reflecting off his pupils. It was after midnight but he wasn't the least bit sleepy. He'd moved his chair right to the opening of the fireplace and had piled on the wood. The random rolling of the flames mesmerized him. He could feel the heat pulling on him, urging him closer. Beads of sweat popped on his forehead but he wanted more. He wanted to take it all in, to feel the power of the burn.

The events of the past week had reignited a different kind of flame that smoldered deep inside his core. Three of those who lived in the cave were out there. Somewhere. Roaming free.

His son was out there. Free. Lucious was free and he envied him.

His time would soon come to an end and he would return.

Literally any day. At any moment.

But for now, for this moment, he was free and full of burning power. And Vaughn O'Leary very much wished he could trade places with him. He longed to feel that kind of unbridled strength. It had been so long. A lifetime ago. But the happenings of the last seven days had brought that former life back close to home. He could feel the burn once again.

He rose and added two more logs to the fire.

There had been no burning, crackling log fire during those years he had spent in the cave. Just a dank, dark, rock-hewn prison of a hole. But he burned nonetheless from a different kind of fire; a roaring deep inside kept him warm. If he were honest with himself – and that is exactly what he was being this very moment – he'd never felt more alive than those years in the cave. There was an untamed strength, an inner power, that coursed through his very being. The simpletons who came to watch over him and the others were so weak and puny. He found himself laughing at the memory of it all. Their "caretakers" thought they were watching the cave dwellers. But the truth is, Vaughn was watching them. Pitying them. They were so frail and stupid. He'd never known such clarity as in those years.

The only thing that held him back were the bars. Those cursed metal bars. He'd been a part of the effort to install them, his own father leading the initiative to "modernize the situation," as he referred to it.

But that was before he understood.

He'd built his own cage and then had come to regret it. He regretted many things during those years. He regretted being so naïve until the disease freed him.

No.

It wasn't a disease.

It was a gift.

A gift from the gods.

How many people ever, in their entire lives, were blessed to know what Vaughn had come to know? That there was a higher level of existence or evolution or whatever one wanted to call it. The answer was - only the residents of Tiamat. And not all of them. Not even most of them. Only a select few. The chosen ones, as Vaughn had come to think of them.

The rest of the town thought of it as a curse. But they were stupid. They were stupid and ignorant and weak because they had *not* been chosen. A curse, indeed. No! It was a blessing and they had been skipped over. The blessing had passed them by and so they were jealous. They were also afraid. Very afraid. They were afraid of losing control. Of losing the tiny morsel of power that they clung to. And the only thing that kept that anemic power alive were those bars. Those stinking bars. Oh, how he loathed them.

But three were free. His son was free. He had the power. He had the blessing. And Lucious was now experiencing something that he, himself, had never known. That he had only dreamed of. Unleashed wild power! Now the dream had been rekindled.

Staring into the roaring fire, Vaughn O'Leary edged even closer. He eased out of his silk robe and removed his shirt. He wanted to feel the flames on his skin. *Oh, the fire!* *Oh, the burn!* More...he wanted more. He willed the heat to consume him - to transition from outside his body to the inside. He closed his eyes and let his mind carry him back to the cave.

He'd been so strong then. He didn't shrink because of the disease, instead he grew. Bigger. Larger. His muscles expanding and testing the limits of his flesh. He could feel his bones harden like iron. All his senses ratcheted to the highest level of animalistic sensitivity. He could hear them. His watchers. Laughing and telling their silly stories. They had their own fire at the mouth of the cave. They had no idea of the fire burning in him.

He could see, oh, how he could see. For the first time in his life his eyes had been opened. The detail of the cave was incredible. He watched from an impossible distance as a centipede made its way up the wall and into a crack. He could count each of its three hundred fifty-four legs. The spindly hairs on each leg, visible to his eyes only, were a marvel to behold. Lack of light was no factor at all. In fact, he enjoyed the darkness more than the light. He could see what others could not. He was superman!

And the smells. A new world had been opened to him. He no longer showered. He had no need. There was no stink. The musk of his own odor added to his strength. Others cowered just in his presence. He could feel the watchers shrink when they brought food to him. *Ha ha*, yes, they served him. They bowed to him. And then they ran from him. Back to their miserable little campfire. Such a pathetic attempt to feel the burn. Their stench the one thing that sickened *him*. As good as his eyes were, he could smell them before he saw them. He could smell them coming. And they each had their own distinct odor. He no longer thought of them by the names they had. He knew them now only by the stink they carried.

That was when he realized that he was no longer Vaughn O'Leary. Whoever Vaughn O'Leary was, he'd passed away, died as it were, and now something new had taken his place. Oh, he was still who he was, but only a better version. The best version. Like an ugly moth that emerges from its cocoon as a beautiful butterfly. The same but different. Wholly and completely different. Yes, that is who Vaughn O'Leary had become in the cave.

The only thing he wanted was to be free from the prison of those bars. To run and leap and hunt and consume and yell with no hindrances.

Instead, he was caged like a pathetic zoo animal. But he wasn't pathetic. He was stronger and wiser than them all. Even the rest of those in the cave with him. He watched how they lay around sleeping - resigned to their lot as zoo attractions for the puny people who watched them.

*Why won't they wake up?!*

*Don't they feel the power as well?*

If they worked together, they could break the bonds of the cage that held them. He was certain of it. But they had no vision. They were as pathetic as the anemic creatures that watched them. Creatures, yes. That is how he had come to view his captors. They loved to refer to him as a creature. Or a beast. Or something worse. As if he were lesser than them. But now he knew the truth. *They* were the creatures. *They* were the beasts. *They* were the lesser-thans.

Not him.

He would never go back. He *could* never go back. Not of his own free will anyway. If he could stay exactly as he was forever, he would do it. With only one exception. The bars. The plague of bars that held him. If he could be free, then he would be whole. He would be...perhaps a god.

Yes...a god is who he was!

But then the blessing left him. His muscles shrank. His bones became frail. His eyes dimmed. He became deaf. And he could smell no more. The curse had returned. The curse of being human. The watchers came and opened the cage. They dragged him out, naked and small. They cut his hair and washed the beautiful smell from him. And then he went home. Back to his wife and a son he'd never known. Born during his touch with the great divine. Now he was simply normal.

But Vaughn O'Leary was not normal. He would never be normal again. A seed of the blessing remained in him. It had been passed on to Lucious who was now free. *Run, Lucious, run!*

He willed the ember inside of him to ignite. He was totally naked now, having stripped off the remainder of his clothes. Just like he'd been in the cave. Oh, so close to the fire. His body glistening with sweat, the tiny hairs on his arms beginning to curl, bowing to the flames. It was all Vaughn could do to keep from crawling into the fireplace. He wanted to be consumed by the burn.

He thought about Phineas Crook. He hated that man. He was a watcher. An outsider looking for a ticket to the zoo. He wanted to trap Vaughn. To cage him like the animal he wasn't. But no! Never again would he be subjected to a cage. The bars would be destroyed once and for all. He would destroy the watcher. He would destroy Phineas Crook and anyone else who got in his way. Vaughn O'Leary was ready to finally be free.

The fire roared.

Vaughn O'Leary craned his neck and released a howl.

# CHAPTER 31

The werewolf pounced on the unsuspecting victim, a loud howl escaping its white-fanged maw. The gun sounded and the wolf flew off of the man, now holding the smoking weapon.

"Got you! You filthy beast of the night!" The playful voice of young Patrick O'Leary filled the breakfast parlor. Phin and Autumn were captivated by his cuteness. He sat right at their feet, a cardboard shoebox open, the contents spilled over the floor. Dracula, Frankenstein, the Mummy, Swamp Thing, and various other action figures. Occupying the attention of his little hands was a G.I. Joe that had just dispelled a werewolf bent on his destruction. "One silver bullet to the chest and *BAM*, you're dead!"

Autumn reached down and ruffled the boy's bang-cut black head. "You like scary things don't you, Patrick?"

"They're not scary to me," he said proudly, his innocent

face capturing Autumn's heart as he looked up at her. "My da says that there's nothing to be afraid of in this world. The only thing to be afraid of is inside of yourself. Not believing in yourself is the only thing we should truly fear." He was strong willed, a clear reflection of Vaughn O'Leary, but less tainted by the scars of life. "Are you going to stay with us for a while? I hope so. I like you and you're not strange anymore."

"We like you too, Patrick. And I think we *will* stay for a few days." Phin was keen on the boy as well. He was easy to attach to – smart, witty, charming. Phin and Autumn had already discussed a tentative plan. Phin wanted to make a short day trip to follow up on the information Jason Morris had shared with them - the amazing theory that the residents of this community were the isolated descendants of Babylonian royalty. But Jason wasn't quite well enough to travel. Plus, they'd all agreed that no one was leaving Tiamat until Jorge was found.

"That makes me happy. Visitors don't stay here very long. I think they get scared and leave. I hope you don't get scared and leave."

"I don't think you have to worry about that, Patrick. We are very brave, Mr. Crook and I."

"Patrick O'Leary! You need to be at school in fifteen minutes. Mrs. McCraery is expecting you at eight-fifteen, sharp. Not a minute late, young man. Now hustle up." Patrick jumped at the sound of his mother's voice. He scooped the action figures into his cardboard box and scampered away. But not until he gave Autumn a wink. She winked in return.

"That was one of the best omelets I've ever had in my

entire life." Autumn Crook sat back, placing her cloth napkin on the marble top of the table she shared with her husband. It was early. Just before eight in the morning and the couple was already showered and ready for the day ahead. The town curfew meant early indoors and early to bed. Cabin fever had quickly set in.

"Patricia, I've gotta tell you, that ham steak is out of this world. And the eggs...what did you do to them?" Phin's compliments on the breakfast, along with his wife's, weren't empty words.

Patricia O'Leary smiled and topped off Autumn's coffee. "Let's just say it's an old secret known only to residents of Tiamat. Pretty much anyone around here can make them just like that."

"I don't believe it," Phin charged. "I've eaten a lot of eggs in my life in a lot of places around the world and these...these are extraordinary." He finished the last bite, his fork clanking on the china plate as if to add an exclamation point.

"I hope you both slept well last night," Patricia directed toward Phin, moving past the breakfast conversation with a blush and a smile. She appreciated the compliment. It was something she was not used to receiving from her own husband. Tiamat got few visitors, so her opportunities to cook for others and hear words of affirmation for her skill were few and far between. It was a nice change.

The Crooks were nice enough, but she knew it was important for them to move along in another day or so. Vaughn never liked anyone staying more than two days, three at the most. Nevertheless, the attention was welcome and she found Phineas Crook a little more than attractive, though she'd never do more than keep such thoughts to herself.

"Yes, the room was very comfortable, thank you." Autumn was curt in her reply. She sensed a vibe from Patricia O'Leary she didn't like. Her radar of protection over her husband was going off. Her intention was not to be rude but she wanted to make sure Patricia knew she was there.

Autumn's response was a lie.

She'd not slept well at all. It was a fitful night, punctuated by rolling and cover-pulling. Phin had slept like a baby, oblivious to Autumn's tossings, the creaking of the old house, and the distant cry of wild animals. The primal animal noises may actually have been part of her dreams as she dipped in and out of a light sleep. It was hard to tell. All she knew was that it had been a very long night and she was relieved when morning arrived. She was jealous when Phin finally opened his eyes and stretched big, an even bigger yawn of satisfaction seeping from his wide-open mouth. It didn't seem very fair. *Ah well*, she thought. It was only one night and Lord knows she'd spent more than enough time sleeping her life away the last three years.

"So, what are your plans today? I could suggest some hiking trails if you like. As long as you're back before dark you should be fine." There was an edge in Patricia's voice that Phin seized upon. He could tell she was steering them away *from* something as much as she was steering them *toward* some destination day hike.

Phin took a sip of his hot chocolate. Always hot chocolate, never coffee for him. "Unfortunately, no time for sightseeing for us, I'm afraid. I believe we'll check in on

Jason this morning and then I'm going to leave Autumn here while I drive back to Dublin. I need to enlist the help of a friend I have there. Should be back by noon tomorrow though." He watched Patricia O'Leary for any sign of dissatisfaction at the mention of "help" in Dublin.

She only smiled warmly at him and began to gather their dishes. "Well, you're likely done here then. Don't want to be slowing you down, now." She excused herself to the kitchen, leaving Autumn and Phin alone.

"What time do you want to get on the road?" Autumn asked.

"Probably in the next hour or so. Should take me about four hours to get to Dublin. Whether or not Sergio can help, I'll spend the night and leave at first light. I should be back well before lunchtime though."

"Sounds good. I'm just going to play the dumb tourist today. Walk around and see what I can see. Talk to as many people as will talk to me."

"Well, good luck with that. Got a feeling you'll get as much out of them as we got out of that Dr. Kelly yesterday. If you get a chance, focus on O'Leary, see if you can get him to give up anything interesting. He's shifty but he might let his guard down around you a bit."

"Phineas Crook! I hope you're not suggesting I flirt with the man." She feigned offense. "I'm a married woman and happily at that." Autumn leaned across the table and gave him a quick peck on the lips.

"Why do you think I'm hustling back by tomorrow morning? I'm not worried about you, my dear. But I do want to make sure nobody moves in on my territory." He gave her a wink.

No, he wasn't worried about Autumn flirting with anyone. He trusted her completely. Their love for each other was pure and undefiled. One of the last few pure things left in the world, Phin believed.

As he looked across at his wife - who was putting on a fresh layer of red lipstick - he found himself overwhelmed by her presence. He'd not spent a night away from her since her awakening four months prior. He didn't want to be separated from her ever again. But one night wasn't separation. It would be a quick trip to Dublin and back. He was fortunate that his private network of "friends" included just the man he needed to talk to without having to leave the country.

He also felt that Autumn actually did have a chance of making some headway with Vaughn O'Leary or another resident of Tiamat without him tagging along. There was a way in which she carried herself that was disarming. If there was a deep secret buried in this town, Autumn Eden Crook would find it. He'd bet cash money on it. They had always worked best as a team in the past, and the situation they now found themselves in reminded him of those good ol' days.

*AHHHHHHH!*

An unearthly shout broke the trance he was in.

Phin shot to his feet as Autumn dropped her lipstick. He made for the lobby of the bed and breakfast. The front door his aim. Autumn had scooped up her cosmetic and rushed to follow as Patricia came tearing out of the kitchen. Another scream. It sounded like someone was in pain.

As Phin ripped open the front door, he saw a small mob had gathered in the roundabout, not fifty meters from where he and the other two women spilled out onto the sidewalk. Phin was frozen, trying to make sense of the commotion in front of him. Out of the corner of his right eye, a figure caught his attention...running at full speed.

It was Vaughn O'Leary and he was carrying a gun.

# CHAPTER 32

Some people instinctively run from danger.

Others run toward it.

For some reason, Phineas Crook found himself running toward the group of people in the traffic circle. He wasn't sure why. It's not like he fashioned himself the bravest man in a gathering of other men. He didn't like to hunt and he owned only one gun, which was stowed in a safe back at his home in Oklahoma. But instinct will cause a man to do any number of things that he normally would never consider doing, like run toward chaos instead of away from it.

Vaughn O'Leary was running toward the chaos as well, but he had a gun. Phin thought that strange because nothing at the moment warranted the discharge of a firearm, at least that he could see.

Autumn was close on Phin's heels. She was one to run toward danger as well. And she was faster than Phin, having been a track athlete in high school. She was fearless. Another quality that he loved about his wife. Sensing her coming up on his rear, he garnered another measure of bravery and increased his own speed.

Vaughn O'Leary beat them both to the small crowd which parted automatically like Moses standing in front of the Red Sea. The head of the town had arrived. Another yell of agony broke forth.

"Get off of me! You stink. You're dirty. All of you, get away from me!" Sitting on the ground was a young man, early twenties. He looked awful. He was drenched in sweat and a pungent odor hit the new arrivals in the face, like walking into a house that had set off a bug bomb.

Phin pulled up, Autumn nearly running into the back of him as she was hit by the same wall of stink. The gears in Phin's mind churned, trying to put what he was seeing into some sort of context.

Eight or nine people gathered around this tortured young man. He clearly was not well. A larger, older fellow was kneeling on the ground, trying to put his arm around him. Maybe his father? A woman stood behind them holding a blanket, tears in her eyes, desperate sorrow on her face. She was chewing the nails of one hand.

The boy had settled some, but was still shrugging off any attempt to be touched by the older gentleman. He looked tussled and dirty like he'd been in a fight. A couple of other men were ruffled as well. Must be the ones who'd chased and tackled him, Phin put together.

"Everybody, step back," Vaughn ordered. Phin noticed that he'd tucked his weapon into the rear of his trousers, up against the small of his back. He got down on one knee in front of the young man, eye level. "Greg, it's me. Mr. O'Leary. Look at me, son. It's okay. We're all friends here. Do you understand me? Your da is right next to you, trying to help you. We're all trying to help you, Greg. Nobody is going to hurt you. I promise."

The boy lifted his head.

Phin's eyes grew wide at what he saw.

Autumn took in a sharp breath.

Greg's own eyes were a bright yellow. Unlike human eyes at all. Phin observed Vaughn's shoulders sag. He clearly saw it too. Greg's face was slack and dirty with bits of grass stuck to the drying spittle around his mouth. Phin noticed that the nails of his hands were unusually long with dirt crammed underneath. That's when he realized the boy had no shoes on, the nails of his feet equally grown out far beyond what was normal. His clothes had clearly not been changed in days, meaning he'd not bathed either. All of this added up to the foul odor leaching from him, except not.

Phin had been around people who'd not bathed for a long period of time. He'd worked in many homeless shelters and food banks in the past. There was a distinct smell of poverty and this was not it. This was something different and it scared Phin. Not the kind of fear that one can turn off, like pausing a horror movie to go to the bathroom or to cook some popcorn in the microwave. No, this was an internal fear that starts small and grows - like a reaction that is out of one's control.

"Come on, Greg. Let's get you on your feet." Vaughn rose, extending his hand to Greg. The young man put his head down but his hand came up. Vaughn took it and gently pulled as Greg's father had his arm around his son.

Working together they both succeeded in getting the boy to his feet. He seemed very calm now, giving the crowd permission to back away some. Vaughn motioned for the woman with the blanket to come closer. She obeyed, laying the blanket around Greg's shoulders. The young man's head hung, those terrible eyes looking only at the ground.

"How long have you known, Jasper?" Vaughn asked the young man's father.

"He got the fever a week ago. We thought...hoped it was only a fever. But it got worse and then he stopped talking to us. Quit cleaning himself four or five days ago and started..." He paused, looking around at the group of concerned observers, as if embarrassed to go on. So he lowered his voice. "Started defecating in his room. And then his eyes turned yesterday."

Phin recoiled at the explanation. As shocked as he was by whatever it was the young man had, he was equally shocked that those standing around *weren't* shocked. Nobody moved quickly away from him out of fear of catching whatever virus he carried. In fact, a few folks nodded their heads in a resigned understanding, like they knew exactly what was going on. Everyone was sad. Greg's mother had tears streaming down her cheeks.

"Come on now, Greg," Vaughn continued in a soothing tone. "Let's get you over to Doc Kelly and he'll get you taken care of."

Greg began to shuffle toward Phin and Autumn who quickly backed away, making room. Phin's sudden movement must have been wrong or too quick. Greg's head shot up, his yellow eyes burning like fire, locked on Phin.

"You!" he shouted and pointed a long, nail-spiked finger at Phin. "It's *your* fault. You've brought the curse to us!" He launched himself at Phin with enormous speed and strength. Phin took the blow like a running back being upended by a massive linebacker. He fell onto his back, hard, the wind knocked from his lungs. He heard Autumn scream in the background.

It was all Phin could do to pull air into his lungs while pushing with all his might, trying to get Greg off of him. The young man was beyond strong. He raved and growled and foamed. He was snapping his jaws at Phin, trying to bite his face. A line of drool strung down and hit Phin across the cheek. And just like that, it was over.

The light faded from Greg's eyes and he went slack. Phin shoved him easily to the side and sat up, panting. Vaughn stood over them both, a gun extended with both hands. It struck Phin as odd that he never heard the shot. That's when he knew there hadn't been one - at least not one like he expected. A tiny feathered dart was stuck in Greg's neck. A tranquilizer dart. More questions erupted in Phin's mind about what exactly was happening in Tiamat.

Autumn was by Phin's side in an instant, wiping the spittle and grime from her husband's face. "Are you alright? Did he hurt you?"

Phin did a quick check and was on his feet without anyone's help. "*What* was that?" He directed at Vaughn, who ignored him.

"Jasper and Dot, I'm so sorry." Vaughn gathered Greg's parents into the wings of an embrace.

Phin realized that Patricia O'Leary had also joined the gathering and fell into the embrace of the couple. There were additional words being spoken that Phin couldn't make out. He and Autumn embraced each other likewise. He was fine but wanted to comfort his own wife after the trauma of the moment.

Vaughn broke away from Greg's parents and began giving orders. "Harv, you and Furman get a group together and take Greg to - " he stopped himself short, looking directly at Phin and Autumn. "You know what to do gentlemen. Just take care of him," he finished.

The two older men, one very weathered-looking and one a bit more refined shot into action like they *did* know exactly what to do - like they'd done it before. Many times.

In short order a group of six were carrying Greg's sleeping body out of the traffic circle where they loaded him into the bed of a truck. The one named Harv jumped behind the wheel and drove away, down the street called Akkadia before turning a corner, and out of sight. Wherever they were taking him, it wasn't to Dr. Kelly's office.

Phin marched up to Vaughn O'Leary, who was in deep conversation with Greg's parents. He put his hand on the man's shoulder and spun him around. It was a rude gesture but he didn't care. He'd just been attacked and everyone was acting like it didn't matter - like he and Autumn didn't matter.

"What's going on around here?" he demanded. "I want an answer and I want it now."

# CHAPTER 33

Phin drove the loop around Phoenix Park twice before navigating onto Ordinance Survey Road. The park was massive, the largest in the city of Dublin, occupying the entire western region out of downtown.

It was midafternoon. Phin had driven hard, stopping only for fuel and a to-go sandwich on his way. The bread had been dry and crumbly and he only ate half of it. His stomach was grumbling, but he imagined that problem would soon be solved. No one ever left Sergio Nardovino's hungry.

He'd hedged on coming to Dublin after the bizarre morning where he'd been jumped by a resident of Tiamat. The strange little Irish town had gotten stranger, and Vaughn O'Leary's explanation was wholly unsatisfactory.

The young man's name was Greg Collins. "He's not well," Vaughn had begun. That was clearly obvious – an understatement for sure. The crowd broke up quickly without anyone else talking much or checking on the wellbeing of Phin. Patricia had taken Greg's parents back to the bed and breakfast, offering something to drink along with some biscuits. Everything about the incident seemed...off. Phin probed as to where they were taking Greg but all he got was that the young man had a condition and that they would make sure he was safe.

Keep *him* safe?

Phin wanted to scream.

What about everyone else? What about Phin nearly having a bite taken out of his face?

The way Vaughn spoke about the whole thing made it sound as if nothing unusual had happened at all, as if Greg Collins running around town all disheveled and manic, jumping on visitors, was a perfectly normal occurrence.

Nothing to see here. Move along.

And what about the yellow eyes and the tranquilizer gun that Vaughn just happened to be carrying? Who carries around a loaded tranquilizer gun? Also, Greg's parents had mentioned a fever for the past week. That sounded a lot like a virus or an infection. Yet, no one seemed to be concerned about catching what he had. No precautions were taken when carrying him away, no protective gear was produced. They'd just literally tossed him into the bed of a truck and driven away. Phin had more questions on top of the questions that already dominated his mind. He gave up pressing Vaughn at that moment, sensing he'd get nowhere.

Autumn had convinced him to go ahead and make the trip to see Sergio. He already didn't like leaving her behind, and the encounter with Greg Collins didn't serve to ease his anxiety at all. She wouldn't be alone, Autumn insisted. Jason was still in town over at Mattie McCloud's house. She would spend the morning there checking on Jason's recovery and see if she could get Mattie to open up. "Woman to woman," Autumn had said with a wink. Her confidence emboldened him. He went back to his room, packed a day bag, and drove away.

He found the driveway to Sergio's house easily enough. "House" would be an understatement. Sergio Nardovino's residence was more like a small estate, nestled into the woods on the edge of Phoenix Park. Very private, which would suit Sergio nicely given his penchant for dealing in illegal antiquities. Nardo, as Phin affectionately called him, never stayed anywhere very long. The nature of his business always kept him on the move, following the latest trove of archaeological trinkets that suited his interests, and his buyer's interests. Because what he did was strictly against the law, he was on the watch list of INTERPOL as well as the law enforcement agencies of numerous other countries.

Sergio had been in Ireland for eighteen months now. About as long as he stayed anywhere. Phin was fortunate, indeed, that his friend was this close, although there was no guarantee that he could be of any help.

Phin had first met Sergio Nardovino ten years earlier when he was traveling through Cairo. He always carried with him, in his journal, a list. A very special list. It contained the names of friends and "connections" that his late father, Adonis Crook, had worked with through the years. His father was a crook, in the very literal sense and not just in name only. Phin had no desire to follow in his father's footsteps but in a strange kind of way, the list had been a way for him to stay connected to his father *post mortem* - his father's friends becoming his friends. They say there is no honor among thieves, which may be true, but there is definitely a comradery. Phin had lost count at the number of times he had heard the phrase, "The son of Adonis Crook is a son of mine!"

Phin parked and made his way up the paver-laden walkway to the massive double front door. He looked up at the three-story monstrosity, it's gray stone masonry and peaks reminding him of a castle. He gave the knocker a whack and waited. Reaching up for a second attempt, the door suddenly opened, more quickly than he would have imagined. The next thing he knew, Phin was enveloped in a massive hug.

"Phin, oh Phin, how are you my boy? So very good to see you!" Sergio spoke and laughed at the same time. Phin was carried along, his body heaving with every chuckle Sergio made. He finally found his release as the Italian stepped back at arm's length to measure him up. "My, oh my, you are so *skinny*. Come in, come quickly...you must eat!" He continued to belly laugh, his voice booming.

"How are you, Nardo?" Phin replied with a smile. It was impossible not to smile when you were around Sergio Nardovino. He was a large man but very short, maybe five feet tall, weighing easily over two hundred and fifty pounds. He was Italian, through and through, with a heavy accent when he spoke English. His face was cleanly shaven as always, sporting a thin black mustache that was waxed into long curls on the edges. His hair was finally showing some salt, to go with the pepper, and was slicked all the way back with some sort of product that Phin had never asked about.

"Oh, me? I'm doing good, my friend. As good as an old man can be in a hard world." He gave a wink. "Now come inside and let's go to the kitchen. As soon as you called, I began to make the pizza. I asked myself, what kind of pizza will I make my good friend, Phineas Crook? And then I knew. It came to me like that." He snapped his fingers and then turned and began shuffling across the entry way toward a set of swinging doors. Phin followed the funny little big man in his baggy pants and untucked long white cotton shirt.

"You still live alone, Nardo?" He marveled at the size of the home. As big as it looked from the outside, it appeared bigger on the inside. *No way he uses all this space*, Phin thought.

"Always, my friend," he called back as he pushed through the doors. "You know my motto: Trust no one. Love everyone!" He laughed big again.

Phin found himself in a lavishly adorned kitchen, very modern considering the age of the house. On the island was a menagerie of pizza toppings and a wad of dough sitting on a dusting of flour. As long as Phin had known Sergio, he had been a connoisseur of pizza. All kinds of pizza. The standard fair of pepperoni and sausage but also gourmet pizzas that no one had ever heard of before. He made them all by hand and was always experimenting with new sauces and toppings. Sergio settled for nothing less than a wood-fired oven to cook them in, and as expected he saw one already bellowing smoke on the patio just through the back exit of the kitchen. Sergio began kneading the dough as the two talked.

"So, tell me, my friend, why is it you have come to me? How can Nardo help you?"

The reason Phin had come to his friend was because of an idea he had. If it was true that the royal family of the ancient Babylonian Empire had fled Babylon upon the invasion of the Medes and the Persians, then a three-thousand-mile trek would have taken a long time – many months and likely more than a year. They would likely have stayed in various locations for extended periods of time. That would mean that they would have exchanged money and bartered for goods and supplies – using *Babylonian* coin and goods. If the theory was true, then there would be a trail of artifacts scattered along the pathway from the Middle East through Europe and beyond. If such a trail existed, Sergio Nardovino would know about it.

The two old friends talked as Sergio built the pizza. He adorned it with an impressive array of meats, cheeses, veggies and a yellow cream sauce of some sort. He called this particular creation The Thieves Bounty, laughing at the irony of serving it to Phineas Crook. Phin thought he simply made the name up on the fly to tease him.

Phin went on to explain what Jason Morris had told him about the discovery of the history of Malphious, his identity as the son of the biblical Meshach. The Italian listened intently as Phin described an exodus of the royal family from ancient Babylon in the year 539 B.C. Sergio asked a few clarifying questions along the way, his focus intensifying once he'd loaded the pizza into the wood fired oven. Nothing to do now but let it cook and listen.

The fat man's eyes grew wide when Phin suggested the notion that this family of Babylonian fugitives may have landed once and for all on the northern coast of Ireland. Phin left nothing out of the tale. He described the town of Tiamat, its oddities, the people all having the look of a common heritage and certainly one that was not Irish. He finished with the attack earlier that morning from the young Greg Collins, unsure if it mattered at all to the big picture, but not wanting to skip over any detail.

Sergio extracted the pizza from his custom oven and cut and served the creation to Phin. The aroma was intoxicating and Phin's hunger reached an apex as the two took up seats at a four-seat table in the kitchen. The sun had finally set and Sergio lit a few candles to go with the incandescent lighting, urging his friend to not wait, but to dive in. Phin had to control himself to avoid wolfing down an entire slice in just three bites. It was delicious. Exactly what he would expect from Sergio Nardovino.

Sergio sat and began to talk between bites of his own perfect slice. "So, my friend. You weave an entertaining tale. Yes, very interesting, indeed. So, let me tell you what Nardo knows and what Nardo thinks." There was a pause. Phin stopped eating and stared, waiting on Sergio to continue. The big man let out a belly laugh, "You are taking this very personally, I can tell, my young friend. Haha, yes, you are. Listen, sit back and relax...eat more pizza and let me tell you what I can. But first I want to retrieve something and I will be back."

Phin helped himself to another slice. Sergio disappeared but was back in his seat in less than two minutes with a small black cloth bundle about the size of one's fist, along with an old book. "I know nothing of Malphious or his history. But that is of no concern. It is a new find, you say. But this idea you have...you've not said it, but I know you are thinking it. That is why you've come to me, no? You want to know if there is a trail of artifacts of Babylonian origin...a trail that leads across the world from Iraq to Europe. And the answer to your question is, *yes.*" Sergio Nardovino's eyes grew wide with confirmation. Phin chewed faster. "I myself have trafficked in such pieces. All from the era of the Babylonian Empire. I found it a curiosity, but the questions such a trail raises are not for me. They are for the archaeologists and the scholars. And I am neither. I am but a humble pizza maker." He let out another bellow of laughter.

"I acquire pizza and I sell pizza. To the highest bidder. It is that simple. And the particular flavor of pizza you are interested in goes for a very high price. It is rare but it exists, yes. And there is good money to be made. I myself have followed this particular trail. You probably have wondered, I am sure, why I am in Ireland this past year plus. Imagine, me? An Italian living here in Ireland! Ha ha. It is not because of the pizza, I can tell you that!" Sergio continued to chuckle. "It is because of the *toppings.*" Phin stopped chewing, willing Sergio to go on. "There is a concentration of toppings coming out of this country. Very curious, indeed. But as I said, such is not my concern. I gather and I sell. That is what I do. But I can tell you something else I know. And I say this because I like to know where my toppings come from. The source is important, you see. There are some unsavory people in my profession who make bad pizza. Let me now ask you a question, young Phineas. You are familiar with the *Enuma Elish,* no?"

Phin knew the story. Every biblical scholar and ancient historian, for that matter, was familiar with the ancient Babylonian epic of the creation of the world. Phin nodded and Sergio continued. "Good. But have you read it?"

"You mean the actual text? Well, no."

Sergio slid the old book over to Phin. "Read this tonight, my friend. I think you will find it interesting and important. That finishes what I know. Now let me tell you what I think." Sergio's countenance took on a sudden and darker tone. "I think you need to be very careful in Tiamat. Not all is as it seems...I *think*. I have one more thing to show you. A topping, we shall call it. It came to me from north Ireland. It is authentic Babylonian, from the era of the empire."

Sergio slid the black bundle over to Phin. He put down his slice of The Thieves Bounty and pulled back the cloth. Phin found himself staring at a small stone relief with an image on it. An image that made his heart skip a beat.

# CHAPTER 34

Autumn was exhausted. She closed the door to her upstairs room and plopped down on the end of the queen bed. Her lack of sleep from the night before had finally caught up to her. Actually, the last forty-eight hours had caught up to her. Just two days ago, she and Phin were enjoying a wonderful time in London. Since then, she'd nearly been hit by a bus due to her own stupidity, Phin's nerves had been set on edge, and the frantic call from Jason had been received. Then came the rush flight from Heathrow to Dublin, a cross country drive in a cramped car, and all the weirdness that was Tiamat.

She had determined that today she was going to get some answers as to what this place was all about. The start had not been promising as her husband had been attacked by one of Tiamat's citizens post-breakfast. The young man had been unceremoniously carted off to who-knows-where, only adding to the mystery of it all.

Autumn's starting point was the McCloud house to check on Jason. She had first seen Phin off on his journey back to Dublin to see his friend, Sergio Nardovino. Phin was anxious to see if he could confirm Jason's theory about the residents of Tiamat being descendants of ancient Babylonian royalty. Once Phin was on his way, she walked straight over to the McCloud's. She met Ross McCloud for the first time. He was leaving just as she arrived. He was a nice warm man who seemed in a bit of a hurry to get to work. But he took time to introduce himself and offer the comforts of his simple home and anything she needed. He was about as normal as anyone she'd met so far in Tiamat. He excused himself quickly, though, and hurried to town. As the local gunsmith, she couldn't imagine what the urgency could be in this sleepy village.

Mattie welcomed her in to make herself at home. Jason was finishing breakfast and the two of them spent the morning talking. Autumn didn't hold back telling Jason about the attack on Phin by the young man named Greg Collins. Mattie listened with curiosity as she cleaned the kitchen but didn't offer any comments. Surely, she knew the young Collins. She imagined everyone in Tiamat knew everyone else.

Jason was healing nicely and anxious to get out of the house once again. Autumn escorted him for a walk that took them about halfway to the town's center before they turned back. Jason had nothing new to offer by way of thoughts. Everything he knew he'd shared the day before. His primary concern was Jorge. He wanted to know if they'd found anything out, which, of course, they had not. Just that local search teams were out looking for him.

The walk had done Jason good but had really taken it out of him. While he went to have a nap, Autumn spent the rest of the morning and lunch talking with Mattie McCloud. This was her woman-to-woman moment she'd hoped would yield secret fruit.

Not so much.

Mattie played the gracious hostess and Autumn peppered her with a series of questions. How long have you lived in Tiamat? How did you meet Ross? Tell me more about your son, Tommy. When is he coming home again? How often do you hear from him? Do you get many visitors? What do you think happened to Jason and Jorge?

The answers were benign. She'd lived her whole life in Tiamat. She met Ross in Tiamat where he'd lived his whole life. Tommy was returning in the spring and the mention of her son lit a spark in Mattie. Autumn asked to see pictures and she was more than happy to oblige. Hardly anyone came to Tiamat to visit. "Just nothing to see here," she'd commented. Autumn wondered why the people of Tiamat stayed in Tiamat if they were so unenthusiastic about their own town. The question about Jason and Jorge got the starkest reaction. Mattie McCloud didn't really have any thoughts on what happened other than the standard line: "Wild animals. Wolves probably." If she did have other thoughts, she wasn't inclined to share them with Autumn Crook.

After lunch, Autumn gave up on Mattie McCloud and decided to turn her attention to Patricia O'Leary. Back at the bed and breakfast, she found their hostess sweeping the back porch. Autumn's arrival was perfectly timed, she'd declared, because it was tea time. Patricia magically produced a tray with tea and biscuits and invited Autumn to join her on the porch. The day had turned off beautiful once again, though a mix of clouds in the distance hinted at something more later.

"Where did they take the Collins boy? I hope he'll be okay. He didn't look well at all." Autumn decided to go for it. She took a sip of her tea and leaned back in the rocker.

Patricia tensed. "Greg is a good young man. He's being taken care of. He'll be fine." It was a cryptic response. Autumn knew there was more.

"Did you see his eyes, Patricia? They were yellow. Bright yellow. I've never seen anything like that before. At least not on a person. What do you think he has that would cause that?"

Another hesitation. Autumn didn't care, she was getting impatient. "There is a fever in these parts," Patricia began, carefully choosing her words it seemed. "It does things. Unusual things. But trust me. Greg will recover...in time. This isn't something we haven't seen before."

"It just seems so strange. Plus, his behavior. The way he attacked my husband. Like some wild animal."

"It would be best if you and your husband took Mr. Morris and left town as soon as possible." The boldness of Patricia's answer surprised Autumn. And then as if to pull back a bit, she said, "I think you would be safer."

"Safer? From what, Patricia? From whatever it is Greg has or from something else?"

As Patricia was about to answer, a crash and bang broke

the moment. Little Patrick O'Leary burst onto the porch, dragging, not wearing, his school backpack.

"I'm home, Mom!" he yelled louder than was necessary. "Oh, good! You're still here." He smiled big when he saw Autumn. "I was hoping you hadn't left."

"Patrick," Patricia started with motherly sternness. "Where are your manners, young man?"

"Yes, I'm still here, Patrick. I don't think we're going anywhere for a while." Autumn eyed Patricia O'Leary who only pursed her lips.

"Oh, good! Did you hear that, Mother?"

"Yes, I heard. Now, let's get you washed up and a snack in you." Patricia took Patrick to the kitchen.

Autumn spent the remainder of the afternoon and early evening after dinner helping Patrick with his homework and playing in the front sitting room with the boy and his action figures and spaceships. Patricia didn't seem to mind and enjoyed seeing her son so happy. Autumn thoroughly enjoyed her time with the boy. He invited her to call him by his nickname – Patty. And in turn he began referring to her as Miss Autumn. It all made Autumn's heart ache even more strongly for a child that she and Phin could call their own. She said a silent prayer right then and there that God would grant them this one wish.

Sitting on her bed now, she prayed that prayer once more. Then she took in a deep breath and let it out.

Alone in the room, she missed Phin for the first time. Hopefully, his trip was yielding the results he wanted, better than what she'd been able to garner. He'd be back after breakfast in the morning and she was strong enough to make it until then. *Strong enough*, she thought. Why was she even thinking this way? Strong enough for what? There was nothing here that was going to hurt her. This was just a sleepy ol' Irish town like dozens of others strewn across the countryside.

Except it wasn't.

In the quiet of her room, the oddities of Tiamat were playing with her mind.

She heard the front door of the bed and breakfast open and close on the floor below her. Voices echoed up the staircase. She decided it was a good time to head to the community bathroom at the end of the hall and to take a quick listen along the way. She grabbed her toiletry bag and shuffled in her socks out into the hall.

Two men.

Vaughn O'Leary and Dr. Boris Kelly.

She'd seen neither of them all day and now that it was dark and the curfew in place, they'd appeared. It was impossible to discern their conversation so she gave up and went and prepared herself for bed. What she needed now, more than anything, was a good night's sleep.

Autumn returned to her room and worked the old-fashioned skeleton key to lock the door. It was tricky and she played with it a bit before being satisfied it was secure. She eased under the covers, pushing thoughts of insecurity to the back of her mind, and slipped away into a deep slumber.

***

Autumn's eyes shot open. She was lying on her back, having kicked the covers off in her sleep. Her heart was beating fast and she was drenched in sweat. Had she had a bad dream? She couldn't remember. She tried to breathe, to calm herself, lifting her head to glance around the dark room.

Clouds must have rolled in, obscuring the moon, because the light coming in through the lace curtain was faint. Only the slightest hint of shadows played across the white plaster walls.

And then she heard an exhale.

Autumn's heart skipped a beat and she held her own breath. Maybe she'd frightened herself with her own breathing?

No. There it was again.

The sound of lungs releasing the pressure of the air within. But it was a short burst. A quick *huff*. Unlike what you'd expect. She continued to hold her breath, straining to hear more.

*Huff, huff, huff.*

Autumn let out a tiny squeal of fear. Someone was in the room with her. But where? She lifted her head higher and that's when her eyes caught the door. The smallest of cracks revealing that it had been opened. She cursed herself for not doing a better job to make sure it was locked. But now that same door was her one pathway to escape. Had her intruder heard the sound she'd made? Did he know she was awake? She assumed it was a *he*. Her mind was racing fast.

A new sound.

Clicking on the hard wood floor.

A very slow clicking sound followed by a scratch.

*Click. Scratch. Click. Scratch. Huff. Huff.*

Fear escalated as sounds moved from the foot of her bed all the way around to her left, between her and the window. Why couldn't she see him?! And then she knew. He was crawling on the floor. Outside of her view. Maybe he thought she was still asleep. Please, Lord, let him think I'm sleeping. She hated the thought of what would happen next if he knew she was awake and might escape. She assumed he, whoever he was, was only there for the worst thing possible.

Her heart beat faster, the perspiration increasing.

She tried to control her breaths, taking in steady air - in and out - trying to make it sound like she was sleeping. There is a certain sound people make when sleeping, isn't there?

A blast of wind hit the crack in the window, blowing the curtain aside. By the time the air traveled across the room to Autumn's face, it had picked up a scent. An awful, inhuman scent. The impact of the smell caused Autumn's fear to spike. It was the musk of an animal on the hunt. That's all she could think of. She had to go. She had to get out of the room. Now. The pathway was clear between the right side of her bed and the cracked door.

Ready. On three.

She began to count silently.

One. Two. Three.

Frozen.

Autumn strained and pulled but it was no use.

Her arms and legs were limp. They wouldn't work. She was frozen by fear. The huffing and the clicking and the scratching and the smell. It worked in awful perfection to paralyze her muscles. Like a rabbit frozen in place by an approaching dog. The prey helpless to defend itself. That's what she had become.

Autumn began to cry, tears running down the side of her face. She let out the tiniest of whimpers. And then another. Louder this time. He definitely knew she was awake now. What would she do? What *could* she do? She longed for Phin. *Oh, Phin, why did you go? Why did I insist on you going?* It didn't matter now. Nothing mattered anymore. All she could do was lay there, helpless. Waiting on him to have his way with her.

*Click scratch. Click scratch. Click scratch.*

The rhythm of the gait picking up pace, as if circling on the floor next to her head. He was getting impatient. She could sense it. Agitated perhaps. What was he waiting for?

And then a new sound.

A low rumble. Like a growl. A hungry growl.

The smell intensified. The fear was overwhelming.

Autumn thought she might lose control of her quivering bladder. The clicking and scratching and huffing moved to the foot of her bed. She was running out of time. He'd be between her and the door in another moment. Her escape route would be cut off. It was now or never. She had to overcome the panic. She had to overcome the fear. It was life or death. She knew it. She sensed that *he* knew it. She counted to three one more time and strained every muscle in her body.

Nothing. Still nothing.

Autumn began to weep uncontrollably. All she could see in her mind's eye was the face of Phin. That's when she felt it. A heavy thump on the foot of her bed. This was it. He was coming for her. She wanted to close her eyes. To block it out. But no! She would not. He might take her but he'd take her with her eyes wide open. Staring strong and proud back at her attacker. She was able to lift her head one more time. Toward the foot of the bed. Toward him.

Two eyes stared back. Two yellow, inhuman eyes. Bright and burning.

Autumn released a blood-curdling scream.

# CHAPTER 35

Phineas Crook slowed his Ford Ka as he arrived at the outskirts of Tiamat. He passed the McCloud house where Jason was staying but kept going. He was anxious to see Autumn, to see how the previous day went and if she'd made any progress with the residents of the town. And he had much to share with her.

After his dinner discussion with Sergio, the two friends had retired to a personal study where his host had shown him a detailed record of Babylonian artifacts that had been moving on the black market going back a generation or more. The evidence pointed to a clear pathway from modern day Iraq, across the Mediterranean, through Europe, and ending in Ireland. All along this route various coins, pottery shards, rings, and other trinkets had been unearthed and traded.

All of Babylonian origin.

Phin had crawled into a fluffy bed covered in fine linen in one of Sergio's many guest bedrooms. "Take your pick, my friend. The house is yours," he had boomed with a big laugh as he waddled away toward his own room. But Phin enjoyed little sleep. Instead, he dove into Sergio's copy of the *Enuma Elish*, the Babylonian epic of the creation of the world. Every scholar knew of the *Enuma Elish*. For that matter every freshman at OBU - or any other Christian college - taking an Old Testament introductory course was introduced to it. It was said to be a competing view to the biblical account of the creation of the world, even though its existence was unknown until English archaeologist, A.H. Layard, uncovered it in 1849 while digging in Mosul, Iraq. Secularists labeled both as competing myths. Phin, however, viewed the biblical account as true while dismissing the Babylonian account.

He knew the general premise of the Babylonian account of creation, that it lifted up the god Marduk as the supreme god of Babylon, and the creation of humans as the servants of the gods. There was a lot more to the story, of course, but he'd never bothered to read a translation of the actual account itself.

Until now.

He sat in bed and absorbed the text until the early hours of the morning. What he read was stunning. He finally forced himself to close his eyes around four in the morning, but sleep was fleeting. He woke early and showered quickly. He had to get back to Tiamat. To Autumn and Jason. Sergio insisted he eat something before rushing off. "Nobody leaves Nardo's hungry!" he proclaimed.

Breakfast pizza, of course. Two slices and it was delicious indeed. Hugs and many thanks to his old friend and then Phin sped away.

Phin made his way around the traffic circle and came to a quick stop in front of O'Leary's Bed & Breakfast. He was proud of the time he'd made; it was just after ten o'clock. He bounded up the few steps and into the lobby. He'd sent a text message to Autumn and knew she'd be waiting for him in the parlor. And she was. Upon seeing Phin, she stood and rushed into his arms. It was a bit more dramatic than he'd anticipated. He eased her away and saw tears in her eyes.

"My dear, what's the matter? It was only one night. It couldn't have been that bad," he gently teased.

"Oh, Phin. It was awful. Simply awful. I didn't know if I'd ever see-" she choked up.

"Didn't know what? What happened, Autumn?" he asked, realizing something serious had happened.

She took his hand and they retreated to a sitting room off the lobby, opposite of the parlor and kitchen area. They sat on an antique sofa and she launched into an account of the night before. The intruder. The overcoming, paralyzing fear. Odd sounds and crawling on the floor. She truly thought she would die - that she'd never see Phin again. And then those awful yellow eyes.

She'd screamed as long and as loud as she could, until her lungs were out of air. And then she breathed in deep and screamed again. Patricia was the first to the room. She burst in, turning on the light. There was nothing. No one else there. Just a frantic Autumn Crook and now, Patricia, in her own night robe and house shoes. She was a bit out of breath, having shot out of bed and up the stairs from her suite on the main floor.

The two women looked over the room. Still nothing. No evidence that anyone had been in the room. Autumn insisted it was real - that someone or something had entered and stalked her. And what about the door? The locked door had been opened. But Patricia countered that the mechanisms were old and didn't always catch like they were designed to do. She'd have Vaughn look at it in the morning and replace it if necessary.

Vaughn arrived momentarily. He'd checked on Patrick whom Autumn's screams had awoken and frightened as well. All was well in the whole house, he declared, not just a little put off by the whole commotion. Autumn began to feel guilty, as if it were her imagination, which the O'Learys clearly thought was the case. "A bad dream," Patricia insisted, taking a more sympathetic approach.

They left her alone and the rest of the night was without incident. But Autumn slept no more. Was it a bad dream? Was her imagination getting the better of her - this strange town and its secrets taking their toll? She was almost convinced it was her imagination...except for one thing. The smell. The odor of the beast. It lingered, if ever so slightly.

Phin listened with a mixture of horror, fear, and anger. Anger at himself for leaving his precious wife alone. He'd been hesitant and should have listened to his instincts. He was also angry at Vaughn O'Leary. Why? He could not answer. He simply felt that somehow he held a measure of responsibility for the quiet chaos that surrounded the façade of peace and tranquility that oozed from this town.

He hugged and soothed his wife. He did not dismiss her account in the slightest. In fact, after what he'd discovered at Sergio Nardovino's he was more convinced than ever they were on the trail that would lead them to the truth in Tiamat. A trail that was growing more dangerous the longer they traveled.

"Listen Autumn, I have much to tell you myself." He pulled away, returning to the urgency that had carried him back so quickly that morning. "We need to go and get Jason and let him know what happened to you, and I need to fill you both in on what I've discovered."

They set off in the Ford Ka. It was not a long walk, but Phin was too anxious and insisted they drive. They parked across the street from the McCloud's house and knocked on the front door straightaway. Mattie was there as expected but Ross was gone for the day, also as expected. Phin still had yet to meet the patriarch of the home. Jason was awake and waiting on them. The three excused themselves, trying not to be rude to their hostess who had invited them to sit and enjoy a beverage of their choice. Phin wanted to get the group away from listening ears.

They loaded Jason into the front passenger seat, and Autumn crammed herself into the too small back seat. They found a park bench in the giant roundabout in the center of town. Better to be hiding in plain sight, Phin thought. *Nothing to see here, move along.* It helped, too, that the people of Tiamat, as a rule, avoided contact with them.

Phin began by filling Jason in on Autumn's night of terror. She added the details to Phin's overview as Jason sat in utter disbelief. Her encounter reminded him of the creature he'd seen at the end of the road outside the

McCloud's house the night he was attacked. Especially the yellow eyes. There was something about those eyes.

Next, Phin pivoted to his evening with Sergio. He explained the trail of Babylonian artifacts, all dating to the time of the empire. The trail ended in Ireland, seemingly confirming the history of Malphious and Jason's theory placing it as the terminal point of the royal migration.

"Have you heard of the *Enuma Elish?*" Phin asked.

"Of course. *You* were the one that taught my OT class, remember?" Jason answered.

"I have no idea what you're talking about," Autumn chimed in. "The Enuma what?"

"Elish. *The Enuma Elish.*"

"It's an ancient account of creation from the Babylonians. Sure, I know all about it, but what does the *Enuma Elish* have to do with anything going on here?" Jason queried.

"You know about the myth, Jason. But I'll bet you've never actually read it, have you?" Phin pushed his former pupil. Jason shook his head. "Neither had I. Until last night. Nardo gave me a translation of the text and I read the whole thing. The focus of the epic is on the Babylonian god Marduk and his supremacy over all of creation. But that's not how the epic begins. The tale begins with two other gods. Two gods that stood above everything before there was anything. Get this...the names of those two gods were Apsu...and *Tiamat.*"

Phin paused to let that sink in.

"Holy cow," Jason let out slowly. "That seals the deal. The people of this town *are* the descendants of ancient Babylon. There's no doubt."

"Listen, I'm just getting started. So Apsu and Tiamat were the two gods that essentially created, or gave birth to, all the other gods in Babylonian mythology. And then a rebellion of the gods took place - like children not wanting to obey their parents. Apsu was killed by these lesser gods leaving Tiamat in a panic. So, what does she do? She creates eleven monsters - eleven otherworldly beasts - who will fight the other gods in hopes of defeating them and restoring power to her alone.

"As the tale plays out, Tiamat's plan fails and she is eventually defeated by Marduk, slain in fact. But the monsters. The key is the monsters. They aren't killed, but instead they are chained and kept. Stone statues are even created to venerate the monsters." Phin finished and sat back, letting the words of the myth sink in.

"What exactly are you saying, hon?" Autumn asked. "What does all this talk of monsters and Tiamat mean for us today?"

Jason was in deep thought, looking around at the smattering of people walking along the sidewalks of the town. *Monsters*, he wondered.

"I have no idea for sure. Nardo warned us to be careful. And then he handed me this." Phin pulled the black cloth bundle from his coat pocket that Sergio had given him. It was a loan to a friend, he'd insisted. "This stone relief came from somewhere up here. In north Ireland. It's labeled in the language of ancient Babylon as 'a monster of Tiamat.'" He unfolded the cloth for them to see the image.

The image of a wolf.

# CHAPTER 36

A plan had been devised.

Phin, Autumn, and Jason walked to the Frolicking Irishman for lunch. Phin laughed as they crossed Akkadia Avenue, pointing at the sign. Akkadian was the native language of ancient Babylon. The signs were literally all around them and he'd missed them until now.

Jason's strength was returning fast, and after hearing Phin recount his evening with Sergio Nardovino, there was no way he was heading back to the McCloud's just yet. The town's only public restaurant sat opposite the large traffic circle from O'Leary's Bed & Breakfast. Upon entering, the trio attracted the immediate attention of a smattering of other residents scattered around the establishment.

They were greeted happily by a pretty young hostess whose name tag read Marilyn. The group introduced themselves and she showed them to a four-seater straightaway. Her demeanor caught them off guard as most people kept their distance in Tiamat.

"I'm so sorry for what happened to you, Mr. Morris. And I'm very glad to see you're getting along well." Marilyn seemed to know exactly who they were and particularly who Jason was. And she knew what had happened to him, at least to an extent. Passing around menus and lowering her voice, she said to the Crooks, "I heard you ran into my fiancé, Malcolm, at Doc Kelly's office the other day. He's been through a lot too but his spirits are up and he'll be out and about in no time, the doctor says. Well, all except for his arm." Her eyes betrayed a sadness.

"Fiancé?" Autumn perked up. "Congratulations."

"Oh, thank you! Yes, we're getting married next summer." She was giddy to talk about her wedding like most brides-to-bes. "It will be glorious. A happy time. And we could use a little happiness around here. The town's gone through a hard spell."

"Marilyn." A firm female voice cut her off. "We have orders ready that require your attention." Marilyn scurried away as if caught doing something wrong, promising to return for their drink orders. "You'll have to excuse my daughter. She sometimes gets carried away, bothering the guests unnecessarily. I keep telling her people come here to eat and not chat about her wedding. I'm Francis Hayes. Folks around here call me Fran. My husband's Furman. He serves on the town council and we own this place. Been in the family for five generations. You are welcome here. I know it can seem otherwise at times." She'd replaced Marilyn, standing over the group with one hand on her skirted hip, black hair pulled up in a bun.

"Oh, your daughter was no trouble at all," Phin replied.

"I just love seeing young people in love," Autumn added. "Thank you for your kindness, Mrs. Hayes."

"Just call me Fran," she said matter-of-factly. "We aren't that formal in this part of the world. Fran and Fur, that's what our friends call me and my husband."

"Well, nice to meet you, Fran." Autumn and Fran talked a bit more, Autumn asking about the wedding. They found that Fran was as chatty as her daughter, if not more so. Phin inquired about Malcolm's amputated arm. He was curious about Marilyn's fiancé. How did it happen? Fran's toned changed somewhat, her eyes all of a sudden looking around the diner at the other townspeople watching. The subject was clearly off limits and she dodged the details by only calling it an accident. Fran pivoted quickly, recommending lunch items that she thought they'd like, and finally excusing herself to the kitchen.

"That's what we run into every time we go deeper than 'Hi, how are you?'" Phin turned a slight shade of red. "Nobody around here will talk to us about anything. We're going to have to force the issue."

That's when the plan was hatched.

Jason's fatigue was catching up to him. He was going to head back to the McCloud's to rest and eat dinner. There wasn't much more he could offer that day. Phin wanted to make a phone call. He had an idea for someone who might be the perfect person to help them in just a situation like the one they were in. And then he and Autumn would play the tourists - take a hike to the famous Irish bluff overlooking the Atlantic and end up back at O'Leary's tired and ready for dinner and an early night. Sometime later, Phin would sneak down to Vaughn O'Leary's private library and take a look at what was inside. He'd already told Jason that he'd spied what he thought was the young pair's backpack and some other gear in the room the first day they arrived. He'd even thought he saw Jason's cell phone.

Jason had been told in no uncertain terms that nothing had been recovered of a personal nature in all the rescue team's searching for Jorge. That was a lie. They knew it. Phin wondered what other secrets that library would reveal. Once he confirmed that Jason's gear was stashed in the room and whatever else he could find, Phin would simply confront Vaughn and demand to know what was happening. If he hedged, he'd call the U.S. Embassy and unleash the power of his own government on the search for a missing American in Ireland.

Phin and Autumn truly did have a wonderful afternoon. The weather was once again perfect, but clouds in the distance portrayed the possibility of something later in the evening. The view of the ocean from the bluffs was stunning. Phin took time to pray with his wife from the summit. He prayed that God would grant them knowledge and truth - over all that was happening in Tiamat - that the truth would be revealed. He sensed a darkness and danger waiting for them. They'd already been touched by it to an extent - especially Jason and Autumn. Phin's fears were his greatest enemy. He could not let the fear win.

Dinner at the bed and breakfast was delicious. Patricia O'Leary served up her own concoction of Irish stew - a mixture of mutton, onions, and potatoes. The soda bread was outstanding as was the carrageen moss pudding for dessert. Phin went on again with his compliments which pleased their hostess. Patrick asked to join them and despite Patricia's protests to leave their guests alone, she relented when Autumn insisted it was fine. Vaughn was apparently gone for the evening and so the lad was bored. Phin and Autumn took notice of the admission, which meant Phin would not have to wait until well into the evening to orchestrate his little break-in.

The Crooks feigned sleepiness, so shortly after dinner and a game of checkers with Patrick, they excused themselves to their room. Phin waited another hour and when all seemed quiet in the house, he kissed his wife on the cheek and slipped out of their room into the hallway. The last words he heard before he closed the door behind him were, "Hurry back, love. I'll be waiting on you." Emboldened by Autumn's words, he set his mind to the task ahead with new energy. He wasn't concerned with being caught. This little operation was amateur hour for someone with his family background. He was a Crook after all. Clandestine activity was bred into his DNA.

The old wooden stairs begged to creak and pop, but Phin made short work of them, his catlike skills carrying him to the landing with ease.

Not a sound to be heard.

The lights in the parlor were off and no light shown under the door leading to the kitchen. Only a lamp with a low-watt bulb sitting on the front desk illuminated the entrance to the guest house. The place indeed looked shut down for the night.

Phin rounded the corner and was at the end of the hall in a quick moment. The door to Vaughn's library stood in front of him. On the off chance that it was unlocked, Phin tried the knob first. There was no give. So, Phin reached into his pocket, extracting his tools of the trade. They represented a path not taken, yet he had retained both the skill and the instruments of the trade.

There was nothing complex about the lock, and a slight click with the use of a small needle-like instrument indicated that he had gained entry. A quick glance back over his shoulder and then he was through the door and in the room. Another small lamp lit the space. Phin was grateful for the light it provided. It would save him using the flashlight on his phone to navigate, and make his work in the room that much quicker.

The library was a quaint space. Shelves layered in books adorned both facing walls. A petite stone fireplace split the rows of books on the west wall, and two tall-back cushioned chairs sat in front of the remnants of yesterday's fire. The largest piece of furniture in the room was a desk made of some sort of dark wood. It was located straight ahead, facing the only window in the room. A colorful rug sat comfortably on the floor, making movement in the room that much easier - the soft layer absorbing Phin's footfalls.

As he took in the whole of the space, Phin thought that this was just the kind of library he would design for himself if ever given the chance. In that moment, he felt a connection to Vaughn O'Leary, as if the two adversaries might not be so different from each other. That thought faded as quickly as it arrived, Phin's eyes falling on the bundle of clothes and gear he'd seen two days prior. He took up the assortment of items and began sifting through them.

A boot, some torn clothes with blood stains, a bit of trash and some camping and cooking gear. He found Jorge's wallet in the backpack. When he turned on the cell phone, it still had a small charge on the battery. Sure enough it was Jason's.

This was the proof Phin needed to confront Vaughn O'Leary. Why had he held this back and not given it to Jason? Why had he insisted nothing had been found in their searches of the area?

Phin pocketed the phone and took pictures of the rest of the items with his own phone. He didn't want it to conveniently go missing and there be no proof. He was ready to leave until one other item caught his eye. He almost resisted the urge to look because he wasn't here for such things. But the ancient book sitting on the small table next to one of the fireside chairs called to him. Phin was a sucker for old books. He would take but the slightest of glimpses and then be on his way. That was his intention anyway...until he saw the title. Written across the weathered leather cover in gold embossed script were four words that froze Phin like a stone pillar.

*The Journal of Meshach.*

This was impossible. Phin reached out in reverence, the tips of his fingers gingerly grazing the title script. Could it truly be? Was this the same Meshach from the Bible? The book of Daniel? The Meshach that had been kidnapped from his home in Israel as a teenager and subscribed to Babylonian servitude? The same Meshach that served the royal family with honor for the whole of his life and then, in the family's greatest hour of distress, had orchestrated their flight to the West?

To Ireland?

To here?

It was beyond comprehension that these could be his words. His story. *The Journal of Meshach.* That such a volume even existed was overwhelming to consider.

Phin eased into the cushioned chair, taking up the tome. He carefully opened its cover and immersed himself in its content.

The first page answered all his questions.

Yes, it was Meshach. *The* Meshach. There could only be one, Phin allowed himself. What he held in his hands was of immense historical importance. He knew it at once. Written in the author's native Hebrew, Phin had no trouble at all reading the story it contained, as he was fluent in the language of the Old Testament himself. The story it contained was magical. Phin was enveloped by a euphoria he had rarely known. How long he sat there he did not know. Time lost meaning in the pages of this peek at history.

Then the story took a dark turn. A familiar cloud revealed itself on the parchment. A cloud that Phin recognized immediately. The same cloud that he'd been under. That they all had been under since coming to Tiamat. And just like that a huge piece of the puzzle fell into place and Phin understood. His heart raced. He needed to tell Autumn. He had to let Jason know.

"Good evening, Dr. Crook." An unfriendly but familiar voice jolted Phin from his trance. "It looks like you and I have much to discuss."

# CHAPTER 37

"Please, keep your seat Dr. Crook." Vaughn O'Leary was standing in the doorway, his features concealed by shadows of the dimly lit room. He held in one hand a steaming kettle of water. "Perhaps some evening tea would be in order. May I prepare you a cup?" His sauntered over to a small table behind the door where an arrangement of chinaware and tea bags were set.

"Yes, of course. I'll have whatever you are having." Phin chided himself internally for being caught in the act, as it were. It was the second time Vaughn O'Leary had caught him unawares. He was better than this. He observed, however, that Vaughn's own movements were whisper quiet. He too was one used to coming and going without notice. In Vaughn O'Leary, Phin felt he had met his match, of sorts. He wondered if Vaughn felt the same about him. Theirs had been a dance the last few days. A game of cat and mouse. Now the mouse was caught. The only question left to be answered was - *who was the cat and who was the mouse?*

Phin remained quiet as Vaughn poured two cups of hot water and slid a tea bag into each. He complemented each pairing with a stir spoon, and passed Phin's to him on a saucer.

A quiet tension in the room was prolonged a bit longer as Vaughn loaded the fireplace with wood and tender. He doused it all in kerosene from a tin can on the hearth's ledge, and then lit the whole thing with a wooden match that resulted in a mighty *WHOOSH!* The tinder caught and the wood began the familiar crackle as Vaughn took his own seat.

"I trust you've made yourself at home, Dr. Crook." Vaughn's voice was even. Measured. He took a sip of tea.

"I thought we were on a first name basis, *Vaughn*," Phin replied.

"Friends are on a first name basis. I'm not sure we are friends anymore. You did, after all, violate the lock on my private library. Hospitality has it limits, even in America, I assume."

"When locks are used to conceal lies and the private property of others, then the breach of those locks is considered by most to be an act of nobility. Even in Ireland, I assume." Phin returned the barb.

As if considering his next words, Vaughn took a moment. "And you shall know the truth, and the truth shall set you free." He gave nod to the book in Phin's lap.

"The words of Jesus. John chapter eight. Speaking to his disciples. Out of context in this instance, but true nonetheless."

"The truth may not always reveal what you hope it will, Dr. Crook." Vaughn sat back, taking a sip of tea before continuing. "Let me ask you a question. What is your greatest fear? What keeps you up at night? What is the one thing that creates dread in you, that threatens to steal the joy of life itself?"

Phin paused at the series of questions. This was not what he expected. For the first time interacting with his host, he was caught off balance. Where was he going with this? Yet, his questioning struck a chord. He chose to follow the line Vaughn was drawing to see where it would take him.

"Death. The greatest fear one has is death." He admitted as a matter of fact.

"No!" Vaughn snapped the teacup onto the saucer with too much force. A clank and a splash of liquid over the side was the result. "Come now, Dr. Crook." He'd calmed himself, his voice returning to its even tone. "That is too easy. A man of your pedigree, of your belief, does not fear death. You are a Christian, are you not? Eternal life awaits you when you die. Or am I mistaken? It is not death that you fear, or that any one of us fears? Death is but the end. The end of that which we all truly do fear."

Phin pondered the riddle and finally whispered the first word that came to his mind. "Control."

"Yes." Vaughn smiled, seemingly pleased. "Now you and I have found a common understanding." Phin still did not know where Vaughn was leading him, but he was starting to grasp where the man was coming from. "We all will die, Dr. Crook. It is inevitable. But *how* we die...now that is what every man and woman who has ever lived truly fears. Because we don't know. And that is what scares us all - terrifies us. You say control, Dr. Crook. But what you mean is *lack* of control. None of us knows or has control over that which shall finally usher us into the by and by. For some it is cancer. For others an automobile accident. Still others are murdered. And then some, the lucky few, die of old age in their sleep. But even those fortunate souls still live in fear. As each day of their aged lives pass, as friends die one after another until they are the only ones left, they wonder when their final day will come. When will death come calling and in what manner? And that...*that* Dr. Crook, is their greatest fear. Because they have *no control.*"

"What is it *you* fear, Vaughn O'Leary?" Phin asked. He was trying to spin Vaughn's words back onto him. "What is it you are trying to control that you cannot?"

"And so now we arrive at the heart of the matter, do we not, Dr. Crook?" Vaughn let escape a mild chuckle as he spoke. "I think you know. Or at least you may think you know. But then again, Dr. Crook, you may not know as much as you think you know."

The circular talk irritated Phin. "It's this book, isn't it?" he said, finally closing *The Journal of Meshach,* gently patting the worn cover. "Let me tell you what I think I know. The residents of this town. All of you. You are not from here. Oh, you are in terms of being born and raised here. But this is not where you are *from.*" Phin emphasized the final word of his sentence. Vaughn's eyes gleamed in the firelight, urging him to continue. "You are Babylonian in origin. Modern day Iraqis, if you will. But you are not commoners in your ancestry. Oh, no. You are all the descendants of the *royal* family of the Babylonian Empire. Going back to

King Belshazzar. Your ancestors were spirited out of Babylon as it fell to the Medo-Persian Empire. All orchestrated by the hand of an old Jew named...Meshach." Phin once again deferred to the large book in his lap. "How am I doing so far?"

"Very well, but go on. You have more to say, I am sure."

"Yes. So, here you are now. In Ireland. On the northern coast. As far as one could go in the known world of the ancients. And here you have stayed. A casual walk around town makes it obvious that you all share a common genealogy. But what puzzles me, and has since I put the pieces together, is why? Why has this community stayed closed to the rest of the world... for twenty-five hundred years? That's a staggering amount of time. It defies all common sense as well as human nature. It's natural for people to spread out and marry. To intermarry and to reproduce. But I suspect no such thing has happened here at all. Everyone born in Tiamat grows up in Tiamat, marries in Tiamat, and dies in Tiamat. Extraordinary measures must have been taken to preserve such purity. And so then again, my question. Why? Why all of this, unless...." Phin stopped, trying to work it out.

"Yes, Dr. Crook. Go on." Vaughn compelled him.

"Control." Phin said. Vaughn nodded. "This whole town is an exercise in control. Which means...there is a great fear here of losing it. So, it's my turn, I think. Tell me, Vaughn, what is it that you and all the people here in Tiamat fear? The one thing you dread and that keeps *you* awake at night?"

"You are holding the answer, Dr. Crook."

Phin looked down at *The Journal of Meshach*. He'd not had time to read it all but he had read enough, and more puzzle pieces were sliding into place. "You brought something with you from Babylon, didn't you? Something that threatens to-"

"Vaughn!" A loud voice thundered down the hall, cutting Phin off. "Vaughn O'Leary, come quick." Ross McCloud burst into the library, out of breath. He eyed Phin but went on. "Vaughn, we have a problem!"

"What is it, Ross?" He asked, rising immediately to his feet.

"It's the Morris fellow. Mr. Crook's friend here."

"Jason?" Phin asked, standing as well. "What's happened?"

"Not sure, but it's not good. He never came home this evening. Thought he was with you all day. I went looking after the sun went down and found this about halfway from the house to here." He held up what looked like an old stick. Phin's heart rose in his chest when he realized what Ross McCloud was holding.

It was Jason's cane.

"Jason left us after lunch. He was headed to your house to rest and finish the day."

"Never made it," Ross said matter-of-factly, concern on his face. "Vaughn, we don't need anything else."

"Show us where you found the cane," Phin demanded.

The three men rushed out of the bed and breakfast and jogged past the roundabout and down the street, headed out of town and toward the McCloud home. The businesses gave way to homes and those began to thin when Ross stopped.

"It was right around here. I came walking toward town to find him. Didn't really think anything had gone wrong. Just thought he was with you and maybe lost track of time. I was going to escort him back to the house, it being dark and all."

Vaughn flicked on a torch and handed another one to Phin. Ross had his already on, having led the way. "Let's fan out and have a look around."

The three triangulated and moved in opposite directions. Phin crossed the road and was sweeping his flashlight across an area of tall grass. He spied a lump of something about five feet away and moved to pick it up.

"Hey, what's going on out here?! It's after curfew." A new figure with his own torch and a large shotgun came jogging out of the night, coming from the direction of town.

"It's us, Harv," Vaughn yelled back to Harv Conner, who was now standing in the road in the center of the three. "I've got Ross and Dr. Phineas Crook with me. Something's happened to the Morris boy. The one staying at Ross's house."

"What do you mean something's happened? Is it bad?" Harv asked, standing his ground.

Phin held up a blue denim jacket in one hand, his flashlight in the other hand illuminating it. It was identical to the one Jason had worn earlier in the day, except this one was torn with a red smear on the inside.

"Yes!" Phin yelled back. "It's bad."

# CHAPTER 38

"Let me see that." Vaughn O'Leary jogged over to Phin, taking the jacket in hand. He examined it under torchlight. "You sure this belonged to Jason?" he asked Phin.

"What do you mean, am I sure? He was wearing a jacket. One just like this. It's lying in the same area that his cane was found." Phin was appalled at the question. "There's obviously a problem with a torn jacket with blood on it no matter who it belongs to. Wouldn't you agree?"

"Give it to me." Ross McCloud stepped in, taking the jacket from Vaughn. "Yep, this is the same one we gave him from our house. It belongs to my boy, Tommy. See here, it has his name on the label. But this red stain isn't blood. It's paint. Tommy somehow got paint on the inside of this jacket back before...he left." He shined his light on his son's name, clearly written in dark black ink from a Sharpie, the dried paint stain also visible.

"Well, I'd say that settles it. The question is, what happened and how long ago?" Phin's mind was racing. How could something happen to Jason again? It seemed too odd for it to be a coincidence. But foul play? Why? It didn't make any sense. Just as he was beginning to figure out what made Tiamat, Tiamat, this strange place threw another curve ball. That it involved Jason made it intensely personal. Phin determined inside himself that he was not going to rest until all was made right.

The priority now was finding Jason. The tear in the jacket meant he was taken by force, and given his fragile state he may even be hurt again. But how badly?

"I'd say it was hours ago," Harv began to answer. "He never made it to my house, like I said. That's why I came looking for him in the first place."

"We have the curfew in place for a reason. It's for everyone's protection. He shouldn't have been out in the first place, and certainly not alone," Vaughn O'Leary charged.

The town council leader's accusatory attitude inflamed Phin - as if it was Jason's fault that he'd been attacked...a second time. "The curfew only applies to the evening, Vaughn. After dark. Jason left me and my wife right after lunch. I'd say around one-thirty, but not much after. Even if he took his time and rested along the way, he'd have been to the McCloud's by two-thirty at the latest. A solid two hours or more of daylight left. You're the head of the town council and the law in this town, Vaughn."

"What exactly are you saying?" Vaughn shot back.

"I'm saying this whole thing stinks and you know it. And don't give me some crap about an animal attack. Not in broad daylight. Somebody, not something, jumped him and took him. The question is why. Why him?"

"You're not suggesting one of us had anything to do with this, are you?" Vaughn gestured broadly, his arm sweeping back toward town.

"Absolutely, I am. Who else would it be? You said it yourself. Nobody comes to Tiamat. Just the occasional tourist," Phin mocked with air quotes. "And last I checked, my wife, Jason, and I are the only visitors you have. So, unless you've got another explanation..." Phin let his last words hang in the air. He'd struck a chord. He could feel it. He could see it in the eyes of each person gathered around him. All members of the town council, he suddenly realized.

The keepers of secrets.

They knew.

They each knew there was more going on. Much more. And now they knew that he knew.

Ross McCloud broke the silence. "I'm gonna go get Furman Hayes. We need to find the boy quick. It's only been a few hours. Maybe they've not gotten far. Harv, why don't you get Buster? He's the best bloodhound in town. Let him smell this jacket and maybe we can follow the scent."

"Hold on a second," Vaughn called for the pause.

"Yes, hold on a minute," Phin agreed but for a different reason. He was still trying to understand. "Who is *they*?"

"Excuse me?" Ross McCloud asked.

"You said, *they. Maybe they've not gotten far.* Who took Jason? You know, don't you?"

Ross McCloud looked to Vaughn O'Leary for direction.

"Why are you looking at him? Look at *me*. Answer *me*. Who did this? What's going on here, Ross? Just tell me."

"We need to tell him, Vaughn."

"There's nothing to tell," the town leader shouted. It was the first sign of him coming unraveled that Phin had seen. "It was an animal. Just like last week. They roam these parts and have been killing our livestock. It's unfortunate but-"

"Just stop it!" Phin matched his volume. "There is no animal. At least none that would do this. What is it that you are hiding here? What are you trying to keep from the rest of the world? I know about this town." He decided to switch gears. "I know about your heritage. Where you all come from." He was looking at Harv Connor and Ross McCloud now - appealing to the two men - looking back and forth at their dark brown middle-eastern eyes. Even in the dim light of a cloudy night, he could see that he was connecting. In that moment he chose to step out on a limb. He didn't understand fully but he had put together enough. A reasonable guess. "Tell me about the monsters of Tiamat."

Harv Connor broke eye contact and looked down at the ground. Ross McCloud took in a deep breath and was about to speak.

"What do you mean by monsters?" Vaughn O'Leary beat Ross in replying to Phin.

"I've read the book. *The Journal of Meshach*. Not all of it, but enough. There's something here, isn't there? Something that was brought here from Babylon over two millennia ago. And now you've lost control. Isn't that what you fear, Vaughn? Losing control of the monsters? Losing control of the secret of Tiamat?" Phin was firing blindly but he could tell some of his shots were hitting the target.

"You know nothing of what we fear, Crook," Vaughn spat in contempt at the college professor from America. "You know nothing about us at all. And what you do know makes you dangerous."

"Vaughn, that's enough." Ross McCloud stepped toward the leader of Tiamat.

"No, it's not. This man comes into our town. *Our* town. Not his. He presumes to know who we are and why we are. And he dares to lecture us on fear. Let me tell you something, Dr. Crook. You know nothing of true fear. But you will."

"Vaughn! Enough! He's right," Ross asserted himself. "We *have* lost control. We've got two people missing now. This has to stop. Now. Tonight. We've got a real chance of tracking Jason Morris. The scent is fresh. We need to move now and we can figure out the rest later."

Phin sensed that Vaughn O'Leary was not used to anyone standing up to him. Especially a simple gunsmith like Ross McCloud. Phin was close. So close to the whole truth. But that would have to wait for now. "Look, Jason Morris is a dear friend of mine. I feel responsible for his wellbeing. I just want to find him and Jorge Ramirez if we can. I'm not interested in hurting this town or the people in it. Truly. Please, I just need your help. I can't do anything without you."

The appeal worked. "I'm going to get Furman and then stop at my shop for some weapons. Harv, get your dog. Vaughn, knock on a few doors on your way back to town, see if anyone heard or saw anything unusual this afternoon.

Let's meet in front of the Lear House in a half hour and head out." Ross McCloud had officially taken charge of the search effort it seemed. Vaughn O'Leary didn't fight back, although his silent seething remained. Phin breathed a sigh of relief.

The four men began the march back to town at a quickened pace. Vaughn broke away first, to knock on the door of a house they passed. Harv Connor pealed off second, heading down a side street toward his own home. Ross McCloud escorted Phin back to the bed and breakfast.

"Mr. Crook," he began.

"Please, just call me Phin. I appreciate your help. I really do. And I'm sorry for how heated I got back there."

"Don't worry about it. We've all been under a lot of stress. But let's find Jason first. And we will." He reached up and gave Phin's arm a warm squeeze and then jogged away toward his gun shop.

Phin felt the tension drain from his shoulders. He hadn't realized the stress he'd carried in his muscles until that moment. He'd had a breakthrough, he believed. Somebody in this crazy town was finally on his side.

He needed to let Autumn know what was going on and to pack a bag for the search. He stepped inside the Lear House. It was dark and quiet. Peaceful. The house still slept. The stress of the last hour began to fade with each step he took up the stairs toward his guestroom. He was still desperately worried about Jason, but he had the feeling everything was going to be alright.

That feeling evaporated the moment he opened the door to his room. The first thing he noticed - the covers of the bed were pulled back. The second thing he noticed was the book Autumn read each night before she drifted to sleep. It was lying on the floor, face down and splayed open. The third thing he noticed was a drop of blood the size of a dime on his wife's pillow. The fourth thing he noticed...Autumn was gone.

# CHAPTER 39

Phineas Crook slammed his fist onto the roof of his rental car, leaving a dent.

He didn't care.

He was standing on the street in front of the Lear House. Vaughn O'Leary was trying to console him but he would have none of it. Ross McCloud was close by with a small arsenal of what looked like handguns. Harv Connor had retrieved Furman Hayes and filled him in on the situation with the missing Jason Morris.

And now this.

Autumn Crook was missing, taken from her room, presumably against her will.

"The time for secrets is over," Phin bellowed. He was loud but he didn't care. Nobody else was out. Instead, the citizenry was abiding by the nightly curfew which descended on the town as the sun set each evening. "I want to know what is going on in this town. I want to know everything. My friend is gone and now my wife. Just in the last hour. Somebody took her and I want to know who. And then I want to find him and...*Ahhhhhh!*" He let out another yell.

"You either tell him or I will," Ross McCloud directed to Vaughn O'Leary. "He already knows where we come from. He knows our origin. And he knows about the...what did you call them, Dr. Crook? Monsters? Well, not exactly, but you might as well know the truth. It does us no good to try to hide it any longer. Too many people are involved now. Too many outsiders. No offense," he finished, looking at Phin.

Ross McCloud's words took the edge off of Phin's frantic rage. He was growing to like this man more and more. He was the one reasonable person, maybe, in the whole of Tiamat. Phin thought that if he could just get some answers, just get his head around what was really going on here, if he could understand what was happening, then he would know better what to do. But regardless, he was at the mercy of this group of men. This was their town, their problem, as much as it was his. They knew the lay of the land. He had no idea where to even start.

He looked at Buster, Harv Connor's hunting dog. He was restless for the hunt, pacing back and forth, but held back by a thick rope in the hands of his owner. Phin was restless too, but could hold himself back if someone in this group was ready to talk, to give him the answers he needed now more than ever. What had started off as a side trip to help a dear friend had become a fight between life and death. Phin tamped down his fear in expectation of finishing the puzzle in his mind.

Vaughn O'Leary nodded in assent. He took a deep breath and began. "What I am about to tell you affects every citizen of Tiamat on the most personal of levels. It's something not for the world, for the world would simply not understand. I think, however, that you might, Dr. Crook...given your religious pedigree. And Ross is correct. You've been pulled into our secret in a way none of us wanted. But, sadly, our reality has now become yours. You call them monsters, but they are not. At least not fully. In essence, they are our children."

Phin took in this stunning bit of information. "You don't mean...your *children?*"

"That's exactly what I mean. You already know the background of how Tiamat came into existence. Two-and-a-half millennia ago, our ancestors fled our ancient homeland of Babylon. Modern day Iraq, if you will. The savagery of the Medes and Persians descended on the great capitol city. But one loyal servant, a Jew named Meshach, orchestrated an exodus for the royal family. He knew from his own experience what an invading army will do. His actions spared the royal family the same indignity they had thrust upon others. And so, our people left - fled in the dark of night, on the same night that the fool king, Belshazzar, was drinking himself under. He died but the rest of us survived."

Phin knew all of this, of course. The history of Malphious that Jason had discovered under the Temple Mount in Jerusalem told the story. The artifact trail of Babylonian remnants backed it up. And Phin's stunning reading of *The Journal of Meshach* had confirmed it all. And more. And it was the more that Phin craved to now know.

"And your people moved across the Mediterranean and Europe and found themselves here, in north Ireland. The end of the world as far as they could know at the time. A place that they believed would be safe and where your ancestors could live at peace." Phin filled in the blanks.

"Yes, that is right. Or at least that was the hope. And in the very beginning it was peaceful. Until we realized that we brought something with us. We call it the King's Disease. It's a curse, really. It began with the great King Nebuchadnezzar. The greatest king in the history of the Babylonian Empire, perhaps in the history of all the world. Legend is all we have to go on, but legend reveals that he came in conflict with your God."

"The legend you're referring to is the Bible," Phin corrected. "What you call legend I call truth and it continues to surprise people even today - and sometimes even me. I think I know where you're going with this, but please continue." Phin's heart was beating faster with anticipation.

The truth was coming out. Finally.

"As I said, your God and King Nebuchadnezzar came into conflict. In a sign of power and superiority, your God inflicted a curse upon King Nebuchadnezzar."

Phin couldn't help himself. "The book of Daniel, chapter four. Wolfman's Disease."

"Very good, Dr. Crook. You are familiar with the curse."

"Well, it's a condition really. A mental state. The medical community refers to it as *lycanthropy*. It's a psychiatric syndrome whereby the person afflicted imagines that they transform into a wolf. In severe cases, victims refuse to bathe, groom themselves, etc. They even quit cutting their hair and nails and they stop eating normal food. They are convinced that they've shape-shifted into a wolf or some wild animal. The Bible records that King Nebuchadnezzar suffered from the condition for seven years until he finally submitted to the will of God – that God was greater than he was."

"Again, I am impressed, Dr. Crook. But what if I told you that this curse was more than a psychiatric condition? And what if I told you that it persisted in the royal family of Babylon beyond King Nebuchadnezzar?"

Phin didn't know what to say. What was Vaughn trying to communicate to him? "You're not saying that people actually turn into wolves, are you? Why, that's ridiculous. Such a thing is not possible."

"And yet your friend and wife are missing. And that same friend and his companion were attacked just over a week ago."

"But not by a...good lord, man...you're talking about a werewolf! A human turned into a wolf. That's the stuff of horror and fiction." Phin was beside himself at what was being suggested. He had never considered such an outrageous explanation. Why would he?

"It's the stuff of your own Bible, Dr. Crook. You even said that you believe it all to be true."

"But King Nebuchadnezzar didn't actually become a werewolf. He just-" Phin stopped himself, trying to recall the biblical account in the book of Daniel.

Harv Connor's gravelly voice entered the conversation, loud and strong. *"Immediately the word of God was fulfilled against Nebuchadnezzar. He was driven from among men and ate grass like an ox, and his body was wet with the dew of heaven till his hair grew as long as eagles' feathers, and his nails were like birds' claws.* Daniel chapter four. We all know the words of the curse. But they are not merely words to us in Tiamat. They are our reality."

Phin absorbed the recitation of his own Holy Scriptures. They spoke to him now in a new way, like looking into the night sky and seeing the stars for the first time.

"We brought the curse with us," Vaughn O'Leary continued in a somber tone. "Our ancestors did. What your Bible does not tell you is that after the curse left King Nebuchadnezzar, it carried on, but only within the royal family. It's not a disease that can be contracted. It's not contagious. It doesn't work that way."

"How exactly does it work?" Phin couldn't believe he was being pulled along in this crazy reality. Yet, these men were not joking with him. And he'd experienced enough in this world to know that matters of the supernatural can cross over in unexpected ways.

"The curse strikes at random. And it strikes the next generation, usually in the late teen years to early 20s, but not always. But it always lasts for seven years," Ross McCloud answered this time. "It begins with a fever - usually lasting a week or more. Then the afflicted begin to lose their minds. They have no desire for hygiene and their taste for normal food fades. Communication becomes difficult and they can be violent. Then the eyes change. That's how we know for sure the curse has taken hold. We call it the *turning.*"

"Greg Collins!" Phin exclaimed. "That's what happened to the Collins boy. He...his eyes were yellow and you said he had a fever. He was...what did you say? Turning. Right?" Phin couldn't believe it. He ran his hand through his hair as was his habit when thinking.

"Yes, you witnessed one of our people turning. It was unfortunate you saw that. No one outside of Tiamat ever has," Vaughn inserted. "It wasn't that we weren't concerned for your wellbeing. I know it may have seemed that way. But our primary concern was for Greg. His parents were devastated, of course. It will be seven years before he returns."

A spark ignited in Phin's mind, like a flash of lightning too close. It jolted him. He looked at Ross McCloud. "You said that your son was *returning* in the spring – Tommy. That's what you said." And to Vaughn O'Leary, "You said your son, Lucious. You said he was returning any day. That he'd been gone seven years." It was all nearly too much for Phin to process at one time. "Not returning...but *re-turning*. That's what you meant, isn't it? That they are changing back. From being wolves!" Phin steadied himself against the little Ford Ka. The men were silent. An almost reverent silence.

"That's right," Ross finally answered. "Seven years and then they re-turn. My wife and I've been waiting for our Tommy to come home for six-and-a-half years. Our wait is almost over. It's really hard, as you can only imagine. Unbearably so at times."

"I'm sorry for your...loss. I'm not even sure if that's the right word. I apologize. I've got so many questions though. How many...how many wolves are we talking about? We've mentioned three so far. Lucious, Tommy, and now Greg Collins."

"Eleven," Vaughn replied straightaway, a very matter-of-fact tone. "There are always eleven. As soon as one returns, another turns. Not immediately, but usually within a week or so. And there's no rhyme or reason to it. The curse strikes who it wills. Totally random."

"Tiamat," Phin whispered.

"Excuse me?" Vaughn asked.

"Tiamat. The name of your town. The ancient goddess of creation."

"I see. So, you know about that as well. Very good, Dr. Crook. Yes, once our ancestors realized the curse had followed them all the way from Babylon to Ireland, they chose the name of Tiamat for the town." After a pause, "It seemed...appropriate."

"The eleven monsters of Tiamat. The eleven wolves." Phin spoke softly again. Then his thoughts shifted back to Autumn and Jason. "These...wolves...they took my wife? They just roam around in the woods for seven years?" He was incredulous at the thought.

"No. Of course not." Harv Connor spoke up this time. The roughness of his voice startled them all. "We keep 'em caged up. Down by the beach just below the bluff there's a cave."

"You keep them in a *cage*?"

"I know it seems savage, Dr. Crook. But you must trust us. This is the best way. Our priority is to keep them safe. From themselves and from others. And to protect this great secret. I can see you are struggling to understand – to believe. Can you imagine how the rest of the world would respond? It's imperative that no one knows. But now you do know, Dr. Crook, and now you must carry the burden with us."

"They broke out, didn't they?" Phin asked. He'd finally put it all together. "That's what happened to Jason and Jorge. That's why the curfew. Something went wrong a week ago."

"Yes," Ross McCloud answered. "Somehow a group of them escaped. They killed one of the two young men guarding them at the time. His name was Blake Lynch. His brother was with him and he's been missing since. Same as your boy, Jason's friend."

"And now Jason and my wife are also missing. But my wife was in her room. Inside the hotel. She wasn't out and about."

"I know. That part is very...troubling," Ross admitted. "Not all of the wolves escaped. Just five. One was killed that same night. A boy named Sid. We use tranquilizers to put 'em down. But...well there was an accident with Sid. We recaptured another one a few days ago."

"So, there are three still out there. Is that what you're saying?"

"That's right. My son...Tommy...is free. And so is Lucious O'Leary, and then another named Vance Talley. Vance isn't going to return for four years yet."

"And we don't know who took Jason and my wife?" Phin didn't say it out loud, but he wondered if Lucious O'Leary had come home and found Autumn.

"No, we don't," Vaughn answered quickly. "But we *will* find them."

Harv Connor interjected loudly, "That's right Crook. Now that we have a fresh scent to work off of, my dog here will track 'em down for us. But we need to get going. Enough talk."

A loud yell broke the night sky. All five men instinctively looked up.

*"Look out belowwww!!!"* the voice boomed.

A dark shadow descended out of the sky at a rapid rate. A black rucksack hit the grassy roundabout, followed by a black clad figure. A thump and a roll and he was on his feet, his parachute billowing in the night breeze.

The group was stunned.

With military precision, the figure unclipped from the chute and stalked right over to the group of men, ripping off his head gear, revealing a buzzed flattop.

"Who in the...who are you?!" Vaughn O'Leary stammered.

Phineas Crook broke into a wide grin and answered before the new arrival could. "This, my friends, is Sergeant Billy Warren."

# PART 3

# ANOTHER LONG
# NIGHT

*The king has lost his mind.*

*Not in the same way as the great king Nebuchadnezzar those many years ago, but then again, Belshazzar is not Nebuchadnezzar. He is a fool king who has surrounded himself with fool advisors. The city is being marched upon. The dread of the Medes and the Persians is coming to us here. Soon the city will be sieged, I fear, and then there will be no escape.*

*Thankfully, not all in the royal court are as delusional as the king. We've all heard the stories of what the Medes and the Persians are capable of. There will be rape and murder. The city will be plundered for its wealth. No one will be spared, including the king's family - especially the king's family. I have lived this before. When Nebuchadnezzar himself, with the power of Babylon, marched on my home. The beloved city of Jerusalem. Nebuchadnezzar was a ruthless warrior. Many in my family were murdered, and the rest of us - the young ones - were taken. I am thankful to my God that I found favor in the eyes of the great king. He softened after the period of the curse and finished his reign with dignity.*

*Belshazzar has no dignity. He drinks until he is drunk. Mighty Babylon has already fallen. He just does not know it. It will soon be the footstool of Persia. Another trophy in the beast's march across the world. Even now the king plans a party for all his fool friends for the night after next. By then, the Medes and Persians will be on our doorstep.*

*There must be action now. We can wait no longer. I was a young man when Babylon came for my family. But now my years are expanded, having reached the mark of eighty. My strength is not as it was. I cannot endure another exodus in chains. I am too old. What strength I have left I will use to serve the king even though he knows it not.*

*Arrangements have been made. Thankfully, others see the folly of this king and have listened to my counsel. They know my story. They know what awaits those who are of royalty when they are conquered by their foes. All has been done quietly and with many whispers, but when the time comes, we will leave. All except the cursed ones, those with the King's Disease, as it has come to be known. It would be impossible to take them. Impractical. Perhaps the Medes and Persians will have pity on them when they observe their horrid condition. I will lead the court and family west. It will be an exodus of another kind. Not by force but by choice. May Yahweh guide us and lead us and grant us favor. I doubt the king will go with us. He will likely die with a drink in his hand.*

From the Journal of Meshach,
Royal court recorder for the king

Twenty-fourth day of the month of Tišritum,
The seventeenth year of the king's reign (539 BC)

# CHAPTER 40

"We're hunting for *what*?!"

Phin had tried his best to explain to Sergeant Billy Warren the situation at hand. That's who Billy Warren was – a situation man. He was all about the mission. So Phin sped through the details of Babylonian history and the migration to Ireland and focused on the problem at hand. His wife and good friend were missing, taken within the last few hours. Time was critical. The hard part was getting Billy to understand *who* had taken them.

"Okay, doc, let me get this straight. We're lookin' for three perps who've kidnapped the missus and our boy Jason. But not just any three perps. We're looking for wolves. But not real wolves. Men who have turned into wolves. Do I have that about right?"

Phin slowly nodded and gave a hesitant, "Yes. Pretty much."

"Holy mother of pearl, Doc. You're talkin' about freakin' werewolves. When you called for help earlier, you didn't say nothin' about werewolves." Sergeant Warren balled both hands into fists, cracking the knuckles on his right. He spat on the ground and pulled a strong sniff through his nostrils.

"I still don't know how you made it here so fast. When I called you said you'd hustle but I had no idea." The call for help Phin made after lunch was to Billy Warren. The two men had a brief but intense history. They'd not always been on the same page or seen eye-to-eye, but traveling to the ends of the earth and facing life, death, and pure evil has a way of bonding two souls. Phin felt very strongly about the friendship he'd forged with Billy Warren and vice versa.

The sergeant was retired military. The Marines. He was hard as nails, outside and in. He'd recently been promoted to special operations coordinator for LaPhage Industries after the deaths of its founder Charles LaPhage and his daughter, Ruth, back in the summer. LaPhage Industries was a research conglomerate with tentacles all over the world. When Phin and Billy Warren had parted ways after the events in the Garden of Eden, the sergeant had exhorted Phin to *call me if you ever need me.* And he meant it. Billy Warren never said anything he didn't mean.

When Phin was faced with the missing Jorge Ramirez and the uncooperative citizenry of Tiamat earlier in the day – that seemed so long ago now – he'd finally decided to call in the big guns. He could think of no bigger gun than Sergeant Billy Warren.

The sergeant picked up on the first ring. After hearing that his friend was in need, his response was simple: "Shoot me a pin drop of your location, Doc. And I'll be there A-sap."

Now that Autumn and Jason were also missing - especially Autumn, his heart twisted in his chest every time he thought about her - he was even more relieved Billy Warren had arrived.

"I was in Germany when you called, Doc. I'd been here sooner but had to nail down some gear and take care of a few details. Once we were wheels up, I was only two hours from your locale. No place to land so the quickest way was to just jump. And here I am." Warren spoke about jumping out of a plane in the black of night over unknown territory as if everyone did it. It gave Phin the chills to think about. The other men only gawked. "But let's get back to this business of the werewolves. I didn't bring no silver bullets, Doc. I hope that ain't gonna be a problem. But if it is, just get me some silver jewelry and I'll melt it down real quick and make some." He was serious.

"Look, good sir," Vaughn O'Leary finally spoke. "I don't know you and you don't know us. But there will be no killing tonight. These aren't animals we are looking for. It's difficult to explain. Your crude understanding will do, but it is imperative that there be no loss of life."

Sergeant Warren sized up the six-foot-tall O'Leary, sharply dressed with hair slicked back and a black crisp goatee on his chin only. He addressed Phin but pointed at Vaughn. "Who is that?"

"Vaughn O'Leary. Head of the town council. He's also the law around here," Phin replied.

"Oh, I get it. A politician. I don't like politicians."

Vaughn O'Leary turned red, but before he could respond Phin inserted himself and explained to the group who Billy Warren was. His background and skill would be invaluable. He could be trusted, and of high importance to the leaders of Tiamat, he was confidential. Sergeant Warren carried his own cache of secrets. Of most importance to Phin, he was someone who was unquestionably on his side. Phin appreciated being initiated into the inner workings of all that was Tiamat – its history and curse – but he was still an outsider. Their concerns were not his. Phin wanted to get his friend and wife back, alive. And he wanted to solve the mystery of the missing Jorge Ramirez.

It was clear that none of the men in the group liked this sudden insertion of another outsider. Just like that, he too knew about the curse of Tiamat. The secret they had so successfully kept for over two thousand years was breaking free under their watch. But the sense of urgency - no, panic - was unmistakable. Matters had grown beyond their control. Three people - three additional outsiders - were missing, and if any one, or more, of them were found alive, the pool of non-Tiamatians in the know would grow.

Phin addressed the men pointedly. "Look, I know that you all are worried. You're worried that you've lost control. That the secret is out. Well, that's true. You have lost control. Your greatest fears are coming true and you are powerless to stop it. At least that's how it feels. Let me just say, I'm scared too. I feel like I've lost all control as well. My wife," he choked up at the mention of his Autumn, "my bride, is out there. Taken by one of the sons of Tiamat. He's not in his right mind, I understand that. So, I want you to know that I don't hold that against him and I don't hold it against any of you. I wish you had been honest from the very beginning, but again, I understand why you weren't. I can't say I would have acted any differently had I been in your shoes. But here's what I do know...the six of us — myself and the sergeant here included — the six of us can fix this. We will worry later about the consequences of us knowing what we know. I can assure you, we have no desire to hurt you or anyone in this town. But whatever has happened here, whatever is going on out there - in the dark of night - with the people we all love...it ends tonight."

Phin's speech seemed to be good enough for the four men of Tiamat. They each broke to the side and began to check the small packs they had brought with them. Phin walked away about twenty feet to find a space all his own. He was sorting through his own pack of gear — a flashlight, extra batteries, and a long, wickedly serrated knife like the one in the Rambo movies. He took it out and threaded the leather sheath through his belt, securing it on his left hip. He had some water and snacks as well. He had no idea how long they'd be out looking for Autumn and Jason, but he had no intention of coming back without them.

He felt a presence walk up behind him. Looking over his shoulder, he knew it was Sergeant Warren.

"What's on your mind, Doc? Something's got you shook. I can tell."

"Thanks for coming, Billy. I really mean it. Thanks. You're timing, as usual, is perfect. Not sure how I'd be getting ready to go out there without you."

"Ah, come on, brother. You're stronger than you think you are. Don't forget, I've seen you in action."

"I'm just so...crap...I don't even know how to say it, Billy."

"Scared. You're scared. It's okay. You can say it."

Phin sniffed and wiped a tear threatening to form in his eye.

"Look, Doc. Everybody gets scared. It's natural. When I was lying in a pool of my own blood in Beirut back when that Akbar chick blew me up, I was scared. And when I woke up in Walter Reed without an arm and a leg...bro, you better believe I'd never been more frightened in my entire life." Warren reviewed his resume for Phin - the terrorist attack he'd fallen victim to years prior, leaving him a double amputee. He now sported high tech prosthetics on his left arm and left leg. LaPhage Limbs, as they were commonly called. They integrated with his brain and functioned, in some ways, better than natural limbs.

"It's my wife, Billy. Autumn. You've never met her. But you know the story. I got her back, Sergeant. Back from the brink of death. And now...I may have lost her again. I just...the whole thing scares me to death."

"Listen, Doc. I'm not the theologian you are. Heck, I don't even know where I stand with God. But I've been around you enough to know that you believe in him. And what about Jesus, dude? I told you once, Jesus is the man. Homeboy came back from the dead. Look, if Jesus can kill death and if you're a Jesus guy, what are you scared about? He's got this."

Phin laughed. In a weird sort of way, Sergeant Billy Warren, agnostic warrior who had spent his life running from all things church and God, just took him back to

Seminary 101. In that moment two words burned bright in Phin's mind.

Two words from God's Holy Word.

Two words repeated in the Bible as a command more than any other two words.

Two words that instantly brought relief and renewed strength.

Those two words...

*Fear not.*

Phin looked into the eyes of his friend, who reached out a hand. Phin took it in a brotherly grasp.

"That's more like it, Doc. Now, let's go find your wife."

# CHAPTER 41

Sergeant Billy Warren knelt on the grass of the roundabout, just a few feet off of the curb. He was sorting the contents of his jumper's ruck, making choices as to what he would need for this mission and what would stay behind. Laid out was a mini arsenal of weapons – a standard Glock 19 9mm pistol, a M27 IAR affixed with an ACOG Squad Day Optic, a Ruger .357 Magnum revolver, and a sawed-off shotgun. The latter was not necessarily standard issue, but Warren liked having it with him just in case.

He weighed both the Ruger and the Glock, one in each hand, trying to decide which one to take. He opted for the Glock over the Ruger. The .357 had more stopping power, but the 9mm held more rounds. There were three beasts out there, Warren surmised.

Werewolves.

*Sheesh*, he was still trying to wrap his mind around that

one. But with three targets to pursue, quantity over quality won out. He holstered the Glock, securing the weapon with a snap.

The next choice was easier. He slipped into the leather holster that mounted between his shoulder blades and, reaching over his left shoulder, slid the shotgun snugly into place. The M27 IAR was a tactical weapon and impractical for the guerilla nature of what they were walking into. The shotgun would be much better in close quarters combat – if it came to that. He prepped several magazines and shells and loaded them into various pockets on his black military-styled pants. He picked up a smaller pack and began to stuff it with other equipment – a headlamp, face paint, water, a lighter, etc.

A figure approached from behind and Sergeant Warren whipped around.

"Sorry." Ross McCloud stood with hands extended. "I didn't mean to surprise you."

"Wasn't surprised. Just cautious. All this talk about werewolves and such has my radar cranked to the max," Warren replied.

"Well, anyway, that's a pretty impressive stash you got there, Sergeant. But I don't think you'll need to use it. I've got one of these for everyone to take." He rummaged in a tan canvas bag he'd been carrying and produced an item that he slapped into the palm of Billy Warren's hand.

"What the heck is this?" Warren stared at what looked to him to be a toy.

"It's a tranquilizer gun. A Crosman Pnue-Dart. Very effective. Here, I've got a pouch of feathered darts as well.

The chamber only takes one round so I'd practice reloading before we head out."

Sergeant Warren laughed out loud, handing it back. "You expect me to use *that*? Uh uh, ain't no way. That's for pansies. I think I'll stick with what I got, but nice try."

Vaughn O'Leary stepped over along with Phin, who'd readied his own gear. "Is there a problem?" Vaughn asked.

"Not for me," Warren replied. "But if you boys run into a werewolf out there and all you got is one of those Toys R Us specials, then you're the ones that are gonna have a problem."

"I'm not sure you get it, Sergeant," Vaughn began. He'd recovered the cocky sternness in his demeanor. "There's not going to be any more killing. Those are not wild beasts that are out there. At least not as you think of a wild beast. Those are our sons. Very literally, our children. It's up to us to protect them as much as it is to recover Jason and Autumn safely. We don't need Vin Diesel or Chuck Norris or whatever American movie cowboy you want to play to come riding in here shooting everything up."

"Why you! Who do you think you are?" Warren puffed his chest out and took a step forward.

Phin stepped up and put a hand on Warren's chest. "Easy, Billy. It's not worth it," he said softly.

"I am the leader of this town, Sergeant. Entrusted by the good people of Tiamat for the wellbeing of Tiamat. I know this town and all the happenings here better than you. The question is – who do you think *you* are? If you want to help, that is fine. But we will do it our way. Now take the tranquilizer gun and stop being a problem. We have enough of those to deal with already."

"Some leader *you* are," Warren replied back. "Maybe if you'd been doing your job better I wouldn't even have to be here. But whatever. Politicians. I told you, Phin. I don't like politicians. When this is all over with, I highly suggest you all elect a new leader," he directed to the other men standing around. "Give me that." He snatched the Crosman Pnue-Dart back from Ross, stuffing it into his pack. "I'll take your little gun along. Sure, no problem. I'll play. But I'm taking a couple of my own toys along as well. For *self-defense*."

"Whatever, I don't have time for this discussion any longer," Vaughn dismissed. "Let's all gather around and talk about how we're going to do this."

The group included Vaughn O'Leary, Ross McCloud, Harv Connor, and Furman Hayes. The head of the Tiamat's town council and three other town councilmen. Phin and Sergeant Warren stood among these men as the outsiders of the group, completing a search team of six. Buster, Harv's bloodhound, would make seven if you counted him.

"I gave Buster a sniff of the Morris boy's jacket. Took him over to where the jacket was found to see if he could get ahold of the scent. He found it alright and it's strong. Took all I had to pull him back over here. I best think we get going." Harv Connor held the rope tight that secured the dog.

"That's good," Vaughn O'Leary agreed. "Let me just say that I am not going with you and I don't think you need to go either, Ross."

"What do you mean, you and Ross aren't going?" Phin raised an eyebrow, surprised. "You two have the most at stake besides me. It's your boys that are out there, along with my wife."

"That's exactly why we can't go. It's against the rules."

"Rules!" Sergeant Warren blurted out. "What rules? This ain't no board game, Mr. Politics. This is real. Life and death real."

Vaughn sighed at Warren's lack of reverence for the situation. "Years ago - generations, in fact, before my time - we established a code of conduct as it relates to those that turn. They are taken to the cave and secured for their own safety, as we explained. Two guards are on duty at all times. We have a rotation system. But it was decided that the family of those that turn could never – *should* never – be the ones that guard the cave. When someone turns, it's best that their parents and siblings just let them go. They should stay far away from the cave and not see their child or brother...in that state. When they return, they are restored. Oh, they need to be cleaned up a bit and they are confused, but the curse has passed and they are no longer..."

"Werewolves?" Warren butted in. "Is that what you were going to say? They're no longer werewolves?"

"That's a crude way to put it, but essentially, yes. They are no longer...that way. They are human again."

"I know it's a rule, Vaughn," Ross McCloud spoke up. "But I'm going. This has progressed too far already. The elders never foresaw something like this when they put the rules in place. My boy, Tommy, is out there somewhere. He's likely responsible for what has gone on. Maybe for Blake Lynch's death...Lord, I hope not. But also, the missing Hispanic guy, and now the Morris boy and this man's wife. Poor Malcom...his arm's gone, chewed plumb off. And Sid Buckley is dead too, shot by accident. This thing has gotten out of control. Tommy is my son, Vaughn. I'm his Da. It's on me to find him and get him back in the cave. Lucious is your boy. You need to find him and get him back to safety. Then we can figure out what comes next."

It was a compelling case. Ross McCloud was not to be denied his chance to set things right this night. He'd followed the rules once before and things only spun out of control. There had been more maiming and loss of life. Plus, there was something not right in the air. Something he couldn't put his finger on. He couldn't sit by another night and let others do all the work. No, this was on him as much as anyone.

"That's fine, Ross. You can go," Vaughn replied, stoic after Ross's impassioned appeal. "But I'm going to honor the rules. They are there for a reason. I'm going to trust the process because I believe it's right. You will have to face the consequences from doing it your own way." Vaughn wiped the palms of his hands against each other. "I've said my peace. My hands are clean."

Phineas Crook observed the whole exchange with curiosity. In the back of his mind, he doubted seriously that Vaughn O'Leary's hands were clean.

# CHAPTER 42

Buster pulled hard on his lead rope. The dog had picked up Jason Morris's scent right at the location where the man's cane had been found and off he went. This time he was unhindered by his owner, held back only by the speed at which the group could travel. True to his word, Vaughn O'Leary had stayed behind. The last Phineas Crook saw of him was his backside as he closed the door to the Lear House behind him.

Theirs was now a group of five: Phin, Sergeant Warren, Ross McCloud, Harv Connor, and Furman Hayes. Furman had spoken the least in the group thus far. Phin recalled only knowing him through his wife's mention of him as the owner of the town's diner, The Frolicking Irishman. The name struck Phin as ironically humorous as nothing about Tiamat seemed frolicking and certainly not Irish. He knew too much now, other than to see this corner of the world as a living shrine to the memory of a forgotten people who now lived under an unforgettable curse.

The bloodhound led the group immediately offroad, back behind what smattering of houses and buildings there were, and into the bush. Buster barked and galloped through the tall grass, and it was quickly apparent that others had come this way recently. The tall growth was bent over in the same direction, indicating that it had been trampled.

They were on the right track.

They stomped across a field of sticky brambles and small bushes that threatened to reach up and grab the heels of the men as they bounded through. Small saplings gave way to larger gauged trees the further they went, and after a good half a kilometer they were firmly surrounded by forest. In short order, they were on a game trail and the going became markedly easier.

Harv Connor slowed his hound and brought the group to a stop. He was breathing hard and shining with perspiration. The rest of the group was grateful for the respite, several downing gulps from their canteens. It was a fast start and Phin wondered how far they would have to go.

"I hunt this trail in the spring. It will take us all the way around the outskirts of town to the far side. There's a dozen other trails that break off from it. We'll just have to follow it and see where the scent takes us," Harv Connor informed the men. "Take another minute to get your breath and I'll let Buster loose again. But we'll take it a little slower now. No sense wearing ourselves out. It'll be a long enough night as it is."

A roll of thunder sounded in the distance. Phin noticed the breeze whipping up, coming from the same direction. He was so turned around after their scamper out of town he didn't have a clue if it was coming from the north, south, east, or west, but it felt good and cool as the wind touched his moist skin.

"I'm very sorry for all that's happened to you and your wife, Mr. Crook. And to the Morris boy. I promise you, we are good people here. I know it may not seem that way, but we are. If you'd come at any other time...well, things would have been different and you would've seen the better side of us." It was the first time Furman Hayes had spoken directly to Phin. In the glow of torchlight, he was convinced of the sincerity of the man. His chocolate colored eyes betrayed a deep kindness. He was being pulled along by this series of unfortunate events as much as Phin and Autumn. This wasn't his fault. It wasn't the fault of any of this group of three town leaders surrounding him. No one else followed up Furman's comment, but their expressions echoed the same sentiment. Phin was grateful.

"Thank you, Mr. Hayes. I appreciate you saying so. And I believe you. If I'm not mistaken, it's your daughter, Marilyn, who's betrothed to Harv's son here. Malcolm...isn't that it, Harv?" The weathered man gave a nod. "Yes, I remember your boy...and his arm. You all have lost a lot yourselves." Turning his attention back to Furman Hayes, "Marilyn's a delight. You should be proud of her as I'm sure you are. Let's do what we have to tonight, gentlemen, to put an end to the nightmare of the last week. And then the healing...for all of us... can begin."

There were nods all around and then the mood was unceremoniously broken. "Okay, Doc! Nice speech and all, but probably should press pause till after we save the world. Time's tickin' and a storm's-a-brewin'." Billy Warren wet the end of his finger in his mouth and stuck it in the air. "Break time's over. Let's get rollin'."

Ross McCloud gave additional instructions. "From this point forward, keep a sharp eye out. We will follow single file, but be sure and look to both sides of the trail. The creatures – as we call them – are smart and crafty. They may circle back around on us. So, keep your guard up. Sergeant," he directed at Billy Warren, "if you wouldn't mind taking up the rear, I think your military training will help us most with our exposed flank." Warren didn't like not being in the lead, but it wasn't his party, he surmised, so he gave the nod. "Good, and everyone keep your tranquilizer pistols ready. These things can spring up on you fast."

Phin looked at the handheld dart gun in his hand. It really did feel like a toy compared to the weighted Ruger the sergeant had given him to wear on his right hip. For all the talk that Vaughn had extolled to the group about there being no need for firearms because there would be no killing, he couldn't help but notice that each of the other three councilmen were armed as well. Harv Connor carried a rifle over his own shoulder, while Ross McCloud settled a shotgun into the crook of his arm. Furman Hayes checked his own pistol, easing it out and back into its holster. The men were clearly ready for more...if more were to come.

Harv Connor gave a grunt and let up on Buster who sprang into action, heading off down the trail. He kept the rope taut, controlling the pace of the march. Phin imagined that it took enormous strength to hold the animal back, but Harv Connor looked all the part of a grizzled woodsman. He likely had arms of steel under his canvas overcoat.

Over the next half hour, the line of hunters worked their way down the game trail with little talk. Occasionally, Phin caught a glimpse of light from town off to his left through the trees and foliage. It seemed the trail would, at times, carry them closer to the village, and then work its way away. As Harv had predicted, various trails shot off in other directions, but Buster stayed on the scent, never wavering on which way to go.

Phin began to imagine Jason being taken this way and his anxiety rose. How had this exactly happened? If these three...he wasn't even sure how to think about them or imagine them, but if these three *people* had truly become wolves, how had they transported Jason? Could one beast carry him alone? He couldn't imagine Jason going along cooperatively so he must have been unconscious, Phin decided. But how could a wolf carry a person? Wouldn't it drag him? And how hard and slow would that be? They'd traveled a good distance so far. Were the wolves able to work in tandem, helping each other out? And even though they'd *turned*, did they still have the use of their hands versus the paws of a true wolf?

The details of the anatomy of the kidnapping played in Phin's analytical mind. As they did, something just didn't feel right to him. The absurdity of what he'd been told began to cast doubts in his psyche. *This is impossible*, Phin finally admitted. People simply cannot become werewolves. The whole thing is the stuff of imagination and Stephen

King novels. Whatever the people of Tiamat thought was happening to their children, this simply could not be it. Yet, they'd been so convincing. And they seemed to believe it themselves. Why would they lie about such a thing? And what would lead a father and a mother to allow their child to be held in a cage inside a cave for seven years? The bizarreness of it all pinged around in Phin's brain like a pinball machine.

"How you doin' up there, Doc?" Sergeant Warren's measured tone shut the flow of Phin's thoughts. As second to last in the line, Phin was directly in front of the sergeant.

"I'm alright, thanks, Billy."

"So, tell me. How have things been going for you these last few months? Since...you know, we last hung out?"

Phin smiled to himself at Warren's reference to their travels across the globe in search of the Garden of Eden, and then their actual finding of it and all that occurred within its boundaries. To Sergeant Warren, all of that was just "hanging out."

"It's been good, Billy. Real good. You obviously heard about Autumn. How we got her back. A true miracle, it was. The university has been great after the return. They gave me the semester as an extended time of sabbatical and so Autumn and I have been traveling and just enjoying being together again. Funny thing is, for me, it was three years. Three long years. But for her, it was like waking up from a long night's sleep. Her last memory was a traumatic one though. You know, of the attack and the shot that nearly ended her life. So, she's been recovering from that...mentally and emotionally. But physically she's fine. And we are fine...well, until all this."

"That's good, Doc. Real good. I'm happy for you. And hey, don't worry. We'll get your girl back tonight. We've got this, okay?" Phin found a strange comfort in Billy Warren's optimism.

Feeling as though he shouldn't be just thinking about himself, Phin asked, "So how have you been, Billy? After we last *hung out?*" Phin knew that the sergeant had taken the death of Ruth LaPhage and Tony Chen at the Garden particularly hard.

"Ah...you know LaPhage Industries. It's a party everyday with those white coats. But they've had me doing some pretty cool stuff. In fact, the reason I was in Germany-"

"Ross...Furman...get up here!" Harv Connor yelled out and brought the group to a stop. All four joined Harv, who was standing in the middle of a much larger trail. "Check out where we are. The game trail dumps out here and Buster is pullin' on me hard. The scent heads down." The four men exchanged grave looks.

"It heads down," Phin began. "Heads down to where?"

Ross McCloud looked at his two friends and then at Phin. "To the cave."

# CHAPTER 43

Jamison Murphy stoked the fire with a long branch. He reached down and added two more logs to the blaze. Sparks flew and new smoke rose into the sky, rolling off the lip of the cave's entrance, adding to the black-sooted stain of the ceiling. It was the first night he'd been on watch back at the cave since...since his world imploded. That had been, what? Not even a week and a half ago. The images of that awful night were burned into his memory. He hoped they would fade with time but he somehow doubted it.

How do you get over seeing someone you've known your whole life just torn to pieces? There was so much gore that at the time he was certain both Lynch boys had fallen to the beast that attacked them - but it had only been Blake he was later told.

It was Blake that he saw splayed out all over the cave.

Sheamus was missing and still had not been found.

Jamison shook his head. He did that a lot these days. Trying to dislodge the images that assaulted his waking hours. He stared across the raging fire and the torment stared back. Malcolm Connor feigned a smile, his arm ending in a bloody stump.

Except it wasn't Malcolm.

It was his younger brother, Drake. And his arm was whole. Malcolm and Drake looked so much alike. Jamison shook his head again.

"You okay, Jami? You keep shaking your head," Drake noted, his eyebrow lifting.

"Yeah, I'm fine. It's just...I don't know. This place. It's not the same anymore. Not since.... Listen, Drake, I'm so sorry about Malcolm."

"Hey, nobody blames you, Jami. It wasn't your fault."

"But I ran. I ran, Drake. And I left him behind." Jamison couldn't look at Malcolm's brother any longer. He watched the flames dance instead. "I was just...so scared."

"Malcolm ran too. You both did. It was horrible what happened here. No one should see...something like that. And Malcolm doesn't blame you for his arm either."

"I know. That's what he told me. Came to my house to check on me even. Imagine that. He's the one that gets his arm chewed off and he comes to check on *me*. You got a good brother, Drake. He's a real good man, he is."

"You're right about that. He's already joking about his arm, too. Told Marilyn that for the wedding he wanted a groom's cake shaped like a hand." Drake's shoulders lifted slightly, accompanied by a short chuckle.

Jamison couldn't bring himself to share the sentiment. A part of him was relieved to know that Malcolm didn't hold against him that he'd abandoned him on the trail the night they were stalked. And he was glad too that Malcolm was handling well the loss of his arm, taking it in stride. He was certainly doing better than Jamison would have been if their roles were reversed. He still couldn't help but feel an intense sorrow for his friend. As long as he lived, he'd have to see Malcolm around town. No one ever left Tiamat, after all. He'd see him and he'd know that one of his arms was a lifeless prosthetic, unable pick up his future daughter properly or throw a ball to his son with it. He'd know, and the guilt would always be there.

"Poor Mr. Lynch." Drake's voice brought Jamison back to the present. "Now he's the one I truly do feel sorry for. Can you imagine? Lost his wife to cancer five years ago and now Blake. A man should never outlive his kids. That's what my da says. It's not natural."

"Nothing's natural about any of it," Jamison broke in. He threw another log on the fire. No way he wanted the fire to go out or even down. Not tonight. Not his first night back at the cave.

"How's that?"

"Tiamat. Nothing's natural about Tiamat. Haven't you ever thought that, Drake?"

The question gave the man pause. Not just the question, but who was asking it. Jami had always been cavalier, rambunctious, irreverent, and jovial. He took nothing seriously and was known for such. Drake understood his dour attitude, given what happened to him —

what he had witnessed. But this was a different Jamison Murphy. Something had changed in him.

"Don't you think it's strange that no one ever leaves? No one. We are born. We live. And we die. In Tiamat. And then...some of us...turn. It's unnatural, I tell you. It's not just those who turn that are cursed. We all are. Malcolm's been touched. His fiancé, Marilyn. Then poor Blake. He's dead, Drake. Dead. I guess that's one way to escape Tiamat. And Sheamus is still out there...somewhere. He's probably dead too, but no one will admit it. So yes. Poor Mr. Lynch. He's fallen under the curse of this godforsaken town." Jami finished by spitting into the fire. It hissed at him like a snake spitting back.

Lightning flashed bright out over the Atlantic. For a split second the light competed with the glow of the fire at the cave's entrance. A moment later thunder bellowed across the sky. Then came the wind.

"A storm's coming." Drake stated the obvious, hiking up the collar of his wool overcoat. It was a cold wind foreshadowing what was to come.

"It stormed that night as well - the last time Malcolm and I came down here."

"This is not last time, Jami," Drake said, attempting to counter his friend. "The creatures are secure. I just checked the cage myself."

"But there's three still out there. I've seen what they can do." Jamison shivered.

"And we've got weapons this time." Drake patted his own shotgun leaned against the log he was sitting on. "It'll be okay, Jami."

The two sat in silence, listening to the continued thunder that followed the flashes of light, the shaking coming more quickly after each round of strikes. They continued to add to the fire, making sure that when the blowing rain finally came it would be no threat to their beacon of safety.

Jamison and Drake would be here at least another two hours before the next shift came to relieve them. The time couldn't move quickly enough for Jamison. He needed to get this one watch under his belt. Like a hitter getting beaned by the pitcher, this was his version of being back in the batter's box, except what he'd lived through - what he'd witnessed in this very cave - wasn't anything at all like baseball. There had been no game the night of the escape.

Jamison caught the whiff of something foul. He looked back into the darkness of the cave but knew it wasn't coming from there. The wind carried this odor.

"Man, what is that?" Drake complained. "Smells like...I don't know what it smells like."

And then Jamison knew.

They say that smell is the most powerful of the five senses, the olfactory nerve having the capability of transporting one back in time as particular odors stimulate the connection between nose and brain. In an instant, Jamison Murphy was transported back ten days to this very spot. The horror of that terrible night crashed into him full force. He nearly fell over before catching himself.

"Jami, what's wrong?!" Drake was on his feet, shotgun in hand.

"It's...it's...." His voice quivered, unable to form the words that cascaded into his mind.

The smell increased in intensity and then a low growl overcame the sound of the crackling fire. Jamison Murphy joined Drake on his feet.

The two men stared past the flames into the night.

And into a pair of flaming yellow eyes.

# CHAPTER 44

The group of five were forced to move more slowly as they made their way down the steep, wooded trail. Buster navigated more easily on his four legs but such was not the case for the men and their two legs. Phin slipped a couple of times, dirtying his rear end. Each time, the sergeant was there to help right him. Another gentle roll of thunder caused Phin to imagine that going up or down the trail would be exponentially harder during a rain.

As before, the party worked single file, careful to keep watch on either side while Sergeant Warren guarded their backsides. Both men and dog were breathing hard, working up a sweat, trying to keep their feet sure and their hearing and eyes sharp.

Another rattle of storm thunder and a horrible howl finished breaking the night sky.

"What the heck was that?" Warren asked from the back. The howl had stopped the march and even Buster pulled up with a whimper.

"It's them," Harv replied. "Still some distance off, but we're definitely headed in the right direction. Come on, let's move it!" He gave the rope a whip, and a command to the hound, who responded with new energy.

The group picked up the pace. The path began to level out and just like that the group burst out onto the beach; the suffocating canopy of the forest was now behind them. Phin felt like he could breathe again.

A cascade of lightning charged the sky from left to right. The beauty of the display over the waters of the ocean was breathtaking. More thunder followed and then another howl from one of the wolf creatures. The wind picked up and ushered the terrible cry up and over the bluffs and away.

"A storm's coming," Ross McCloud observed. "The cave's on up a bit. Let's go."

The sand was not the easiest to slog through, but the openness of the terrain made movement swifter now, plus visibility was no longer an issue. The group put away their torches and still there was enough ambient light reflecting off the low clouds to cast night shadows.

Phin lost track of time, but after what seemed like another ten minutes of swift movement Furman Hayes cried out, "There! Just up there. They've got a fire really going tonight."

Phin strained to see and then it came into view - an orange glow about a hundred meters ahead. He missed it at first because the glow was higher up than expected, flashing through a covering of trees. As they drew closer, he discerned a path that led up to a small thicket of foliage. The entrance to the cave must be behind it. The casual observer could easily miss it all together, which, he realized, was the point to having a secret cave in the first place.

The men began to eagerly scamper up the path toward the face of the bluff. Harv Connor aggressively brushed aside branches, leading the way, Buster barking incessantly. The party crested the top of the rise and powered through the foliage after Harv and his dog. Phin and Billy Warren were the last to push through and as they emerged, stopped short at the scene in front of them.

The first thing that struck Phin was that Buster had quit barking. The dog was hunkered down, trembling. The group had stopped a mere twenty feet from the raging campfire. Two young men were opposite the blaze, one as white as a bleached sheet, the other leveling a shotgun in the group's direction. But his aim was not at them...it was instead on a beast, the likes of which Phin had never seen.

A prickly feeling overcame him as he stared at the backside of the creature. It stood frozen, looking at the human with the gun. It was unlike any "wolf" Phin had ever seen in a National Geographic magazine or on Discovery Channel.

The creature was covered in matted brown and white hair, crouched on all four legs. It was a huge animal with a hunched appearance, the rounding of the back showed a bony spine that parted the hair to each side. The hair around its head was especially long but from his angle, Phin couldn't make out its face. He noticed that the two hind legs ended not in paws but in large gnarled feet. The nails protruded in a kind of vicious claw. Likewise, the front legs ended in a type of hand, again the nails forming a slashing claw-type feature. It was clearly a mixture of human and wolf, Phin thought.

The werewolf became instantly aware of the presence of the five men and dog that had come up behind it. It was trapped. Nothing was worse than a trapped wild animal.

"Easy, Drake," Harv Connor called over to the man with the shotgun. "Careful son, if you miss, the scatter will hit us."

"This thing got Malcolm, Pa. It took his arm. We have...." The young Drake Connor was scared. He was pleading with his father for direction.

"Maybe so, son. But lower the gun. We don't need an accident. We've got it cornered and outnumbered."

Phin noticed that the beast was breathing hard. And then he caught something else. The pitiful thing looked emaciated. There was a bony appearance to the whole of its body. It was breathing hard, not out of excitement but out of what seemed like fatigue. Phin had not known what to expect when encountering one of Tiamat's hidden monsters, but this was not exactly it. This creature didn't look fit to fight, much less attack and drag a body through the woods.

The werewolf began a slow turn toward Harv Connor's voice. As he made the circuit, the frontal view revealed his face. Phin recoiled in pity.

"Man, oh man," Sergeant Warren let out softly. "That is one ugly mother."

It was a true mix of human and animal. Phin could discern the brow of a man, but a snout had clearly, somehow, grown to protrude where a normal mouth should be. He imagined the beast had the jaws to match. But the creature's yellow eyes signaled something other than rage.

This monster was defeated.

He was tired and he looked to be starving. Phin realized in that moment that he'd just mentally shifted from thinking of the beast as a *he* and not an *it*. The beast let out a sigh to match his demeanor and then he did something unexpected. He sat back on his hind legs, a sign of submission.

A light airy *THUNK* made Phin flinch. He was unclear as to what made the sound until he saw the fluff of feathers jutting out from behind the werewolf's neck. The light faded from his yellow eyes and then they closed altogether as he simply lay over and went to sleep.

"Got you," the other young man said, teeth clenched in bitterness. He was holding one of the tranquilizer pistols they each carried, both hands wrapped tightly around the grip.

Drake Connor reached up and eased the discharged weapon down. "That's right, Jami. You got him. It's okay now." He led his friend off to the side and sat him on a log.

Sergeant Warren sauntered over to the sleeping werewolf and gave him a nudge with the toe of his boot. Furman Hayes joined him and kneeled. He took the head in both hands and looked at the beast hard for a moment before fishing around in the mane of his hair. Phin knelt down and noticed that he was wearing a leather collar of some sort.

"It's Vance," Furman announced. "Vance Talley. That means Tommy is still out there. Him and Lucious." Ross

McCloud looked down. He'd hoped this had been his son, that he'd been put down safely.

Harv Connor put his hand on the man's shoulder by way of consolation. "We'll find him, Ross. We'll find your boy." Turning to his own son, "What happened here, Drake?"

"You saw nearly the whole thing, Pa. Jami and I were just logging time, waiting our shift out, and he comes walking up. Caught us completely off guard. We expected him to attack but...man, he doesn't look so good to me."

"This person...thing...sheesh, I don't even know how to refer to him." Phin was still examining the werewolf he knew now to be Vance Talley. "He's in no shape for a fight. Did you see how he looked at us? It's almost like he's been wandering around out here for over a week and now he's had enough. So, he came...home."

The group acknowledged the obvious, that Vance was no threat. But what did that mean for the other two werewolves still out there? And what did that mean for Jason and Autumn? Phin turned on his torch and walked all the way to the back of the cave, leaving the others as they discussed the situation. They filled in Drake and Jami on why they were out there in the first place – two more missing people.

What Phin found at the back of the cave sickened and saddened him both at the same time. There were eight in all – behind thick iron bars. Vance would make nine, plus the two still out there.

The eleven monsters of Tiamat.

Phin felt like he was looking at some anemic version of ancient mythology come to life. But the creatures he was looking at appeared far from ferocious. Some of them were sleeping. Others paced back and forth. All looked well fed. As a whole they seemed thoroughly uninterested in Phin, as if his presence was a non-factor. Occasionally, one would give him a lazy glance. The whole scene reminded Phin of one of he and Autumn's numerous trips to the zoos across America - just another animal exhibit, albeit a sad one.

Something here didn't add up. The picture presented to Phin was not what he had expected. He knew that more was going on, he just didn't know what. These thoughts dominated his mind as he made his way back to the mouth of the cave.

"So, what's the plan?" he called out as he approached the group. "Jason and Autumn aren't here, so what's next?"

"That's what we were just discussing, Doc," Sergeant Warren answered.

"I pulled Buster off the scent to come up here. But he's still got it, and strong. Jason, for sure, came through here recently. I suspect your wife too." Harv Connor pointed back toward the beach trail.

A bolt of lightning and loud crack of thunder jolted the cave. The closest one yet. In response a werewolf howled. Then came a second howl. The same but different - two distinct voices - in the distance but closer than before. Everyone looked at each other until Buster barked and bolted out of the grasp of his owner. He was gone in an instant. Harv Connor cursed and took off after him.

"Sounds like our cue, boys!" Sergeant Warren commanded with a big grin on his face.

# CHAPTER 45

A puddle drop slammed into Phin's forehead. The storm that had been brewing out over the ocean was ready to make landfall. Phin gave no regard to the rain and thunder, though. The storm he was concerned with was up ahead.

He could feel it.

They were close now.

He wiped the splash of water from his face and carried on.

There were only four of them now. Harv Connor was chasing after Buster with Sergeant Billy Warren on his heels. Phin and Ross McCloud were doing their best to keep up. Furman Hayes had stayed behind at the cave to help the two young watchmen secure the werewolf that had been tranquilized.

The group traversed the sandy beach for a good half a kilometer. There was no discernable trail now - clearly no one ever came this far up the shore. The path they had followed previously had ended on the rise where the cave entrance had been hidden. Slowly, the sand gave way to rocks, and eventually they found themselves scrambling over a bellowing of old volcanic rock. It slowed the progress considerably. Phin had to use his hands to steady himself in what became more scrambling than running. The touch of the rock was sharp and threatened to slash open his clothing and the flesh underneath if he fell. It was a balance for the four men between speed and safety.

The whole way, they could hear Buster barking between thunder rolls. Every time there was a flash of lightning, a terrible howl tore through the darkness that was now becoming ever darker as storm clouds arrived. Sometimes a second howl would sound after the first. Both were horrible sounds, very much like a wolf but longer in duration, with a grating quality to the scream. It was the howl of a werewolf, Phin thought.

Half wolf, half man.

The stuff of legend come to life.

In the movies people ran away from werewolves. How odd it seemed that they were running *toward* these beasts? But it really wasn't about the werewolves. At least not for Phin. For him it was all about Autumn. He was going to get his wife back. He couldn't lose her again. He'd lost her once but then God had performed a miracle and now she was back. Surely God wouldn't strip her from him a second time. And not so soon. It had only been a few months but nothing is guaranteed in life. We all die eventually. Autumn had tried to tell him that just a few days ago.

*Fear not.*

The two-word command from the Bible echoed for a second time in his head that night, as Phin slipped and clawed his way over the rocks. He was desperate to keep up with the other three men. God had placed those two words in *his* Holy Word more than any other two words because he knew that man was prone to fear - fear of all sorts. Everyone has their own fear that grabs them and shuts them down - holds them in their own private cage hidden in some cave. No two fears may be the same, but fear is fear nonetheless.

Vaughn O'Leary had been right - all fear flows from a lack of control. At the heart of man is the desire, the yearning for control over every facet of life.

Phin hated to fly. Why? Because he was afraid of crashing. But the real fear came from the fact that when he flew, he wasn't in control. He wasn't the one in the cockpit. He'd rather drive ten hours than fly to the same place in two. When he drove, he was in control - nothing to fear. At least that's how it felt. The reality of control is all an illusion, Phin realized now. He had never been in control at any point in his life, he'd only thought he was. Phin hated to fly, but he did fly. He was able to do so because he could take the voice of fear and kill it on the altar of trust. He had to make a choice to trust the pilot, a person he'd never met and could not see - someone he may actually *never* see, except in a casual hand wave exchange after the flight is over, as he exited the plane.

Phin saw Ross McCloud slip and roll on the rocks. He popped up again and kept going. Phin's own foot rolled on a loose patch and he also went down. He too was back up quickly, ignoring the scrapes he now had on his knees under his jeans.

*Fear not.*

Gotta keep going, he told himself. Run toward the fear and not away from it.

Gotta find Autumn.

And Jason, too. He couldn't forget about Jason.

The lightning flashed, the werewolves howled, Buster barked. And still they kept running.

Phin prayed as he ran. And then two more words flashed through his head. They came to him almost like a spoken voice. Not from within him, but planted in him from someone else. Someone on the outside. Someone who *was* in control.

*Trust me.*

Phin shuddered at the two new words. It had all come to this. He had to release the control he didn't have. It was his only option. Trust God. Trust the one flying the plane.

Fear not. Trust me.

*Fear not. Trust me.*

Two words spoken thousands of years ago. Two words spoken tonight. Both commands for him. For this moment. For every moment. Both commands from the same Author.

Phin had to make a decision. Would he? Would he trust God? Would he release his fear? He couldn't have it both ways. He had to embrace one and let the other go. Either fear would win and trust would lose. Or trust would win and fear would lose.

Phin made up his mind. He chose trust.

He gathered himself for a burst of speed and caught up

to Sergeant Warren. The wind was strong now and more drops of rain were blowing into them.

"Great job keeping up, Doc!" Warren cried out over the sound of the wind. "This terrain ain't no joke."

"Buster!" Harv Connor was calling for the dog. They'd closed the gap between themselves and the hound. His barking was definitely closer. And then the dog began to bark incessantly, like he'd cornered a fox on the hunt.

The barking grew louder and fiercer as they carried on. The dog was definitely not running anymore. The group rounded a point on the beach and pulled up.

They'd found Buster.

No more than thirty meters ahead the rocky shore rose up to a point - a small hill of sorts. Buster was at the base, barking with all his might, crouched back on his hind legs as if ready to pounce.

And on top of the rise...a werewolf.

It was a massive beast - terrible in appearance. It's yellow eyes glowed bright. The sky flashed and the creature lifted its head, craned its neck, and let loose one of the most horrible cries Phin had ever heard. Even at this distance, the group took a step back.

*Fear not. Trust me.*

Phin willed his legs to take two steps forward.

The dog worked his way back and forth, scooting to the right and then to the left, as if measuring up the werewolf. He continued to bark, unphased by the creature's night howl. This was the same kind of beast they'd put down back at the caveside campfire – the one named Vance Talley – but different. This wolf was larger by a considerable degree, and he was well fed - *healthy*, Phin thought. There was nothing in this beast that signaled compliance or defeat. He was ready to fight. And just like that, the werewolf leapt off the rocky top, pouncing on the much smaller bloodhound.

"Nooo!" Harv Connor let off three blasts of his shotgun, pointed over the heads of the two animals now embroiled in a maul. The shots did nothing to dissuade the werewolf from its attack. "You sonuva...let go of my dog!" Harv moved to charge into the melee but was restrained by Sergeant Warren.

"Won't do no good, mister. It's already over."

Warren was correct.

The great werewolf clamped down hard on the neck of the hound and began thrashing the poor dog back and forth like a ragdoll.

In that moment, the wind stopped whipping and everything became silent save the snarling of the wolf and a dying whimper that eased past the dog's vocal cords. The werewolf stood on its hind legs, Buster limp in its grasp, and with impossible strength reared back and threw the dog toward the group of men. It traveled the full distance, landing with a sickening thud at Harv Connor's feet. There was something in the act that felt intensely personal.

Harv fell to his knees. He took the beloved hunting dog in his arms. The werewolf, still standing on its hind legs, let out a final howl of victory. A charge of lightning struck behind the wolf, illuminating the whole scene in a flash of horror. And with that the creature bounded around the small rise and was gone.

Ross McCloud walked over to his friend and laid a hand

on the man's somber shoulders. "You saw where he's headed, Harv...where we have to go."

"Yeah...I saw. Makes sense, I guess. If you want to hide something."

"Or someone."

"What are you talking about?" Phin asked, pleading in his voice. "Where's he headed? Where's my wife and Jason?"

Harv rose to his feet and looked Ross in the eyes. He got a nod in return. "To the tombs. The ancestral tombs of Babylon."

# CHAPTER 46

The wind continued to blow. The weather had transitioned to a downpour of rain – heavy sheets of water slapping at the men. The storm had made landfall. The miserable conditions matched the mood of the situation and in short order everything was soaked. Clothes, bags, feet, hair - all a sloppy mess. Phin used his wet hands in a futile attempt to wipe the water from his face and eyes.

It did not take long to arrive at the tombs.

It was only a short distance further but the group took extra care, not wanting to be ambushed by the massive beast that had crushed Buster.

Phin was trying to sort out what he'd already seen in the span of only an hour. The curse of Tiamat was real. People were transforming – turning – into wolves...werewolves. He'd now seen the proof with his own eyes. But apparently not all werewolves were equal. The difference between the one that had sauntered back to the cave and essentially laid down and the one they'd just encountered was striking. What they were dealing with now was an apex creature - something at the top of the food chain. And there was still another one of them free and roaming close. The back and forth howling made that clear.

Ross McCloud and Harv Connor led Phin and Sergeant Warren to a chasm in the face of the coastal bluff. The black sky crackled with electricity, illuminating the ominous slit in the earth. The famous Irish bluff rose straight up from the sandy beach where they stood, at least three hundred feet, the gap matching the rise from bottom to top.

"The ancestral tombs are through there," Ross McCloud shouted over the storm. He was soaked as well, his black hair straight and stuck to his brow. "No one...no outsider has ever been to the tombs. I must have your promise. You must swear it, that you will never reveal its location. You are only here now out of necessity."

"I swear it!" Phin called back. "All I care about is my wife and Jason."

"And you, Sergeant? Swear it."

"Yeah sure. Cross my heart and hope to die! Stick a needle in my eye...knack-knack patty wack give a dog a bone!"

Ross and Harv both looked at Phin, confused. "That's just his way of saying he swears it. We're all good. I promise."

The four men stepped into the blackness of the chasm.

The wind and the rain abated considerably after walking only a dozen feet inward. Phin measured the gap between the two walls of the chasm to be maybe ten meters wide, and it looked as if it stayed that way as far as the path traveled in front of the group, to the boundaries of their combined torchlight. It was easier to hear and be heard away from the whipping of the surging storm.

"Follow us and stay close. Be sure and run your lights along the walls as we go. Lots of nooks and crannies here – places to hide and spring from." Ross McCloud gave the instructions in a monotone voice and proceeded into the depths of the chasm, Harv Connor at his side. Phin and Sergeant Warren paired up behind them and stayed close.

About a hundred meters in, Phin perceived a low whistle as the wind worked its way lightly through the pass. It made for an eerie march that became all the more eerie as a monstrous howl punctuated the air. It echoed off the walls like a ping pong ball, impossible to tell how far or close the wolf beast was.

"Why do you think he brought them here? Jason and Autumn?" Phin questioned the two men of Tiamat.

"Because we would never look here." Ross was the first to answer. "Would never even think of it honestly. This is sacred space to our people. To bring your wife and the Morris kid here is a sacrilege."

"And because it's a tomb," Harv offered as a second. His rocky voice the opposite of inspiring. "If he plans to kill them or leave them for dead and never wants them found...well, this is the place."

"But that's what I don't understand. It's the town tomb. So, don't you come here every time someone dies and needs to be buried?"

"Oh, not anymore," Ross said, surprised, understanding now what Phin and the sergeant must have thought.

"These tombs haven't been used in over a thousand years, at least. We started burying our dead in a localized cemetery a long time ago. When I said no one ever comes here, I mean no one *ever* comes here. It's forbidden. The only time I've ever been here was when I was a kid and a bunch of us snuck down here one day in the summer. When my father found out...well, let's just say he made his point and I've never been back."

"We're here, Ross. This is it." Harv Connor brought the group to a halt. Phin had been so caught up in the conversation that he had not noticed the change in the canyon wall on his right. The black of the chasm was so complete that he would have missed the opening in the side of the mountain were it not for being escorted.

Phin wasn't sure what he expected, but a simple rectangular carved opening the size of a double door was not it.

"Holy cow, Doc," Sergeant Warren uttered in awe. "Check this place out."

Phin couldn't understand what was so impressive about the entrance until he realized the sergeant wasn't looking at the entrance, at least not directly. He was holding his torch out and up and sweeping it back and forth as high as the light extended.

When Phin's gaze joined his friend's, his mouth fell open. Carved into the face of the rock was the edifice of a temple. Stone pillars each topped with animals - all wolves - were the primary feature. Between the pillars were carved human figures each twice the height of a normal man. Some held their arms outstretched, touching the shoulders of the figures on each side, while some held their arms against their hips or across their bodies. Phin had to step back to the opposite wall to take it all in. The masonry involved here was massive in scale. He could only imagine the numbers of decades that had gone into its creation.

"Reminds me of the scene from that Indiana Jones movie, Doc. You know, the one where they go lookin' to find that holy cup?"

"Holy grail, Sergeant. It was the holy grail. And you're talking about Petra."

"About what?"

"Petra. That scene was shot in the Jordanian desert refuge of Petra. It's a real place carved by the Nabateans about two hundred years before Christ. This place...this place is easily twice the size of the carving at Petra. And it's distinctly Babylonian in its architecture. Amazing. Simply amazing."

"The tomb is inside. Let's go." Ross McCloud interrupted their temple gazing. He was clearly not as impressed as the two visitors.

The four men stepped through the double doorway and the darkness became even darker still. But the four torches they carried did an impressive job of illuminating the interior. They were in a long hallway around ten feet tall and the same width as the double doorway they'd just stepped through - all rock hewn. Phin commented again at the amount of time it must have taken to excavate where they stood. Harv Connor explained that according to the town history, this was originally a cave with natural tunnels branching in multiple directions. When their ancestors settled the area, their excavation for the tombs simply built off of what was already here. It would have been hard work but not as hard as it first appeared.

The tunnel ended in a large circular chamber. While the walls were smooth, the ceiling had a dome-ish appearance but was clearly natural rock. They were in a cavern with four separate tunnels that branched off in different directions. The prominent feature of the room was four stone rectangles on matching pedestals, each the size of a medium U-Haul box.

"What do we do now?" Phin asked. He pointed his flashlight at each of the black holes indicating a new passageway.

"Easy," Sergeant Warren answered. "Four tunnels. Four of us. We split up and each take one."

"I don't like the idea of splitting up." Ross McCloud scratched his head. "Safety in numbers."

"It'll take us four times as long to check all these out if we stay together."

"Twice as long if we go in pairs," Harv Connor weighed in. He was nervously bouncing his right leg. The man was itching to keep going. "I agree with the sergeant fella. We need to divide up. No time to waste."

"That settles it." Billy Warren was quick to latch onto Harv's agreement.

"But-"

"You'll be alright, Doc! Use that Ruger I gave you if you need it. No fear. Remember?" Before Phin could object further, Sergeant Warren sprinted away, swallowed up by the black hole on the far right, as if he'd fallen into a bottomless pit. Ross McCloud relented to Harv's judgment and took the second tunnel, while Harv disappeared into the third.

Phin was left alone in the chamber room. As he moved toward his own tunnel, a thought tickled the back of his mind. He cautiously moved to the center of the cavern where the four stone boxes lay. Not just any stone boxes, he realized now that he was looking directly at them.

These were ossuaries – bone boxes. When an ancient person of great importance died, their body was placed in a tomb for a year or more, whatever time it took for the flesh to decay. Then a tomb keeper, priest, or family member would come and take the bones and place them in one of these, an ossuary. This allowed for the bones to be buried or easily moved and relocated should the need arise.

As Phin stared at the first ossuary he saw a name carved into the top of the box. Phin's heart jumped. Another impossible revelation in this impossible story he was living.

In clear Akkadian script: *Nebuchadnezzar*.

Phin could feel the blood drain from his face; his ears began to ring. He was staring at the final resting place of the great king of Babylon – in of all places, a tomb carved into the side of a bluff in north Ireland.

Phin's torch played across the other three ossuaries.

Expecting to see the names of family, maybe his queen, he was completely unprepared for what he saw next.

Three stone boxes.

Three names.

Three names he'd heard his whole life going all the way back to the Vacation Bible School his friend used to invite him to each summer. Three names. A shared destiny. A shared resting place.

Shadrach. Meshach. Abednego.

# CHAPTER 47

Sergeant Billy Warren moved swiftly through his tunnel.

What began as a smooth manicured passageway had transitioned to natural rock after a hundred feet or so. The floor remained flat, which aided in the speed of the search. Warren found himself rushing past dozens – perhaps hundreds – of recessed enclaves carved into the side of the tunnel. Each hole contained smaller versions of the stone boxes in the master cavern where the four tunnels originated.

Occasionally, and at random, the tunnel would open into a larger room that was ornately decorated with smooth stone reliefs in the walls and larger stone boxes in the middle. The pictures and scenes made no sense to Warren and he didn't care. He imagined the doc would be unable to resist himself and lose his focus. But the focus had to be the mission. Find the missing subjects and eliminate any threats. Simple. Clean. No need to muddy things up with sight-seeing. He continued on through a tunnel opening on the opposite wall as quickly as his feet would carry him.

Coming to another cavern room, he quickly noticed that it had two tunnels splitting off from it. Warren checked his mapping display clipped to his belt. The prototype device was an advanced type of GPS in the beta stage for LaPhage Industries, his employer. When the sergeant got the call from Phin and knew they would be searching for missing persons, he'd grabbed this model just in case. It was ideally designed for above ground use where it could pick up a satellite signal. But it had an advanced underground application that Warren was putting to the test. A sensor was embedded into his headlamp and communicated via Bluetooth to the mapping display. As he moved through the tunnels, the infrared sensor scanned ahead, creating a 3D display that could be accessed later. The immediate benefit to Warren was that it created a roadmap of sorts. He could move down any passage with confidence, knowing he could navigate himself back without getting lost. This made his decision easy. He'd explore both tunnels. Picking the one on the right, he shot into the gap at full speed.

He was knocked off his feet before he saw the creature spring at him. He slammed into the unforgiving rock of the cave wall, knocking his head hard and sending his headlamp flying. A glimpse of hair and sharp teeth flashed in front of him before the lamp was extinguished, plunging him into total darkness. The last thing Sergeant Warren felt was the puncture of those same teeth clamping down hard on him.

\*\*\*

Phin found himself drawn to the countless stone boxes that lined the walls of his tunnel. This ancestral tomb was really a catacomb. If each tunnel was the same as this, there would be hundreds, probably even thousands of ossuaries down here, each containing the bones of the Babylonian royal family and their descendants. The cavern rooms he periodically came to likely represented some particular branch of the family tree.

It would take archaeologists years to work through the various chambers and tunnels. He was confident he was walking through only a fraction of the total number. Each stone box was neatly labeled with a stone carving of name and family origin. The carvings on the walls of the chamber rooms depicted historical scenes of great importance to the royal family. He observed that some of them may even tell the story of their migration from Babylon through Europe, all the way to where they finally settled.

This was the kind of stuff that could fill the Met in New York City, drawing scholars from around the world. It was also the kind of stuff that could change his career - put him on the map. Books would be written. Papers presented to Biblical Archaeology Review and other secular journals. History would be rewritten based on what he was looking at. Yes, Phin thought. It was all so tempting. But he'd promised the two men helping him search for his wife and friend. He'd given his word. Phin clenched his teeth. He wasn't here for this - for any of it. He was here for two reasons. Autumn and Jason.

A scurrying sound caused him to whip his torch around. He caught a flash of skin and hair darting through the chamber room at the end of his tunnel. He seized up. It didn't look like a werewolf, more human in appearance. His first thought was Jason. He sprinted toward the chamber.

"Jason," he whispered loudly, lips pursed. "Jason, is that you?"

Phin shot into the large room, eyes covering the space as quickly as the light of his torch could scan. More noise to his left caused him to jerk. A silhouette moved more quickly than his beam of light could follow and the figure was gone into one of two tunnels on the opposite side of the room. Why would Jason run from him?

A howl echoed back at him by way of an answer. Phin stopped short, the hairs on his arms tingling. What to do? He'd not seen a werewolf; he was sure of it. But the howl. If that was Jason, was he running right into one of the beasts? But again, why would Jason run from him? Unless he was running from one of the wolf creatures and had mistaken Phin for one of them. He could also be lost and suffering injury, not thinking clearly. In any case, there was danger ahead and whoever it was just ran into it. Phin tamped down his own sense of terror. *No fear.* He ducked into the tunnel, completely unaware of the evil that awaited him.

***

Sergeant Warren emerged from his tunnel back in the main chamber room where the group had started. Harv

Connor and Ross McCloud emerged from their tunnels at the same time. All three looked surprised to see each other.

"I heard a shot, like a canon going off," Harv bellowed.

"That was me." Warren held up his arms to calm the two men. Their eyes grew wide at the sight of his left hand. Half of it was missing – the thumb and the index and middle fingers, along with most of the palm. What was left showed a mish-mash of wires and gears. He saw their reaction. "Easy boys, its mechanical, the whole arm. And my leg too...long story. Point is, I was jumped by one of y'all's werewolves. I think it was the one that killed your dog, Harv. He was even bigger up close...and strong. Threw me against the rock and took my light out. Bit my hand clean off before I could pull my 9mm and let off a round. I'm pretty sure I winged him. He screamed and ran off. This way I thought. Did you boys see anything?"

"Not me." Ross McCloud was still looking at the sergeant's hand as he replied. "I followed my tunnel all the way to the end and...nothing. Just a lot of burial boxes along the walls and in several larger chambers."

"Same here," Harv added. "My tunnel basically ended. There's been a collapse way back in there. I climbed to the top of the rock pile. You might be able to squeeze a small person through and go down the other side, but no way you could get two unwilling people to do it. I think it's a dead end."

"I didn't have a chance to finish my tunnel. I came to one of those chamber rooms you all mentioned, but it had two branches off of it. The werewolf got me in one of 'em. Didn't have a chance to go down the other."

"So, we need to finish that or–"

"Wait! Where's the doc?" Sergeant Warren cut off Ross McCloud midsentence.

A weak-sounding howl oozed out of the fourth tunnel in the master chamber. The same tunnel Phin was exploring.

"Crap! Let's go boys!" The sergeant bolted into tunnel number four with the two men from Tiamat on his heels.

The three of them moved together. Their lights and drawn weapons created a boldness that none of them would have felt alone. Warren led the way in a crouched military pose. He swept each chamber room they came to with precision, like urban warfare. That's exactly what this reminded the sergeant of – sweeping the city of Mosul, Afghanistan, for ISIS scum.

When they spilled out into a chamber that had two other tunnels exiting it, they stopped. "This is what my tunnel did." Warren's voice bounced off the high rock ceiling of the room. "Exactly the same. We'll need to go down both but I don't think we should split up this time."

Ross's eyes grew wide with recognition. "Follow me!" he exclaimed. "It's the one on the right. I know where they are. It's all coming back to me now." They looked at him, confused. "Remember? I told you I came here as a kid." He shot into the tunnel on the right before Sergeant Warren or Harv Connor could protest. The two men looked at each other. Harv gave a shrug and plowed in after, followed by Warren.

They wound their way down the dark passage. Something was different about this tunnel from all the others, and Warren finally put his finger on it. No stone boxes. This tunnel was not a part of the tomb. There had never been any burials here. Warren could sense that they were getting close. Close to something important.

And just like that, they spilled into a high-vaulted chamber room. But like the tunnel, this room was different from any of the others he'd passed through. On the far side of this chamber was a hollowed-out grotto with ancient-looking bars covering it. A cage, Warren recognized.

He also recognized two of the four people inside.

"Billy!" Jason Morris jumped to his feet.

Sergeant Warren rushed toward his friend but pulled up short.

Between him and the cage doors crouched a werewolf.

# CHAPTER 48

Phin was in trouble.

The tunnel had split and then split again. He wasn't the best at following directions and in his haste to follow Jason or whoever was running from him, he'd feared he was now so twisted that he might not be able to find his way back out without help.

His concern was heightened further by what he thought was the report of a gunshot ten or fifteen minutes prior, somewhere way back. It was impossible to tell for sure because of the way sounds bounced and carried off the hard angles of the mountain rock he was traversing. Something more was happening with the others, he felt certain.

He'd begun to feel he was being led somewhere instead of chasing someone who was in trouble. And he'd become fairly certain that who was leading him wasn't Jason. He'd called out his name several more times and the only response he got was a weak-sounding howl, not exactly like the others the group had heard earlier. Phin chided himself for not taking a bit more time to process all of this before he'd run after whoever or whatever he'd seen. Now he was twisted around and probably lost.

He came to a yet another chamber room. This one also had two tunnels exiting it. *I can't go on like this*, Phin thought. "The further I go the harder it will be to make my way back," he said to himself. He needed help. He couldn't do this by himself. One half of him wanted to continue on, to solve the mystery. He was close and could feel it. But the other half, the wiser half, told him to turn back and wind his way out of the maze he was caught in.

Phin listened to the wiser half and turned around. A cranky howl let loose this time. Almost like a child whimpering, but more animalistic. He whipped back around. It was close and Phin believed he was being watched. He stood firm and took a hard look into the inky blackness of each tunnel. Which one had the sound come from? He imagined someone looking at him from one of the black holes, standing just far enough back so as not to be seen by him, wanting him to follow, wanting him to continue the pursuit.

Phin resisted the urge. Turning yet again, he took off back the way he'd come. Hastening his steps, he didn't want to waste any time. If that had been a gunshot he'd heard before, then one of the others might actually need *his* help. He just prayed he could reason out which tunnels to take as he backtracked his way out.

He skidded to a stop in a domed chamber room. They were all beginning to look the same – three or more ossuaries on pedestals in the center, walls covered with stone pictorial reliefs. There were two tunnels. One was the tunnel he never went down and the other was the tunnel he'd originally come from. His head swung back and forth between the two. "Think, Phin, think!" he ordered himself. Why had he not done a better job marking his route? A shuffling sound came from the tunnel behind him, then a low growl.

Phin picked a tunnel and ran. There was no reason other than instinct. His mind raced as his feet carried him. The whole thing had been a ruse. He'd been lured, pulled along like a lamb being led to the slaughter. He'd only *thought* he was the one chasing whoever or whatever. The reality of it all was that he was the one being hunted the whole time, drawn into a maze designed to twist and turn him to the point that he was hopeless to save himself. He only hoped he'd not gone too far, that he could retrace his steps until he was free. He also hoped that his flashlight would not die. If it did, he was doomed. Funny, he thought, how he'd not given the reliability of the light a second thought until his life was now threatened.

The noise from his own footfalls made it hard to tell but it felt like he was being followed. There were sounds of pursuit behind him - scratching and padding. It was difficult to know for sure. He couldn't trust that his imagination wasn't playing tricks on him. His heart pounded in his head as well.

Then another howl. Not far.

Yes, he was being chased. But by what? He'd not seen a werewolf when he started the chase. It had been a man, right? He really didn't know what he'd seen. The fear was rising in his chest as the bile rose in his throat.

"God, help me!" Phin cried in prayer. It wasn't a thoughtless exclamation such as is repeated on television and in the movies *ad nauseum*. No, this was a genuine plea, a prayer to the Almighty that he loved and was convinced loved him. Phin was in deep. This was – whatever this was – bigger than himself. He wanted to know the truth. He wanted to untangle the final knot of this web called Tiamat. He wanted to get his wife back and rescue his friend. But in order to do any of that, he needed to survive this moment.

Phin spilled out into yet another chamber. This one had five ossuaries in the middle. There was something about this room that actually looked familiar. "God, please let it be true," he prayed again. Two exiting tunnels, just as before. Which one had he used when he originally came this way? And was this really the way he'd come? Maybe he chose the wrong tunnel back at the last chamber and now he was hopelessly lost.

A barking laugh issued from the blackness behind him, like an evil hyena.

Phin froze.

This was a game to the thing chasing him. He willed his pursuer to reveal himself, just so he could know what or who he was facing. But yet, he wanted to flee and get away.

A thought. He looked at the floor of the chamber.

There were clear shuffled steps imprinted in the fine layer of dirt that had settled in the chamber. Steps made by him when he'd come this way the first time. He *had* been here before. His heart soared. He wasn't lost. The markings in the dirt led right to the tunnel he'd come from. That was his exit. His pathway to freedom.

"*Yoouu...wiiilll...nooot....essscaape....*" A malevolent voice drew the words out like a hissing snake ready to strike. Phin was about to bolt for the tunnel when he saw the eyes - two yellow eyes piercing the blackness of the tunnel he'd only a moment ago emerged from. Two hovering yellow flames of fire.

The yellow orbs began to bob, then slowed. Up and down. And they grew brighter, more defined. The beast was walking, taking its time as it approached the burial chamber. Phin was transfixed. He could have run, but he knew now that it was too late. The thing would catch him and have its way. There was no longer a choice. Fight or flight had come down to one inescapable option. Phin would have to fight.

Ever so slowly, like the shadows that recede in the morning dawn as the sun makes its rise, a figure began to form. The eyes had a face - a face framed in long matted hair, oily and mangy. And the face was clearly human. Phin recognized the features. He'd seen this face before.

In the Lear House. A family photograph.

It was the face of Lucious O'Leary.

The young man had returned. Re-turned. Or at least he was in the process of returning. The curse still had a hold on him. The body that emerged into the chamber came crawling on all fours. The nails of both hands and feet were long and jagged, but his naked body was clearly human in appearance. He was a filthy, pitiful mess, and a horrid stench came with him. But he had none of the features of any of the other werewolves he'd seen back in the cave or like the mighty creature that had so easily dispatched Harv Connor's dog. There was no coat of hair covering the body - only skin. The muscles of his arms and legs were taut and wiry-looking. There was strength in them, and it was human strength. But the look in his eyes...that look was still the look of an animal.

Lucious entered the room in full view, still on all fours in a careful crouch like a lion stalking its prey. Phin positioned himself with the four stone ossuaries between his body and Lucious.

This elicited another laugh and then a howl.

He sounded like a person *trying* to sound like a wolf. This was what Phin had heard back when the chase had begun. There had never been a werewolf or a helpless person in this set of tunnels. Only Lucious, playing the part of both, tricking him, drawing him in.

"*Iiii...haaave...yooouu....*" he hissed. And then Lucious sprang upon the top of the ossuary formation. He growled and shook his head from side to side. Phin backed away. He'd made the mistake of allowing Lucious to come between him and the tunnel that led to freedom. He was trapped. Sensing victory, Lucious stood on his hind legs proud and tall. With arms out to his sides he craned his neck and let out an awful howl.

Phin cowered back but then remembered the Ruger that Sergeant Warren had given him. Why had he not thought to draw it yet? He reached down to pull the weapon but as he did so, Lucious sprang. As if in slow motion he launched himself into the air, teeth bared wide, hands extended with claw-like nails ready to inflict their terrible toll. Phin raised his hands to cover his face, but it was unnecessary.

A second figure flashed into view.

A mass of raging hair slammed into Lucious, sending both of them careening onto the rocky floor just feet from Phin. A werewolf snarled and bit as Lucious clawed and pulled and sunk his own teeth into the neck of his surprise attacker. No one was more caught off guard by this turn of events than Phin. He was paralyzed watching the two beasts fight. That's what they were - two beasts - although one wore the body of a human.

As if in planned rhythm, both dualists pushed away from each other. Separated by only a few feet, they each measured the other up. The werewolf on all fours, fangs flashing. Lucious also on all fours. And then he rose up on his legs again, still hunched over with arms and claws extended, as if to intimidate.

*BOOM!*

A deafening blast sent Phin to the ground. He saw Lucious's chest explode, blood and gore spraying as he slammed into the back wall of the chamber. Phin gaped at the lifeless body, his ears ringing from the blast. He broke his gaze to see where the shot had come from.

Standing in the rocky frame of the tunnel was Sergeant Billy Warren, gun leveled, still smoking. With him were Harv Connor and Ross McCloud.

# CHAPTER 49

Phin scrambled to his feet and frantically drew the .357 magnum from its side holster. He pointed the Ruger at the werewolf and was in the process of squeezing the trigger.

"Stop!" Ross McCloud yelled, sprinting toward Phin in desperation.

"Don't do it, Doc. It's not what you think," Sergeant Warren ripped with command. It was Warren's voice that gave Phin pause. The sergeant and Harv Connor moved swiftly into the room as well.

Phin lowered his weapon only slightly, allowing himself the first good look at the creature that had saved his life. That's what had happened, Phin put together incredulously. The wolf creature had actually come to his rescue. He'd purposefully launched himself into Lucious O'Leary, shifting the fight from Phin to himself. Phin looked at the animal and he saw something he'd not seen before. There was a softness. Not weakness, but a compassion in the creature's yellow eyes. He appeared...almost human in his expression.

The beast sat back on his haunches like a dog obeying its master. Despite his massive size, there was no threat here. Ross McCloud raced to the animal's side, placing himself between the beast and Phin.

"It's Tommy, Mr. Crook. Tommy McCloud. Ross's son," Harv Connor announced. He took in a deep breath, relieved that disaster had been avoided.

Phin's own mind struggled to sort out what was going on. He reholstered the gun and stood to his feet. "I need a little help here. What's going on?" He observed Ross McCloud sit on the ground as "Tommy" – a half-wolf, half-man creature – eased his head into his father's lap. There was no category in Phin's experience for any of this.

"We found 'em, Doc. Your wife and Jason and the others."

"What? Where? Take me to her. I need to see her, now!" Panic flooded Phin. "Is she okay? Tell me she's not hurt."

"She's fine, Doc. The others are more or less okay too. They'll live. We left 'em back in the cage."

"The cage? What cage? You left them in a-"

"Just relax, will you? It was safer there until we could find you and take care of the werewolf thing."

"I don't understand. Somebody, please tell me what's going on. What *others* are you talking about?" Phin pleaded. He wanted to see Autumn, uninterested in the virtue of patience in that moment.

"They're not far from here, Dr. Crook." Ross McCloud

stood. He gave the wolf at his heels a good rubbing on the head. "A branch of this tunnel leads to a chamber that was never used for burial. In fact, before these tunnels were ever used as tombs they were originally used as a place to keep the cursed ones."

"He means the werewolves, Doc," Warren butted in. Phin shushed him, beckoning Ross to continue.

"Somewhere along the way, it was decided that if these tunnels were going to be used as a burial ground that the...werewolves," he gave Warren a look, "needed to be relocated. That's when the cave came into use. Most folks don't even know about the old cage down here. I found it many years ago when my friends and I came exploring. It took me a while, but I recognized the tunnel we were in and it struck me that that is where your wife and Mr. Morris might be."

"And sure enough, that's where they are, Doc. But we got more than we bargained for when we found 'em. Low and behold, our boy, Jason's buddy, is in there too."

"Jorge? You found Jorge Ramirez?" Phin was shocked.

"Yep, sure did. He's in pretty rough shape. Hungry and dehydrated most of all, I think. And we also found one of the boys from town that's apparently been missing."

"Sheamus Lynch," Harv Connor answered with his gruff voice. "We've been looking for Sheamus since the night the...okay, I'll say it...werewolves broke free." Sergeant Warren smiled and nodded. "His brother was killed by one of them. But Sheamus apparently ran and was eventually captured and thrown into the cage down that way. We didn't get the whole story but that's the general makings of it all." He pointed back to the dark tunnel.

"The Sheamus kid is in the worst shape of all. He's been chewed on, Doc. He needs a real doctor pretty quick. No offense...Doc." Warren twisted up the corner of his mouth in an embarrassed sort of half smile.

"I still don't understand. Who did all this? Was it...Tommy?" Phin pointed at the animal at Ross McCloud's feet. He'd now stretched all the way out on his belly, his front legs out in front of him. He looked completely harmless, yet he'd just witnessed what the creature was capable of.

"No," Ross McCloud was quick to say. "You saw for yourself, Dr. Crook. Those who have turned are mostly harmless. They are primitive and animals, but gentle once the turning has set in. We very rarely have issues with those in the cave. But something happened ten days ago. They got out. Lucious became the ring leader. I am sure of it. He takes after his father that way. Full of himself and overflowing with ambition. Been that way since he was a little kid. I don't know for sure, but what I think happened is that Lucious began to re-turn about the time of the escape. But he fought it for whatever reason. Four others escaped with him. You know about Sid. He was accidentally shot and killed that same night. Marco was captured a few days ago. He was docile when we found him. You saw Vance Talley a bit ago. He too was gentle. They may have had some fight in them at first, emboldened by being out and free, but after several days or a week, they were tired and ready to go back. Tommy here." He reached down and rubbed the creature's mane again.

"Tommy intentionally stayed close to Lucious. Jorge said that Lucious was a full-on werewolf a week ago, but he watched him turn back to the way he is now. His body anyway, but not his mind. He's been mean and vicious the whole time - before and after the returning - like he's unwilling to let the curse leave him. Jorge told us that Tommy has stayed close the whole time. As a protector. He scuffled with Lucious any time he felt he was crossing a line in his treatment of them. Tommy even went and scavenged food from town and brought it back to them. Jorge and Sheamus would probably be dead by now if it weren't for my...boy." Ross choked up referring to his son.

"Amazing," uttered Phin. "It's like they operate with a pecking order. And in spite of this...turning, the essence of your son or the essence of Lucious is still there. They're not themselves but they are. The best and worst of who they are they bring with them, even though they aren't of right mind."

Phin walked over to the body of Lucious O'Leary. The young man was crumpled and dead. Sadness swept over him at the loss of life. Had this really been who Lucious was in the core of his being? A crazed animal intent on caging and torturing innocent life until that life faded away to nothing? For that is what surely would have happened to his wife, Autumn, and the three other lives hidden away – caged – in these catacombs. He thought of Lucious's mother and father. And little Patrick who had never really known his big brother. The family would endure heartbreaking sorrow once they brought him back and reported the happenings down here.

Phin looked over at the wolf still laid out on the ground next to his father. Tommy McCloud had stayed close on purpose. He had protected and saved the lives of four people. It was impossible to imagine, because though he looked very much a wild animal, in a matter of months, he would return as well.

*In the spring. Tommy comes home in the spring.*

Those were the words uttered by his mother, Mattie McCloud. For the first time, Phin truly understood the hope behind those words. He made up his mind then and there that he would have to return to Tiamat in the spring and properly thank this young man.

"We still got a problem, Doc." Sergeant Warren's voice was grave.

"Problem? What problem?" Phin replied. He suddenly felt weary.

"Lucious here wasn't the one that kidnapped your lady and the others."

"I don't get it. What are you talking about?"

"He had help, Dr. Crook," Ross McCloud added. "Lucious couldn't have done all of this by himself. Especially in the state he was in a week ago before he re-turned. And there's no way he could have come into town in the condition he was in now, all naked and filthy, without someone noticing." It was true. Phin had actually wondered the same thing. How would a creature on all fours drag two people like Jorge and Sheamus all the way down here? "And the escape. We've been scratching our heads for a week and a half about how they got out of the cage in the first place. But now we know. Sheamus and Jorge told us."

Phin looked at the three men as if to say, "Go on. Spit it out."

"It was Vaughn O'Leary," Harv Connor growled. "He opened the cage and let 'em out. And he took your wife. He took them all."

"And he didn't want to come with us tonight either, remember?" Ross McCloud reminded Phin. "That's because...he had other plans."

Phin pondered this news. It all made sense in a bizarre sort of way. "Well...that's a problem indeed, isn't it?"

"Oh, it's more than just a problem, Doc," Warren jumped in. "He's also one of 'em. He's a stinkin' werewolf."

# CHAPTER 50

Phin was frantic as he worked the skeleton key to the lock on the cage door. Rust and grime covered the ancient bars but he succeeded, yanking the door wide and enveloping Autumn in his arms.

"Please tell me you're okay. He didn't hurt you, did he?" Tears had welled up in his eyes, but they were streaming down Autumn's cheeks.

"I'm fine. I'm fine. Just a little bruised and sore but overall okay."

He stepped back, arms on her shoulders, looking her up and down. Her hair was a mess but her face was as beautiful as ever.

"I'm not exactly sure how it all happened or where we are. The last thing I remember, I was in bed reading my book. Then I woke up here, with Jason and the other two. I'm not even sure where *here* is. Can somebody please tell us what's going on? There was a horrible naked man, acting like an animal. And then...a giant wolf-like animal of some sort." She became emotional and buried herself in the protective arms of her husband.

Phin and Sergeant Warren spent the next few minutes filling the group in on what they knew and what had happened with Lucious O'Leary. They had questions of their own. Some Jason and Autumn were able to answer and others not. Harv Connor and Ross McCloud had not arrived in the cage room yet but were on their way. As soon as Phin heard that Autumn had been found, he couldn't wait to get to her. He'd sprinted ahead with the sergeant showing him the way.

Jorge Ramirez had more information than Jason and Autumn combined. Both of them had been rendered unconscious and had woken up behind the bars, disoriented and confused. They'd only been here for a matter of hours. Jorge, on the other hand, had been imprisoned along with Sheamus Lynch for the last week and a half.

"So, you're Jorge." Phin extended his hand, but Jorge grabbed the college professor in an embrace.

"Si. Muchas gracias, hermano. Thank you so much for coming to save us."

Phin recognized the Spanish word for brother. "You are welcome, my brother. A lot of people have been looking for you. We never gave up hope."

Sergeant Warren hadn't been lying when he said that Sheamus was in rough shape. He had multiple puncture wounds that showed signs of infection. Phin examined the young man and confirmed a fever. Jorge had played nurse since they were dumped here, doing his best to keep the young man alive, hoping for a rescue.

"He comes and goes - mumbles a lot. He came to when the others found us... more than I've seen him in the last few days. Was able to tell them about how we got here and who did it."

Phin nodded. He understood. "You've done a good job, Jorge. I don't think he'd have made it without you. But we need to get him and all of you out of here. Sheamus needs Dr. Kelly as soon as possible."

Autumn screamed.

It was piercing in the close quarters of the chamber room, causing everyone to flinch. A werewolf had emerged from the darkened tunnel. Harv Connor and Ross McCloud followed the creature into the room.

"It's okay, Autumn," Phin reassured. She'd taken a step back, putting Phin between herself and the beast. "He's harmless. He saved me from Lucious." She relaxed realizing there was no threat, but the beast became restless, almost as if he knew his presence made them uncomfortable. He bolted through a tunnel and was gone before anyone could react.

"Tommy!" Ross McCloud made chase after him.

Harv Connor grabbed his friend. "Let him go, Ross. You'll never catch him. It's okay, he can take care of himself. We'll find him later." Ross relented but a profound sadness hovered over the man.

Phin and Warren filled in the two new arrivals on the condition of Sheamus. Proper introductions were made related to Jason and Jorge and then talk turned to how to proceed. Sheamus was in no condition to move on his own, he would need to be carried. Likewise, Jason was still recovering from his leg injury and hiking out was not a wise move, especially with the storm still raging. There was also the issue of Lucious's body. They couldn't simply leave it here. It needed to be returned and a proper burial performed.

And that led to the final problem of Vaughn O'Leary.

He was still out there and apparently he had turned as well. Harv Connor and Ross McCloud had no explanation. It was common knowledge to everyone in Tiamat that years ago, when he was a young man, Vaughn had turned and then returned seven years later. He'd already endured the King's Disease. The curse had visited and gone away. There was no record of anyone ever being inflicted twice. It was inexplicable if what they were being told was true. Yet, the caged Jorge Ramirez confirmed that Vaughn O'Leary had appeared earlier in the day, dropping off an unconscious Jason Morris and then Autumn Crook.

The turning had already begun, according to Jorge. He was agitated and twitchy and shirtless. Unusual hair growth was visible on his chest and exposed arms. What looked to be a snout was already taking form and his hands were twisted unnaturally, the nails protruding and sharp. Jorge had been horrified and too frightened to challenge the man as he unlocked and then relocked the cage, having deposited his two new captives.

Based on all this, the others were near certain that the wolf-man they'd seen crush Harv's dog was, in fact, Vaughn. He'd been a massive beast. He was powerful and ferocious and ready to kill.

So, Vaughn O'Leary was out there.

Somewhere.

Maybe he was in the tunnels. Maybe he was on the beach.

But he was free and he was dangerous.

He'd clearly been working some diabolical plan. A plan that was now exposed and thwarted. It was anyone's guess as to what he was capable of doing next. A trapped animal is a dangerous animal.

Vaughn O'Leary was both.

After much debate, it was decided that Jason and Sheamus must stay behind. It was too risky to move them and everyone expected that Vaughn would not just let them leave unchallenged. This was his Alamo. His last chance to regain the control that had slipped from his grasp.

The group needed help from town. A lot of it. A small, well-armed group that could move quickly and make it back to Tiamat was essential. Jorge would stay back with Jason and Sheamus. He was starved and lacked the energy to be of use. Ross McCloud volunteered to stay back as well. The four of them would lock themselves inside the cage for protection in case Vaughn had a notion to come for them. Ross was also armed. That left Phin and Autumn, Sergeant Warren, and Harv Connor as the group of four that would go for help. Phin tried to persuade Autumn to stay back as well, but she'd have none of it. She reminded him that she had a black belt and could take care of herself.

Sergeant Warren reached over his shoulder and brandished his sawed-off shotgun. "Here you go, sweetheart." He placed the weapon in her hands. "Take care of this baby and she'll take care of you." He gave her a quick lesson on how to hold the weapon and what to expect if she pulled the trigger. "Whatever you do...don't drop it."

She furrowed her brow and gave him a nod. "Sir, yes, sir!" Warren growled and walked away as she smiled back.

The group made sure the cage was secure and readied to leave. Ross McCloud reached through the bars and gave Harv Connor's arm a squeeze. No words were exchanged. Just an understanding between two old friends. They left the chamber room, and using Warren's mapping display, wound their way back to the main burial room where the four primary tunnels broke away.

A primal cry of anguish ripped through the opening of the tunnel they'd emerged from. Phin looked at Harv and Warren. "Lucious."

"If he's found his son..." Warren didn't finish.

"We need to go...now!" Harv Connor moved as quickly as Phin had seen the weathered man move yet. They raced down the tunnel to the exit of the tombs. Phin made sure he kept Autumn in front of him. Another howling cry sounded behind them.

"I'm gettin' real tired of that sound," Warren complained.

"Just keep moving," Phin barked back at the sergeant.

"Ain't no way we'll outrun him. We're gonna have to stand and fight."

"Just go!" Phin pleaded.

# CHAPTER 51

The wind had picked up in the chasm as they spilled out of the catacombs. If it was blowing this hard in the shelter of the gap of the bluff, Phin dreaded to think of what it was doing, fully exposed on the beach. Even the rain was making its way into the crack in the earth in ways it had not when they'd come this way earlier.

Now free from the suffocating rock of the tunnels, the four of them sprinted toward the chasm's end. Perhaps they could make it to the cave where Furman Hayes waited with additional weapons and the two young men were keeping guard over the other werewolves. The more they could fortify themselves with bullets and additional numbers the better.

They were a mere forty meters or so from the exit to the canyon and still running. With every flash of lightning, they could see the silhouette of the walls on either side, and the blowing trees and surf that lay beyond. In one spectacular flash of electricity the group pulled up short.

Outlined in black was a figure.

One that had not been there a moment before.

Standing tall and powerful was Vaughn O'Leary. The shag of his wolf-like mane was wet but still full, only adding to the impression of his size. He was on his hind legs, the muscles of his arms bulging. He didn't look like the other wolf creatures that were caged at the cave. Whereas they looked more wolf than man, Vaughn appeared more man than wolf, but had clearly transformed into something that was neither. He had become the monster of Tiamat. Unmatched by any other.

Somehow, he'd cut them off – perhaps an alternate exit to the tunnels. That didn't matter in the moment, though.

In his arms he carried something. A limp figure.

Autumn gasped. "Oh my...no. Lucious. He has Lucious."

Vaughn lifted his head to the sky and let out a screeching howl of pain. The scream of a father who had lost a child. He gently eased the body of his son to the ground. Rising back to full height, the sound of his woofing and panting was audible even over the whistling of the wind. The beast that was the head of the Tiamat town council kicked backward with each foot, like a sprinter preparing for the shot that would signal the start of the race. And then he released and rocketed toward the group.

"Charge!" Sergeant Warren drew his 9mm and sprinted toward Vaughn O'Leary, seeking to match the intensity of the wolfman. Not to be outdone, Harv Connor followed next, his old legs doing their best to scamper toward the inevitable clash of titans.

Two loud reports pinged off the chasm walls followed by a crushing blast that echoed up and out. Warren had popped off two rounds as Harv pulled the trigger on his shotgun. One or both shots landed. Vaughn released a cry and jerked to one side. Warren hoped that this would only compound the damage his previous shot had inflicted back in the tunnels. But the beast carried on, and if anything picked up speed. He closed the distance with inhuman quickness. All three figures crashed into one another as more shots from both Warren and Harv exploded.

The melee was over in a matter of seconds.

A massive hairy arm dispatched Harv Connor as it swept him into the darkness. Only the sound of a thud hitting the rock wall indicated that the older man was finished. Autumn winced, her fingernails sinking into Phin's arms, drawing blood even through his jacket and shirt. They watched in helpless horror as Vaughn took hold of Sergeant Warren's head with both hands. He lifted the Marine into the air, arms extended. Warren scratched and beat the back of Vaughn's hair-laden hands, desperate to compel a release. He kicked and thrashed at the wolfman but Vaughn held him too far away. All of Sergeant Warren's attempts to fight back were futile.

More lightning revealed an evil grin on the snout of the beast. He was enjoying himself. The power in his muscles was sickeningly impressive. Vaughn let loose a victory howl and then he slammed Warren's body to the hard earth. Before the sergeant could rise, the beast bent his legs and jumped with malevolent intent, landing on the torso of the poor Marine with a sickening crunch. Sergeant Billy Warren didn't move as Vaughn stepped off of the man, turning his full attention now to Phin and Autumn.

"Run!" Phin screamed. "Back to the tombs!" They ran and flew into the dark entrance, plunging once again into the depths of the ancient burial grounds.

They were quickly back in the central chamber room. Four tunnel options. Was it possible to pick one and confuse Vaughn on which way they'd gone? He doubted so, but it didn't matter. On the heels of their arrival in the chamber, Vaughn O'Leary appeared behind them.

The only light that illuminated the chamber was from Phin's torchlight. Out of instinct he shined it directly at the wolfman's eyes. What was he thinking? That he'd blind the beast and make his escape?

The creature laughed at the feeble attempt.

He leapt at the couple, landing on the collection of four ossuaries holding the bones of King Nebuchadnezzar, Shadrach, Meshach, and Abednego. He used the perch as a springboard to launch himself over the heads of Phin and Autumn, landing directly behind them.

His movements were so fast, so calculated. He was one step ahead of them, and before they could react Vaughn snatched Autumn from Phin's protective cover and backed away. She dropped the shotgun Warren had given her and screamed as she reached both hands up, trying to dig into the hairy arm that was now wrapped around her neck. Vaughn squeezed hard, putting pressure on her windpipe, cutting off the flow of oxygen.

Phin knew that the beast could snap her neck quicker than he could move to rescue her. Vaughn breathed hard against her neck and bared his teeth. A line of feral drool leaked from the corner of his fangs and oozed down Autumn's cheek. He opened his jaws wide in a mocking gesture as he slowly placed his fangs on the soft pink of her neck. He could bite down, ending her life in that moment. But maybe he was just playing with Phin.

"What do you want, Vaughn?" Phin asked. He wasn't thinking, he was only acting, going with the first thing that came to his mind. "You want *me*? Is that what you want?" His mind raced until it landed on Vaughn O'Leary's one weak spot.

"You've lost control, Vaughn. The one thing you fear has come true. Your secret is out. You can't kill us all. Someone will survive and make it back to town. Soon, everyone will know that you are a monster. Isn't that what you're really afraid of? That people will see you for who you really are? A hideous beast! A cursed freak of the gods. A pitiful, self-consumed creature from the pit of hell."

Vaughn's eyes grew wide and he squeezed Autumn's neck harder. Her eyes rolled into the back of her head. She was losing consciousness. Phin was running out of time.

"Yes! That is what you are Vaughn O'Leary. Blame me if you want. Blame the town. But it's not my fault. It's not anyone's fault. It's your fault, Vaughn. You are the one that lost control of yourself. And look what has happened. Lucious is dead. Your own son is dead. And it's all...your...fault!"

Vaughn lost himself at the mention of his son. He howled loud and long. With singular focus he threw Autumn to the side and overwhelmed Phin as he launched himself with all the might he carried in his wolf-enhanced body. He landed full force on the college professor from Oklahoma, pinning the man to the ground, knocking the full measure of breath from his lungs.

In the next instance, a quiet settled over the burial chamber and several things happened at once. Phin tried to overcome the blow to the ground and the weight of Vaughn's massive body - to pull just a bit of air into his lungs.

Vaughn lay on top of Phin, his face inches from the professor, eyes wide with a look of shock.

Phin felt a gush of warm liquid envelop his right hand. Vaughn's eyes grew wider still at the realization of what was happening. Phin held the hilt of the serrated knife in his grip and pushed one more time for good measure. The blade had penetrated in an upward motion, just under the rib cage. Phin imagined that the tip had pierced Vaughn O'Leary's heart. He looked into the yellow eyes of his nemesis and stared in wonder as they phased back to their original brown color. A sadness fell over Vaughn's face and then those brown eyes could see no more.

Phin pushed the limp form of the wolfman off of himself. It rolled onto its back as Phin pushed up, regaining his feet. Autumn came to Phin's side, taking his arm. The couple looked down at the lifeless body of Vaughn O'Leary. Half wolf. Half man. Consumed by an evil that had now been extinguished.

Neither said a word. Autumn only leaned her head on her husband's shoulder and they both breathed a sigh of relief.

# CHAPTER 52

The sun had risen on a beautiful day in Tiamat. The blue sky almost glowed with brilliance after the previous night's storm. There was not a cloud to be found.

It was lunchtime at The Frolicking Irishman. There was only a smattering of patrons besides the one large group huddled in the back around two tables that had been pushed together.

Phin and Autumn Crook sat across from Jorge Ramirez and Jason Morris. Phin couldn't quit looking at the Hispanic man. He'd been missing for well over a week but seemed no worse for wear after a good night's sleep and some hot food. Sergeant Warren filled up one end of the table gathering while Ross McCloud sat at the other.

Fran and Marilyn Hayes loaded up the tabletop with a buffet of fixins from the menu. Potato bread and scones complemented the cottage pie, black pudding, barmbrack, and, of course, Irish stew.

"You sure you're okay, Billy?" Phin asked. The sergeant kept working his head from side-to-side, flexing his neck.

"Oh, yeah," Warren croaked. "Just workin' out the kinks. Nothing that a helping of home cookin' won't drive away." He eagerly dove in, scooping spoonfuls of everything onto his plate. His prosthetic hand was still mangled, but he'd put a glove on so it wasn't so noticeable.

Phin was grateful that his friend had recovered from the vicious stomping he'd endured the night before. He had feared the worst but Sergeant Billy Warren was one tough grunt. "How's Harv doing?" He looked at Ross McCloud.

"He's gonna be okay as well. Worst part was the blow his head took against the rocks. Probably has a mild concussion but I checked on him this morning and he was already up and about. His wife is insisting he stay close to the house and just rest for a few days. That'll be hard for a man like Harv Connor but I suspect he's more afraid of his wife than he is anything else. He'll be a good patient."

It had been a long night. Sergeant Warren had wandered into the burial chamber after the death of Vaughn O'Leary. He was clearly in rough shape but still mad that he'd missed the final "showdown," as he called it. He'd already checked on Harv Connor and confirmed that he was alive, instructing him to stay put until he could bring back help. The three of them - Phin, Autumn, and Sergeant Warren - went and released those waiting in the cage and told them what had come of Vaughn O'Leary.

Ross McCloud joined the trio. The foursome collected Furman Hayes and the two young men at the cave. The whole crew hiked back to Tiamat in the downpour that came on the backside of the thunderstorm. The lightning and thunder had moved off and by the time they arrived back in town, the rain had stopped as well. Ross and Furman roused a small army of men - young and old - and the whole party raced back to the tombs.

It was a chaotic scene for a time. Most of the townspeople had never even been to the ancestral tombs. There was a lot of confusion surrounding the deaths of Vaughn and Lucious O'Leary. Phin could sense that rumors were already forming. It didn't help that when they arrived back at the tombs Vaughn had re-turned, his nude body showing no signs of ever having become a werewolf. There would be a lot of explanation required to answer the questions in people's minds.

The discovery of an alive Sheamus Lynch was a victory, however. His father had joined the rescue and smothered his son in hugs and kisses as soon as he made it to the cage. He personally joined the escort as part of a smaller group of four that carried his son's wounded body back to town. It didn't take as many as four people, but Jason and Jorge both needed assistance in hiking the steep trail off the beachhead. Harv Connor reluctantly accepted some help as well. It was deep into the early hours of the morning when everyone was back and the nightmare had ended.

Today, the cleanup would begin. The collateral damage would be massive for this small community. The loss of the leader of the town, along with his son, and the circumstances surrounding it all would take time for this little town to come to terms with.

"Where do you all go from here, Ross?" Phin asked. He felt a bond with the man. What they had collectively endured the last twenty-four hours had forged an understanding among the group at the table.

"Well, there's obviously a lot of explaining to do. I've been approached by multiple people already this morning. Everyone wants to know if it's true. Did Vaughn O'Leary really open the cage and let the cursed ones out? Did he play a part in the death of Blake Lynch and the loss of Malcolm Conner's arm? And did he really hold Sheamus prisoner in the ancestral tombs? Most people are hearing just bits and pieces. Nobody knows the whole story yet, except us and a few others."

Phin thought about Patricia O'Leary. When he'd seen her just a couple of hours ago, she was already dressed in black, the color of mourning. She'd not spoken to him or acknowledged his presence. She just slipped into the kitchen of the Lear House, letting the door swing shut. He could only imagine what she was feeling. She'd lost her son and husband, both in the same night. He wondered if she knew that it was Phin who'd been responsible for Vaughn's death. Although, he wasn't responsible, really, but still....

"It will be a lot for the folks of this town to accept," Ross went on. "Vaughn wasn't exactly loved by everyone, but he was respected...trusted. What he did...what he became, is a violation of everything we are and everything we are trying to protect. It's still a mystery to me as to *how* he was able to even turn again. Not sure we'll figure that one out. And don't take this the wrong way, but most people aren't going to care too much about what happened to you all. They still see you as outsiders. And from their perspective, everything was fine until you two showed up." He pointed to Jason and Jorge. "And then when you showed up, Dr. Crook...well, that's when everything really spun out of control. It will take a while for people to see Vaughn O'Leary for what he really was...and accept it. It's probably best you don't hang around very long."

"Oh, don't worry. We're planning to leave right after we finish this feast." Phin smiled at Fran Hayes as she refilled their drinks. She knew the whole truth. Her husband, Furman, had told her the whole unbelievable story after he got home in the early hours before dawn.

"I've called a town meeting for midafternoon," Ross continued. "It'll be the first chance to tell most people the whole truth. I'm hoping Sheamus is in shape enough to come. He's really the key. He's the one that will identify Vaughn as the one who came down to the cave when he and his brother, Blake, were on guard duty. It was a violation of the 'rules' for him to be there since his son was in the cage. But he was the town leader after all, so they didn't feel it their place to question...until they saw him opening the cage. Blake tried to stop him and that's when Lucious attacked him and...well, you know what he did to Blake. Sheamus ran and was able to hide for a few hours until Vaughn and Lucious caught him. Chewed him up good. They were working together. And that's when he first saw Vaughn partially transformed. Not all the way, just enhanced size and strength and some wolf-like features. He dragged Sheamus to the tombs and imprisoned him along with Jorge who was already there. The rest I think you all know."

"I still don't understand how he was able to take Jason and Autumn without a scuffle. Without them screaming or fighting back," Phin said.

"That's right," Jason inserted. "I was just like Autumn. Walking back to the McCloud house, taking my time, and the next thing I know, I'm waking up in the tombs, behind bars."

"That's an easy one. It was the tranquilizer guns we use on the cursed ones."

"Werewolves," Sergeant Warren butted in. "Why can't you guys just call 'em what they are? Werewolves." He took another giant bite of barmbrack.

Ross ignored him. "Vaughn had been carrying one of the tranquilizer guns on him for over a week. Made no sense to me at the time. But that's what he used on you both. Shot you from behind, likely, and then he probably just eased the door open to Autumn's room and fired the dart before she could look up from the book she was reading."

It all fit, Phin realized. All the pieces to the puzzle nicely in place. Yet, he still felt uneasy and he didn't know why. That probably just meant it was time to leave. The group finished their lunch, enjoying some small talk about lesser things. They endured the suspicious looks of the others who came and went over the lunch hour.

When they were done, they rose and walked outside as a group. Fran and Marilyn Hayes gave them each a hug and whispered well wishes in their ears. Mattie McCloud had also come to bid them farewell, as had Dr. Boris Kelly.

There was a sadness that dampened the mood of a beautiful day trying to assert itself. Phin understood. This place may never be the same.

Autumn, Jorge, and Jason crammed into the too small Ford Ka. Phin stood at the driver's door, thinking it a comical mess. "Billy, I'm sorry my friend, I don't think we can fit you."

"No worries, Doc. Wasn't planning on being a sardine. Don't worry about me. I'm just gonna walk that way." He pointed out of town. "Make a phone call and all will be well. I'll be back in Germany by bedtime. Don't you worry a bit about ol' Sarge."

Phin knew he didn't have to. "Thank you, Billy. I mean it. Don't know what we'd done if you hadn't come."

"It's what I do, Doc. I take care of people. Especially my friends." He leaned down looking through the open windows of the tiny car. "Nice to meet you, little lady," he directed to Autumn. "Take care of this guy. He finds trouble easier than most. You too, Jason. Take care." Straightening up, he said, "And call me if you need me!" He turned and began the march out of town.

Phin turned to get in the car, but one other thing caught his eye.

A little boy.

Patrick O'Leary.

He was sitting on the front porch of the Lear House by himself, wearing a black t-shirt and matching pair of shorts. He had his shoebox of action figures dumped out in front of him - escaping from reality into a world of make believe. The little guy looked up, right at Phin. There was no expression on his face. Phin's heart broke and he could only wave at the young child. Patrick responded by lifting a tiny hand...and then he went back to playing make believe.

Phin got into the car and started it. He drove straight out of town without looking back, leaving the sadness of Tiamat in the rearview mirror.

# PART 4

# HOME

$W$<sub>e</sub> have no king.

But we have a home. We've come to the end of the world it seems. The land literally drops into the sea. I've taken to spending the night on the bluff, enjoying the cool breeze and gazing into the distance as the sun sets. We can go no further and our pursuers left us long ago. Just over two hundred of us survived the journey. We are spent and weary. The exodus took its toll and we lost many along the way.

The green of this strange land is beautiful to the eyes. There are not many who live in this land, and those that do are simple people, clannish in nature. I doubt we will attract much trouble. The sentiment of the royal family – I suppose I should say no more about royalty because those days are gone. The king is dead and Babylon the Great is no more. There is no more royal family. We are all just family now, even myself. Somewhere along the journey something changed. I went from being a mere servant to being one of them. It is a good feeling - the first time I have felt the warmth of brotherhood and family since those years so long ago when it was all taken from me - by the great grandparents of many of those I live with now. I was fifteen at the time.

But as I was saying, I am so easily distracted these days as my mind wanders in its old age, the sentiment of the family is to be left alone. We have all endured enough adventure for ten lifetimes in the *two years that it took us to find this place. We have walked many miles, sailed many waters, hidden in caves and fought off bandits. We've bartered away what little treasure we took with us just for food and new sandals. We are now nothing more than a simple family of people. We only want to be left alone and to build a new life in the peace and quiet of this beautiful land. My only concern, and others share it with me, is that the curse we had hoped to leave behind has followed us to our new home. Time will tell, of course.*

*I once thought I would live my whole life in Jerusalem and be buried with my fathers in the royal tombs. Then the Babylonians came. I then thought I would live my life in Babylon and be buried in some servant's grave. Then the Persians came. Now I know that I will finish my days here and be buried among...family. The days are drawing nigh when I shall breathe my last breath and will write no more. Perhaps one day, many years from now, the children's children's children of our people will read these words and understand that no matter where one may lay their head, in that place, the God of Heaven still watches over.*

From the Journal of Meshach,
Recorder for the remnant of Babylon

Eighteenth day of the month of Dumuzu,
The second year of the great exodus, the first year of hope
(537 BC)

# CHAPTER 53

Phin leaned forward and slapped the tabletop. "I'm telling you, Max, I was right there. I was able to touch it, just like I'm touching my desk. I actually traced the carved name with my finger. Nebuchadnezzar." He was wide-eyed with enthusiasm as he unpacked the details of his unexpected adventure to the town of Tiamat in north Ireland. His best friend, Max Allred, listened, shaking his head in disbelief, interrupting only to ask a question here or there.

The two men were sitting in Phin's cramped office on the second floor of Montgomery Hall on the campus of Oklahoma Baptist University. Cramped only because the space was filled, wall to wall, with all manner of books and memorabilia. Phineas Crook was a collector. He didn't like to throw anything away. The office had grown in clutter over the last few months as Autumn had insisted that much of what he'd used to decorate their home on Broadway Avenue really belonged in his campus office. Now that she was awake and back, she had other plans for how a house should be properly decorated. They had reached a compromise with about two-thirds of his collection finding a new home on a bookshelf, the top of a filing cabinet, or some other flat space inside the four walls of his home away from home.

Max Allred had accompanied Phin on a number of his unusual excursions through the years, but nevertheless, the tale he told now stretched credulity. "I'm sorry, buddy, but you're moving too fast for me. Let's go back to the other part."

"Other part?" Phin queried. *What other part?* he thought. The whole three-day event was all one in his mind.

"The part about the werewolves. That's the part I'm really having a hard time getting my brain wrapped around." The assistant dean of the Hobbs College may have been Phin's best friend, but he also had an interest in the well-being of the school's faculty. He didn't need a professor who'd lost touch with reality stepping in front of a class of impressionable freshmen. Max scratched his head, the same hand brushing his brown hair to one side. He was still trying to sort it all out. He was an average-looking man, nothing really spectacular about his appearance at all. But he was intensely loyal, and for that Phin would be eternally grateful. He owed much to his former college buddy, now colleague and quasi-boss. Phin went through the whole timeline of happenings one more time, a shortened version, by way of review.

It was late afternoon and the fall sun would be setting soon. It didn't matter though, as there was no window in Phin's office. This helped to ensure a sense of privacy as the topic they were discussing was not only sensitive but could lead a casual eavesdropper to suspect insanity.

"So, you're serious about all this, aren't you? You're not yanking my chain. I can see it on your face," Max conceded.

"Look, you can ask Autumn if you like. She'll be here after a while to get me. You *know* she doesn't lie. And I can put you on the phone right now with Billy Warren. That man is incapable of not telling the truth. Code of honor and all that stuff. You know how he is." And then shifting gears because that's how his brain worked, "Oh, I wanted so badly to open the top of that ossuary, Max. To see his bones...take pictures of them. Can you imagine? And then the other three. Shadrach, Meshach, and Abednego. Straight out of the Bible and right in front of me. I was so close I could touch them...I could almost feel their presence."

Max sat back in the simple leather chair opposite of Phin's desk. He let out a lung full of air. "You realize what you've discovered here...I mean there...in Tiamat. Well, it changes the history books. You get that, don't you?"

"No, it doesn't." Phin was stern with his answer. "I gave them my word, Max. Their secret is something I promised I'd protect. I'm only telling you because, well, I needed to tell someone and I trust you."

Max didn't push it. He knew to do so would be fruitless. When it came to his good friend, Phineas Crook was stubborn if nothing else. "I get it. Sure. Your secret - their secret - is safe with me. So, what am I supposed to do now? Just carry around inside of my head the knowledge that there's a modern-day colony of pure descendants of the

Babylonian royal family in north Ireland? And that at any given time eleven of them are werewolves living in a cave for their own protection?" Phin's friend oozed with sarcasm.

"Let me put it this way, Max. If you decided to do anything about it, who'd believe you?" Phin laughed. "You'd sound like a crazy man and I doubt the dean would let you keep your position."

"Touché, my friend. And what exactly do you think *you* sound like? If I hadn't been with you, to see some of the things you've seen in this life myself, well...maybe you'd be the one without a job. I gotta tell you though, Phin, there's something about you. I mean you attract crazy like someone out of a Twilight Zone episode. And let me just say one more time...werewolves? It sounds too fantastical. It's some kind of genetic disposition – has to be. It needs to be studied, in my opinion. There might even be a way to cure those who are impacted."

Phin sat in silence after Max was finished with his mini-diatribe. He let it linger a bit longer than necessary, just enough to start feeling uncomfortable. "You're wrong, Max." Phin's tone took on a reverent seriousness when he finally spoke. "It does not need to be studied. It does not need be diagnosed. It needs to be left alone. Some things in this world defy explanation. They are, in fact, not of this world at all. At least not the natural world. They belong to the *super*natural world. You of all people should understand this." Phin let that sit. A clear allusion to their tour of the Garden of Eden not even five months past. Max seemed to understand and didn't return to the topic.

The two friends chatted just a bit longer until the five o'clock hour. "Well," Max announced. "Time for me to head home. Shelly's cooking homemade chili for dinner tonight. Good stuff, amigo. You said Autumn's coming to get you, right? You don't need a ride home?"

"No thanks. I've got some work I want to catch up on. And, yes, Autumn will swing by. I think we'll grab a late dinner at Van's."

"I still can't believe you're trying to pull off the one car thing. I told you I'd sell you my truck. You've always said you'd love to have it."

"Probably soon. Autumn and I are still getting settled back into things. She's discovering the big metropolis of Shawnee. I'm good hanging out on campus most the time, or at home. I don't officially have to be back till J-term anyway."

"Gotcha. Well, when you're ready, say the word and we'll work it out." Max stood and slipped into his tan corduroy jacket. As he began to leave, he turned back. "Oh, and Phin." His good friend looked up from the laptop, which had already drawn his attention away. "I'm glad you're back, and most of all, I'm glad you're okay." He winked and disappeared, closing Phin's office door behind him.

Phin took his time catching up on email and a few other odds and ends. He stood for a good stretch and walked out into the hall. His body had nearly recovered from that long night...let's see...he did a quick calculation in his head...two and a half weeks ago or so it had been since he and Autumn had returned from Tiamat. He still had a few scratches and his pants concealed the healing scabs on his knees.

Thinking back on that night on the beach and in the tombs, it could have been so much worse. He walked to a window overlooking the Oval of the campus and noticed that a full moon lit the ring of buildings beautifully.

Satisfied everyone had gone home for the evening, he ventured back to his office and closed the door. He punched the lock for good measure. He eased into his leather highbacked chair and fished around in the pocket of his Harris Tweed, fingering a set of tiny keys. He used them to unlock a safe box he kept under his desk. It contained but one lone item. He withdrew it and set it carefully on top of his desk. Pulling back the linen covering, his eyes gleamed at the title: *The Journal of Meshach.*

He'd not stolen it, although it was tempting and would have been an easy thing to do. No, instead, he had asked permission of Ross McCloud. The man had agreed, indicating to Phin that he'd crossed over to a new level of how he was viewed. He was an outsider in Tiamat no longer, at least not to Ross McCloud. Phin promised to return the volume in the spring – on the planned trip to come back and meet Tommy McCloud properly...and thank him for the night he intervened with Lucious O'Leary, likely saving his life.

Phin never had the time to read the whole journal the night he'd broken into Vaughn O'Leary's library and discovered its existence. He'd seen just enough to verify Jason Morris's theory, that the residents of Tiamat were the descendants of ancient Babylon, and that they had carried with them from their homeland something called the King's Disease. Phin looked forward now to reading the volume in its entirety. He'd never be able to tell anyone about it but he had an insatiable curiosity that begged to be satisfied. He just had to know the whole story. Maybe at some point down the road he could tell Max about it. Maybe.

And quite a story it was. Much he had already learned from his adventure in Tiamat and from what Vaughn and the other men had told him. But there was more. Much more. Phin was pulled along on a roller coaster of excitement as he read one page after another. There were other secrets of Tiamat. And the sojourn for the royal family - when they fled the Medo-Persian invasion of Babylon - had not been without incident. It was all there. Recorded in meticulous detail by the biblical figure, Meshach. Phin made furious notes, scribbled in a fashion that only he'd understand. At some point down the road, he'd have to search this all out. The adventure of Tiamat, it seemed, might only be beginning.

Losing track of time, he broke loose to the bang of a door slamming shut down the hallway, harder than necessary. Most likely the cleaning crew. He checked his watch. It was almost eight o'clock. He was surprised Autumn had not called to check on him by now. But then, she didn't like to disturb him when he was working. He reached for his cell phone sitting next to the journal when it rang. Probably her, he thought. Autumn's patience must have run out and he didn't blame her. He was set to apologize when he noticed it wasn't her number. In fact, he didn't recognize the number at all.

Pressing the green answer button, he said, "Hello." Another loud bang. An office door just down the way from his. He wished they'd be more careful. He had a mind to step out and say something.

"Dr. Crook. Is that you?"

"Yes, this is Dr. Crook. Who is this?" Phin opened the door to his office and stepped into the hallway. There was a rustling coming from an open office door just three doors from his. Whoever it was was being rough. Too rough for his tastes and rougher than he wanted them to treat his office. He walked toward the open door.

"Dr. Crook! This is Ross McCloud." The connection wasn't the best, being overseas and all, but he recognized the man's Irish accent. "Listen, Dr. Crook. You're in danger. Do you hear me, Dr. Crook? Danger."

Another bang as if something had fallen over. Phin wrinkled his brow, about to yell at the cleaners that enough was enough. Something in Ross McCloud's voice gave him pause. "What do you mean, Ross? What danger? What are you talking about?"

"There's another one, Dr. Crook. It's worse than we thought."

"Worse than you thought? What are you talking about, Ross? Another what?"

"Werewolf, Dr. Crook. There's another werewolf...and we think it's coming for you."

Phin froze. He lowered the phone to his side. Ross was still talking but Phin's focus was on the open office door. Phin was only a few feet away.

That's when he heard the growl.

# CHAPTER 54

Phin ran.

He thought for just a moment about trying to barricade himself in his office but decided against it. He remembered the power of Vaughn O'Leary when he had transformed. The last thing he wanted to do was find himself trapped with no way out. Instead, he slammed into the release bar on the fire door at the end of the hall and thundered down the steps. He dared a quick glance to his rear as the door was slowly easing shut and caught what looked like a dark blob rounding the corner and heading his way. It might have been covered in hair but he didn't wait to confirm.

He shot through the door into the first-floor lobby of Montgomery and stopped. He was already breathing hard. What to do? Where to go? He wished desperately he had the F-150 that Max had offered to sell him. He heard the slam of the stairwell door as it banged against the stop.

No time left to contemplate.

He bolted through the front doors, opting for a more public option of the campus's Oval versus a dark and empty parking lot in back of the building. Perhaps a campus police car would be checking the girls' dorm and he could flag it down. He couldn't remember if they were armed or not, though. He raced down the few steps and sprinted across University Drive into the center of the Oval.

No police cars to be seen on Oval Drive.

Phin silently punished himself for the decision.

A few students were walking across the Oval as well. He didn't want to create a panic, but at the same time, if one of the monsters of Tiamat had come to the United States to seek him out, he doubted it would be dissuaded by the presence of a few co-eds.

He ran past a clump of girls strolling close to the Oval Fountain. "Girls, there's an intruder on campus," he yelled. "Get to the dorm as quickly as you can." They complied and moved quickly toward WMU Residence Center.

Thinking that the werewolf should have exited Montgomery by now, he chanced a look back. Nothing. He began to feel foolish. Maybe he'd overreacted to the whole thing. He'd never actually seen anything upstairs. He'd only heard banging and what he *thought* was an animal growling. The mind can play tricks on its host, especially in moments of high stress. Maybe it *was* just the cleaning crew. Loud music coming from headphones can sometimes sound like a growl to those a few feet away. Maybe. And he'd just sounded the word that an intruder was on campus. Most likely the frightened girls would have called campus security by now or even 911. How would he explain himself?

But Ross McCloud had not called for nothing. *Danger.* That's what he'd said.

*It's a lot worse than we thought.* Phin recalled the man's words.

Phin was in danger. Him specifically. Another werewolf. But how? It didn't make any sense. How would one of the creatures even get to the United States? Certainly not on a plane. But a ship? And then it would have to cross the country to get to Oklahoma. It was impossible. Unless...unless it was someone who could transform at will. Like Vaughn O'Leary had. Such a person could buy a plane ticket. Plan the whole thing out. And then strike. Phin would never expect it. And what about Autumn? Would it stop with only him, or would it go after his precious wife?

Phin looked up at the full moon for the second time tonight. It beamed down bright, casting its brilliance across Bison Hill, as the OBU campus was known. He was tempted to walk back to Montgomery and meet whatever waited for him head on. And if it really was someone from the cleaning crew, the sooner he called campus security and cleared the whole thing up, the better.

Just as he was about to make the move back, he changed his mind. A hairy flash burst through the front doors of Montgomery. Definitely not the cleaning crew. Thoughts of meeting the challenge head on evaporated in a fit of self-preservation.

Phin sprinted again.

The beast must have sensed his movement because it flew off of the steps in pursuit. Phin found himself ducking into the shadows of various trees that dotted the expanse of the Oval. Even in late fall with most of their leaves gone, the trunks and limbs cast a tangled maze of shadows, perfect for Phin to disappear into. He found one particularly large oak tree on the far side between Shawnee Hall and WMU. He slammed into its girth, using his left arm to sling around behind it. He was panting now, sweat soaking his forehead despite the cool of the autumn evening.

Squinting, he frantically scanned the Oval for sight of the beast. It was nowhere to be found. Rather than comfort him, Phin's heart only pounded that much faster. Where was it? He jerked his head wildly, checking his backside. Nothing. He could see the glass wall of the Geiger Center, the student center and hub of the campus. Dozens of students were relaxing inside – watching TV, drinking Starbucks, or chomping on Chick-fil-a sandwiches – totally unaware that evil had slipped its way onto their campus home.

Phin looked back toward the Oval. Still nothing.

Then came the howl.

The terrible sound he'd heard too many times in Ireland echoed across the campus. His eyes found the horrible creature. It was perched not forty yards from his position, on a brick pillar right in the middle of the Oval. On top of the pillar was a painted gold bison, the mascot of the university. And on top of the bison, using the statue as a foothold, the wolf-like beast looked like a grotesque extension of the landmark. It stood on its hind legs in much the same way as Vaughn O'Leary had. In fact, it looked just like Vaughn, very human legs and arms covered in muscle and hair. The head was a mane of shaggy hair, and the silhouetted profile revealed the characteristic snout of a wolfman. But Vaughn was dead. Phin was sure of it. He'd been the one to do the horrible deed.

Phin observed more closely and noticed that this new creature was different, a bit smaller and sleeker in appearance. But the terror of the beast was the same. It arched its frame against the backdrop of the full moon and, raising its head, bellowed another awful howl. Phin heard students scream behind him. The beast snapped its head to the sound and in an instant found Phin - his body behind the tree but his head exposed. The yellow eyes of the werewolf hungrily bore into his own. It had found its target.

Leaping from the bison, it landed on its two powerful legs and stood staring at Phin. It began a deliberate walk toward him and then crouched into a sprint on all fours. Phin pushed away from the trunk of the tree and ran for the only shelter left open to him. His only option - the Geiger Center.

He motored down the grassy rise, fully exposed now. No more cover or shadows to hide in. He didn't look back. He didn't need to. He knew the monster was behind him and he could feel it closing the distance. A concrete pad met him as the grass ended and he flew around the corner of the building. A student was exiting the glass doors that greeted him. Looking down at his phone, the young man wasn't paying attention as Phin barreled into him.

"Back inside!" he commanded. Phin physically turned the student and sat him down in a chair as he sprinted across the open space of the main room. He crashed into a few more chairs in an unsuccessful attempt to not attract attention. Several students looked up from laptops at the sudden entry.

"Yo! Dr. Crook. Whassup?" someone called to him.

A massive thud crashed into the bank of glass walls. "Oh, geez!" the same student exclaimed. The hairy wolf threw itself into the glass a second time, splintering the wall in a tangle of white lines.

Screams followed as students sitting next to the glass fell over themselves to get away. Others moved closer out of curiosity. Phin was about to yell for them to run when the third hit from the creature shattered the wall. Glass flew as students dove for cover. The werewolf stood fully exposed in the fluorescent lights of the student center and howled with all its might.

Chaos ensued.

A couple of brave students launched chairs at the beast who summarily flicked them away like it was swatting at gnats. Most ran, but a few pulled out their phones to capture the whole thing on video.

The beast scanned the room as Phin raced away. He found himself running past the campus bookstore and up a set of steps that led outside. Raley Chapel stood proud and tall in front of him as he exited the building and found more steps, these leading down to the grassy lawn between the Geiger Center and the chapel.

The wolf creature ripped one of the doors off its hinges as it followed Phin out of the student center. Phin heard the crash and whipped around. He was fully exposed once again. Nowhere to hide and, this time, nowhere to shelter. There was no way he could outrun the monster to the chapel. It was too far. Plus, it would likely be locked at this hour.

This was it and Phin knew it.

Only him and the werewolf.

Just like the tombs in Tiamat.

But this time he had no weapon with him. No gun. No tranquilizer. No knife. Nothing. His strength was no match for one of these monsters and he knew it. He backed slowly away from the Geiger Center, not taking his eyes off of the hairy wolf. Sensing the chase was over, it took its time walking down the steps, not on all fours, but on its hind legs. Just like a man. But not. A wolfman.

The werewolf reached the bottom of the steps and continued its slow stalk toward Phin. There was malicious intent in its eyes. The creature's tongue licked its snout and it smiled wide as it snapped its jaws at him. Phin prayed to God. Perhaps his last prayer before meeting the Lord in person on the other side of eternity. In that moment he found strange comfort in two words.

*Fear not.*

The same two words that had seared themselves into his heart back in Ireland emerged again in this last moment. Phin stopped backing away and stood his ground. Whatever came next, he would not fear.

The creature stopped. Sensing a renewed boldness in its prey it released a hideous laugh as if humored by Phin's pathetic attempt to stand and fight. And then it launched.

Phin fought the urge to close his eyes and was glad he did. For in that next instance the attack was halted.

The loud honk of a horn caused the wolfman to hesitate. The headlights of a car bounded over the curb of the adjacent parking lot. The vehicle clipped the side of a fountain but hardly slowed its speed as it plowed right into the beast. The werewolf screamed in pain or anger, Phin wasn't sure. Its torso was splayed over the hood and it attempted to claw its way toward the windshield. But the attempt was for naught as the car slammed full speed into the brick wall at the base of the Geiger Center steps. A sad squeal escaped from the creature and then its body went slack, crushed between the grill of the car and the wall.

Phin was stunned as he stared at the scene. Steam rose from the front of the car, painting a grizzly image he would never forget. He was stunned again as the driver's door flung open and Autumn Crook stepped out.

"I got a call," she could only say. "From Ross McCloud. There was another one, Phin. Coming for you, Ross said. I just jumped in the car and drove. And I prayed. I didn't know what else to do." Tears formed in her eyes. Phin rushed to her, embracing her in hugs and kisses.

"You did fine, Autumn. You did perfect." He pulled away from his wife. "But I don't understand. Who..." he stuttered. "Who came after me? And why?" Autumn just shook her head.

They turned to look at the macabre scene. Sirens could be heard in the distance. The help they no longer needed would be here in a moment. Phin gazed down at the wolfman and in that moment he had an answer to his question. The re-turning had already begun.

Not a wolfman.

A wolf-woman.

Patricia O'Leary.

# CHAPTER 55

It was another beautiful day in Tiamat. The crisp wind coming off the ocean bit anyone out for a walk, hinting that fall was ending and winter was just around the corner. Phin and Autumn strolled across the grassy roundabout, arms linked. Ross McCloud joined them as they took their time.

Fran and Marilyn Hayes had doted on them over lunch at The Frolicking Irishman. "Anything you want from the menu today," they had said. "It's all on the house." Autumn chose the traditional Irish fry up. It was a breakfast dish but she didn't care. Phin went with Fran's delicious Irish stew, and their hostess brought a few other goodies they didn't order for good measure. Furman Hayes joined them for a bit, as did Harv Connor and his son, Malcolm – although Phin suspected he'd come as much to see his fiancé, Marilyn, as anyone. Harv and Malcolm gave the couple hearty handshakes before bidding them a good day and even inviting them to hurry back.

Phin and Autumn couldn't help but notice that the general tenor of the citizens of Tiamat had turned more friendly toward them. They received numerous smiles and head nods from the other patrons in the town's diner. One of the biggest surprises of all was a visit from Dr. Boris Kelly. Sharply dressed as always, he was warm and hospitable. He even offered to pay for their lunch but was told to put his wallet away by a hovering Fran.

Any vibe of suspicion or coldness they had felt from their first visit was gone. The people of Tiamat knew. They knew what the Crooks had been through - what they had endured - because of their secret, yes, but mostly because of Vaughn and Patricia O'Leary.

"Thanks so much for opening the Lear House for us last night, Ross." Phin hiked up the collar of his peacoat to shield his neck from the breeze. "It was strange being back in the hotel, and especially now that it's empty. But I don't know...there's a peaceful quiet about it now."

"I just love the place and I love this town. I know we weren't here under the best of circumstances last month but what you all have here is special in its own way." If it sounded like Autumn was overly kind, she wasn't. It was truly how she felt. She was the eternal optimist, always seeing good as outweighing bad.

"I appreciate you thinking of us that way. You both have every right to see us...I don't know...as a freak of nature I guess." Ross McCloud didn't give himself or the town of Tiamat enough credit, Phin thought.

"Look, what happened to us was not yours or anyone else's fault. It was always about Vaughn. He had become something...different. I suppose that's what you'd say.

Have you all been able to figure out what happened with him and why?" There was a mystery that still surrounded the O'Learys and was part of the reason Phin and Autumn had returned to Tiamat. That, and they had agreed to escort Patricia's body back for burial. And then...there was one other important matter to be settled which was why they were headed toward Ross McCloud's house.

"After you all left, well, the whole town wanted to know what happened and why. Most folks blamed you two for bringing trouble our way. As you can imagine, it's pretty quiet around here most of the time. But the real truth is that trouble had been brewing for a long time - or at least it had been in the Lear House. Dr. Kelly first noticed Vaughn's odd behavior, going back a couple of years ago. He'd begun to make it a point to stay close to him. Stop by for regular tea and such. Vaughn didn't have any true friends to speak of, so while everyone respected him, nobody really knew him. Dr. Kelly would have been the one person who came closest to knowing what was inside of Vaughn."

"And what *was* inside of him? I mean, based on what you've told us about the curse, it's a random thing. Strikes when someone is young and lasts seven years. At any given time, there's always eleven, no more and no less. And once those stricken return, that's it, right? It's over. So, what happened to Vaughn and Patricia?"

"Dr. Kelly found a personal journal of Vaughn's in his library. It gives some insight but there are still a lot of holes we've had to fill in on our own. Vaughn contracted the King's Disease in his early twenties. Went away for seven years, just as you know. Those who return don't ever have much to say about it. I never got the curse so I don't know, but those who do say it's like being in a dream-like fog. They have flashes of memory, a few nightmares afterward, but for the most part, once they return and realize what happened to them, they just want to leave it all behind. But that didn't happen with Vaughn. His journal is a series of mad ravings. He apparently became obsessed with the turning seven years ago when Lucious contracted the disease. He began to make it a habit of breaking the rules. You know, the one about family not going to the cave. It's thought to be better if we don't see them in that state. Vaughn would go, though. Often. He became fixated on Lucious being free. Somewhere along the way...well, he crossed over. He wanted the curse to take him again. He wanted the ability to turn at will but this time be free and not caged. As you read his entries it's clear he was losing his mind.

"We suspect he dove into occult practices and became a worshiper of Tiamat herself, the mother of the eleven monsters of myth. He turned himself willingly over to the curse. It's likely he had been turning into a monster, on and off, for some time. We've had a lot of unusual activity with missing animals for the last couple of years. We all chalked it up to wild wolves and Vaughn went along with that. But now...well, let's just say in the last month, it's been pretty quiet."

"What about Patricia, Ross? What happened to her?" Autumn asked. They could see Ross's house just coming into view as they made their way down the asphalt road.

"Yes, that's the big question we all have. No one knows for sure. The whole town is aware...that she could turn at will, that is, and that she came after you. It's remarkable, really. No one, and I mean no one, ever leaves Tiamat for long, and certainly none of us have ever traveled that far from home."

"But she did. And it was personal, Ross. You should have seen the look in her eyes as she came after me. There was hate and evil there." Phin had filled Ross and a few others in on the details of Patricia's rampage. The police were obviously concerned and thought the Crooks to be crazy when they said a wild animal had chased Phin across campus, especially when what they found, instead, pinned between the car and brick wall of the Geiger Center, was a nude female, crushed and dead. But numerous cell phone videos from students and the university's own security cameras told a different story. It was inexplicable but what was clear was that Phin's life was threatened and the ramming of the car had been an act of self-defense. Phin suggested that the police just file the case away with the X-Files. They didn't think that was very funny but they let it, and the Crooks, go.

"I think it's possible that Patricia was the one pulling the strings the whole time. I can't be certain and it's just a personal theory, but rather than Vaughn wooing her, I think she may have wooed him to the curse. I grew up with Patricia. With both of them. We even dated for a while when we were kids. There was always a side to Patricia. A dark side. I'm convinced that her coming after you was an act of pure revenge. In her mind, she lost both her son and husband because of you. I don't know, that's just me and we probably never will be able to sort it all out. But it doesn't matter now. It's over."

"Yes," Phin agreed. "It's over. So, where do you go from here? I mean, who's going to be the new head of the town council and the law of the land?'"

Ross McCloud looked down. A smile cracked his two-day-old stubbled face. "Well, as a matter of fact, you're looking at him."

"Hey, congratulations!" Autumn clapped her hands and broke from Phin to give him a hug.

"Wasn't my idea, I can tell you for sure. My name just came up and Mattie insisted I let myself be voted on. It was near unanimous, so I guess that's that."

Phin suspected the gunsmith was more excited about leading his village and stewarding its secret then he let on. It was a good choice, though. Phin could think of no one better.

"What about Tommy? Have you all found him yet and gotten him back to the cave?" Phin asked.

"Nah...we decided to leave him alone. He's clearly no danger to anyone. Never was. None of them are really – you saw. It was only Vaughn...and Patricia." The new leader of Tiamat looked sad. But then brightened. "Tommy can take care of himself. He'll either roam around, staying close, or he'll get tired and go back to the cave on his own. I'm not worried. Not anymore. And in the spring-"

"He returns," Autumn finished with a skip in her step.

"Yep. My boy returns."

They arrived at the McCloud homestead. The conversation switched gears entirely. This was the main reason...the real reason Phin and Autumn had come back.

"He's inside?" Autumn asked.

"Yes. Been with us since his mother left. It's a sad thing really. He's a good kid. But the O'Leary name isn't thought of very highly here anymore. It will be hard for him."

"Well...that's why we came," Phin said. Everyone wore somber expressions.

"How's he doing? Is he scared or...worried?" Autumn continued to quiz.

"He's brave. And good natured. Always has been. He's not like his parents."

"And there's no other family?"

"None."

"Well, then..."

"You do realize...one day...he might turn." Ross looked worried.

"We know," Phin acknowledged. "We'll cross that bridge if and when we come to it."

"If you're ready then." Ross climbed the steps and opened the door to his house.

Autumn smiled at her husband and took his hand as they crossed the threshold. Mattie McCloud was sitting on the floor, a cardboard shoebox and action figures dumped out in front of her. She looked up and smiled, winking. Hearing the door open and the arrival of guests, a little black haired head turned as well. Patrick O'Leary smiled big at the sight of Autumn and Phin, but mostly Autumn.

"How are you, Patrick? Have the McClouds been treating you well?" She beamed at the little boy.

"Yes, ma'am, they have. They've been very nice." There was a sadness behind his smile, and maybe some apprehension too.

"Have they shared with you our idea?"

"Yes, ma'am, they have," Patrick's unusually timid voice replied. Phin's heart flipped.

*Fear not. Trust me.*

He could the hear words speaking to him anew.

"And what do you think of it?" Autumn went on.

"I don't know, Miss Autumn. What do you think of it?"

"I think it's a splendid idea," she announced. "I think that somehow, in spite of all the sadness, that we were meant for each other."

Patrick O'Leary jumped up at Autumn's words and sprinted into her arms, squeezing her around the waist with all his might. Phin looked on. This was right. He could feel it in his bones.

Patrick pulled away and looked at them both. "It's a little scary, you know," he pronounced, not sounding scared at all. "But I can trust you, right?"

"Yes, you can, Patrick. You can trust us." Phin rubbed the boys head.

Autumn reached down, taking his little hand in hers. As if to finish the chain, Patrick took his free hand and grabbed Phin's.

"Come on," Autumn said. "Let's go home."

# EPILOGUE

American Airlines flight 295 touched down at Atlanta's
Hartsfield-Jackson International Airport. It had been a
smooth flight across the Atlantic. Phin looked down at
Patrick, who was sleeping soundly. The gentle thud of the
landing had not prodded him to wake up. The pilot had
done a good job.

It may have been close to noon in Atlanta but it was
after dark back in Ireland. Their body clocks told them it
was time for dinner, but, of course, they would be eating
lunch once they were in the terminal. Phin always thought
it was a bit easier to adjust coming from Europe to America
than the other way around. For them, today would just be
one long day and then they could go to bed and wake up
refreshed. At least, that's how he hoped it would work.

They still had one more leg to go to reach Oklahoma
City and then the short drive to Shawnee and Patrick's new

home. Autumn smiled at Phin and gently caressed Patrick's cheek. He stirred and his eyes squinted open just a crack.

Phin pulled his phone from the seat pocket in front of him and took it off of airplane mode. It could be a long taxi to the jetway and he felt compelled to check any texts and emails that may be waiting for him after the nearly nine-hour flight. The device began to frantically ding as messages started flowing in. He thumbed the switch to vibrate and gave an apologetic smile to the lady across the aisle who seemed disturbed by the noise.

The only text of importance was from Max asking for a picture of the new family. Phin laughed and held the phone at arm's length, clicking a selfie of the three of them, Patrick still looking groggy. No other threads begged for a reply so he moved on to email. A few administrative messages from the school, a couple from Max as well, lots of SPAM. He scanned through it all and then stopped. The FROM field read: Oklahoma State Penitentiary.

Phin felt a shot of adrenaline surge through his system. He'd not heard from his brother in months. Remus had cut off all communication and he'd not had the opportunity to go for a visit and force the issue, whatever the issue was. Phin opened the message to read it, but it wasn't from his brother. It was from the office of the warden.

Autumn saw the blood drain from Phin's face.

"What's wrong? What are you reading?" she asked.

"It's from the prison. It's about Remus."

"Your brother? What's going on? Is he okay?"

Phin shook his head, balling up his fist. "No," he began, looking straight at Autumn. "He's most definitely *not* okay. He's escaped from prison."

*Phineas T. Crook will return in...*

*Search For The True Cross*

# ACKNOWLEDGMENTS

I've always loved a scary story. I grew up on werewolves, vampires, and mummies - much like little Patrick O'Leary in our story. When I set out to write a "sequel" to *Finding Eden*, knowing I wanted to do an exploration of fear and trust, I thought it would be a nice homage to my youth to use one of the classic bad guys of the horror genre. But could I really pull off a modern-day werewolf tale without it coming across as "cheesy" or "already tried"? An obscure few verses from the Bible in Daniel 4 became the perfect backdrop for what has become *The King's Disease*. As it turns out, *lycanthropy* is a real psychiatric condition whereby an individual believes oneself to be an animal. Certainly, Nebuchadnezzar fell ill to this rare delusion...but perhaps, there was more going on. Only you, the reader, will be able to judge whether or not I pulled it off. Nevertheless, it was fun to write.

I must thank the many people who helped me bring this story to you in the best form possible. Most of all, I am grateful for my wife, Julie. She is an editor extraordinaire and her hundreds of marks, notations, and suggestions took this novel to a whole new level. Thank you, dear, for putting up with my crazy mind and for being gentle with my ego through our lively "discussions" related to edits. My daughter, Madison (for whom this book is dedicated), served as a proof reader as well and it was a joy to share this story with her first. A big, big thanks also to a couple of ladies I am privileged to work with in my office: Gayla Oldham and Jill Langham. Thank you for your interest in my work and for reading and providing additional proofing and edits. I am also grateful to my big brother, Colonel (Ret) Bobby G. Crawford. As retired U.S. Army, he's been a good check for me as it relates to the military technical lingo, plus he's always good for an opinion about pretty much everything else. :) We grew up on the same diet of fantasy, horror, and sci-fi, and he loves a good story as well as anyone. It's a joy to have him along for the ride. And, finally, thank you Millie

Cooper for an amazing book cover. Millie sat and listened early on as I explained the premise of *The King's Disease*, and then she went to work and brought it all to life in an extraordinary image.

Most of all I am grateful for my Lord and Savior, Jesus Christ. I am grateful for a God of creativity who loves to see his children create. This novel, along with everything I write, is my creative expression in honor of a God who loves me more than I deserve.

# ABOUT THE AUTHOR

Jeffrey S. Crawford is teaching pastor and lead pastor of ministries at Cross Church in northwest Arkansas, one of the largest and fastest growing megachurches in North America. He holds a Doctorate of Education in Leadership from the Southern Baptist Theological Seminary, a Master of Divinity degree from Southwestern Baptist Theological Seminary, and a Bachelor of Arts in Philosophy from Oklahoma Baptist University. He has served for over thirty years in churches across Arkansas, Texas, Oklahoma, Louisiana, Utah, and Tennessee and enjoys traveling the globe on missionary journeys and interacting with the peoples of the world. He and his wife, Julie, have raised their four children in the foothills of the Ozarks where they make their home.

Made in the USA
Middletown, DE
27 September 2020